REVIVAL

A Folk Music
Novel

Advance Praise for Scott's Novel, Revival

"A terrific, cathartic, hard-to-put-down read that I look forward to being able to share with friends."
—Mark Moss, editor, *Sing Out! The Folk Music Magazine*

"*Revival* captures the heart of the singer/songwriter scene with this story of love, ambition, and artistic integrity. The characters are so believable that you want to go hear them in concert after reading the book. Clearly written by someone in the know, *Revival* allows the good, the bad and the ugly elements of the folksinger's experience to be witnessed without glossing over anything."
—Catie Curtis, singer-songwriter

"Wow. Scott Alarik has told a moving story set in the modern trenches of the urban folk music world; the coffeehouses and bars where tradition meets ambition and sometimes spawns lasting art. This is very close to the way things were for us in the sixties; really, just shuffle some tables and chairs around and you've got the same scene he paints so beautifully in *Revival*. I recommend it very highly."
—Tom Paxton, songwriter, author

"Scott Alarik has done such a masterful job capturing the New England folk scene that, months after finishing the book, I still find myself wondering about the fate of the characters. *Revival* is a highly entertaining and informative glimpse into the inner workings of the business of folk music. I highly recommend it."
—Alison Brown, Grammy-winning musician and Compass Records founder.

"If I wanted to make someone understand why folk music has been my own greatest passion, I'd be likely to hand them a copy of *Revival*. . . . Readers who love listening to folk music . . . will enjoy how the story pulls them into that fascinating world. Those of us already immersed in that world will . . . be inspired by Scott's eloquent description of why folk music moves his characters—and him, and us—so deeply."
—Bob Blackman, host of "The Folk Tradition," WKAR Radio, E. Lansing, MI.

"I ran the open mic at Folk City in Greenwich Village and felt right at home in the novel's pub. I loved reading about the regulars who come back week after week —and I want to hang out with Ferguson! Beyond that, this is a special love story because it also shows the love shared by volunteers at folk venues everywhere, the love of discovering new talent, and the spirit of community that nurtures those feelings."
—Sonny Ochs, WRPI program host for 18 years and heard on SiriusXM Radio, organizer of Phil Ochs Nights concerts, self-described "professional volunteer."

"Compelling . . . broad appeal . . . a behind the scenes look at the musician's life and work from someone as knowledgeable as anyone about the modern folk world . . . Alarik is the PERFECT person to write this book. . . . I have a strong feeling that many, many artists would get behind this book, and that many, many of their fans would as well."

—David Tamulevich, music manager-agent, The Roots Agency

"I didn't read this book, I devoured it . . . thrilled to see that each character was masterfully developed, with the subtlety and complexity that real people deserve . . . parts of this book are very funny. . . . When I travel around the folk world today, I am constantly reminded of characters I met in *Revival*. . . . For those outside the community, it's as good an introduction as I've ever seen."

—Don White, songwriter, humorist, author

"Scott Alarik's novel *Revival* is like a folk song. There's a sense of familiarity with the characters and the situations that makes you feel involved, like you are a part of the story and the community. That familiarity shows the universality of the story—and the stories within the story. You don't need to know anything about folk music or the folk community to feel that you are a part of what's happening—and to love the story and characters. Truly an outstanding first novel. Hell, it would be an outstanding tenth novel."

—Matt Smith, Club Passim manager

"A must-read for anyone who enjoys character studies, has an interest in the working of creative people, or thoughts of being in the music world . . . a highly entertaining novel . . . deals with . . . the music business in ways I have never read before . . . amazingly real. . . . My wish is that this story is passed around like the songs we love that live on for years."

—Ralph Jaccodine, music manager, Black Wolf Records executive

"Through the pages of *Revival*, I was able to loathe this brutal business, laugh at its absurdity, admire the sincerity of folk music and the hardworking-ness of its people, question what is in store for us in the future, and delight in the simple love story of a man and a woman navigating through it all the best they can."

—Michelle Conceison, management and marketing, Market Monkeys

A Folk Music Novel

We come of age more than once

Scott Alarik

Songsmith
an imprint of
Peter E. Randall Publisher
Portsmouth, New Hampshire
2011

ISBN13: 978-1-931807-91-3

Library of Congress Control Number: 2011925166

Published by
Songsmith
an imprint of
Peter E. Randall Publisher
Box 4726
Portsmouth, NH 03802

www.perpublisher.com

Book design
Grace Peirce
www.nhmuse.com

For more information: www.scottalarik.com

For the volunteers,

who give so much, and give up so much, to keep folk music alive. You open the doors, turn on the lights, set up the chairs, put up the stage, bake the cookies, book the shows, spread the word, pamper the performers, fold up the chairs, take down the stage, switch off the lights, and close the doors.

You are what you have always been: folk music's beating and gracious heart. This story could not have been written without you, because without you, what story would there be to tell?

Author's Note

This is a work of fiction. No character is based upon, or intended to resemble, any person living or dead. Any similarities are purely coincidental. The stories told about actual folk musicians, however, are true, as far as I know.

—Scott Alarik

About the Songs

Credits for songs referred to in this book are listed on pages 314–315.

Book One

*Some
lone
hollow*

One

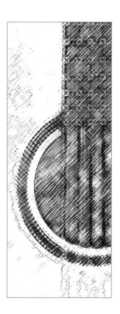

Such a short way up, such a long way down.

The thought always struck Nathan Warren at some point during his Tuesday chores: while he was lining up the microphones in neat, straight rows, adjusting the dials of the sound system, or sweeping the remains of last night's fun from the old stage.

For almost fifteen years he had hosted the Tuesday open mikes at Dooley's, a small pub just outside Cambridge's Porter Square. Anyone could come down, sign up, and play a couple of songs on a real stage, in front of real microphones. On Wednesdays, Nathan hosted a jam session there, mostly bluegrass, some Celtic. Again, anyone could come down and play along to assorted jigs, reels, waltzes, and the occasional weepy folk ballad.

Dooley's was a dark-lit, frayed neighborhood bar that was to Nathan the perfect landing place for the long, downward slide of his musical career. Water finds its own level. So did he.

Once—and it never felt as long ago as it really was—he was soaring to stardom so fast it took his breath away. A short way up. And now, here he was, scraping someone's old gum off the small stage: a career open-miker, as close to a professional amateur as it is possible to be.

On this early August Tuesday, the thought struck him while he inspected the mikes, snapping his fingers in front of them to make sure they were all on. He noticed a broken guitar pick beneath his feet and kneeled to pick it up. A tidy stage is a happy stage. He was, if nothing else, still a pro.

He almost lost his balance as he tried to scoop up the pick and had to push a hand and knee down on the stage. There he froze, half standing, half kneeling, and felt the thought come. Such a short way up, such a long way down, long, slow, and stupid.

He waited for the emotional pain that always followed. He closed his eyes and waited; long ago, he'd learned that it passed more quickly if he tried not to think. It once burned through him, almost paralyzing in its intensity. Now it came only as a dull ache, washing coldly over him. Such a short way up and then this, years and years and years of this.

Nathan Warren was once the boy wonder of the Boston folk scene, the guy everybody said was going to be a star. He had it all: the looks, the voice, the chops, the songs, and the swagger. It was almost as if "future star" was his nickname; he even saw it on posters advertising his concerts.

To everyone in the scene, including Nathan, it seemed like his career was charmed and national success a foregone conclusion. The first time he played New York City, it was at Carnegie Hall. Sure, it was a fluke, a revue of mostly obscure songwriters financed by a naive guy who was trying to become the next great folk impresario. But Nathan was the one singled out by the New York papers. And like everyone else back then, they dubbed him a star in the making.

After a tiny Massachusetts record company released Nathan's debut album, he was signed to a major label amid much media hoopla. The story of how the label executive sought him out at a neighborhood coffeehouse while visiting a daughter at college became part of Boston music lore. The local papers all wrote about the album before it came out. It was even whispered about in *Billboard*. This kid is going places.

But his star-making album was never released because of a staff shake-up at the major label. The executive who signed Nathan was fired for reasons that had nothing to do with Nathan or his album. But no one who remained at the label wanted to help somebody else's discovery become a star. If it became a hit, who could take the credit? And if it was a hit, questions would be asked. What happened to the guy who signed our big new star? Why isn't he at the label anymore? In short, the album's potential became a reason to not release it. Now, more than twenty years later, it still sat in the label's archives, on some dark, silent shelf.

That was what made Nathan the craziest through all the long nights he spent wondering why. It was the idea of his music rotting in a warehouse, never to be heard by anyone, along with the aching and certain knowledge that it was the best of him: the best work he had ever done, could ever do, would ever do. It was as if that body of songs was a person, a loved one that he somehow betrayed and left to die, alone and unwanted. That image, of a dark shelf in a moldering warehouse, gnawed at him deep down inside, until the raw places became reddened, then hardened, and then numb.

The failure of that album sent Nathan into an epic tailspin, years of drinking and depression that he was only now beginning to climb out of. Or had he just made peace with it, deciding that failure and numbness were not the worst fates, as long as he could still call himself a musician?

Now, every week at Dooley's, he watched others with the same stupidly certain dreams he once had, as they convinced themselves they were one song, one guitar lick, one big break away from it all coming true. He always tried to be kind, helpful, but also to never build false hope. Because he knew, more than any of them, how much harder the fall is when the hope seems real.

It took Nathan less than an hour to get everything set up for the open mike, but he always got to Dooley's at least four hours early. Back in his drinking days, he said he wanted to get his game face on, by which he meant having a few pops with Jackie, the bartender, and the handful of hard-core regulars who slouched sleepily at the bar.

Nathan quit drinking several years ago but he still liked to be there early, to answer phone calls and personally greet the first open-mikers. The ones who came early were often the most nervous; it sometimes helped to say something encouraging, tell the first-timers how things worked, tell the frightened ones to just have fun.

Nathan told himself that was why he showed up early. But the truth was that the only time he felt even remotely alive these days was when he was at his work, whether that was playing guitar or peeling a wad of yesterday's gum off the stage.

The Dooley's gig was the closest thing to steady work Nathan ever had. He also taught guitar, which he enjoyed but took as another sign of his failure—those who can't do, teach, right?—and he still played sporadically at small coffeehouses in the Boston suburbs. Usually, he was hired by someone who knew him way back when, and seemed less interested in hearing his music than in remembering the good old days. Still, a gig's a gig.

Nathan stepped down from the Dooley's stage and walked over to the mixing board, which sat on a small table beside the stage. He looked at the levels, then turned everything off and listened to the quiet. He liked the old pub this time of day, before the after-work crowd came in with their hurried, blowing-off-steam chatter.

To Nathan, there was something wonderfully lived-in about Dooley's. It was a one-room bar, a long rectangle painted in dark greens and browns, with a worn wooden bar lining most of one wall, small tables in the middle, and a long row of bench seating and tables around the back and side walls. The stage was in the far front corner, jutting out to face both the bar and tables. Across the high brown ceiling exposed construction beams and heating ducts were decked with strings of tiny holiday lights, red and green and white. They'd been hung up there some long-ago December, looked good and never came down. No one could remember when that happened.

There were lots of things like that around Dooley's, mementos of forgotten moments, the lost history of departed patrons. Behind the bar, there was a clutter of knickknacks attached to stories nobody could remember anymore: a large plaster moose with an antler chipped off, a ship in a bottle, autographed softballs from summer-league teams, a half-deflated football, faded snapshots, postcards wishing the staff could be here.

It's the stuff gourmands of old saloons call "character," as in "Don't take that down, it gives the place character." Drunk or sober, Nathan was one of those gourmands.

He gazed out the window beside the front door, at the glaring summer sunlight. The open mike was such a waste of time in August, when it seemed like most of Boston was on vacation. Driving to the gig, you would have thought it was Christmas Eve, with none of the jostling, nervous traffic he usually had to navigate. Where does everybody *go* this time of year? They can't all be on Cape Cod, for god's sake; this is a city of four million people.

He climbed back onto the stage for the finishing touch, winding the mike cords carefully around the stands. It made the stage look more professional and kept anxious open-mikers from tripping over them. Turning around to survey his work and deciding all was ready, he stepped down from the stage and walked over to the bar.

Nathan sat on a stool by the bend of the bar, leaned his head heavily on his hand, sighed, and again gazed out the window. It's like a ghost town. This is supposed to be rush hour. You can't even stage a decent traffic jam this time of year. What am I *doing* here? He smiled and shook his head, thinking, good lord, what kind of Bostonian sits around missing the traffic? He sighed again, louder than he intended.

"I'm coming, I'm coming," Jackie said as she walked up the bar. "Keep your shirt on."

"Sorry, Jackie," Nathan said. "I wasn't sighing at you. Just a general maintenance sort of sigh."

She laughed. "Yeah, a lotta that going around these days."

Jackie was the anchor at Dooley's. It was as if she came with the place. She was already working there when Murph bought the bar, and that was over thirty years ago. She had long, thick white hair, tied back in a ponytail in defiant disregard of anything approaching modern fashion. It suited her weathered face, with its startlingly bright blue eyes. She usually wore some form of work shirt over a white T-shirt tucked into faded blue jeans with rolled-up cuffs.

No one but Murph seemed to know her last name. Whenever anyone asked, her stock answer was "Just call me Jackie—that was good enough for my first two husbands." Nathan had been there almost fifteen years and still didn't know her full name.

He thought she just enjoyed having a secret that the regulars could tease her about. Jackie was very savvy about the culture of saloons and knew that a few ongoing secrets made people feel more like they were part of the place. Insiders.

"Go ahead, ask her what her last name is," a regular would tell a newcomer. So the newcomer would ask, get the "first two husbands" line, and giggle knowingly. It made both patrons feel more at home, like they knew something special about the place.

To Jackie, bartending was not a service job; it was a trade. She observed the ancient etiquette of the tavern and lamented how few people knew such things today. She always rapped her knuckles on the bar when she picked up a tip and scowled at patrons who hollered for service. A raised glass was all right, as was a raised finger. A simple wave of the hand was her preference. But shouting for her attention, especially after the music began, was either ignored or scolded. "I'm not your friggin' dog, honey," she'd say. "Just wait your turn."

Jackie was the only person outside of TV cop shows who Nathan had ever heard actually use the word *friggin'*. Swearing was a vital part of her punctuation, but she had long ago reconciled that with her respect for the bar as a public place. Words like *friggin'* and *Jeez Louise* became her profanity placebos. If she needed to actually swear, she would lean over the bar, right into the ear of whomever she was talking to. People were always flattered the first time she did that, another sign they'd become a regular.

Now, on this sleepy August Tuesday, Jackie poured Nathan his usual: a large mug of root beer, no ice. Since he'd given up alcohol, it was his drink of choice. He didn't miss drinking; lord knows, he'd done enough of it. But it felt awkward to hang around a bar without something dark and sudsy in his hand.

Jackie shoved the mug over to him. He was still sitting, head in hand, staring out the window. "You look as bad as I feel, ace," she said.

Nathan sat up straight and smiled. "Really?" He said. "Dash of the old soldier's disease? Touch of the plague?"

"Just the usual." She smiled sheepishly. "Aunt Jackie had too much medicine last night. Gotta head like a blowfish."

"Ah. Been to that movie," Nathan said, sipping his root beer. Another of the many odd little things about Dooley's. Root beer on tap. Who uses root beer as a mixer?

"What's got you all mopey?" Jackie asked.

"The usual with me, too. Wondering why the hell we do this. So tell me, oh wise one, why do we do this?"

Jackie tapped her hand on the bar and squinted her eyes, as though hard in thought. "Ooh, ooh, gimme a minute," she said. "On the tip of my tongue."

She popped her eyes wide and raised a finger. "Got it. Money?"

Nathan laughed. "Oh yeah, that. I keep forgetting. But seriously, why does Murph keep this open mike going in August? I mean, it's a ghost town around here. He can't be making any money."

"Yeah, but you know Murph. It's all about the regulars. He likes to keep everything the same."

"Makes sense, I guess. Even if he loses a little money now and then, people know what to expect when they drop by."

"It's more than that with Murph," Jackie said, topping off Nathan's root beer. "He's old school, he's neighborhood. Got it growing up in Southie. It's not just for the customers; he likes to see the same faces around here all the time. Even sour old faces like yours. Like a little family. You think he keeps you around for your looks?"

"I don't know why he keeps me around, Jackie, I really don't."

"Aw, don't start with me with that crap. Not this early. Save the pity for last call, will you? I can handle it better when I got a few pops in me. He likes you, Nathan. And he happens to think you're a heckuva musician. And so do I. So don't argue with me; I will peel your friggin' face right off."

"Yup, that's me," he said. "A natural-born open-miker."

"Jeez Louise, don't start with that stuff! I mean it. I got my own troubles. Woke up feeling like the whole Russian army camped in my mouth overnight. Marched around in their stocking feet. Yeww, I think they're still in there."

She stuck out her tongue and said, "Hup, hup, hup." With her tongue out, it sounded more like "huth, huth, huth."

Nathan laughed, took another long swallow of his root beer, and stood up. "Well, hair of the dog for you, m'dear. I'm going for my afternoon stroll."

"Take care, darlin,'" she said, picking up his mug and wiping the bar with her towel.

Nathan walked into the late-afternoon sunlight and was immediately hit by a chill wind that belonged more to October than August. It had been like this since the weekend.

Strange summer. A week ago it was so hot you could smell the tar on the streets. Last night it was so cool Nathan pulled his old patchwork comforter out of the closet. He could have simply shut the windows, of course, but the comforter was nice. In August, it felt like an indulgence. A comforter. God, he was getting old, wasn't he?

He smiled, stuffed his hands into the pockets of his black denim jacket, and looked up at the sky. A single huge cloud filled the horizon above the squat storefront buildings across the street. It was white around the edges, but the rest was an ominous slate gray. Above it, the sky was turning that quiet azure it becomes as day turns to twilight. Too early for twilight, though; that cloud is doing it. Might rain. Maybe not. These late-summer clouds often just tease. All blow, no bite.

Out of the corner of his eye, he noticed a young couple who'd stopped about ten feet away, then turned to stare at him, whispering to each other. Who was that? Was he somebody?

Nathan was used to this; he'd been getting those stares for years. Even before he was, briefly, a somebody, he would see people starting at him in supermarkets and on street corners. Something about the way he looked, and the easily confident way he carried himself, made people think he might be well known or important. Some actor in town for the American Repertory Theater? Maybe he's in a band, an eccentric software mogul, or some noted author guest-lecturing at Harvard.

Nathan had that kind of look. His hair was mahogany brown, nearly black, lightly speckled with gray. But it was still thick and wavy, worn just long enough to spill over his ears and collar. His eyes were often what drew people first, even from a distance. Like his hair, they were almost black, and despite the tired, sad lines around them, they remained piercingly bright and boyish. They were eyes that seemed to take in everything and to be thinking, always thinking. So when those bright black buttons fell on people, they were at once flattered and a little intimidated. His gaze made people think they were getting his full attention, whether or not they were.

But there was something else in his face, a sense that beneath all the intensity and self-involvement that comes with being an artist, and beneath the long years of cynicism and self-doubt, he genuinely liked people, enjoyed getting to know them and hearing their stories.

He was middle aged now, but his body, like his eyes, remained oddly boyish: slim-waisted, narrow-shouldered, and angular, making him look leaner than he was. In his youth, it was the kind of physique that made older women want to feed him. Now it conspired with those piercing eyes to make him look years younger than he was. Funny about that, because it had been just the opposite when he was in his twenties. Back then, he was always taken for an older and more worldly man, a lucky trait for a kid trying to look like a hard-traveling folksinger. Just good genes, he told himself, the one good thing his crazy parents left him.

If it's possible for a voice to match someone's eyes, Nathan's did. He had always sensed that people simply liked the sound of it, whether he was singing or talking. He could speak softly and command attention when others had to shout. In fact, he'd learned that the softer he spoke, the more people leaned in to hear.

It was not a beautiful or trained-sounding voice, but a warm baritone with a caramel resonance that made everything he said sound kind and credible. It felt like fine old suede and now that it had picked up a little gravel, it was even more honest and intelligent. It was a nice-guy voice, with a thick stillness beneath it and a beguiling halt to the cadence, suggesting the workings of the poet within. People were often flattered to simply hear that voice say their name; it implied a confidentiality that was often unintended. And people were inclined to believe whatever that voice said.

There was another quality, both indefinable and defining, that made people stare at him, whether he was on a stage or standing idly on a sidewalk. Everything Nathan did seemed to have some silent music to it. It wasn't simply that he was graceful and easy in his movements, it was as if every motion was set to a rhythm that only he could hear. It made him very attractive to watch, though no one ever quite knew why.

He looked down from the teasing cloud, across the street at an old café where people gathered around outdoor tables and conversations often broke out between complete strangers. So rare these days. A lavishly tattooed teen couple in black leather talked intently with a tweedy professorial type, a large black man dressed entirely in denim, and two elegant old men wearing berets. Old men in berets always struck Nathan as the sign of a genuine bohemia. God, he loved Cambridge.

Porter Square was one square north of Harvard Square and had always been something like the country cousin among Cambridge's several squares, ever since its origins as railhead for the cattle yards that once speckled the area. The square was named for one Zachariah B. Porter, who owned a nineteenth-century hotel there. Some historians said that was how the porterhouse steak got its name, though New York City and a small town called Flowery Branch, Georgia, also had stories claiming they were the birthplace of the porterhouse. Nathan enjoyed little mysteries like that, especially when they had no answers. They were like the old folk songs he loved so much; no one knew who wrote them or why. The mystery was part of the allure.

Boston was a big city, but Nathan might as well have been living in a tiny town like Flowery Branch. His life existed within about a square mile these days, from his home outside Harvard Square to Dooley's, up a few blocks to the music store where he taught guitar, and back home again. It seemed like the older he got, the smaller his life became. It wasn't supposed to go that way, was it?

Nathan strolled up Mass. Ave., Cambridge's main artery, and into Porter Square, enjoying the waning afternoon, thinking about nothing in particular. He'd been alone such a long time, years and years. That didn't bother him as much as how comfortable with it he'd become. Aloneness was an addictive thing. He was disappointed but not surprised that he'd never had his own family. His career had been such a roller coaster, with steep downslides and few climbs, or even level stretches, in which settling down could be considered. And since the long fall from his short stardom, it was all descent. All those dark, lost years.

But perhaps the seeds were sown before that, in a childhood he seemed to remember entirely in black and white. Watching his parents, there had been little to recommend the idylls of family life. He was still not certain if they had even liked each other, much less been in love. As a child, he saw their life together as a joyless burden to them both.

Perhaps it started there. He'd spent so much time alone as a child that he came to enjoy his own company, his vivid and intellectually adventurous interior life. He never felt lonely when he was alone, only when he was around people he didn't know. That may have been why he first started drinking, to make himself want to be around the eager strangers the touring life threw at him night after night. As his star rose, that eagerness grew more intense, and so did his drinking. He thought now that failure had made him a drunk; it actually began at the peak of his success.

Music always felt like home to Nathan, almost like a family. He fell in love with folk music before he knew what it was, before he discovered the mystical thread that connected his dad's old blues albums to his kiddie records of cowboy songs, sea chanteys, and "Ye Merry Olde Ballads of Colonial Days." He felt real people moving inside the old songs, like veins beneath the skin, and he wanted to know them. He always dug to the roots of whatever music he heard, trying to scrape to the bone, the source, what the Irish call the pure drop.

And music is always heard alone, no matter how many people are around you. Whether sitting in a crowded concert hall or in front of his dad's record player, listening to some long-dead blues guitarist, music traveled into Nathan's most private places. And he traveled with it.

Later, as he grew accustomed to his aloneness, he learned to take great pleasure in living by his own lights. He'd set out to live a radical life, an outsider's life. At least he succeeded at that.

He found himself well past the square, almost halfway to Harvard. He looked at his watch and turned back toward Dooley's, wondering who would show up. He liked to game-plan the open mike, just like he would a concert. He was, if nothing else, still a pro.

With a few exceptions, the current crop was a pretty motley bunch of squirrels, as Jackie liked to call them. Years ago, Nathan had referred to a particularly bad open mike as "a squirrelly lot," which Jackie found unaccountably hilarious. From then on, she referred to all open-mikers as squirrels. Inside jokes like that pleased her immensely, whether or not anyone else understood them.

It was always easy for Nathan to distinguish the would-be songwriters from the would-be stars. That never changed. Some came in week after week, working on their craft, trying to write better songs. Others were certain this was a game of attitude, of getting the right look, the right hairdo, hat, pose, or vocal affect.

The leader of the poseurs these days was a strutting peacock called Ryder. His name was actually Seth Ryder, from the affluent western suburb of Wellesley, but "Seth" didn't have that hard-traveling, folk-hero ring, so he went by his last name. He always held court at a long table near the stage, surrounded by a surly pack of fellow wannabes who flitted around him, sure that they were courtiers to the Next Big Thing in Boston's long line of Next Big Things.

There were also a few perennial squirrels who had no ambitions at all, but simply enjoyed the *craic*, as the Irish call the convivial vibe of shared music. To Nathan, there was a humble beauty to the way they played, however badly. It was so free of pretense and ambition.

Then there was Kit Palmer, the only regular who showed any real promise. Nathan thought she had both the physical attractiveness and distinctive sound that it took to have a career. But she also had a severe case of stage fright, so bad that it often made it impossible for her to complete her sets. Nathan's old instincts told him there was genuine potential there if she could overcome those shattering nerves. But that was a big if.

The first time she sang at Dooley's was a disaster. She'd come in for a few weeks without a guitar, huddling in the back corner, listening and writing in a journal. Nathan suspected she was summoning the nerve to sign up, so when she finally brought her guitar, he made a point to welcome her and try to put her at ease. Tell her to just have fun. It didn't work.

Her first song got off to a promising start but soon dissolved into a mess of missed chords and lyrics that trailed off into silence. Regaining her footing for a few measures, she would suddenly puff out a breath instead of the lyric, then seem to forget the melody. Staring helplessly at the audience, playing muted chords and shrugging in defeat, she would wait for the verse to begin again and try to hop back on. For a few lines she'd be okay, then the process would repeat, always beginning with a puffed breath and a missed word, followed by a missed beat and a painful silence.

Her skin was an almost ivory white, even more striking against her black hair and dark brown eyes. So when the stage fright hit, there was no hiding it. Splashes of bright red appeared on her cheeks and forehead, visible to everyone in the audience. She would shrug helplessly and stand there, blushing and huffing those awful breaths, waiting for the verse to come around again. Nathan often saw those moments coming before she did and suffered right along with her. If only he could do something to help.

Nathan wandered back into Dooley's around six-thirty, a deep quiet filling him after his evening stroll. He paused at the door, letting his eyes adjust to the sudden darkness. Dooley's was that rare bar that still smelled like a bar, even after Cambridge banned smoking in public places. Nathan guessed that the odor of tobacco was so deep in the wood that even without new smoke, it retained the musty scent, mingled with the musk of hardwood floors, spilled suds, and the slight but unmistakable pungency of what can only be described as regular patrons. Nathan loved it. Character.

He checked with Jackie but there'd been no calls. Another dead night. Murph, the owner, was holding court in his regular spot, a small table in the far back corner. As usual, he had a large checkbook, ledgers, and piles of business papers in front of him. His eyes darted back and forth between the bar and the Red Sox game on a TV mounted on the wall.

Before the music started, Murph would pay bills, look over receipts, watch TV, and chat with customers. As soon as the music began, however, he would turn off the TV. Music time was music time.

Murph was thickset, thought not at all fat, with a physique that suggested he'd once been an athlete, or at least a tough guy. The hair was nearly gone on top of his head, making his ruddy face look even larger than it was, and drawing attention to a fleshy mouth seemed to be smiling even when it wasn't.

He waved Nathan over with a shout of "Hey, been looking for you." Nathan smiled and nodded. He liked Murph. As Jackie said, he was old-school. He saw the bar as a business, of course, but even more as a little neighborhoods unto itself. "It stahts with the reg'lahs," he'd say in his thick South Boston brogue.

For nearly twenty-five years, he'd featured the same weekend act, an old rocka-billy singer who had a minor hit decades ago. Over time, the old singer's cornpone show became a cherished local institution. College students were told they simply had not done Cambridge until they'd seen that geezer twang his big pink guitar.

Keeping the old singer around was good business, but only because Murph stuck with him through some lean times. Murph believed loyalty was good business—how old-school was that?

So when he hired Nathan to start a Tuesday open mike, he didn't drop the idea when the first blush of popularity waned. Instead, he doubled down, asking Nathan to come up with something for Wednesdays. And he'd been rewarded: almost immediately, the Wednesday jam became popular, which helped to build up the Tuesday audience.

Murph was also a fan of Nathan's music, though he was never able to convince him of that. He constantly pestered Nathan to sing more, which Nathan took as simple kindness. They'd actually had some hot arguments about it, with Murph insisting he was speaking as a businessman and Nathan ridiculing the idea that having him sing more would make the cash registers *ka-ching*. Over time, it developed into a fond and manly ritual they both enjoyed. But Murph could never make Nathan play more than two or three songs.

"How ya doin', pal?" Murph hollered, grinning as Nathan got to the table.

Nathan smiled, still foggy from his quiet walk. He could fall so deeply into him-self these days. Or had he always been that way?

"Hey, you know what?" Murph said.

"No, Murph, I have no idea what. I never have any idea what."

Murph laughed like that was the funniest thing he'd heard all day. "You kill me, pal. Well, I'll *tell* you what. I been humming one of your songs all day. That one about being tongue-tied?"

Nathan nodded. "Not mine. It's an old Chris Smither song. 'Footloose.'"

"That's the one. Smither song, huh? Well, like I said, I been humming it all day, so would you sing it tonight?"

"I don't know, Murph. I haven't played it for a long time. Not sure I could remember it."

"Getting old, are you? Having trouble with the old memory?"

"No, I don't think…I mean, yeah, but—"

"Me, too," Murph said, nodding his head slowly. "I been having trouble remem-bering stuff lately. Like right now I can't remember, do I pay you for this open mike?" He grinned at Nathan, tapping his pen on the checkbook.

"Well now, Murph, you make a persuasive point there," Nathan said, rubbing his chin. "I think I could probably remember the song, now that you put it that way."

They laughed and slapped a high-five. Ah, male bonding. Rut, rut, hug, hug.

"Seriously, I'd love to hear it," Murph said, "if you think you can."

"How can I say no to the man who writes the checks?"

Murph chuckled and glanced up at the Red Sox game. "And people say you got no head for business."

They watched the game together until Nathan saw the first open-mikers arrive. He brought them the big chalkboard he always hung over the stage, and let them sign their names to it. It was a kick for them to see their names up there, even if it was just in chalk and they'd written it themselves. In fact, a few years ago, Nathan bought a chalkboard with a frame that looked like a theater marquee, to enhance the effect.

Kit Palmer walked in around seven, shyly smiling at Nathan as he handed her the sign-up board. She seemed nervous, signing her name and commenting on the chilly weather, but scurrying to her usual spot in the back before he could reply. Nathan decided that if she didn't fall apart tonight, he would have a chat with her, try to make her feel a little more at home. Maybe that would help.

Promptly at eight, Nathan walked to the mikes at center stage. He began, as usual, by chatting a little about his day. To him, folk music was a personal art, and the between-song talk was as important as the songs.

He had a disarming way of teasing himself, usually about being too dense to get the point. For example, he would say he was confused by the philosopher Henry David Thoreau's most famous words of wisdom: "Simply, simplify."

"So how come he said it twice?" He'd say, shaking his head uncertainly.

He also liked to mock his aging folk-star status. "I'm actually a very famous folk-singer but nobody knows it," he'd say, as if it made perfect sense. It never got the big laugh at Dooley's that it did with older crowds in the suburbs, though.

Nathan assumed that was because the younger crowd at Dooley's didn't know about his brief flirtation with fame, but he was wrong. It didn't strike them as funny because they enjoyed the idea of someone being secretly famous. And that's exactly how most of them saw Nathan Warren.

He was the only musician they knew who'd even gotten close to the starry heights most of them dreamed of reaching. His hard fall from those heights, which they all knew about, only made him more of a mythic figure, like the star-crossed lovers in the sad old ballads he sang.

To many of them, folk music was the anti-pop, a perennial outcast from the commercial music industry, so it stood to reason that it would have anti-stars. For Nathan to have fallen so far was proof to them that he'd never sold out, never offered his music to the highest bidder. He'd never let a big label dress him and coif him and tell him what to sing. Anyone like that was bound to wind up at a battered old joint like Dooley's, singing for his supper.

So the Dooley's crowd saw that joke more as a worldly boast than self-mockery. The smiles and nods he read as sympathy were in fact awe, sprinkled with the usual open-miker's portion of envy.

Nathan closed his set with Murph's request, the Chris Smither song he'd learned almost 20 years ago. He hadn't been completely honest with Murph about why he didn't want to do it. Nathan found it a little painful to sing; it hit too close to home, with its wincing portrait of a life stuck in neutral.

> *I've lost my shoes but I don't feel like walking.*
> *If you find them and they fit, they're yours for free.*

Nathan accompanied the song with a wistful, circular chord pattern, sliding fluidly to higher notes on the guitar neck when the chorus came around.

> *Tongue-tied and turned around*
> *Footloose with your feet stuck in the ground.*

"Footloose" had been a standard for Nathan during the worst of his depression and drinking, but he'd never seen how closely it mirrored his own sad little life. Back then, he just thought it was a great song and that audiences liked his intricate guitar work.

> *I know my name, now I know it ain't no secret.*
> *If you know it, I will claim I'm not to blame.*
> *I'd be mad to seek it.*
> *Seemed to grow some wings and sail away.*

He sang almost in a whisper, looking at the neck of his guitar or glancing around the small crowd. A few years ago, when he began to find the song uncomfortable, he did not stop singing it. Instead, he decided he would only do it on request. Like so many things in his life, things that were much more important than which songs he sang at an open mike, he let the world decide for him. He liked to think of that as some kind of mature contentment, but it was really more of a surrender, wasn't it? He could always find a reason to not do something; that had become his forte.

> *The sinking sun and rising sun are most amazing*
> *When the difference doesn't matter much to you.*
> *Just blazing cloud horizons*
> *Going in and out from red to mainly blue.*
> *This confusion ain't for nothing.*
> *It's what you get for something*
> *That you could have done but never seem to do.*

Wasn't that the track of his own great retreat from life's daunting promises to its small, reliable comforts? Despite himself, Nathan winced and looked away from the crowd as he finished the song with a series of light, wet slides down the strings. It almost sounded like the guitar was trying to stop sobbing, sighing to regain its breath before resolving into an elegiac strum of the root chord. Nathan let it ring out, like fading bells in the night air, and the crowd remained silent until all the sound had vanished.

He looked down at the stage, shaking his head slowly back and forth, blessedly aware of only the fading music, the sensual feeling of it slowly leaving his bones as the final notes echoed through the old wood of his guitar.

The applause started quietly, almost timidly, then strengthened in volume. Nathan lifted his head suddenly, as if startled by the sound, and broke into a warm, open-mouthed smile. He nodded his head a few times, thanked the crowd, then waved the applause down and introduced the first open miker.

He did not notice that when the song began, Kit Palmer looked up from the journal she was always writing in and leaned forward in her seat, listening to the song with a hand over her mouth. At the end, she leaned back, exhaled hard, and applauded loudly. Then she turned her head back down into her journal and began to write furiously

The open mike was slow, only a dozen had signed up to play. When the college students were in town, there could be twenty-five or more. And it was pretty bland; only a few stood out from the strained sound of clumsy beginners who all try the same tricks, find the same cool-sounding chords, and make the same mistakes.

Ryder certainly stood out; the question was whether that was a good thing. Lately he seemed to be wrestling with the great and troubling career issue of hats. Last week he'd worn a huge Stetson cowboy hat but did nothing to break it in. Its wide straight brim, along with his large Roman nose, stringy brown hair, and thin frame, made him look curiously birdlike, which was probably not the look he was going for.

This week Ryder was sporting what appeared to be either a wool derby or a stocking cap with a brim. Nathan guessed he saw it as a negotiation between the hat and the more affable cap, but its floppy shape and tiny visor left him looking like a cross between an Andean peasant and a Victorian tea merchant. Again, probably not the look he was after.

The quest for the perfect hat must have taken up Ryder's time, because he sang the same two maudlin songs he'd done the week before. Still, Ryder's obedient squirrel pack applauded fiercely as he strutted off the stage, hips swaggering, certain he'd knocked 'em dead.

Ryder was followed by Randall Cahill, a middle-aged MIT professor who liked to be introduced as Ramblin' Randy. He was one of the most loyal regulars, and Nathan fondly thought of him as the Charlie Brown of the open mike. That was partly because of his round face, but also because of the sublime pleasure he took in singing for people.

At MIT, he was something of a legend, a professor of something so complex that Nathan couldn't understand it, despite several patient attempts by Randy to explain. All Nathan knew was that it had something to do with germs and computers. And that Dr. Cahill had led MIT research teams that won major science awards.

So Ramblin' Randy was no fool. He was also no musician. But he took such exuberant joy in performing that he seemed to not comprehend, or at least not care, that he often sounded foolish. In his youth, he'd probably toyed with being a folksinger but realized he had no talent for music. He compensated for that with an almost manic enthusiasm. Nathan liked him a lot.

Randy knew scores of old American folk songs, but for some reason he'd latch on to the same two and do them week after week. Then he would come in with a fresh pair and repeat them for several weeks.

Nathan once asked him why he did that, since he knew so many songs. "Gotta get 'em down," Randy said, with such an earnest nod that Nathan could only reply, "Of course, of course. Gotta get 'em down."

For weeks, Randy had been fixated on a boisterous sea chantey and "Remember the Alamo," which sounded traditional but was actually written in the 1950s by a Texas folksinger named Jane Bowers.

Randy worked hard to make the chestnut seem topical. Every week, after solemnly pushing his old straw cowboy hat back on his head, he reminded people that many Hispanics had died "alongside Crockett and Bowie in that doomed fort in 1836."

And with that, he was off, his right arm moving in wide arcs, pounding the chords in loud, tick-tock beats. Above that, he hollered:

Heyyyyyy-ooooop, Santy-Annaaaaaa
They're killing your soldiers below-ow-ow
So the rest of Texaaaaaassss will know-ow-ow
And remember the Ala-mooooo."

That last word came out sounding distinctly bovine, "*Ala-moo,*" which made it difficult for even Nathan to listen with a straight face. The first time Randy sang it, however, people began to *moo* along, so he now gleefully exaggerated the *mooing* even more. Randy was happy whenever—and however—the crowd responded to him.

The cockier squirrels, like Ryder, loved to overreact to Randy, their cheers dripping with sarcasm and condescension, made all the louder by the secret fear that they were not, in the end, so different from him. Nathan didn't know if Randy picked up on the sarcasm. He was a very smart man; maybe he just didn't care. Why should he?

The highlight of the evening, for Nathan at least, was Kit Palmer's set. She seemed to be trying to focus her stage fright fears around her breathing, taking long, careful breaths as she introduced songs and during instrumental passages. It helped a little; the red patches made only brief appearances. But she was still in terror of the fright returning. And so, of course, it would.

Nathan wished he could tell her something that would help, but it was like a kid learning to ride a bicycle. You can't tell them how to balance, you just keep pushing them along and then—*voilà!*—they're riding and wondering how they ever had trouble with it before. It's nothing you can explain, nothing you can teach. All you can do is be there.

With her nerves somewhat under control, Nathan could focus more on her songs. There was real potential there, a flowing sense of melody and a knack for vivid details that invited listeners inside her songs: a lover stealing the covers, a face reflected in a moonlit window.

Her lyrics could sag into obscurity, though. She often spoiled the mood with distractingly artful images, like a lover's farewell that was like a "*cinéma-vérité* sonnet." It made her sound smart—she knew about *cinéma-vérité* and sonnets—but what did it mean? Screw you in French?

Between songs, if she could manage to talk at all, she was shyly endearing. Singing or talking, she had a way about her that people trusted. You believed what she said because you thought she believed it. She spoke to audiences at eye level, not looking up from a cloying, insecure place or lording down from a feigned star posture.

And she was pretty, very pretty. The folk biz was still show biz, after all, and that mattered. Even better, she had a distinct prettiness, the kind that made her seem at once mysterious and knowable. She had the makings of classically beautiful features: an oval face with almost impossibly white skin, a few light freckles, and very dark brown eyes. Her hair was jet black, cut a bit above shoulder length, with just enough wave to always look a little tousled.

Yet something was just irregular enough to set her apart, and alluringly so. Her mouth was a little wider than you would expect for her narrow face, making her seem both sensual and waifish. Her eyes were not unusually large, but her black lashes were, drawing attention to her dark pupils. She was not tall, but her lithe, angular frame made her seem both taller and more delicate than she was.

Her voice was soft but resonant, a shade deeper than you would expect, rippling with intelligence and friendliness. And she knew how to use that voice. There was not a trace of affect to her vocals; she sang sustained vowels exactly the way she spoke them, rare for a beginner. In everything she did, from hitting beautiful vocal sustains to crumbling like an old cookie from stage fright, she always appeared to be utterly her-self. Nathan knew enough about stardom to know how important that was, especially in the cozy, up-close world of folk music. People did not just like Kit Palmer; they *wanted* to like her.

Nathan's favorite part of the open mike came after everyone who signed up to play had gotten their chance. Years ago, he'd dubbed it the witching hour, for reasons he could no longer remember, and the name stuck. After the final open-miker left the stage, usually around eleven, Nathan announced that the official open mike was over but the stage would remain open to anyone who wanted to share a song, story, or poem. Then Jackie would ring her tip bell, a small bronze replica of an old ship's bell. The *clang, clang* officially launched the witching hour. Jackie never rang the tip bell while musicians were onstage. Music time was music time, though she claimed she simply never had the opportunity on folk nights, since as she put it, "You folkies are the worst tippers I've seen since I catered a Republican fund-raiser in Hyannisport."

People chatted throughout the evening, but tried to be attentive during the official open mike. When the witching hour bell rang, however, all pretense of that was gone. The talking lamp was lit. Heads snapped toward the door whenever it opened, because the witching hour was when local folk stars were most likely to drop by, try out a new song, or just pay their respects to Nathan. He had given most of them early opportunities to perform, and words of encouragement or advice they recalled now as golden moments in their careers.

Of course, Nathan acknowledged none of that; to his mind, he had seen no one rise from his open mike who did not succeed entirely by their own talent and will. That negated any debt, or even gratitude, someone might feel toward him. He often brushed aside such comments so aggressively that people worried they had offended him.

Nathan enjoyed the witching hour because the only thing he loved as much as playing music was talking about it. Not biz talk, career talk; he was quickly bored by that. But he relished conversations about the art of music, the discipline and tradition. It was one of the things that had first drawn him to folk music: the people who played it felt deeply about it, thought hard about it and cared so much.

The witching hour was also when Ferguson usually rolled in. His byline read Ryan Ferguson, but everyone just called him Ferguson; it suited him. He had been the folk critic for one of the local newspapers for nearly two decades and Nathan's friend even longer.

He rarely missed a Tuesday or Wednesday at Dooley's but he came for the talk, not the music. After a day spent poring over new CDs, interviewing musicians, and writing about music, the last thing he wanted to hear was a parade of open-mikers stumbling through their songs because they saw him in the audience and wondered if their big break had finally come.

If he came in early—and he did like to keep up on the local talent—he slipped in the back door and sat quietly at Murph's table. When Jackie rang the witching hour bell, he would saunter to the bar as if he'd just come in, and sit down on the stool Nathan always saved for him.

Ferguson was a small thick man with dark gray hair and a light gray beard he cut with the seasons, but not the way you'd expect. He kept it long in summer and short in winter. "The first time some kid points to me and says, 'Look, Mommy, it's Santa,' I grab the scissors," he'd say.

He often came in with something he wanted to say, something that had been buzzing in his brain that day. Nathan and Jackie could tell when that was the case; he was antsy, fingers tapping on the bar, eyes darting around the room. At other times, there was a stillness to him that Nathan enjoyed being around. It was the kind of stillness that came from having done hard work, work worth doing, and knowing that you did it well.

Tonight, Ferguson was antsy, and Nathan watched to see how he would steer the conversation toward whatever it was he wanted to say. As Ferguson gulped his first rum, his eyes darted around the room, then fell on Ryder.

"Good lord," he said, slapping his glass down on the bar. "What is that thing on Ryder's head? It looks like a fungus."

Nathan laughed. "I have no idea. He's been fidgeting with it all night; I don't think he can get the angle right. Jaunty? Slouched? Casually askew? The toils of the modern-day troubadour."

"Same goose-fart songs, I suppose."

"Oh, yeah."

Ferguson finished his first rum and motioned to Jackie, who was already pouring him a second. He always drank his first two rounds quickly—Mt. Gay Rum and a beer—then nursed his drinks for the rest of the evening. Around the time Nathan quit drinking, Ferguson made his own peace with the physical realities that every pleasure drinker must deal with, or die from. He loved the first convivial buzz of alcohol, and it calmed his mind after a hard day of writing. He decided to allow himself that and nothing more. Since then, Nathan had almost never seen him drunk.

"A few weeks ago," Nathan said, "I told Ryder he shouldn't worry about all that image stuff, that it would take care of itself."

"What did he say?" Ferguson said, lifting his beer bottle.

"Nothing. I think he just tried to figure out if it was a compliment."

"Jesus. Well, like George Bernard Shaw said, 'Youth is wasted on the young.'"

Nathan smiled. "He also said the only thing we learn from experience is that we never learn anything from experience."

Ferguson laughed. It always made Nathan feel smart when he could make Ferguson laugh.

Ferguson heaved a long sigh, a sign that the rum was kicking in. "Perhaps if I spoke to the lad," he said. Nathan eyed Jackie: here we go. She grinned.

Ferguson waved to Ryder, motioning him to come over, which he nearly tripped over himself doing. An interview, perhaps? Something in depth, my formative years on the mean streets of Wellesley?

"Hi, Ryder," Ferguson said. "I thought about you and some of the other open mikers today, while I was reviewing a CD by a new Texas songwriter. It got me thinking about things I've noticed about you and some other open mikers. We're just talking here; this isn't for publication or anything."

"Okay," Ryder said. He winked in recognition of Nathan without actually looking at him. This kid's annoying even when he's being polite.

Ferguson cleared his throat and spread his hands along the bar. As he began to speak, he closed his eyes, measuring every word. "Well, what I wrote about this guy's music was that it sometimes felt like he was writing songs about other songs. Kind of a cookie-cutter approach: here's my wistful highway song; here's my lost-my-lover song; here's my got-a-new-lover song. I wondered if the guy had anything he wanted to say or if he was doing what he thought people expected a songwriter to do."

He smiled at Ryder. "I hear a little of that in your music, too," he said. "Don't get me wrong, it's a great way to learn. I'm not criticizing here."

Ryder cocked his head, grinning nervously.

Ferguson cleared his throat dramatically and drank a healthy swig of rum. There's the windup; here's the pitch.

"Well, this is what that Texas songwriter got me thinking," he said. "I wasn't able to get it into the review, but I thought you might find it useful, Ryder. If you'll indulge me."

Ryder nodded, swallowing hard.

Ferguson again closed his eyes and spoke in a measured cadence. "As near as I can tell, the difference between art and craft is that art is always trying to tell the truth. Any old chair is not art but a Shaker chair is. Why? Because a Shaker chair tells us something about the people who built it, who they were, what they believed, how they lived their lives."

Ferguson opened his eyes, smiled at Ryder, and said, "That Texas guy made me wonder if there was anything he really wanted to say about himself. Anything true, anything real. Anything that made him so sad or happy or pissed-off that he wanted to shout it out loud to see if anybody else felt the same way."

He gently poked Ryder's chest with his finger. "Doesn't anything piss you off like that, so much that you want to howl it for the whole world to hear?"

"Like what?" Ryder squeaked. He was in way over his head.

"Like *what*?" Ferguson bellowed, then reined himself in. Jackie cleared her throat to keep from laughing. Nathan smiled at her.

"Like what?" Ferguson repeated, his voice gentle and reflective. There really was a touch of the actor in him. "That's a good question, actually. Like what? Well, look around you. What's wrong with things today? It seems to me that talented young artists like you gather at places like this, singing for no money because you want something more than you can get from pop music. Something that feels real, that's about *you,* not what some Madison Avenue marketing company thinks you are. Right?"

Ryder nodded excitedly. He thinks I'm talented?

Ferguson continued. "You want something real, but all you get from pop culture these days—from music, movies, TV, whatever—is cynicism, aloofness, the cultivated snicker. It's as if seeing through the shit means you're not part of the shit. But you are. Unless you point your finger at it and say, 'Look, it's shit,' then you're just swimming in it with everybody else."

Ferguson took a long sip of his beer. Ryder stared at him but said nothing.

"But it's not life that's wrong," Ferguson said quietly, staring into his beer. "What's wrong is what we're being told life is. As if nothing that's not for sale is worth our attention. And that's just not true."

He patted Ryder on the shoulder and smiled. "Anyway, what I wrote about that Texas songwriter was that he should find his fine young rage, howl at the moon a little, and take some chances. And so should you, Ryder. Find your rage and aim it at the people who think they've got you figured out. The people who want you to believe that life is just a big goddamn shopping mall where you go to work during the day, making other people rich, then return at night to spend what you've earned, making the same people even richer. Doesn't that *piss* you off?"

Ryder nodded. "Yeah, yeah," he said, almost shouting.

"Good. A little food for thought, that's all, some things I wanted to get off my chest. You're a good kid, Ryder, just keep writing. I guess all I'm saying is, don't be afraid to dig a little deeper. You might like what you find down there."

Ryder nodded, shook Ferguson's hand, and sauntered back to his adoring squirrels.

Nathan smiled. "I do enjoy your sermons, Brother Ferguson," he said.

"Well, we must do what we can to keep the little ones amused. Think I was too hard on him?"

"Maybe, but he'll get over it. There are depths to that boy's vanity that he has not begun to plumb. Look at him over there. He's probably telling his pals you think he's a talented young artist."

"You think that's all he heard? Really?"

"I don't know, man. I never know with him."

Twirling his beer bottle in his hand, Ferguson said, "Getting old is frustrating, but not for the reasons you think it will be. You get these opportunities to whisper a warning to your vanished youth as it swishes past: beware of vanity, it lies; beware of ambition, it's never enough. But youth struts by, oblivious, arrogant, and perfect, straight into the mine fields."

Nathan took a thoughtful sip of his root beer. "You suppose people warned us, way back when?" he said. "And we were that stupid?"

Ferguson glared at him. "Were we that stupid?" he barked. "Is *that* the question?"

"Ah. Point taken. Sorry I asked."

"Were we that stupid," Ferguson repeated, chuckling and shaking his head. He waved his empty beer bottle at Jackie, and she reached into the cooler behind the bar.

Ferguson asked if any of the open-mikers had impressed Nathan. He motioned toward Kit Palmer, alone on the bench against the far wall, her journal open in front of her, peering at her iPhone.

"She's certainly pretty enough," Ferguson said. "She's the one with the stage fright?"

Nathan nodded. "Yeah. She did okay tonight. I'm pretty sure she'll get over it; the trick is convincing her."

"The only thing we have to fear is fear itself."

"Exactly. That's exactly it. Actually, I was planning to go over and talk with her tonight, see if I can calm her down a little." They looked at her, sitting alone, head down, in her own world.

"I really think she's got some potential," Nathan said, "if she can get past those nerves."

Ferguson spread his hands on the bar and straightened his back. "So she rates a royal visit, eh?" he said, grinning. "Very impressive."

"Oh, drink your drink," Nathan said, getting off his bar stool.

Ferguson was referring to the way some open-mikers believed there was a pecking order to how Nathan treated them, and that a visit from him moved them up a step on some imaginary career ladder. Such nonsense. He obviously had no ability to advance anyone's career or he'd advance his own, right?

Still, if they wanted to believe it, he'd play along; and Kit Palmer could use some royal treatment. Ryder and his crew had been particularly patronizing to her tonight. Ryder actually patted her on the back as she left the stage, saying, "You'll get 'em next time, honey," in a voice dripping with superiority. Nathan was not going to sit with her in order to worry Ryder, but the fact that it would certainly pleased him.

He walked past Randy, who was sitting with a few older squirrels at a large table in the middle of the room. "I love the way you play that Smither song," he told Nathan. "I tried to figure out those little guitar patterns once, but they're trickier than they look."

Nathan was always a bit startled when Randy wasn't doing his Ramblin' Randy schtick. His voice was so erudite and, well, professorial. He must fit right in at MIT.

"Come in early next week and I'll show you," Nathan said. "It's pretty simple once you know how."

"Like most things in life, eh?" Randy said.

Nathan smiled and walked back to Kit Palmer. She had her journal open but was tapping something on her cell phone.

"Hi," he said. "Mind if I sit down?" She put down the phone and slid over on the bench, but not far, so he had to sit closer to her than he would have.

He glanced at her open journal. She must have listened hard to "Footloose," because she'd written, "Footloose with your feet stuck on the ground," with the alliterative *F's* underlined. She'd also written the line, "If you find it just amuse it. Every time I try to use it," circling the inner-rhyme of "amuse" and "use." In big letters, she'd written "blazing cloud horizon going in and out from red to mainly blue," with four exclamation points beside it. Nathan smiled. She's right, that's a killer line.

She must have been eavesdropping on Ferguson's talk with Ryder, too, because she'd also written "diff. art + craft: telling the truth," and "find your fine young rage." At least someone got the point.

He glanced at the facing page, where she'd critiqued her set. In big letters, she wrote "TOO MUCH TALK." He pointed to it as she closed the journal. "Sorry to poke my nose in there," he said. "But I don't think you talked too much."

"You don't?"

"Any talk can seem like too much at an open mike, looking out at all those people who want you to finish so they can get their turn. But it's important to work on what you say between songs. In a folk club, people want to think they're getting to know you, and I get that from what you say between songs. It feels real."

He cleared his throat and shook his head. Lecturing again. Harrumph. God, he was as bad as Ferguson. Shrugging his shoulders, he said, "So if you ask me—not that you did but *if* you did—stick with it. It works for you."

"Thanks," she said, seeming both pleased and nervous. She really was pretty. Nathan asked how she got into folk music.

She told him she'd grown up in Connecticut, with very liberal parents who used to play a lot of old folk records. She'd liked the music but not how much they played it and how young they always acted when they did. She said she used to tease them by calling it fogey music, as in, "Aw, Mom, don't play those fogey songs again."

She looked suddenly at Nathan, her eyes startled and wide. "No offense," she said with a nervous puff of breath. He'd noticed that before when she talked between songs; it seemed to be some kind of nervous tic, a milder version of those heavy breaths that announced her stage fright. It was as if the puffs popped out involuntarily, almost like silent hiccups.

"No offense taken," Nathan said, smiling at her.

"I mean, I don't think that way about your music at all."

"None taken."

"I think you're a great singer. And songwriter."

"None taken."

She puffed another little breath and stared at the table. "I'm always telling people I wish you'd sing more," she muttered.

"None taken, Kit. So how did you get into folk music? Playing it, I mean."

"Well, you're going to think this is, like, really stupid," she said, "but my mom wanted me to take classical violin and I hated it. All the emphasis on technique and *virtuosity*." She said that last word like it was a skin rash.

"So my mom said, 'Why don't you try fiddling? It's more social, and you can hold your bow any way you want.'"

"Cool," he said.

"What?" Kit said sharply, as if what he'd said was a non sequitur.

"I think that's cool," he said, laughing a little. "I mean, good for your mom. It's important for kids to have fun with music. So what did you play, Irish, bluegrass?"

"Scottish mostly. I did a few contests, you know, when I was eight or nine." She bobbed her head on each syllable of the word contests, to be sure he saw how dumb she thought it was. "I hated the competition but I liked the social part, getting together to play tunes. And I loved those melodies. But I gave it up when I got older. Not hip enough for high school, I guess. I was pretty stupid back then."

She said she'd gone to college in Boston, considering a career in theater or writing, then got interested in poetry. She tapped her journal.

"That's when I started carrying around one of these," she said. "But I thought, like, who reads poetry? Just a bunch of other poets. It all seems kind of ingrown, you know? Like classical music."

"I know what you mean," Nathan said. "Pete Seeger said we've become a nation of experts, poets writing for poets, novelists writing for novelists, songwriters writing for songwriters. We go to the food expert for dinner, the car expert to fix our cars, and the wood expert to cut our wood for us. We don't do things for ourselves like we used to and we don't do things together. We just take turns being experts for each other."

She thought about that a minute. Clearing her throat, she said, "Well, *any*-way, after I graduated, I tried all kinds of things. I even thought about acting, but I figured it might be a drawback that I can't stand on a stage for five minutes without making people want to call the paramedics." She laughed a little.

She straightened her back and slapped her hands on the table. "Then, at twenty-five, I had what I call my 'precocious midlife crisis.' I decided I had to stop being such a dabbler, pick something and just go for it. I thought maybe I didn't stick with those other things because I wanted to do something with music. I got a guitar in college, wrote some songs, so I started checking out the open mikes. I thought, well, this way I can do my poetry, use my theater stuff a little, and be a musician. All in one neat little package."

She looked up at him, as if to see if she'd answered correctly, then shrugged and spread her hands. "So, here I am."

"Hmm," Nathan said, nodding and smiling. "That's not far off from how I decided to be a folksinger. Plus, I love those old songs, the traditional ones."

"I can tell when you sing them," she said softly, with a smile he'd never seen before, warm, tender, almost maternal. He thought about making a crack about fogey songs, but didn't. He didn't want to do anything to make her uncomfortable. He was enjoying this.

"So you're a fiddler," he said. "How come you never bring your fiddle down here?"

"I don't know. I still have it, play a little for myself once in a while. I guess I didn't think it had anything to do with this music." She waved a hand around the room. "I mean, all you see is guitars."

"Yeah, but it's all folk music, just different flavors. You should come down here on Wednesday and join the jam. Very different scene, very social. You wouldn't even have to get on stage; people sit at the tables and play along. There's no pressure and lots of fiddles."

He gave her a surprised look, as if he'd just thought of something. "Actually, that'd be a great thing for you to do," he said. "Get back to the fun of social music, so you're not always thinking about the spotlight and worrying about getting nervous. You were better tonight, by the way."

"Thanks," she said. "But I'm still thinking about it all the time, nervous I'll get nervous." She shook her head, staring down at the table. "It's so frustrating, Nathan. But like you said, I'll probably just get over it. Sometime." She puffed another breath, but hotter, deliberate. She was mad at herself.

They were quiet for a moment. He realized he had enjoyed hearing her say his name, and that he liked her. She was very smart, but in a humble, personal way, watching the world around her, processing what she saw. There was a lot going on with her. And something else, he thought. A good person, just a good egg.

"But the jam is bluegrass, isn't it?" She said suddenly. "I never played that."

"Well, it's called a folk jam, but it's mostly bluegrass. Same basic tunes, though: jigs, reels, hornpipes, waltzes. Most of those old Southern tunes started out in Ireland or Scotland. A lot of Celtic players come down, actually. I think you'll pick it up pretty quickly. Different groove, but the notes will be friendly."

"Friendly notes. I like that."

"So we'll see you tomorrow?"

"You bet. Dust off the old fiddle."

She nodded her head slowly. "I really do like your music," she said quietly, smiling that warm smile again.

"See you tomorrow then," he said. She waved her fingers as he walked away.

A little after closing time, Nathan stood on the stage, taking the microphones off their stands but leaving the cords carefully hanging on the mike holders. Tuesdays were nice; he didn't have to take down everything since he used the same basic setup for the jam. He had to put up more mikes, though; the stage would be crammed with jammers.

He enjoyed the bar after hours, the intent quiet. Jackie was restocking the shelves and making notes for the day bartender. Murph was in the back, counting the cash and getting his nightly deposit ready. Like the afternoon, this was a time for the workers, and Nathan liked to think of himself that way.

He thought about his set and remembered something had been wrong with the guitar on the chorus of "Footloose." One of those slides up the neck had knocked it out of time. He sat cross-legged on the stage, holding the guitar in his lap, playing the chorus and mouthing the words silently.

That's it, that transitional chord. He slid it too fast. He played it again. But he liked it that way; the wetness gave the whole chorus a nice motion. Maybe if he lengthened the pause before the slide. He tried that and it worked. Like the tumblers of a lock falling into place, the chorus clicked back into time. Ah. Nice feeling.

He played it a few more times, then carefully put the guitar into its case. He remained cross-legged on the stage, resting his forearms on his knees, remembering Kit's set. Some real promise there, beneath the stage fright. He wondered if she had what it took for a real career. She was obviously ambitious; she wouldn't be putting herself through all this if she wasn't. But talent and ambition aren't the whole package; they're just the starting blocks. He'd learned that much from Joyce.

Nathan was married once, for barely a year, but it was a marriage he was never quite able to escape. Her name when they met was Joyce Houghton, but she was still using her married name when she moved to Los Angeles, right after their divorce, signed a major label deal, and became the big star everyone in Boston had thought Nathan would be.

Ever since, her "brief tumultuous marriage" to "a minor cult star in Boston" was a standard part of Joyce Warren's biography, popping up whenever she was profiled in a newspaper or celebrity magazine. The "minor cult star" didn't bother Nathan—it was true, wasn't it?—as much as the "brief tumultuous marriage." Brief, yes, but tumultuous? Hell, they barely spoke after the first three months. He had no hard feelings about how it ended and neither did she, as far as he could tell. She'd even suggested he come to L.A. after her second album came out, because she thought she could get him a record deal. But he was still waiting for his big record to come out.

He thought the main reason they got married was that everybody expected it. They were the two bright stars on the Boston scene—it was *kismet*. He'd been passionately attracted to her, lord knows, but he didn't think he'd ever loved her. He wasn't even sure he liked her, though he enjoyed her quick intelligence and almost cheerful cynicism about the music business.

Which was not to say that Joyce Warren was not the genuine cloth. She was a terrific songwriter who used her earthy beauty to create an exotic sexual persona, but never at the expense of her music. In fact, she could have been a bigger star if she'd played by the pop-star rules more than she did. She was still regarded as a renegade within the industry, renowned for her stubbornness and independence. And it had cost her; the music business was not a renegade-friendly place these days.

When Nathan finally quit drinking, he searched his memories of Joyce to try to figure out what had gone wrong with his career. He saw more clearly how different they had been. He realized, a bit sadly, that there really was such a thing as star quality, and that talent was only part of the mysterious compound that created it. It was a hybrid fuel of talent, attractiveness, ambition, discipline, and a relentless singularity of purpose. It was as if becoming a star, and then remaining one, was all Joyce Warren was.

When they were together, she was constantly on the phone, writing letters, meeting one dead-end agent after another. Nathan stayed home, playing his guitar, writing songs, serenely certain that his purer path would be rewarded in the end. It was not.

He had been the bigger local star when they married, and, yes, perhaps she used that to help her career. But Joyce had been an undeniable talent and she always used her stardom well: shining her light on other songwriters, reminding people that she did not emerge from a split-pea shell, as she liked to put it, but from a long tradition of folk songwriters. She was always touring on behalf of good causes, from fighting AIDS in Africa to land-mine removal to endangered birds in the Yucatán, and the lobbies outside her concerts were littered with displays from grassroots nonprofit groups. And yes, perhaps she used those things to help sustain her career. More power to her.

Nathan had recently read that she was leaving her label of nearly twenty years. She said she was tired of being its "token integrity artist," to be trotted out whenever the label was accused of not being committed to good music.

It was classic Joyce: true, but neglecting to mention how much her sales had declined, or that she'd been in an artistic slump for years, trying to wriggle her aging sensibilities into the tight fit of today's youth-obsessed pop market. She'd essentially been writing the same songs over and over, filled with a romantic angst that seemed increasingly puerile as she grew older. They became even more laughable when she actually became a grandmother, thanks to a son from her equally brief second marriage.

Nathan glanced over at Jackie to make sure she wasn't ready to lock up. Still busy, giving the bar a good rubbing. She looked at him and winked. No hurry.

Did Kit have that kind of, well, whatever it was that Joyce had? Could she, under all those jitters? It didn't just happen to her on stage; Nathan recalled those nervous puffs of breath when they talked. He leaned back on his hands, dangled his feet over the stage, and smiled, remembering what Kit did the first time she played at Dooley's.

Her set had been a disaster. She must have wanted to run out the door that night and never come back. Instead, she had walked up to Nathan, awkwardly thrust out her hand, and said, "Hi, I'm Kit Palmer."

"I know," he'd said, smiling and shaking her hand. "We've met, remember? When you signed up to play."

She nodded and the red patches appeared again. "Of course," she said softly. "But I mean, like, we never actually…well, *anyway*…I'm sure you saw what happened up there. Quite the train wreck, huh?"

"Oh, it wasn't that bad. A lot of people get nervous their first time. The stage can be a scary place. But I liked your songs."

"Thanks," she said. The red was suddenly gone from her face and her dark eyes stared directly into his. The compliment didn't seem to surprise her. Some real confidence there. Good.

She was obviously trying to impress him that there was more going on with her than she showed on stage, which was another good sign. A certain self-regard, even cockiness, was part of this job.

"I thought maybe you could give me some advice about how to keep from falling apart up there," she said, her voice stronger.

"Well, I'm flattered that you'd ask," he said, smiling when she rolled her eyes shyly. "I know it sounds funny to say so soon after—what did you call it?—your train wreck, but I'd say don't worry about it."

Her eyebrows arched, and she looked at him quizzically.

"It's mostly adrenaline," he continued. "Stage fright is usually more of a physical thing than a confidence thing. Adrenaline is a powerful drug. You've probably heard stories about farm women who lift tractors off their husbands after accidents. That's adrenaline; it's strong stuff. So my advice is to keep getting up there, on every stage you can. One day you'll learn how to ride it instead of it riding you. And then you'll see that adrenaline is our friend. A nice buzz, actually. Cocaine is basically synthetic adrenaline, you know; that's why so many entertainers and athletes like it. They get to be adrenaline junkies."

He realized he was spouting and reined himself in. "So try not to worry about it, Kit," he said softly, leaning his face into hers. "Hard as that is right now, don't worry. You'll get past this, I promise."

They small-talked for a moment, then Kit bundled up her guitar, wrote for a few minutes in her journal, and left by the back door.

That had impressed Nathan and he didn't care how calculating she'd been. If she was merely trying to show him there was more going on with her than she showed on stage, that was smart. And if she thought she could benefit from her disaster by asking for advice, so much the better. There was some strength, some real confidence, lurking below the shyness.

She came back every week, always waving but never approaching him again. Each Tuesday, however, she seemed a little friendlier, as if following some private ritual. The wave would be accompanied by a mouthed hello, then a big smile and a "Hello, Nathan." It had now gotten to the point where they would chat a little while she signed up, though she often hurried to her spot in the back before he could reply to her small comments about the weather or the crowd or something she'd seen in the news.

More importantly, she showed musical improvement every week. But the stage fright was always there, like some invisible Harpy hovering around her shoulders. You could never tell when it would pounce, or why. As often as not, it derailed her when she was singing well. Funny stuff, adrenaline.

Still sitting on the stage, lost in thought, Nathan heard Jackie clear her throat sharply, the first sign she was getting ready to lock up. If he didn't respond, she would crisply remind him that *some* of us had homes to go to.

He put each mike into its little case and laid them in an old blue suitcase, where he'd already put the mixing board. He carefully folded a thick towel around them, tucking everything snugly into place. He was careless about so much in his life, but when it came to the music, even its accouterments, he was as tidy as a surgeon.

He heard Jackie clear her throat again, louder this time: "Ahmm-*hemmm*!" He looked up and grinned.

"Jeez Louise," she said. "I start the day with you whining about why you're even here and now I can't friggin' get rid of you."

He stood up, bowed, and laughed as she tossed him the keys to the storage closet with a wild, sidearm toss, the way an irate Red Sox fan might throw an empty beer cup at a Yankees outfielder. As Nathan locked everything in the little closet, he smiled, trying to imagine Kit Palmer with a fiddle crooked under her chin.

Two

Nathan woke up Wednesday the way he always did these days. As he stretched the sleep from his body, feeling the first sweet flush of wakefulness, he realized he felt good. And then, with a shiver of pleasure, he remembered that he no longer drank, no longer had to negotiate his daily deals with alcohol. It was those ceaseless negotiations, more than anything else, that led him to quit: How much did I drink last night? How bad will I feel today? Should I drink tonight? Do I want to drink tonight? Old habits die hard; they also become pests.

Nathan had become a very disciplined person, if habit and discipline are the same thing. As he grew accustomed to being sober, he developed daily routines he now relished. Doing small things to make himself feel better seemed like an extravagant luxury after all the years of touring, staying in cheap motels or strangers' homes, waking up in places where nothing around him was his. It was so nice to have everything there for him in the morning, right where he'd put it, because that's right where he wanted it.

He began his day with a few herbs that a pretty clerk at Whole Foods told him we all need when we get a little, um, older, not that you look, um, old or anything, sir. Then he would put the coffee on. One cup, two at most, because he'd realized it made him cranky as he got, um, older.

Sipping the coffee, savoring the glorious little rush when the first caffeine kicks in, he would look out the window and ponder his next steps. Chores or running? He liked to get outside in the morning, do something to wake up the body, get the blood pumping. Another one of those "as we get a little, um, older" things.

This morning he looked out at the creamy blue of the morning sky, lovely against the soft greens of late summer. No chores seemed to need doing; nothing ever does in August. So he ran a few blocks past the grand old homes and close trim lawns of Craigie Street, where he lived. It was a bit warmer, but still chilly, with a steady breeze. Odd summer.

Nathan lived in a small Victorian carriage house, a few blocks north of Harvard Square, in an old and posh part of Cambridge. Not that he belonged there, needless to say, and friends liked to tease him about what a folksinger was doing in that upper-crust neighborhood. His eccentric little home was another one of the things that made other musicians think Nathan had it made—and that made him feel like a failure.

During his brief stardom, he'd lived in a large apartment building in Harvard Square. When the landlord died, a notoriously ruthless real-estate tycoon, his properties were divided among his several children. Nathan's building fell to an estranged daughter who, like her husband, was a socialist professor of economics. At first the couple resisted taking the six buildings she was bequeathed, but they relented when a radical friend suggested they use them to prove that you didn't have to do business the way her father had. The couple determined to be thoroughly progressive landlords, a promise they had mostly kept.

They were delighted to discover that Nathan Warren, one of their favorite singers, was among their tenants, and they became friends. When Nathan's career faltered, he asked if he could move into a less expensive apartment. The couple began moving him through a series of smaller apartments in their shabbier buildings, always charging him the lowest rent they could argue him into accepting. As his career continued to decline, they lowered the rent further by having him do minor caretaking.

When a sudden real-estate boom hit the city, however, the couple couldn't resist the temptation to upscale their properties. They had children approaching college age and were beginning to view her father's attitude toward business in a somewhat more sympathetic light.

Soon, even the basement studio where they had put Nathan became worth more than he was able to pay. He suggested moving out, but they said, "We wouldn't dream of letting you leave us; you're just like family."

Instead, they showed him a small carriage house behind their own huge Victorian home on Craigie. "You're pretty handy, Nathan," the husband said. "If you want to fix up that place, you can live in it for nothing. We never use it and we'd love to have you as a neighbor."

Nathan spent one of his favorite summers fixing up the old place. Without noticing it, he began to exert a mature will over the worst of his old habits. It meant so much to feel a sense of ownership over some part of his life, even if it had been doled out to him as a favor. It also felt good to be part of a larger household, although the couple were almost never home and timidly respectful of his privacy when they were. To them, he was still their celebrity tenant and a dear friend. To Nathan, he was, finally and fully, a charity case.

With some help from the couple's maintenance men, Nathan had divided the place into a three-room home that still sported the carriage house's original brick interior walls and broad wooden beams, with black iron girding.

It was a great place for music parties, far enough from the main house and other neighbors that late-night noise wasn't an issue. For a long time, he hosted parties every Wednesday after the jam. People could sing ballads in the bedroom while fiddles and banjos twanged out dance tunes in the kitchen. Nathan usually held court between the two sessions, on a large sofa in the living room, swapping a few songs, then trying to get a lively chat going.

After a few years, however, he got tired of the parties. He often spent the waning hours of the jam longing to be alone in his little house. But people enjoyed the parties, so he decided to not decide, as he did with so many things in his life. He would leave it up to someone else to suggest a party. Of course, jammers felt awkward inviting Nathan to a party at his own house, so they rarely happened anymore. He could always find a reason to not do something.

Nathan also liked Wednesdays because he could feel like a musician all day long. He was in mid-gig. Tuesday nights, he would leave his guitar in the storage closet at Dooley's, which pleased him more than it should. It wasn't that toting the guitar was a chore; it was just that *not* having to tote it made him feel like he had steady work. And so he always looked forward to his leisurely Wednesday stroll through Harvard Square, then taking the Mass. Ave. bus up to Dooley's. Another working man off to ply his trade.

He left his home around three. It had warmed a little, but still felt unseasonably cool. He usually heard the traffic on Mass. Ave. and veered off for a shortcut that wasn't much shorter, but it was a lot quieter. Traffic was so light this time of year, however, that he forgot to turn and strolled over to Mass. Ave.

As he walked, he was acutely aware of the birds chirping in the trees. Why did they sound louder? It wasn't like there were more of them; they seemed to have more on their minds.

He stopped by a tree especially thick with birds. What had them hopped up? Maybe with the streets so quiet, he could hear them better. But there was something else: the birds sounded agitated. Their chirping seemed hurried, more high-pitched and shrill. Maybe the cold snap was throwing off their internal clocks. Maybe they thought it was fall, time to begin their long migrations.

He stared up at the tree so intently that a few passersby looked up, too, but they saw nothing. Nathan wasn't looking; he was listening. What were the birds saying to each other? Arguing whether it was time to go? Weather reports? Departure times? This is *my* branch, assholes?

He smiled, shook his head, and hooked right on Mass. Ave., past the ancient Church Street cemetery and into the heart of the square. Only then did he realize that he had not taken his shortcut.

He still adored Harvard Square but hated how it was changing. It had once been among the most famously iconoclastic places on earth, and Nathan loved to think that he belonged there. Many of the storefronts had been purveyors of eccentric stuff that only very smart or very odd people would appreciate. Rare books, antique clothing, vintage comic books, doodads from distant lands.

Now, the winding streets were full of chichi chain-store boutiques, their display windows hawking only vanity and its necessary colleague, fear. Artfully tattered jeans were showcased in one window, in carefully considered degrees of disintegration: from casually frayed to knees-poking-through to the more risqué flashing-a-bit-of-thigh. Good lord, Nathan thought, people can't even be trusted to wear out their own jeans anymore; it must be done for them by fashion experts, for just the right exposure, just the right degree of skin peeking through.

The mannequins in the windows were, of course, inhumanly thin, to ensure that the young women walking through the door knew they were congenitally inadequate for the fashions of the day, biologically unlovely, and in need of all the help their over-extended credit cards could buy them. Jesus, he hated what the square had become. Or was it just what a curmudgeon he'd become?

He looked at the huge clock over Mass. Ave. and decided to hop the bus for Dooley's. He'd be early, but the phone might ring. He glanced from the big clock over to the second-story offices of Tom and Ray Magliozzi, hosts of the popular public radio show, *Car Talk*.

Emblazoned on their office windows was a small but splendid reminder of the grandly funky place the square had once been. In impudent gold lettering, for all the stuffy and the chichi to see, they had painted one of their favorite *Car Talk* gags: Dewey, Cheetham & Howe, Attorneys-at-Law. Lord bless and keep the Magliozzi brothers.

The Wednesday scene at Dooley's was a world away from Tuesday's. The open mike could be such a sullen parade of wannabes. The tense audition vibe and sour scent of ambition always hung in the air. Almost everyone played solo, making it seem even more solitary and competitive.

Wednesday, on the other hand, was a real jam session, what the old folkies used to call a hootenanny. Amateurs and professionals all gathered together for a big music party. Tuesday was all about self-expression and the quest for stardom; Wednesday was all about shared expression and the quest for the common chord. People didn't worry about what hat they wore to the jam.

Nathan rarely sang more than a couple of songs to begin the jam, usually old traditional standards to set the right mood. Within moments, a core of regulars would commandeer the sound system and take charge of who got on stage and when to shift to a new bunch, in order to ensure that everyone got a chance behind the microphones.

The rest of the jammers played along wherever they were sitting, standing, crouching, or leaning. It was a glorious mess.

At first Nathan had tried to resist the weekly coup of regulars. But then he realized that this was the whole point of a jam. At the dawn of the sixties folk revival, these kinds of informal evenings were often called Come-all-ye's. That was partly a riff on those ballads that began something like

> *Come all ye saucy sailors, I'll sing for you a song*
> *It's only sixty verses, so I won't detain ye long.*

But the name also proclaimed that folk music belonged to everybody and that everyone was welcome at its table. So having the regulars run things meant that the jam was working on the most elemental level.

Nathan listened closely to the jammers, especially the new and struggling ones, and offered advice or praise whenever he thought it might help. He would sometimes tell the regulars when he thought a newcomer was ready to "call a tune," which meant to choose what the jammers would play next. In bluegrass jams, Irish seisiuns, and come-all-ye's of all stripes, that was a cherished rite of passage, a moment of initiation and acceptance. Whoever was at the mike would say, "Amy, you're sounding good tonight; why don't you call a tune for us?" Amy had arrived.

Over the years, Nathan developed little rituals for the folk jam, just as he had for the open mike, aimed to make everybody feel more at home. He would introduce the first group of musicians on stage as the Early to Rise String Band and the final group as the Last Stand Band. He closed every jam with Woody Guthrie's song, "So Long, It's Been Good to Know Yuh."

> *I've sung this song but I'll sing it again,*
> *Of the place that I lived on the wild windy plains,*
> *In the month called April, county called Gray,*
> *And here's what all of the people there say:*
> > *So long, it's been good to know yuh;*
> > *So long, it's been good to know yuh;*
> > *So long, it's been good to know yuh.*
> > *This dusty old dust is a-gettin' my home,*
> > *And I got to be driftin' along.*

It didn't take long before the jammers started singing it on their own, which was fine with Nathan. It became their closing song, just as the jam became theirs. It never occurred to him that he was losing an opportunity to perform. The point was the song, not who sang it.

Ferguson believed this innate egalitarianism had lessened the glow of Nathan's stardom during his glory days. To Nathan, there was only one litmus test for membership in the big folk club, and that was love for the music. He saw no useful distinctions between stars and fans, venue owners and backstage volunteers.

But performers who cultivated a distance from their fans, as Joyce had, created more of a star aura around themselves and often had their music taken more seriously. Ferguson thought Nathan seemed like too nice a guy to be as much of a star as his talent should have made him. Nathan fiercely wanted stardom, but he never developed those harder qualities that people who know them call "the killer instinct."

As Nathan struggled to understand what had gone so terribly wrong with his career, he realized that Joyce had that instinct and he didn't. Not right, not wrong, just real. It's simply the way the world works, just as all wild places endure because some are predators, some are prey, and the rest mind their own business.

After making this cold peace with the world, which he regarded as a surrender, Nathan took keener interest in his work at Dooley's. He learned to savor the cacophony of a new generation, like clumsy, eager lovers, taking possession of the old music, putting their stamp on it, making it their own. As his generation had done, and the generation before it, and the one before that. As things had always been done, and needed to be done, if traditions are to survive. Once Nathan learned to recognize that sound, he heard it as the most beautiful music that humans can make.

Kit Palmer showed up around nine-thirty, clutching her fiddle under her arms, eyes darting around the club, mouth in a tight line. When she saw Nathan sitting with Ferguson at the bar, she waved briefly and nodded her head once. Then, head down, she scurried to the back bench, just as she did on Tuesdays.

Nathan thought about walking over but she seemed to need to get her bearings. Her head turned this way and that, so intent and poised that she looked a little deer-like. He smiled. Give her some time to figure this out.

More than a dozen jammers crowded the stage, all laughing as they moved their fiddles and banjos and guitars out of each other's way, with varying degrees of success. They were pounding out "Cluck Old Hen," a quick Appalachian ditty. Everybody shouted the title line whenever it came around, then laughed and whooped together.

> *Cluck old hen cluck and sing*
> *Ain't laid an egg since late last spring.*
> *Cluck old hen cluck and squall*
> *Ain't laid an egg since late last fall.*

Pockets of jammers stood by the stage and around the room. A few played by themselves, seated around the back and side walls. They were the shy ones; Kit fit right in.

Staring uncertainly at the stage, she took out her fiddle and began to play quietly to herself. When she seemed a bit more at ease, Nathan strolled over.

"Having fun yet?" he asked.

She smiled weakly. Not yet. She still looked nervous, or at least uncertain. "I really can't play this stuff," she said. "I'm just laying on a little harmony, some countermelody."

"Harmony, countermelody, all good," Nathan said, nodding and smiling. "It's nice. What you're doing, I mean. A little like your own songs, actually, those nice long lines."

She smiled more broadly, and a little red splashed on her cheeks. He smiled back. "Didn't mean to embarrass you," he said.

"Oh, you mean the red cheeks?" she said. "You can't help that. God, that happens to me all the time. Want to sit down?"

He did, and listened as she played. It really was like her songs, that same floating melodic sense, as if her fiddle was commenting on the quickstep tunes being hammered out on stage, but quietly, reflectively. She was playing more to how the music felt than to its tempo or melody.

"Save my seat," Nathan said suddenly, and went off to get his guitar. He hurried back, sat down, and turned into her so he could hear better. What he'd heard was a tune within the tune the jammers were playing: another, gentler melody was emerging in Kit's long bow strokes. It was her tune that he began to underscore with soft, fingerpicked chords.

Kit smiled as she realized he was responding to her fiddle lines, not to the main melody they were accompanying. He smiled back, and they settled into the close, wordless conversation of shared music.

When the jammers stopped, Nathan and Kit continued a moment or two, seeking a coda to what they'd been playing. She slowed into a resolving line, which he followed with a descending guitar run that didn't quite work. They both laughed at the clumsy ending.

"Do you ever use the fiddle when you write songs?" Nathan asked. "You've got such a nice, open sense of melody. It can sometimes get kind of boxed in by guitar chords, you know?"

Kit thought about that. "I haven't used the fiddle, no," she said, "but it's a good idea. Thanks."

"Just asking, that's all. I like the way you play. Always something familiar there, but also something that's just you."

She cleared her throat but said nothing. Just as the silence became awkward, the band struck up a quick, bluegrassy waltz, and they joined in again on fiddle and guitar. As before, they were soon responding only to each other's music, lost to what was happening around them.

Over the next few weeks Kit became a regular at the jam. As Nathan hoped, it brought back the casual fun of sharing music she knew as a child and took her away from the pressure she felt standing alone on a stage, with all eyes—and expectations—on her.

Kit soon discovered the back room jam, which became her regular haunt. It was a large function room Murph had never known what to do with. Apart from occasionally renting it to groups for parties after weddings, wakes, and softball games, he kept it locked.

When the jam got popular, people complained there weren't enough places to play. Isn't there someplace more informal that they can go? The stage dominated everything in the bar; you had to play what the people behind the microphones were playing. So Murph opened the back room to jammers.

There was no stage, no sound system, no center of attention. People gathered around small tables or stood in tight circles by the walls. One group would play swing tunes, another Celtic jigs and reels, another bluegrass. There was always one table that played a mix of vocal songs and instrumentals. That became Kit's table.

She never sang, however. She only wanted to play her fiddle, blend in with what was happening around her, and not be the center of attention. She was still unfamiliar with most of the tunes and rusty with the ones she remembered, so she played softly, almost to herself, adding simple lines that underscored the emotion of the melody.

Every week, Nathan brought his guitar into the back room and jammed with her. They always played the way they had that first time, ignoring the main tune and huddling into their private music. As they found their own common chords within the swirl of sound around them, they exchanged the knowing smiles and nods that musicians often do when sharing the wordless dialogue of music.

Between tunes, Kit would ask him about the folk scene, the mores of the jam, and the origins of the music. He was struck by how comfortable she was with her youth and with being a newcomer. Most young musicians wanted to seem hip and in-the-know; he'd certainly been that way when he was young. But Kit enjoyed learning about the music and often reacted to Nathan's simple answers with raised eyebrows and sly grins, as if he'd shared some great secret with her.

And in a strange way he had. By asking him all these things, she seemed to understand something about Nathan that few others at Dooley's did. He disliked being seen as the boss of things; he thought of himself as more of a tour guide, helping people to find whatever music was inside them and learn to enjoy it. More than anything, he wanted to be treated like just another musician. Since that first time Kit had asked for advice about her stage fright, she seemed to know that about him. So the way she smiled when he walked over with his guitar meant more to Nathan than she probably knew.

One Wednesday in late August, a jammer told Nathan that it was his birthday and asked if they could have an after-party at his house. Nathan agreed and immediately thought of inviting Kit. It would be a good way for her to get to know a few of the regulars.

He walked down the back hallway, up a short fight of stairs and into a large rectangular room with something fuzzy on the floor that probably used to be a carpet. There were about fifty people there, divided into several jams, each with a handful of musicians and a few people just listening. Dim overhead lighting cast a yellowish glow on everything, like a lamplit room in an old house.

Kit sat with a half-dozen jammers at a small table by the far end of the room. They had finished a tune and were laughing and talking in the time-honored way of the jam. Applause is considered bad form because it suggests a performance atmosphere. So after a tune, there's a period of idle chatter, sipping beers, laughing, and shuffling chairs, until somebody begins another tune.

There is an unspoken order to all this, but nobody really knows what it is. It's simply the way it's always been, since the first caveman noticed his neighbor beating on a rock, wandered over, and said, "Hey, I got a stick, too."

A young guitarist in a faded Boston Celtics jersey, neatly trimmed beard stubble, and Martin Guitar baseball cap, suddenly began to sing a traditional cowboy song, "Colorado Trail." Nathan walked closer, putting a finger over his lips when a few people started to say hi. He wanted to listen.

> *Weep, all you falling rains,*
> *Wail, winds, wail.*
> *All along, along, along,*
> *The Colorado Trail.*

You could almost hear the slow padding of horses and cattle in the easy gait of the song. It vaguely tells a story about a pretty girl named Laura, whom the cowboy loves and misses. But the song never explains who she is or what's happened to her. She's simply gone away.

As a young man, that drove Nathan crazy. He tried to learn the song a few times, but without knowing what happened to Laura or even what her relationship was to the cowboy, he didn't know how to approach it. Now he thought those omissions were brilliant, because the song really isn't about Laura or even the lovelorn cowboy. It's simply about being alone in a lonely place and wishing that you weren't. Nathan certainly knew what that felt like.

> *Ride through the lonely night,*
> *Ride through the day.*
> *Keep that herd moving on,*
> *Moving on its way.*

The young singer was putting more Texas drawl into his voice than anyone in a Celtics jersey should. Nathan moved closer so he could hear what Kit was doing. She had her eyes closed, her bow hovering uncertainly above the strings of her fiddle. Then, with a long, soft downstroke, she began to play.

> *Ride through the stormy night,*
> *Dark is the sky.*
> *Wish I'd stayed in Abilene,*
> *Where it's mighty warm and dry.*

Kit played low notes that underscored not only the melody but the loneliness of the lyric. Nathan had noticed before how quickly she was able to zero in on the basic emotion of a tune and wrap her playing around it. It was as if her fiddle knew the unsaid things in the song, the feelings beneath the words: the mix of sadness, homesickness, and tiredness that cowboy had felt so many years ago, riding night herd on some rainy prairie, singing to himself.

> *Weep, all you falling rains,*
> *Wail, winds, wail.*
> *All along, along, along,*
> *The Colorado Trail.*

Bobbing his head lightly to the beat, Nathan closed his eyes and wondered what it was about sad songs that appeal to us so much. Do we like being sad? Even the uptempo songs at the jam were usually about train wrecks, dead mothers, ghastly murders, and ghostly lovers walking these hills in long, black veils.

Maybe it's like those actors who say they prefer playing villains because they're more interesting. Our dark feelings have more complex palettes; at least in art they do. But Nathan had learned that form usually follows function in traditional music. Perhaps our unhappy feelings are more in need of examining than our happy ones. Who needs to solve happiness?

We need to understand the dark sides of life; that's where the dangers are. Why else would cowboys have sung all those sad love songs? It was the one time they could display their inner-selves, explore their feelings, and share them with friends. And those deeper feelings need attention, even on a cattle drive. Leave them alone too long, unexamined and unexpressed, and they fester like an untreated wound. Maybe that's why "Colorado Trail" leads us away from the particulars about Laura and the cowboy. Laura becomes everybody's absent love, and the cowboy's loneliness becomes everybody's loneliness. And doesn't the simple act of sharing that in a song make us a little less lonely?

Nathan opened his eyes because he heard Kit's voice. On the final chorus, she'd stopped fiddling and was adding a high vocal harmony. It was the first time he'd heard her sing at the jam and he smiled. The magic of the jam was working; she and the music were becoming friends again.

After the song ended, he invited everyone to the after-party. A red-haired woman with an old mandolin quickly accepted and offered a ride to anyone who wanted to come. Nathan looked at Kit and said, "Why don't you come, too? You could get to know some of the regulars."

"I'd like that," she said, smiling and nodding her head.

The party was in full swing by the time Kit arrived with the mandolin player and the guy in the Celtics jersey. Nathan was staked out on his couch, guitar by his side. She walked around a little, smiling at a few people and accepting a beer from a jammer stationed by the refrigerator. Nathan waved her over with a swing of his head.

"Sit down," he said, picking up his guitar. "I've been saving a seat for you. Somebody asked me to sing this song, but I wanted you to hear it."

"Really?" She said, sounding a bit surprised. "Cool. What is it?" She sat next to him.

"It's a really old American folk song called 'Pretty Saro,' probably from colonial days." He began to sing, his deep voice soft and low, almost whispering. The room hushed.

Down in some lone hollow, in a lonesome place
Where the wild birds all whistle, and their sounds do increase.
Farewell, pretty Saro, I must bid you adieu,
And I'll dream of pretty Saro, wherever I go.

My love, she won't have me, and I understand.
She wants a rich merchant, and I have no land.
I cannot maintain her with silver and gold,
To buy her the fine things that a big house will hold.

If I were a merchant, and could write a fine hand,
I would write my love a letter that she'd understand.
I'd write it by the river, where the waters o'erflow,
And I'll dream of pretty Saro, wherever I go.

After the song, Kit looked pleased but puzzled. Why sing that for her?

"It reminds me of the way you write, Kit," he said. "Kind of impressionistic." She smiled. Ah, another music lesson.

"You think my songs are impressionistic?" she asked.

"Sure. You'll focus on an emotional moment, like the guy in that song, and then look at it from different angles. I mean, why does he start the song in a lone hollow? It has nothing to do with what the song is about, except that—"

"Do you think your songs are impressionistic?"

"I don't know…some of them, I suppose—"

"Because I really like the way you write. And I always know just how you feel. I mean, how your songs feel."

"Thanks…I…you know, like the guy in that old song—"

"I wish you sang more at the open mike."

"Thanks, but I just—"

"I tell people that all the time. Really. I love your voice, too. It's so warm. I keep thinking it's like somebody's voice that I know, but I think it's just the way you sing. You know?"

"Yeah, I think I do." He cleared his throat.

She leaned into the couch and turned toward him. "So you think my songs are impressionistic, huh? I never thought about them that way."

"Definitely," he said. "Like when you write about seeing a face reflected in a window. It's not part of the story you're telling, but it helps people feel what the song is feeling. Like the lone hollow in that old—"

"You really love them, don't you?" she said softly. "Those old folk songs."

"Yeah, I do." He leaned closer to her as the jammers in the kitchen launched into a loud reel. "There's something different about traditional songs, the ones that were passed along from singer to singer. Like the one I just sang. Not a word wasted. It tells this guy's life story in about four lines, and the rest is about how that life feels. Like an emotional landscape."

He took a deep breath. He didn't want to wheeze off into a lecture. "So yeah, I'm much more into them now than I was way back when. Back in the day."

"Back in the day," she repeated sarcastically. "I mean, *really*. You're not so ancient as you want people to think. I'm on to you, you know." She wagged a finger playfully under his nose, then poked him in the arm and laughed. Was she flirting with him? What's going on here?

"Right, you got me," he said. "It's all a stunt. I put the gray in my hair to make me look…uh…distinguished."

"It works," she said, arching an eyebrow. Good lord, she *was* flirting with him.

He laughed and then, as if by some unconscious will, poked her arm in return, grinning mischievously.

Good lord, he was flirting with her, too. What's happening here? He was probably twice her age, old enough to be her…uh-uh, don't need to go there. But old enough. Why didn't that feel like it mattered? Maybe because it didn't seem to matter to her. Even at her shiest, Kit had always spoken to him eye to eye, like a friend, a peer.

After a quiet moment, she said, "I wasn't just buttering you up, you know. I really like your songs. I was asking around about you, and I heard about what happened with your big record deal. God, that must've been awful." Her smile fell and she looked concerned. "Is it all right to talk about this?"

"Sure," he said with a tired smile. "Everybody knew about it back in the…ah… back when it happened. My great crash and burn; Nathan Warren's five seconds of fame. Long time ago, though."

"How did you ever get over it?" Kit asked, shaking her head slowly. "Something like that would just kill me."

"It damn near did." he said, gazing off at the jammers in the kitchen. "Damn near did." After a moment, he added, "I guess I got tired of being dead."

He smiled at her. "So here I am. Most people try to go from open-miker to star. My career plan was the reverse. Different drummer, huh?" He shrugged.

She took a breath as if to say something, but didn't. She looked at him for a long time, a curious half-smile frozen on her face.

"I don't know much about that stuff," she said finally, and Nathan worried that he had pushed her away. "I'm pretty new at this. It must have really hurt, though. So unfair."

Nathan scolded himself for laying all this on her. What the hell was she supposed to say? Suddenly her eyes widened and she grinned.

"But I know more about you than that," she said. That teasing tone was back in her voice. "I went to the used-record store on Mass. Ave."

"Stereo Jack's?"

"Yeah. Cool place. I found a copy of your first CD, that local one you made before the major-label deal. And I love it, Nathan. Really. Jack said you were quite the Mr. Big Deal back then."

Mr. Big Deal? Was she flirting again?

"Oh yes, way back when," Nathan said. "Me and Bix Biederbecke, side by side forever in the racks of Stereo Jack's vintage-record store."

Kit let out a sharp cackle. "God, the way you talk about yourself. Because you don't seem old to me at all. You sure don't when you sing. You should sing more at Dooley's, you really should. Everybody wishes you would."

"Everybody?"

She nodded firmly.

"Ryder?"

She exploded into laughter, such a free, almost feral sound. He realized that he liked making her laugh. She was different when her guard was down, when the shyness was at bay.

"Well, almost everybody," she said. "We mustn't expect miracles." She smiled at him, shaking her head, still laughing. They looked at each other for a long moment.

"Back to your songs, Kit," he said, clearing his throat. "I think they're best when you're looking for that emotional moment. Like the one you wrote about coming through your depression, how the colors were so bright they hurt, the 'sudden greens and reds.' I love that line because it's something everybody can see. You know? It's describing this intimate moment, but you let everybody know how that moment feels. When you're beginning to come out of that kind of darkness and everything seems so bright. Sudden. You nailed it."

As he spoke, Kit's eyes widened. She took in a quick breath. "How do you *know* that about me," she whispered, "that I was in a depression? Nobody knows that."

"From your song, Kit. You can't make something like that up. 'Sudden greens and reds?' You couldn't have written that if you'd never been there. It's too real, too true."

She stared at the floor. "I didn't think anybody knew about that about me. Except like, my family and…" Her voice trailed off.

"You better get used to people figuring out your secrets. That's what happens when the writing's honest. When it's real. And that's what you want, isn't it?"

She stared at him. "How do you know all this stuff about me?"

He shrugged, his smile a bit cocky and a bit sad. "I'm a songwriter, too," he said. But that wasn't the whole truth, was it? He also knew because he'd lived in that same gray world.

Their talk became more personal then, about his own long bout with depression, which he believed he'd never entirely overcome. About her freshman-year depression, which she had believed she would never get over but did, with the help of a campus psychologist.

She told him about her parents, who were as much pals as parents, and who called her the "artistic sheep of the family." They urged her not to make the practical career choices they had, at least not at first, and supported her completely when she decided to be a songwriter.

As Nathan and Kit talked, they leaned more closely into each other on the couch. They played a few songs together but quietly, for each other, as the party swirled around them.

Nathan wasn't sure when he realized what was happening between them. Her eyes changed, becoming at once deeper and softer, and he knew she felt about him the same way he was beginning to feel about her. Even after so many years alone, he knew that look in a woman's eyes, and what it meant when she kept turning the conversation back to him.

Long silences, intense and yet comfortable, seemed to continue the conversation, not interrupt it. Why wasn't he stopping this? Why wasn't he changing the subject, now that the conversation had become so dangerously lacking in subject? Why didn't he reach for his guitar, rejoin the party, ask if she wanted another beer? Why didn't he use any of the old tricks he'd mastered, so long ago, to push distance into the warming air between them?

The last of the jammers walked by them on their way home, thanked Nathan for a great party, and said they guessed *he'd* had a good time, too, with knowing twinkles in their eyes as they glanced back and forth between him and Kit.

"I'll show you to the door," he said and stood up. He turned to Kit, leaned over and said, very softly, "You'll stay? I mean, I'd like you to stay."

She closed her eyes, then opened them and smiled. "Of course I will," she whispered.

Nathan woke up the next morning and surveyed the lump beneath his sheets. For one bleary moment, he thought that, once again, he'd fallen asleep with his guitar in the bed. Gonna roll right over on top of it one of these days.

Then he remembered it was Kit, lovely Kit, and smiled. He pushed himself up against the backboard and looked down at her. He tried to stoke some "Good lord, what have I done?" reactions, as he would have years ago, but they didn't take. He was entirely glad she was there, sleeping beneath his summer sheets.

Nathan would soon learn that just as Kit did everything intensely, she was a consummate sleeper. On all but the warmest nights, she ended up completely beneath the covers and awoke thickly, dreamily, for long, warm moments before she kicked into a sustained level of energy that even Joyce would have had trouble keeping up with.

He wondered, looking down at her now, if he had ever fallen into bed with a woman more comfortably, even when he was young and notoriously carefree, and how that could possibly be, after so many years alone. Last night had felt like one long conversation, naturally growing in intensity and intimacy, until words were no longer needed.

He was skittish at the first romantic contacts, less because of the sexuality than the sheer strangeness of being touched. He clenched at the first light kisses and flinched at her feathery touches; his fingers fluttered at the first feel of her soft skin. She leaned into him and stroked his cheeks reassuringly—or was it approvingly?—probably taking it for shyness.

Soon enough, though, the old motors kicked in. It's true what they say, he thought, smiling, it's just like riding a bicycle. After a few swirling moments of surprise, all he could think about was her. And then he did not think at all.

He looked down at the curled-up lump next to him and knew there were strong and real feelings growing inside him. And, to his surprise, he welcomed them. That was strange, not like before, when walls shot up at the first pangs of tenderness, warning bells he'd trained to ring at the first moment of strong emotion.

Back then, it was usually rising feelings in him, not the woman he was with, that made him pull away, leaving her wondering what had happened, what she had done? It was such a contrast from the easy, confident romance in his songs, and he remembered how that had secretly shamed him.

Why did it seem so different now? Her? Him? Both? So much passing, wasted time in his life? Later. That was a brood that would take him through some bad places. It needed to be done, but not this morning. Enjoy this now; enjoy her now. He looked down at Kit and smiled again.

He felt such an odd mix of things about her: musical comradeship, respect for her talent, a tenderness enhanced by her innate cuteness, and a keen sexual attraction. Something else, too, something about him being older. Not paternalism, God knows, but he was nearly twice her age, and that was certainly not a fact either of them ignored. He wanted to teach her things, and she seemed to want to learn them. That was a big part of what drew them together. Why didn't that make the other feelings seem more, well, *strange*? He didn't know; he just knew it didn't, and was glad.

She stirred beneath the sheets but didn't show any signs of surfacing. God, he liked this woman, liked knowing he was around her. He wriggled down in the bed and softly squeezed Kit's shoulder. There was no reaction, so he dove beneath the sheets. She was facing him, curled up in a ball, eyes shut tight, almost kitten-like. Adorable. She even sleeps cute, he thought, and stroked her shoulder until she began to open her eyes.

Apparently, she had her own bleary little moment because she jerked with surprise when she saw his face so close to hers. Then she smiled bigger than he'd ever seen her smile, which filled him up.

"Howdy, bub," she said, her voice husky with sleep. "New in town?"

"Yeah, doll, but I like it here," he said, and kissed her lightly on the mouth. He caressed her arm. "I'm glad you're here, Kit, glad you stayed." He said it somberly, as if it was important for him to say now, at once. His seriousness surprised him. She purred and burrowed her head into his shoulder, and they were quiet together, not moving.

Along with her genius for sleep, Nathan would also learn, rather to his relief, that Kit was an intent but quiet and undemanding lover. She was sensual and very affectionate, but rarely indulged in sweet nothings. He didn't think her placid attitude about sex came from not enjoying it; she clearly did. It was more that sex was a means to an end for her, and that end was a more complete closeness. Sex was not a destination, but a pleasant journey to where she wanted to go with her lover.

As he grew comfortable with her, he realized this was how he had always wanted sex to be: a shared passage. In his hurried youth, it had always been an end in itself, the skyrocketing, wave-crashing, be-all and end-all it never quite measured up to being. For Kit, sex was not the goal but the gateway to the goal. For Nathan, seeing it this way made both sex and what it led to more pleasurable. What he would never know for certain was if it had been him or those he'd been with who kept him from ever realizing that before.

Kit also enjoyed the conspiracy of sex: sly smiles, winks, and raised eyebrows exchanged while other people were around. She loved the shared secret of sex. At first, Nathan wondered if she was still a bit enamored with the novelty of intimacy, but she seemed comfortable as a lover. It probably had more to do with her seeing sex as a continuing conversation. And is there anything that makes us feel closer than the secrets we whisper to each other, the things that only we know?

But on this warm August morning, everything about her was new and shiny. As he held her, all his senses seemed sharper. He was aware of her scent, how differently her black hair smelled from her lightly freckled shoulders, the softness of her skin, its lovely whiteness, even more striking in her nakedness.

When they emerged from bed, Kit immediately began talking about food, with a lip-smacking longing that suggested she hadn't eaten in weeks. He walked to the nearest market for rolls and coffee—store-bought coffee always was like a treat to him, even though his own was usually better. And this was a day for treats.

When he got back, he found that she'd made coffee anyway. As he walked in the kitchen door, she was at the table, coffee mug in her hands, smiling and chanting, "Food. Must. Have. Food."

Once Kit refueled, they spent a deliciously lazy morning. Remaining at the kitchen table, they played music together. Kit picked up her fiddle to accompany him, then took his guitar and sang while he added harmonies.

There in the kitchen, free of the unnerving glare of the spotlight, her songs impressed him even more. They were richly composed, with elegant spaces that insinuated the emotions beneath the surface. She was completely unafraid of silence in her music, rare for such a new songwriter.

It must add to her stage fright, Nathan thought as he listened. Her songs were so bravely written, not only in their confessional honesty but in those daunting melodic spaces. They were riveting to hear, but they must be terrifying to get through on stage. The temptation for beginners is to hurry, fill every space with sound. In old show-biz circles, it was called "dazzling 'em with footwork." Keep the tricks coming so they won't see the frightened soul behind them. Kit often fell apart on stage, but he'd never seen her rush a song to avoid it.

After a third cup of coffee, which he worried might be a mistake, Nathan got spouty and took Kit on a carpenter's tour of his old carriage house. This is where there used to be a big furnace, and over here the beams had to be replaced. She followed along, suppressing an indulgent smile with varying degrees of success, but always asking the questions he hoped she'd ask and commenting on how well everything turned out.

As the tour moved outside, she told him about her situation. She was making ends meet with two part-time waitressing jobs at Davis Square in Somerville, a couple of miles from Nathan's house. She shared a huge duplex near Davis with five female students from Tufts University.

She complained bitterly that it was impossible to get a moment's peace there, much less to seriously practice her music, except in the morning when they're all away at *class*. She groaned that last word, as if it proved the utter indignity of her situation. In some ways, he thought, she really was a bit spoiled.

She made it clear that the "my place or yours" issue would never come up, because she had no intention of letting him see, as she put it, "that toxic waste dump I call my room."

Then she spread her arms expansively toward the little carriage house. "Besides," she said brightly, "who wouldn't want to hang out in a cool cottage like this?" Despite himself, he puffed up like a schoolboy who found a gold star on his science report.

He motioned her over to a series of large, flat stones that marked the path to his door, and told her how hard they'd been to find, much less to match up. She either didn't notice or didn't mention that they didn't seem to match up in any way other than being large and flat. Lifting a black stone by the kitchen door, he showed her a key hidden underneath.

He said, "I put that there back in my drinking days, so I could get in if I left my keys somewhere or had them taken away by some bartender. If you ever need a place to be alone and quiet, or to work on your music, you can come over here and let yourself in, even if I'm not home."

She stared at him, her mouth falling open.

Nodding firmly, he said, "I mean it. You know, you can call first if you want; but if I'm not home, come on over anyway. Really." He shrugged and smiled. "It'd be nice to find you here. Make yourself at home."

"Yeah?" She said uncertainly. "You sure?"

"You bet," he answered serenely while a voice inside his head hollered, "*Who are you? Why have you invaded the body of Nathan Warren, and what have you done with him?*"

But he meant it, he actually meant it. How about that?

Over the next week, Nathan spent a lot of time worrying how this new and sudden relationship would define itself and just as much time worrying about why that didn't worry him more. He quickly realized that he was less anxious about Kit than he was about simply having been away from the game for so long. What are the ground rules these days? Are there ground rules these days? Don't people have "the talk" anymore?

The one about where they stand and how they really feel, usually followed by the dreaded "I'm not sure where this relationship is heading."

He braced himself for that moment with Kit, listened for hints that she wanted a more serious talk about what was happening between them. But it never came—or was his radar simply not tuned in to the same frequencies she used? She seemed entirely comfortable with the way things were developing. Was he missing something? No, rephrase that. How much was he missing?

It used to be that whenever he became romantically involved, he immediately grew terrified about what he privately thought of as "the talk," with its demand for emotional availability he wasn't prepared to offer. Now, he found himself worrying that "the talk" wasn't happening.

Perhaps it's up to me, he thought, because I'm so much older. Yes, perhaps as free and independent as Kit seemed to be, she was still the young one in this relationship, and didn't want to force his hand, to intrude on his life or his feelings. But boy, that sure didn't sound like anyone named Kit Palmer that he'd been hanging around with. She acted as if she'd known him for years, and Nathan savored that familiarity. She would look directly at him, right into him, and then smile. It left him giddy.

Maybe women today refuse to carry the emotional baggage for both people, so it's up to him to make his own feeling clear. Lord, he hoped not; that had never been his strong suit. Except in his songs, of course, where they could be carefully camouflaged—what the politicians call "plausible deniability."

Again, that didn't seem to be what was happening. Perhaps it was simpler than all of that. Perhaps Kit was one of those women who didn't need to have "the talk," who assumed that emotional clarity existed from the first intimate touches, and for whom the very need to have "the talk" marked the beginning of love's end.

Nathan had known a woman like that, years ago. She was sort of an earth-mother type, which was one of the things that attracted him. She had a smoldering sexual freedom once she set her cap for a man; and he had never, before or since, felt such pure physical lust for a woman: something about that earthiness, that unspoken assumption that love opened all doors, and the way she believed that deep feelings gave sex both its pleasure and purpose.

When they finally talked about their relationship, he brought it up, because he was becoming scared about their emotional closeness. He began by enforcing his usual distance, offering hackneyed excuses about career, the musician's solitary lot, and the need for "freedom," by which young men usually mean the right to sleep with as many women as possible.

As he spoke, he watched all the promise leave her eyes. They grew dull with disenchantment, then distance, and finally disinterest. He knew there would be no way to relight the flame he had just extinguished.

"Whatever," she'd said, her voice horribly bare of feeling. "We all got our own row to hoe."

They never spoke again.

There are few things as intimately shattering to a man as watching that change come over a lover's face. It feels as if it can be measured by degrees—*tick, tick, tick*—as the love drains from her eyes. And then it's gone. There is no light left in those eyes for you. Whether or not a man is in love, witnessing that kind of withdrawal claws away at the core of what he thinks, what he needs to hope, that he is.

A shudder came over him at the memory. He never wanted to see that look in Kit's eyes—*never*—which brought back all the old mumbles: stop this now, retreat, you're not ready for this. But just as on that first sweet morning when he woke to find her beneath his sheets, the mumbles didn't take hold. He wasn't afraid of the closeness, only of losing it. Hmm, now there's a sea change in your little universe.

He closed his eyes and thanked the memory of that old, lost love for the lesson she'd left him. He hoped she was well, wherever she was, and with someone who was a better judge of hearts than he had been. He would not make that mistake again, not with Kit.

Still, he continued to ruminate, as if he was trying to find something to worry about. For so many years, that had been his way of approaching everything, his dark comfort: brace for the worst, dig in, hunker down, because the safe bet is that worse weather's coming.

But those old cautions didn't feel like they applied to Kit. She was different from any woman he'd known before; and he was certainly a different man than he'd been. Wasn't he? Of course he was, or he wouldn't be having this conversation with himself.

And then the thought hit him, so unexpectedly that he actually looked upward, as if something had physically fallen on his head. He was sitting at the kitchen table, sipping his second cup of coffee, after having driven Kit to one of her waitressing jobs in Davis Square.

Gazing out at the yard, it occurred to him that perhaps they'd already had "the talk." Perhaps it came that first morning, when he lifted the stone outside his door and offered her the keys to his life, saying, "Anytime. Really. Anytime."

He caught his breath and looked down, thinking, God, I hope I don't let her down. Then he felt a sense of peace, a sense that maybe everything was alright. Shaking his head, he marveled at what a new feeling that was.

None of this stopped him from worrying, but it did tend to move his worries to a more mundane level. He became ridiculously anxious about saying or doing something so antique that Kit would laugh and say, "Good lord, you are old fashioned, aren't you?"

For example, what do couples call themselves these days? Significant other? Domestic partner? My First Among Equals? These monikers can change so quickly. What is the *nom du jour* for romance?

And so it came as an enormous relief when Kit first referred to him as her boyfriend. On Saturday, with a strong breeze blowing, they walked hand in hand around Harvard Square. The wind swirled and rose into sharp gusts, blowing candy wrappers and ATM receipts across their feet.

An old college friend of Kit's hailed her from across Mass. Ave., then dodged the traffic to stop them in front of the brown bricks of the Harvard Coop. The pair immediately began to chatter away, oblivious to the world, slipping into affected voices that surely had been their secret language in the campus days.

"Oh!" Kit said, as if remembering something she'd meant to say. "This is my new boyfriend, Nathan."

It pleased him on many levels as he grinned foolishly and shook the friend's hand. First, it resolved the nettlesome semantic problem he'd been fretting over, and in a way that suggested he might not be as out of step as he feared. Second, it was a dear term of endearment, especially coming from Kit; and she said it so matter of factly that it implied considerable affection. Third, it thrilled his vanity to be described that way by so beautiful a woman, especially to another woman nearly as attractive, who offered an approving nod and a very complimentary arch of her eyebrow. And finally, any day a man of his years got called a boy was a good one.

One issue that didn't need worrying about was whether to keep their relationship secret. Nathan figured this out before Kit did, however. It may be a big world, but folk music is a small town. After the way the last jammers left the party Wednesday, giggling and grinning at the two of them, he knew the regulars would all hear about Nathan and that pretty young open-miker. And there was enough spillover between the jam and the open mike that the word would spread like kudzu among Dooley's regulars.

Sure enough, when Nathan wandered in the following Tuesday, Jackie was beaming at him like a kid who knows a secret. She paid him more attention than usual, wearing the same silly grin whenever he caught her looking at him as he swept the stage and set up the mikes. The old pain swept over him as he crumpled up an out-of-date concert poster that had been taped to the wall, but it passed quickly.

Nathan checked the mikes and walked to the bar. He frowned at Jackie, who was staring at him, arms folded, grinning and clucking her tongue.

"Oh, get it over with," he said. "Please. Get it over with."

"Who, me?" Jackie said, pointing a finger at herself.

"Just get it over with, please. It's like waiting for popcorn to pop. Very annoying popcorn."

After a bit more grinning and feigned innocence, she leaned over and said, "About friggin' time."

"Huh?"

"You and that pretty open-miker. I worry about you sometimes, so it's about friggin' time, that's all."

She handed him his root beer, patted his shoulder, and said "I'm happy for you, binky." Then she sauntered up the bar, singing under her breath. He listened to the tune. Yup, it was "People Will Say We're in Love."

A little before eight, Kit wandered in, guitar case slung over her back, apparently determined to make a show of this being Just Another Tuesday. She pointedly stopped inside the door and moved her eyes around the club—*la-di-da*—finally settling on Nathan. She nodded curtly, lowered her head, and walked quickly past his seat at the bar on the way to her usual perch in the back.

"Where do you think you're going?" Nathan said as she passed him.

She leaned her head over without looking up, whispering out of the side of her mouth, "I didn't want you to feel like…you know…I thought I'd just—"

"Kit, do you honestly think there's anyone around here who doesn't know we're an item? This is the folk world; most of them probably knew before we did. Remember the party last Wednesday?"

She smiled and looked at him, nodding her head.

"Okay," he said. "Do you think we were particularly subtle? Do you think we were in any way subtle?"

She shook her head and her smile widened.

He patted the bar stool next to him. "So stop being silly and sit down. Unless you want people to think we've already had our first spat."

"So *everybody* knows about us?" she said, continuing to whisper as she put her guitar down and climbed on to the bar stool.

"Look for yourself," he said, pointing his head toward Jackie without bothering to glance her way. Sure enough, there she stood, with that same knowing grin, her eyes darting back and forth between Nathan and Kit.

"Ahh, I see," Kit said in her normal voice. No need for whispers here.

"Well?" Jackie said to Nathan. "Well?"

"Jackie, I'd like you to meet my new girlfriend, Kit Palmer." There, now he'd said it, too.

Jackie thrust out her hand. "My sympathies, darlin.' He's a load."

"Thanks, I guess," Kit said, laughing softly. She shot an embarrassed glance at Nathan: what do I say?

"Just nod and say yes when Jackie speaks; that's the lesson we all learn, sooner or later. Nod and say yes."

"You're not as dumb as you look, Nathan," Jackie said, then winked at Kit. "Now, what'll you have, dear?"

It was a fairly uneventful open mike, unless you counted the whispers and pointed fingers directed at Nathan and Kit. She sang her first song strongly but stumbled badly through the second. She was gaining musical confidence every week at the jam, but it wasn't helping her at the open mike. The stage fright was always hovering, always ready to pounce. Nathan usually saw it coming before she did, and was angry with himself for not being able to help

Ryder didn't show up. Nathan figured he was either still in quest of the Magic Hat of Stardom or ducking Ferguson until he could decipher his criticisms.

Ramblin' Randy did a boisterous version of "Remember the Ala-moo," but eschewed his sea chantey in favor of a curiously calypso-like version of the sappy Scottish love song, "Wild Mountain Thyme," with its refrain of "Will ye go, lassie, go?" Wiggling his eyebrows, he dedicated it to "A certain couple we've been hearing about all week." Sheesh.

Nathan was looking forward to Kit meeting Ferguson, for a couple of reasons. He was certain they would become good friends, but Ferguson had a way of taking new people lightly, particularly young ones. He liked to test their mettle. He would be unable to resist doing that with Kit—cute little Kit, shy little Kit—and Nathan expected some fine fireworks. He was learning that the confidence he'd sensed beneath her shyness was very real.

As Jackie rang the witching hour bell, Ferguson rolled through the front door, sweeping majestically to where Nathan and Kit were sitting at the bar.

"Aha!" he said, dramatically waving a hand between them. "These must be our mystery sweethearts. The entire town is abuzz."

"Jeez Louise, how long have you been lurking out there?" Jackie asked.

"Just long enough to miss the music," he said, then looked at Kit. "No offense. I hear too damn much of it while I'm working. Music, music, music; don't you people know how to do anything else?"

He laughed, then held out his hand to Kit. "I'm Ferguson. You must be Kit."

"Hi," she said, shaking his hand tentatively. "I guess I must be. The press is never wrong."

"Don't try to get on my good side," he barked as he sat on the stool Nathan had saved for him. Then he winked at her. "You're already there."

Taking a healthy swig of his first rum, he said, "I've heard you sing, you know. A few weeks ago. Sometimes I steal in the back door, catch a few sets. You have a lovely voice. And you *are* lovely, if I may say so."

Kit heaved a loud sigh. "Omigod," she said, "I remember that night. I was awful; I just sucked, totally. I even dropped my pick in the middle of a song. I... I... and then, like, I saw you in the back and thought, 'Well, that's that. It was a nice little career. Maybe I can try another city, somewhere far, far away, where they don't get newspapers.'"

"Nonsense," Ferguson said, finishing off his rum and waving the empty glass toward Jackie. He picked up the beer in his other hand. "You forget that I'm a highly trained professional." He laughed. "This is an open mike. I don't judge performers the same way I would at a big concert hall."

"That would be unfair?" Kit asked.

Ferguson tilted his head thoughtfully. "Yes, I suppose it would be, now that you mention it. Mostly, it would be stupid. It's an open mike; people are supposed to be stretching their muscles, trying new things."

"Like getting through a whole song without dropping their pick," Kit said, shaking her head.

"Oh, all you need is a little road wear, kiddo," Ferguson said, his tone airy and patronizing. "Get a few miles on you, the way this old soldier has." He pointed to Nathan, then nodded happily as Jackie refilled his rum glass.

Taking a swallow, he smacked his lips and sighed dramatically. "Yes, the road is a hard teacher, but a good one," he said. "You young songwriters have it too easy here in Boston. You get pampered because the audiences are so nice. You don't have to earn your stripes."

He was obviously teasing her now, baiting her, talking down to her.

"Yes," he said in a world-weary tone that dripped of sarcasm. "Get some hard miles under your belt, kiddo, and you'll be fit as a fiddle." He winked at her. "Right as rain."

"Gee, Ferguson," Kit chirped, her voice so squeaky and childlike that it startled Nathan. It sounded like she had a whistle stuck in her throat. "Nathan says the only thing he ever learned from the road is that there's no such thing as casual sex."

"Nathan said that?" Ferguson said casually. He swallowed some more rum.

"He says if it's casual, you're not doing it right."

Ferguson choked on an ice cube. Jackie reached over, laughing, and patted him on the back. Ferguson could manage only a hoarse, wheezing, "Huh?"

"I agree with him, like, *totally*, don't you?" Kit said, fluttering her eyelashes sarcastically.

Ferguson coughed and sputtered, then glowered at Nathan. "You could have warned me about her," he said. "Why didn't you warn me about her?"

"Didn't have a chance," Nathan said. "Besides, would it have done any good?"

"Did you really say that to her? About the road?"

"Well, she spruced it up some."

Ferguson looked at Kit, eyeing her up and down, as if processing an entirely new opinion. Then he smiled and held out his hand again.

"Hi, I'm Ferguson. A pleasure to meet you."

Kit laughed, shook his hand again, and winked in a way that was so friendly that Ferguson blushed a little. Taking a deep breath, he spread his hands wide on the bar.

"You know," he said slowly, "I was channel-surfing the other night and came across one of those music infomercials, for the greatest hits of the eighties."

He took a dramatic breath and straightened up on his stool. Time for the weekly rant. Jackie moved closer.

"Well now," he continued, "I listened to three or four of those greatest hits of the eighties, and thought, 'I must try not to be so hard on myself for having decided to spend that decade drunk.'"

He put down his beer with a thump and, eyes twinkling, looked at Nathan. He and Jackie were laughing very hard, shaking their heads at each other.

With a firm nod of his head, Ferguson said, "Ahh, good to get that off my chest. That's all for tonight, my children. You may resume normal activities; please feel free to unfasten your seat belts and move about the hovercraft."

Kit was laughing too, but uncertainly, glancing between Ferguson and Nathan. By now, Nathan was slapping the bar, moaning, while Jackie sang, "Do you really want to hurt me; do you really want to *seeeeeeee* me cry?"

"Bad time for music, huh?" Kit said.

Ferguson looked at her with surprise, then smiled. Most young musicians would have bluffed along, pretending to understand. Or at least kept their mouths shut. He was impressed.

"I'm sorry, Kit. You probably missed that decade, lucky you. Yes, it was a terrible time for music: disco, videos, heavy metal, arena rock. Most pop music went from being melody-driven to rhythm-driven. The age of the drum machine. *Brrrr-rap-rap-rap.*"

"And big hair," Jackie said, spreading her arms around her head. "Very big hair."

"Yeww," Kit said.

"It ended up being a good time for folk music, though," Ferguson said. "It was revving itself up again, after the commercial folk revival fell apart. Getting comfortable with life in the underground."

Kit leaned closer to Ferguson, intrigued, and Nathan excused himself to make the rounds. He wanted them to get to know each other.

Ferguson told Kit how it had really begun in the seventies, as folk music lovers got back up on their hind legs after the industry abandoned folk as a commercially viable form. The same thing was happening all over the world, he said, in a thousand little scenes, a thousand different ways. People in Ireland and Scotland formed hip traditional bands, and activists brought them together in big open-air festivals, sparking the Celtic music revival.

The same thing was happening with bluegrass in the South, as it became clear that mainstream country music was never going to accept its rootsy forebear. Fans staged huge summer festivals to show what a vibrant form the old mountain music was. The idea quickly spread northward, proving there was a strong audience for bluegrass outside the South.

Throughout the Third World, lovers of indigenous ethnic music were forming contemporary-style bands, just as Celtic musicians were, reinventing their traditions for modern ears. Afro-pop, world-beat, and the world music movement were born.

Small record labels—Rounder, Philo, Flying Fish, Shanachie, Carthage, Hannibal—sprouted up to service these new folk revivals. They wouldn't dump folk music overboard at the first sign of bad weather, because they *were* folk labels, run by fans, for fans.

"Folkies started to realize that their big mistake had been trusting the music industry in the first place," Ferguson said. "Of course those corporate swine would drop folk music at the first opportunity. Of course they wouldn't understand it, care about it. The whole notion of a tradition, of timeless music, is incomprehensible to people who see everything in terms of quick hits and quarterly profits. How do you put a bar code on a song that's been around for a thousand years?"

Ferguson scowled at his beer, then smiled conspiratorially at Kit. "The secret," he said, almost whispering, "was to do everything ourselves. Not just helping the artists, but creating a whole support system independent of the industry: our own labels, radio shows, managers, agents, sound engineers, recording studios. I like to call it an ecosystem; everything you need to sustain life outside the mainstream."

Kit was coaxing all this out of Ferguson, peppering him with questions. Partly, he knew, she was being ingratiating. He was accustomed to that. He was the big folk critic in town, and young performers wanted to get on his good side. But she also seemed to genuinely want to know these things.

"And let me guess," Kit said, wagging a finger under his nose. "Somewhere in there, you figured out how to become a folk critic. Just another fan looking for a way to keep it going. I mean, it really feels that way from how you write."

Ferguson grinned and raised his beer bottle to her. "Nice to be read, better to be understood. You're exactly right; I'm just a folkie. I used to play a little myself, you know, back in the day. There's something about folk music makes you want to pitch in and do your bit."

"You're a musician, too?" Kit said. "I didn't know that."

"Oh, I wouldn't say that. I just played a little. I'm certainly not a musician, not the way he is." He pointed at Nathan, who was in the back, laughing about something with Murph.

"But if you can play, you're a musician, right?" Kit asked.

"Musicians can talk; it doesn't make them writers."

Kit narrowed her eyes but said nothing. Ferguson smiled.

"Music is a language, Kit," he said. "It took me years to figure that out. It's another human language, created because there were things we couldn't say to each other in words. Mostly emotional things; how life *feels*."

Kit smiled at that, nodding her head.

"When I figured that out," he said, "I realized I would never be a musician, not the way Nathan is. I understand the language, but it's not my native tongue."

He took a long pull from his beer. "Winifred Horan, a great Irish fiddler, said that the first time she hears a melody, she begins hearing countermelodies. From the first note, her brain begins breaking down the melody into patterns, hearing things moving over it, under it. I'm just the opposite: I plow through all of that to get to the core idea. I want to see everything flat, linear, ordered. Not good, not bad, just different. Makes life interesting. And it makes me a writer."

Kit nodded. She looked down at the bar, smiling vacantly into her beer.

After a moment, Ferguson leaned close to her ear. "Yes," he said softly.

She looked up at him. "Yes? Yes what?"

"Yes, you're a musician, a real one, the way Nathan is. I knew it the first time I heard you, dropped pick and all. Just because you flub the words doesn't mean you don't speak the language. You do, Kit, fluently."

"Thanks," she said, reaching over to squeeze his hand. "May I buy you a drink, perfesser?"

"You may indeed. Just one. Work day tomorrow."

From then on, "perfesser" became Kit's pet name for Ferguson, and he basked in its teasing familiarity. He would find that she didn't talk to him the way most musicians talk to critics, in guarded ways aimed at creating a favorable impression. She treated him more like a kindred spirit, the way Nathan always had.

After Ferguson became a critic, he never detected the slightest difference in the way Nathan felt about him. One night, both in their cups, he'd said to Ferguson, "You're not changing jobs, you're just changing tools. Job's still the same, for both of us. Job's the music."

That was one of Ferguson's most cherished memories; for if he could pick one musician to understand that about him, it would be Nathan Warren. Even after all these years as friends, Ferguson was still a bit star-struck around him.

Ferguson and Kit both looked over at Nathan, still chatting with Murph. "He used to be King Hell around here," Ferguson said, almost to himself, and Kit's head snapped to him. "Back in the day, I mean. He walked on water, and he knew it. He wasn't always so damned self-effacing, you know; he used to be cocky as hell. Never mean or arrogant, and he disliked people who were. But he knew how good he was; he sure knew that."

Ferguson leaned over to Kit, his eyes excited. "Did you know he played Carnegie Hall? First time he ever played New York, and it's at Carnegie-for-god's-sakes-Hall."

"I didn't know that," Kit said. "He didn't tell me."

"Of course not. He wouldn't. Don't get me wrong; it's not like he *achieved* Carnegie Hall or anything. It was a very fluky thing. Some guy inherited some money and rented out one of Carnegie's smaller halls for this big revue of new songwriters. There are three concert spaces in Carnegie Hall, you know."

He shrugged. "But that's folk music for you," he said. "It's a very fluky world. Things don't rise and fall on hits, market trends, demographic shifts. Somebody retires and opens a coffeehouse in their church. A record label starts up because some fan wants to record his favorite songwriter, and fifteen years later, he's staring out the window, trying to figure out how the hell he became a record mogul with a catalog of three hundred albums."

"A guy gets some money and Nathan plays Carnegie Hall," Kit said with a touch of impatience. She was very interested in this.

"Sorry," Ferguson said. "Yes, Carnegie Hall. And he gets a standing ovation. I'm pretty sure he was the only one who did. One of the big New York papers reviewed the show. The gist was that the critic was unconvinced this show heralded any big new folk revival; but he was convinced of one thing, and I quote: 'The young and remarkably talented Mr. Warren is someone we will all be hearing from very soon.' That's how that record exec heard about him, you know, the one that signed him to that disastrous contract. You heard about that?"

Kit nodded. Ferguson shook his head and looked down at the bar. "Such a tragedy," he said, "such a goddamn waste. And of course, Nathan blames himself for all of it. He feels like he never did anything with his life; his music can't be worth anything because look what happened. But he's still Nathan Warren, still the best pure, pound-for-pound folksinger I ever saw walk on a stage."

He looked back at Kit, and his eyes were burning. Reflexively, she reared back a few inches. In a low whisper, Ferguson said, "I'm not saying that because I'm his friend. It's the goddamn gospel truth. I've written it in the paper, and they don't pay me to be anybody's friend down there. The best I ever saw."

As Nathan walked back toward the bar, Kit leaned over to Ferguson and said, "Could I get together with you some time, talk to you more about…um…this stuff?"

"You mean Nathan?"

She nodded and drew in a breath. Had she crossed a line?

But he patted her hand. "Sure," he said. "It's a good idea. Because he won't tell you much. Especially the good stuff; he won't tell you anything about the good stuff."

"Why not?"

"Because he doesn't think there is any," Ferguson said, and slipped his business card under her palm.

Three

Nathan sat on his bed, strumming the chords to "Footloose." Since Murph requested it, the song had been running through his head, and he thought he might rearrange it. Or maybe he just needed something to do. He sighed, listening to Kit through the closed bedroom door as she moved busily from guitar to fiddle, trying melody lines, softly singing lyrics. So hard at her work.

This was how he and Kit often ended up on days she didn't need to work, run errands, or rush off to one of the two classes on folk music she was auditing at, of all places, Harvard University (who knew?).

The day would begin with a long, chatty breakfast, followed by a walk or some chores in the yard. Back at the kitchen table, one of them would pull out a guitar and the other would rush off to get theirs. They would swap songs for awhile, then Kit would grab her fiddle to play along to one of Nathan's songs, and he would return the favor by accompanying one of hers on guitar, maybe finding a nice harmony.

At some point, usually without anything being said, Nathan would go into his bedroom, closing the door behind him, leaving Kit to work by herself in the living room. At first, she tried to argue about having the larger space, saying she felt like she was kicking him out of his own house. But Nathan liked the solitude of the small bedroom, and she'd found a favorite spot in the living room, sprawled on the floor in front of Nathan's stereo.

"What's that?" she asked one morning, pointing to a rectangular box with a towel over it on top of Nathan's CD player.

"My stereo," he said.

"No, I mean on top of the stereo," Kit said. "What's that box on top?"

Nathan laughed. "That's an honest-to-god stereo. A record player."

She looked bug-eyed at him. "You have record albums? Like, vinyl?"

"Absolutely colonial, isn't it? Goes with life in a carriage house."

He showed her the stereo perched on top of his CD player and the cabinet underneath, full of old folk albums. The collection had begun with his dad's vintage blues records, which were about the only thing the two had enjoyed together. After he died, Nathan took the records home and began to build on them, scouring used-record stores. He particularly liked albums made just before the commercial folk revival of the 1960s. There was a sweetness to them, a melodic innocence and purity of purpose. Before folk music realized it was a business.

Unlike Nathan, Kit listened to music while she wrote. She would often put on an old album or a new CD, listening through Nathan's big headphones. She called it priming the pump, and before long she was off on new song ideas. Following Nathan's suggestion, she'd begun using her fiddle as a barometer of melodies and arrangements. She would hum and strum chords for a while, then pick up the fiddle to hear the melody by itself.

Now, on a warm September afternoon, Nathan heard her play a sweet fiddle trill over and over. She was probably trying to figure out how to play it on the guitar. Sure enough, she was soon searching out the same notes on her guitar.

Everything about Kit's music was new to her, fresh and full of discovery. He looked down at his guitar and suddenly felt very tired. When did he learn "Footloose?" Fifteen years ago? Twenty? He slid his fingers silently up and down the strings. So long ago.

Where did all that fine eager fire go? It once burned so hot in him. Perhaps too hot; sometimes the hottest fires burn themselves out. And then they are cold for such a long time, with nothing left to rekindle the flame. Just ash and ember, the memory of wood.

He looked at the door, hearing Kit beyond it. She was still trying to turn that fiddle trill into guitar chords. She hit a seventh chord, which sounded sappy. "Oh, *yeww,*" she said, and he smiled.

How long had it been since he wrote a song? He couldn't even remember. While he waited for his album to come out, it seemed wrong to write new things, as if he was getting ahead of himself. Or maybe that was just his excuse; maybe he had nothing left to say, nothing about his sad little life worth singing about.

He shook his head sharply. That's a bad thought, and it's never true. Folk music taught him that our most ordinary mornings can be the stuff of song. So why could he no longer find music in his ordinary mornings?

He felt the old thought return—*such a long way down, long, long, long*—and the ache it brought was worse than usual, bending him over on the bed. So much of his life, his past, was numb to him now, like it had all happened to someone else. Why did this pain feel so sharp, like he was feeling it for the first time? Why today, why now?

He heard Kit again, playing the guitar more forcefully. The fiddle line was now woven into the guitar, surrounded by thick chordal patterns. As if it had been there all along. She's a quick study, isn't she?

He looked down at his guitar. Maybe he could find a starker chord for the middle of the second verse, something bare and sudden to underscore the surrender of the lyric. His fingers sought a chord, raising up where he knew he would find open, droning notes. He strummed with his right hand—yes, that's it—and began to sing, barely above a whisper:

> *I know my name, now I know it ain't no secret.*
> *If you know it, I will claim I'm not to blame.*
> *I'd be mad to seek it,*
> *Seemed to grow some wings and sail away.*
> *I for one have seen it fly.*
> *It never screams. It only sighs,*
> *And makes me cry each time I hear the sound.*

Ferguson came into Dooley's a little after eleven, looking disheveled and mumbling to himself. Kit was doing a late shift at one of her waitressing jobs, and Nathan was talking with Jackie at the bend of the bar. Ferguson sat down heavily. He'd had a terrible time with an editor at the newspaper, he said.

He'd been worried about his position there for more than a year, since it was purchased by a national media corporation that Ferguson would refer to only as "the mother ship." The paper was losing the uniquely Boston flavor for which it was famous, taking on more of a generic, Anywhere, USA, feel.

In most towns, folk music was underground to the point of being virtually invisible to mainstream media. But this was Boston, and Boston had always been a folk town. The question was, did they know that five hundred miles away in the offices of the corporation that now ran this paper, and a dozen others around the country?

So far, Ferguson's position seemed fairly secure, but the paper was not doing well. Most of what was going wrong, he thought, was the usual miasma of huge corporations, a distant management style that trickled down from people too far away to know what was really happening on the ground.

After taking a sip of his first rum, Ferguson told Nathan that a few days ago he'd filed a story for a new editor, who e-mailed him back: "This is the most pristine copy I've ever received. It will run as is."

Praise like that was rare from busy editors. "Usually," Ferguson said, "when they're happy, you don't hear anything because nothing needs fixing. It's a busy place."

Earlier this evening, however, he'd received an e-mailed copy of the story. It had been so heavily edited it was almost unrecognizable. The editor asked him to offer suggestions about what was wrong with the edits. That was also something editors rarely did; but it was obvious the story was now in trouble.

"He ended up taking out some of the most basic newspaper stuff," Ferguson said, staring into his rum. "It's a trend piece about ethnic foods at a local folk festival, so I interviewed a lot of the immigrants who cook it. Some of them weren't even identified: where they lived, what country they came from, why they were in the story. The editor had just gone over it and over it, editing, editing, editing, until nothing made sense. And he knew it; that's why he asked me for help."

"But you said he liked it," Nathan said.

"Pristine. Yup. I sent him back a version that reinserted most of the basic stuff. It's not as good as the original, but at least it's coherent."

"So what the hell happened?"

"He told me that his new boss, this guy the mother ship brought in from another paper, had been 'auditing' the section. God, what a terrible word—like it's your taxes or something. He would come down and dissect every story, saying this was no good or he didn't want that."

Ferguson picked up his beer but put it down without drinking. "You won't believe what my editor told me next," he said, shaking his head. "I mean, this ought to be in some journalism textbook, under the heading 'Signs of a Management Crisis.' He said, 'Every week my boss tears the section apart, but I still don't know what he wants. All I know is what he doesn't want—and that keeps changing.'"

"Jesus," Nathan said. "How can you even function that way?"

"Exactly. My editor started preemptively tearing the story apart, trying to anticipate everything his boss might complain about. But he didn't know what to change because he thought the story was fine. Pristine. So he was just guessing: maybe he won't like this; maybe he'll complain about that. And he kept guessing until he realized he'd ruined the story."

Jackie delivered Ferguson's second rum before he'd finished his first one. She rapped her knuckles on the bar, signifying it was on the house. Jackie knew when her regulars needed a little pampering. Ferguson smiled gratefully at her. She looked quizzically over at Nathan, who mouthed the word *paper*. She nodded sympathetically and walked away. She also knew when her regulars wanted to be left alone.

Ferguson emptied his first rum in two big gulps, then picked up the second. "I seem to be falling behind in my work here," he said, trying to laugh. But it came out like a weak cough.

"You ever wonder why they never hired you as a staff writer?" Nathan asked.

"I know exactly why. I never wanted them to. I mean, it would've been nice to be asked, but I never angled for it. I only want to write about folk music; I'm a folkie, you know? I can see why they wouldn't want to have a full time staffer doing that. Years ago, an editor coached me on how to get a shot at getting hired, but it was all about branching out, showing I could write about mainstream stuff, pop music. I just wasn't interested."

Nathan nodded and smiled.

"But they've always gotten it that folk is important in this town," Ferguson said. "The way they used to put it is, 'It's one of the things that makes Boston Boston.' And the paper used to be all about that: what makes Boston Boston. Now it's being run from another city, by people who don't know this town and are completely invested in proving that you don't have to know that to run a paper here. Or else, why did they buy it?"

"Jesus," Nathan said. "That's just like the music industry. If you have to know about music to run a record label, then why is Sony running Columbia?"

"Exactly. So Sony tries to prove that the music business is like any other business: that it's all about marketing and accounting, and you don't have to know the difference between reggae and ska to know the difference between a band that will make money and a band that won't."

"I don't know the difference between reggae and ska," Nathan said, grinning.

Ferguson squinted at him. "You don't know the difference between making money and not making money either."

"Good point."

Nathan didn't like seeing his old friend this way. He usually blew into Dooley's like a Yankee schooner under full sail. "What you do down there is important, you know," Nathan said.

Ferguson shrugged. "Oh, I know. Everybody needs a little press attention. I just—"

"That's not what I mean. I mean the way you write. So many critics focus on the career stuff: how hard the touring life is, how our fans made us what we are, and we've finally got a label that understands us. They never get into how the music sounds."

Nathan pointed a finger at Ferguson. "But you do. Like the line you wrote a while ago, about that quiet singer. You said her voice sounds the way eyes look when they're darting. Man, you nailed it; that's *exactly* what she sounds like."

"Thanks," Ferguson said. His mouth moved as if he was searching for more to say. Picking up his beer bottle, he cleared his throat a couple of times and said, "Thanks."

For a long time, Ferguson twirled the bottle slowly in his hand. "I'm getting scared," he said, so quietly Nathan had to lean closer to hear. "You can feel the current flowing upward down there. Like that editor I told you about. He's not thinking about readers; he's worried about what his boss is going to say. And the boss is worried about what they're going to say at the mother ship. The energy is all flying up. Up and away."

A little later, the conversation turned to Kit. Ferguson said he liked how unafraid she was to ask him questions about the music. A lot of young songwriters tried to bluff him about how much they knew; it showed confidence that she didn't try to impress him.

"That impressed you," Nathan said with a coy smile.

Ferguson laughed. "It did, now that you mention it. You think that's why she did it?"

"No, she really wants to soak it all up; she's auditing two folk music classes at Harvard. But she's smart about people, too. I'm sure it's not lost on her that you might be impressed. She knows I am."

Nathan confessed that he sometimes had strangely conflicting feelings about her, because of her passion to learn. One minute he'd be so proud to see her using something he showed her, then he'd be kissing her, or wanting to, wondering if this was all a little, well, dirty-old-mannish.

Ferguson chuckled dryly, shaking his head.

"What?" Nathan said.

"Only you, Nathan. As God is my witness, only you."

"What?"

"Only you could find some way to make this seem like a problem. I swear, somebody could give you a million dollars and you'd worry about the taxes. Angelina Jolie could stick her tongue down your throat and you'd worry if she had a cold. You are a piece of work, my friend, a certifiable piece of work."

Nathan laughed but didn't quite get it. Why would Angelina Jolie stick her tongue down his throat?

On a Saturday in mid-September, Kit asked if she could bring some things to Nathan's house and spend the day getting ready for her first really important gig, at the Home Baked Coffeehouse. She said she needed some peace and quiet.

The Home Baked was one of the best of the suburban coffeehouses, and always began its season with its New Voices Showcase. The couple who ran the place liked to haunt the suburban open mikes, trawling for Next Big Things. They caught Kit on a good night, at a tiny open mike in Concord, and hired her on the spot.

Because the showcase happened before most of the suburban coffeehouses started their fall-to-spring seasons, other coffeehouse managers came to check out the new talent. The Home Baked had a reputation for debuting people who went on to bigger things, so a successful set at the showcase usually led to other gigs.

Nathan was delighted at the thought of accompanying Kit to her first big gig, but he was also worried. She'd been jumpy all week, as if the lack of stage fright on the night the Home Baked folks saw her guaranteed it would derail her this time. The more she dwelled on it, the more likely it was to happen.

After a quiet breakfast on Saturday, Nathan figured that Kit needed some time to herself and said he was going to wander around Harvard Square. He warned her not to sing too much; her voice could get tired.

"And drink lots of water," he said. "Hydrate, hydrate; keeps the throat fresh and juicy."

"Fresh and juicy, right," she said, puffing a breath and staring at her set list. He doubted she'd heard a word.

"I'll see you in a few hours, unless Harvard Square hits an iceberg," he said as he opened the kitchen door.

"Right, okay, bye," she muttered. Just as he closed the door behind him, he heard her say, "*What?*" He smiled and walked down Craigie Street toward the square.

It had been hot and humid for the past week; but the weather report said a cold front was coming down from Canada, and when it collided with the heat there could be thunderstorms. They were expected right about the time Nathan would be driving Kit to her gig.

Nathan walked around and around the square, thinking about Kit, worrying about Kit, convincing himself she'd be okay, then worrying some more. Ferguson was right; he could worry about anything. And when all else failed, he could do what he was doing now: worry about worrying. He smiled and shook his head.

He sat at one of the areas designed for people to relax, a semicircular stone structure on Brattle Street, with wide, sloping steps. He enjoyed watching people, imagining what their lives were like, what they were thinking. After a while, he noticed a woman busking, or singing for spare change, in front of a trendy pizza bistro. He wandered over.

Nathan had done some busking in his younger days, but back then almost nobody used amplification. Nowadays, everybody had a portable sound system with mikes and small amplifiers. To him, that defeated both the charm and the value of busking.

The streets were the world's oldest stage, and they had much to teach. Back in his day (god, there he went again), he learned the precious arts of eye contact and how to move your body to create visual interest without distracting from the song. He would engage the crowd by singling out certain passersby, especially children, and walking over to sing for them. He learned things that cannot be taught, the mystical ways your physical energy can be pushed out into the world and draw people in. How can you learn those things huddled behind a microphone?

He watched the busker, pretty but very thin, in a loose sleeveless tank top and faded jeans, her brightly dyed orange hair trailing in strands over her face. Her eyes were closed, and she was muttering an old Paul Simon song in a way she probably thought sounded troubled and interesting. But her voice was barely audible over the loudly strumming guitar.

Nathan looked at the crowd. No one was closer than ten yards. A mother with two small children sat down, pointing to the music. The smaller one, a toddler, waved shyly at the busker, but her eyes were still closed, perhaps imagining herself in some grand theater. Damn.

The older child was a girl of four or five with a flaring pink skirt, almost like a tutu. The mother gave her a coin to put in the busker's guitar case. The child walked timidly forward, clutching the coin tightly in her hand, then stopped. With the mikes so loud and the busker eyes shut tight, the little girl actually felt like she was intruding. She looked uncertainly at her mother, who pushed out her hands, coaxing the girl forward.

Nathan shook his head sadly, watching the child squirm up to the guitar case, drop the coin in, then run clumsily back to her mother while the crowd laughed. The singer never noticed, never opened her eyes—another magical moment of art meeting life, missed and now gone.

Oh, grumble, grumble, piss and moan; you're such an old fart these days. Jesus, so the kids want to use microphones. He remembered how he'd sworn he would never end up like one of those curmudgeons who waved their canes at the changing world, and called young people hooligans and whippersnappers. He was becoming just like that. Next thing you know, he'll be saying "You call that music? Why, you can't even hear the words!" Jesus, what's happened to you?

But it wasn't the microphones he minded. It was the distance they created between the street singers and their streets, between their deeply felt dreams of art and the possibility of actual art that passed them by, unseen and unanswered, while they sang only to themselves. Art is communication, whether the vocabulary is words, notes, or brushstrokes on a canvas. All this technology keeps people from seeing that, keeps them apart, keeps them from using their art to touch each other.

He got up slowly, suddenly feeling very old. Who was he to curse the newfangled? He put a dollar bill in the busker's case and walked into the heart of the square. He looked at the big clock above Mass. Ave. and figured it was time to go back and see how Kit was doing.

He turned up Mass. Ave. to walk home. After a few steps, he stopped, as a great sadness swept over him like a cold, aching wave. It came with no thoughts, no meaning, only a dull shiver of pain. He stood frozen to the feeling, thinking nothing, then shook his head as if batting away morning cobwebs, and began to walk home.

"What do you think?" Kit said, looking in the bathroom mirror and turning her head this way and that.

"Well," Nathan said, "I think you're lovely, just—"

"I mean the hair. What do you think of the look? For tonight, I mean."

"I like it. Sort of a country lass thing."

She stared at him, narrowing her eyes. "Country lass?"

"You know, folksy, down-home." Trying to rebound, he added firmly, "But hip, definitely hip. A hip country lass."

"You're not a real coiffeur kind of guy, are you?"

"Not really, no."

She smiled, patted his cheek, and turned back to the mirror.

"What about makeup?" she asked. She'd already done her lashes and put on some eyeliner, and it looked incredibly good, widening her eyes and making her long lashes seem even longer and blacker.

"The eye stuff is great." He cleared his throat. "I mean, really great. I've never seen you with it before. You look great. Really…great." He was nodding foolishly, stammering. She grinned at him in the mirror.

"But I wouldn't put any face makeup on," he said, "any powder or anything. You want to look natural at these places. Dressed for company, but not dressy, you know?"

"Yeah? I thought a little makeup might cover the—"

"Red cheeks? Kit, if you wore that much, they'd think they were reviewing the corpse at a wake. 'Gee,' they'd say, 'she just looks like she's sleeping, doesn't she?'"

"All right, I get your—"

"But I don't remember her ever *smiling* that way.'"

"All right! You made your point. Gee, you just keep cheering me up, don't'cha?"

"I'm sorry, but it's true."

She frowned in the mirror. "Maybe you're right about the hair being too much."

"I didn't say it was too much; I said I liked it. I…"

But she wasn't listening. She thrust her fingers beneath her hair, spread them, and began raking it in a circular motion. Then, with a strong toss of her head and a few strokes from a skeletal brush, the hair billowed and fell back, now looking artfully tousled, what a Newbury Street stylist would probably call "urban."

She scrunched the hair in front into her fist, then pushed it to the side, and the bang effect suddenly became thick strands that seemed to have carelessly fallen forward over her face. A few flipping strokes with a wide-toothed comb, a spritz of spray, and it was done. A completely different look. You'd think she spent the whole day on it.

"Better?" she asked.

"How did you do that? Yeah, it looks terrific. And you're right, it's better for tonight. Still obviously done up, but more casual. Coffeehouse-y."

He shook his head, still wondering how she changed her hair so quickly. "You did that in a minute," he said. "If I hadn't seen it, I wouldn't believe it. And it looks great. Great. Just …really…um…great." He was stammering again.

She smiled and turned to him. "So, if I get you right, you're saying it looks… um…great? You can be so sweet when you're not…I mean, country lass. Really?"

She laughed, punched his chin lightly, and was off into the bedroom to figure out what to wear. He thought she'd want to be alone now—at least he hoped so—but she immediately hollered his name.

"Absolutely not," he said, as she pointed at several ensembles laid out on the bed. Good Lord, did she bring her entire closet? "Not on your life. That's up to you. Whichever one I choose, it'll come back to haunt me. No, no, no. They'll all look terrific on you, and there's no dress code at a coffeehouse. Wear whatever will make you feel the most comfortable. They're all perfect, just perfect. *Perfect*."

"Oh, but Nathan, you could just—"

"Not a chance. You choose. Jesus, I just about ended our relationship a few minutes ago by saying I *liked* your hair. You think I'm going to weigh in on your wardrobe? You always look great, Kit; I'm sure whatever you decide will be the perfect choice."

"God, you sound just like my parents."

"Yeah, well, they had to live with you for a long time; I'm sure they've learned how to handle moments like this. You are on your own."

She began to grumble the way she did when she wasn't really angry but wanted to keep the mood. Then she turned toward the bed, folding her arms and considering her choices.

Good time for an escape. Nathan went into the kitchen to make tea. A little afternoon caffeine. Long night ahead.

She emerged fifteen minutes later, dressed casually, with a garment bag in her hand, and announced she was ready to go.

"Guitar?" he asked.

"Oh, yeah." She blushed and turned, shaking her head in some private scolding, and walked back to the bedroom to get her guitar. Nathan followed.

"I know you're getting nervous, Kit," he said, "nervous about getting nervous, and I know how much that sucks. You're going to get on top of this stage fright; I know you are. If not this time, next time. Soon."

"Oh, thanks. If not this time? You trying to jinx me?" She slung the nylon guitar case around her shoulder harshly, as if it had misbehaved.

"No, but you have to be ready for it if you're going to control it. And you're not going to do that by pretending it won't happen, pretending you're not thinking about it, worrying about it."

Her shoulders sagged, and she looked down at the floor. She fumbled with the shoulder strap of the guitar case.

"Remember, Kit," he said, "it's only adrenaline, something coming from inside you. It's just part of you."

She looked up, and her face was miserable, as if she'd already tried and failed. He walked over and held her.

Then he stepped back, spread his arms wide, and took an exaggerated breath, as if gathering in the air with his arms. "Just remember, it's all part of you. Your natural juices. Once you learn to ride it, it's a very pleasant drug."

"Yeah, yeah, just like cocaine. Well, maybe I'm not a cocaine kind of girl, Nathan. Can we go now?"

The Home Baked was one of a couple of dozen community coffeehouses in the suburbs of Boston, ninety minutes or less from Nathan's house. A little before five p.m., they turned onto I-93 North in Nathan's old Subaru. The promised thunderstorms were coming. The sky was so dark it seemed like twilight, and Nathan turned on his lights. The clouds were grim and threatening, every color but gray. Patches of slate black were streaked with ominous shades of green and dark purple, rimmed by a dried-blood red that didn't look like it was kidding around.

A few huge drops slapped against the windshield, and then it was as though a great faucet opened, streaming down sheets of water. Everyone on the freeway turned on their lights and slowed to about twenty, a rare tribute to weather in this town.

"Great, just perfect," Kit muttered, shaking her head as she stared out the side window.

"It's only rain. We won't be late."

She made a simpering kind of acknowledgment, as if she'd started a sarcastic sigh, then tried to pull it back. He looked over, and she managed what would only pass for a smile in a police mug shot. This was not good.

As they pulled up in front of the colonial church where the Home Baked was, the rain was still heavy, pouring straight down. The torrents drove some green leaves off the trees, and they swam crazily in the street. Nathan could see through the windows of the function hall beside the church tower. The premature dusk made the lights inside the white wooden church look yellow and warm, like an old Norman Rockwell painting. Volunteers were busily setting up tables and chairs, putting up the temporary stage, plugging in the sound system.

They parked in front of the church, across the street from the small town common. Nathan leaned over the steering wheel, resting his head on his arms and looking into the church. God, he loved folk music. All these good people—doctors, teachers, computer engineers—spending their Saturdays creating a venue so the music they loved could be heard in their own hometown. And today, they were doing it all for a bunch of singers no one had ever heard of. It was such a group effort these days, keeping the music alive. Maybe it always was, and we just forgot that for awhile.

"Are you waiting for someone to open the door for us?" Kit said, trying to be funny but sounding edgy and impatient. "I mean, wanna go in?"

Still leaning on the wheel, he looked over at her and smiled. "Relax, will you? These are all nice people. They're not here to size you up or look down their noses at you."

"It's called a showcase, Nathan. How is that not sizing me up?"

He nodded in agreement, straightened up, and turned off the engine.

"I know, sweetie," he said. "But people come to a place like this expecting to like what they hear. It's personal. They want to feel like they're hearing songs from a friend, not a star. You're going to be just their cup of tea."

She shook her head, puffing a nervous breath. "Okay, okay. I'm sorry, Nathan, but you know how this feels. I'm a wreck. Can we just go in and get it over with?"

He smiled. "You bet. Here we go. Ready?"

"No. But I'll never be readier."

He nodded approvingly. "Good answer. Let's go. Wait until I get over there with my umbrella. Mustn't drench the star."

The crowd arrives very early at the Home Baked, which performers often mistake for enthusiasm about their music. In fact, everybody wants first crack at the fresh pumpkin cake for which the coffeehouse is named. It was so famous locally that a Halloween-colored banner across the stage read, "The Home Baked Coffeehouse: Folk Music and Pumpkin Power." Alongside the slogan was a drawing of a jack-o'-lantern playing a banjo. Ah, folk music.

Nathan used to play there regularly but hadn't in years, ever since a performance at which he didn't think he was drunk, but everybody else did. Hoping to lighten Kit's mood, he told her the pumpkin cake was so good it should be registered as a controlled substance. She smiled weakly, but it probably reminded her of cocaine, which reminded her of adrenaline, which reminded her she was going to get stage fright tonight.

As they walked in the door, the couple who ran the coffeehouse rushed over. "Nathan, what a nice surprise to see you," the wife said, while the husband nodded and held out his hand. They both waved hi to Kit, and the wife gave her a light hug. Kit smiled briefly, then stared down at the floor, nervously adjusting the guitar case slung over her shoulder. Nathan was holding her garment bag.

After an awkward silence, Nathan said, "Dressing room still in the same place?" The couple nodded and pointed them toward the pastor's office in the rear.

The coffeehouse was held in a large, almost square room, seating more than a hundred, with dark wooden walls, and large windows that looked out on the town common. All the tables had orange-checked tablecloths and orange candles in black casings. A pumpkin motif. People were talking quietly, eating pumpkin cake or brownies, sipping coffee, herbal tea, and Whole Foods soda.

Nathan took Kit's hand and said, "You're gonna kill 'em tonight, sweetie. I predict." Kissing her cheek, he left her at the dressing room door and walked to the back of the hall to find a seat. He loved the pumpkin cake but was much too nervous to eat.

Kit would perform first, the most unknown of all the unknowns. On the bright side, that meant her torment would be over quickly. But it also meant that the crowd would be cold, perhaps wondering if a concert of beginners was still a good idea, now that they'd had their pumpkin cake.

Kit emerged from the dressing room wearing a white blouse with a few light ruffles down the front, suggesting both a folksy and dressy look. Over it was a shimmery blue coat, like a blazer but shorter and very feminine. She had on dressy blue jeans that were just tight enough to, well, you know…but not the least bit show-offy. He'd been right about letting her decide what to wear; she certainly knew how to dress for the stage. Maybe she'd be fine tonight.

During the third verse of her first song, however, the red patches appeared and with them a hot puff of breath, almost a gasp, that threw her completely off rhythm. The elegant spaces in the melody became clumsy silences; she missed chords, fumbled over lyrics. The song was met with polite applause, but the crowd wriggled in their seats, pretty sure that listening to this "New Voice" was going to be an act of charity.

Kit stared at the floor, and Nathan went from worried to scared. Could she even continue? If she retreated now, she might never get over it. She shot a terrified glance at him, and he made his exaggerated deep-breath motion again. It meant nothing; he did it merely to remind her that the adrenaline was hers to control. But she mimicked the motion, waving her arms and taking a deep breath, then letting it out so loudly that it popped in the microphone.

"I guess you can tell I'm nervous, huh?" she said with a shrug. The audience laughed sympathetically; there was kindness in the sound. A few whispered "That's okay" and "We don't mind."

"People can always tell when I'm nervous," Kit said. "Because of these." She puffed out her cheeks and pointed to the red patches. The crowd laughed louder now, more comfortably. She poked her cheeks, puffing the air out of them with another loud microphone pop, and the laughter grew. "I light up just like a Christmas tree, don't'cha think?" And then she smiled.

"I could never get away with anything when I was a kid because of these," she said, pointing again at her cheeks. "My mom would say, 'Who broke the red rooster vase Aunt Tildy gave me?' She'd look at my red cheeks and say, 'Kit, how many times have I told you not to run through the dining room?'"

The audience howled at that, a few clapping their hands in delight. Some leaned forward in their seats, grinning. Nathan felt like he'd forgotten to breathe and could now begin again. As she told the humbling story, the red disappeared from her face, and the next song billowed with all the sweet space and tantalizing rhythmic irregularities that made her songs feel so intimate and natural. She began to sway to the rhythm, and emotional purpose returned to her phrasing. She was not just singing the words now; she was telling a story.

Every song received sustained applause, and she was enthusiastically brought back for an encore, which the hosts said almost never happened at these showcases. "So we're going to have to bring Kit back real soon, aren't we?" the wife said. The audience cheered again, all the louder for the good feeling they shared, knowing that they'd helped Kit to do well.

Nathan settled into his seat and grinned. She was riding the beast. She would get nervous again; the battle wasn't over. But now she knew the way out. He was so glad he'd been there to see it.

More important, she turned the fact of her stage fright into a performance tool. She took the audience into her confidence, shared a secret with them, made them feel part of her bad moment. She wasn't performing at them, but with them. That's a trick some of the biggest stars never learn. In folk music it's not about dazzling audiences; it's about befriending them.

Kit was becoming an entertainer, and now he knew what he'd only suspected: that she would become a very good one. Her humor fit right in with her songs, that same vivid, quirky eye for detail. She hadn't broken a plate or a window, but "Aunt Tildy's red rooster vase." Brilliant.

After the show, the hosts asked her if she'd come back in a few months to do an opening set for a popular local songwriter. She was the only one of the New Voices asked to return so soon.

Because of the Home Baked's reputation for discovering new talent, Nathan knew Kit's triumph would lead to other gigs in the suburbs. He'd seen several people approach her, giving her business cards or scribbling phone numbers on the bright orange napkins.

The rain had stopped midway through the evening. The night air was cool and clean, but you could still smell the rain. After they got in the car, Nathan reached into the back seat and pulled out a red rose he'd bought in Harvard Square and hidden away for this moment.

"For the star," he said. Kit took it and beamed, her eyes glowing at him. Then she mouthed "Thanks" and kissed him.

On the way home, tapping the rose on her lap, she talked nonstop, the adrenaline still doing its stuff, but happily now. Nathan savored the contact high from all that excitement. He was so glad he'd been there, and genuinely pleased that he didn't feel a whiff of envy. Gee, he'd always envied Joyce.

"I haven't let you get a word in, have I?" Kit said about halfway home.

Nathan laughed. "But enough about me, what do *you* think about me?"

"God, am I that bad?"

"You're always going to be full of yourself after you kick the way you did tonight. Might as well get used to it. We'll both have to, because this is going to start happening a lot."

"You think?"

He started to explain how important her set had been and the other gigs it would lead to, but she smiled absently and turned to gaze out the window. She didn't want to think about that now, about biz things. She wanted to savor the moment, let tonight stay tonight. So much smarter than he'd been when he was starting out.

"I have to ask," he said. "Aunt Tildy's red rooster vase?"

She laughed. "Absolutely true, I swear. My mom glued it back together, but not very well, so all the scars showed. Elmer's-Glue white, y'know? And there it sat, on the dining room bureau, for everybody to see: this poor little crippled rooster that Kit tried to kill. I think she put it together sloppy like that to teach me a lesson."

"A cautionary rooster," Nathan said thoughtfully, as they turned off I-93 onto the long, winding off-ramp that led to Storrow Drive and home.

Kit laughed, a deliciously open-throated laugh, a laugh that said she was comfortable with him, unguarded, open.

"It felt true," he said. "That was a good instinct. You didn't fight the stage fright, you used it. You turned it into something to draw in the audience, get them on your side. You made them feel comfortable by telling them how uncomfortable you felt. You included them. And that's it; that's how it's done. The secret is that they want to be on your side. And now you'll always know that."

She thought about that. "What they wanted was me," she said finally, "not an act of me, not me being all polished and perfect. They liked what I said because it sounded like me. Yes?"

Nathan nodded. "You were sharing something with them, trusting them, taking them into your confidence. And one other thing."

"What?"

"It was real, Kit, like your songs. They believed you."

She was quiet for a long time, staring out the window, stroking her mouth with her index finger. Nathan could almost hear the wheels churning in her head.

As they turned onto Craigie Street, past the big old houses, dark and silent now, she began clapping her hands softly. "God, I love it when they love me. I'm sorry, but I really do. I *love* it!"

"Get used to that, too, sweetie."

"Yeah?" She was beaming again.

Nathan grinned and nodded. She gazed back out the window as they pulled up the winding driveway. He'd left the kitchen light on and was glad; it looked white and welcoming against the dark night.

"Sorry about being cranky earlier," she said, her voice sounding more sincere than it needed to. "When I was getting dressed, I mean. I'm sorry I snapped at you. I was so nervous."

"That's okay, sweetie. I know how that feels. And I'm sorry about the country lass thing. I guess my fashion advice is a little, um, retro."

She laughed and leaned toward him. "So I'm your country lass, huh?"

"You're anything you want to be."

She was startled by the serious answer, and her smile dropped. She moved closer and cupped his head in her hands. "You are a lovely man, Nathan Warren, do you know that?"

"Even when my fashion advice is right out of the sixteenth century?"

"Especially then. I like you just the way you are."

Four

Twice a week Nathan taught guitar lessons at a music store in Porter Square, a few blocks from Dooley's. He liked to teach, especially beginners. Most of the teachers preferred more advanced students, so novices became Nathan's specialty, even though he was the best guitarist at the store. He liked being around the excitement that new students felt as they played their first chords, learned their first songs. It reminded him of his early passion for folk music, the wonder of it, the sense that this was music that everybody could share.

Lots of kids came to him on the verge of giving up. Their troubles often began by getting a guitar at one of the chain music stores that offer free lessons with the purchase.

The teachers were often not guitarists and would begin students the same way they would for piano, violin, or trumpet: learning the scales. After the free lessons were over, these poor kids thought they'd never be able to play the songs they liked.

The store where Nathan taught advertised that its teachers were professional musicians, so parents would say, "Maybe it'll be different with a real guitar player. Just try it for a few weeks, and then you can quit if you still want to."

Nathan knew the neck of his guitar the way a carpenter knows his hammer, but even he had never mastered the scales. If you want to accompany songs on the guitar, you need to begin with chords, not scales. Nathan knew the notes in relation to the chords.

He would call new students before their first lesson and ask for the names of a few songs they liked. That always confused them. Why does the teacher care what kind of music I like? He'd watch them come in for their first lesson, discouraged and wary. They'd never be able play a real song; they were too stupid and clumsy.

Then he would pull out the chords and lyrics to the simplest song they'd suggested, and begin showing them the chords. He would tell them to forget about scales, and watch their little faces begin to sparkle when he said, "You'll learn better if you're playing songs you like."

Within minutes, students would be tentatively strumming along, searching out the next chord while they sang, growing excited and confident, because they knew they were making progress. It's much easier to learn when you're already familiar with the song. Students knew when they made mistakes because they knew how the song was supposed to sound.

By the end of the first lesson, they would be so happy and hopeful. They were playing music. Nathan would smile as they hurried out, imagining the scene when they got home, pulled out their guitar, and said, "Look, Mom, I can play a song!"

Nathan liked intermediate students less and advanced ones least of all. Most of them weren't having fun anymore. There was usually some fatal flaw in their playing, often a simple lack of talent, that they thought they could fix with more work, more work, more work.

Nathan felt like a fraud taking their money. Music had become the mountain they could not climb, the enemy of their dreams. They sat stiffly in their chairs, frowning at their betraying fingers, grimly determined to overcome obstacles they probably knew, deep down, that they never would.

Nathan wanted to tell them to accept their limitations and enjoy how well they already played. But the few times he did that, students got angry and went to other teachers. There's nothing quite so hard to give up as a dream that can never come true. Nathan knew something about that.

A few days after the Home Baked gig, Nathan returned from teaching to find Kit sprawled on the floor in front of his stereo. She was listening to an old Woody Guthrie album, her head burrowed in the liner notes. There was a notebook on her lap, guitar on her right, fiddle on her left.

"Aha!" Nathan said. "Caught you listening to that fogey music."

"Not fair!" she said without turning around. "You know I don't think about it like that anymore."

"Sorry," he said as he put his guitar down in the kitchen. He sat down next to Kit, her head still buried in the album's liner notes. He looked at what she'd been writing: "so simple," "repeats key words," and "chorus makes song about us." She'd underlined the word *us* three times. He loved how her mind worked.

"This guy is amazing," she said. "I always heard how radical he was, writing all these political songs. But they're really not. I mean, like, they are, I suppose, but they're so personal. They're really almost like…like…love songs." She glanced at him, wrinkling her nose doubtfully. "Yes?"

"Absolutely," Nathan said. "I never thought about it that way, but you're right. Personal."

They listened together. Guthrie was singing "Pastures of Plenty," an ode to the itinerant workers of the Great Depression.

It's a mighty hard row that my poor hands have hoed,
My poor feet have traveled a hot dusty road.

When it was over, Nathan said, "Oh, Kit, you have to hear this."

He took the needle off the turntable and went through his CDs, until he found a reissue of a 1963 Judy Collins record. He slipped it in the CD player, saying, "Woody never recorded this; I think it was one of the last songs he ever wrote."

He played her Collins's version of "Plane Wreck at Los Gatos," also known as "Deportee," about migrant workers who died in a 1948 airplane crash at Los Gatos, California, while being deported back to Mexico. It was haunting, hopeless, wrenchingly simple. And Kit was right, Nathan realized as he listened. What made it powerful was that it was not a polemic on the injustice of immigrant labor; it was a love song, about people caught up in events far beyond their control.

Goodbye to my Juan, goodbye, Rosalita.
Adios, mis amigos, Jesus y Maria.
You won't have your names when you ride the big airplane.
All they will call you will be deportee.

When the song was over, Nathan pushed the pause button, and they were quiet for a while. Kit played the song again, then said, "God, that's beautiful. It's so earthy; everything he writes is. Even when he's singing about outlaws and power dams, it's really sensual."

She picked up the Guthrie album cover and studied his picture: his head cocked a bit arrogantly, eyes closed, eyebrows raised, hair tousled. "I'll bet he was a frisky little fella," she said, pursing her lips.

"Do you mean that the way I think you do?"

"Mmm," she said, which either meant yes or that she wasn't listening to him. She was staring at the album cover in her lap.

"He definitely had a way with the ladies, if that's what you mean," Nathan said.

"Yeah?" she said and wiggled her eyebrows at the picture. "I'll bet he did."

"Woody felt like he was a journalist more than a poet, telling stories of people who couldn't tell them for themselves."

She looked at Nathan, brushing a shock of hair from his forehead. "It doesn't sound like that, though," she said. "It's more like it's all happening to him."

"I think he probably felt like that. Politics was personal to him, everything was. It was about what was happening to the people he knew, his family, neighbors. Even 'This Land Is Your Land.' You know that one?"

Kit heaved a sarcastic sigh. "Of course. We always sang it in school. I thought it was kind of hokey, to tell you the truth. No?"

"Well, there's verses that don't make it into your basic high school textbook." Nathan picked up Kit's guitar and hit the pause button on the CD player.

"Ah, now we're getting somewhere," she said, rubbing her hands conspiratorially. "The forbidden verses."

He tuned a string, strummed a few chords to find his pitch, and sang:

On Sunday morning, in the shadow of the steeple,
By the relief office, I saw my people.
Some stood there starving, and I was wondering,
If this land was made for you and me.

"*My* people," Kit said softly. "God, that's so sad."

Nathan was struck by how differently she heard things. He'd always focused on the symbolism of the steeple, the irony of poor people starving in this wealthy Christian nation. But she heard something else: "*My* people." Woody had made it intimate, personal: this was happening to him. Like a love song.

Kit put on "Deportee" again and hummed along. After a couple of verses, Nathan said, "You should learn that. It's perfect for your voice."

"Mmm," she said vacantly, which Nathan took to mean, once again, that she was either agreeing or not listening to him.

She leaned closer to the speakers, listening intently, eyes closed.

"I wonder if I could use the fiddle with it," she said, mostly to herself. "Some droning strokes during the verse, little trills in between, maybe kind of Mexican-sounding."

She looked at him, and he half-expected her to say, "Oh, are you still here?" Instead, she smiled and touched his cheek. "Whaddya think?" she asked. Her look was tender, fond, and searching.

"That'd be great," he said. She continued to stroke his cheek. "I'd love to see you, um, work the fiddle into your show. And that would really be a different way to do that song; I think people would love it. Yeah. Um, I know I would. Yup, I think… "

He realized he was stammering. Kit looked into his face, smiling and trailing her fingers along his jaw.

Suddenly she straightened up and slapped her hands on her knees. "We should do an experiment," she said.

"Yeah?"

"Yes. An experiment. We should put on a bunch of Woody's albums and pretend they actually *are* love songs; see what kind of effect it has on us."

"Ahh, I see," Nathan said. "Sort of a behavioral study experiment. The effect of Guthrie's implied sexuality on the glandular reactions of the postmodern primate."

"Exactly," she said, slapping her hands on her knees again. "A behavioral study. Exactly my thought. We'll study each other's behavior."

Nathan nodded. "I'll get the lights."

To the pleasant surprise of them both, Nathan thought, they made love twice that night. As Kit trailed off to sleep, burrowed under his sheets, he worried again about their age difference, his ability to keep up with her astounding energy level. Once again, he tried to feel anxious about it, to stoke up some of the old dark mumbles; but as always, they didn't take. He simply didn't sense that it was a problem for her, and it certainly wasn't for him.

After all, it's not like a man Kit's age would be likely to keep up with her, either. She didn't seem like the kind of person who minded others moving at their own pace while she whirred through the world. She probably always knew she was a little smarter, a little faster, more driven—more effective—than most people.

She must have, he thought, because while there was not a shred of arrogance in her, there was that deep-set confidence he'd noticed the first time they talked. Even as a child, she probably figured out that she moved through life a little quicker than most people. Hell, she just went to a few open mikes and thought, "I can do that." And she was right. If she'd had the same reaction watching a hospital show on TV, she'd probably be doing appendectomies in six months.

He wondered if that might be where her shyness came from, that inward loneliness that always seemed to lurk behind her eyes. Being that smart, that certain of your abilities, sets a kid apart on the schoolyard. And with her innate cuteness, she was probably every teacher's pet, whether or not she liked it.

There's a special kind of loneliness that comes from knowing all the answers, always being ahead of the class. It can make a child feel like a stranger in the world as surely as never knowing the answers can. Maybe that's where her empathy came from, that ability to write intimately but in a way that felt like she was singing our song, not just her own. Maybe it came from years of watching others move more slowly, more painfully, through life and secretly wishing she was more like them. More average.

Nathan opened his eyes to look at her, curled up beneath his sheets. As to their sex life, she knew what she was getting, didn't she? She must have known that it would be different with a man his age, a little more, well, *serene*. She seemed to have a good time; he was pretty sure he could still tell when that was real in a woman. She would expect a slower pace with an older man. Much older? He settled for considerably older. And besides, what's wrong with slower?

Kit emerged from the covers, purred and stroked his cheek. "What're you thinking about?" she said with a sleepy smile.

"We never really talked about our ages."

"A little late to card me, don't'cha think?" she said.

"You know what I mean," he whispered, but she was already slinking back under the covers, chuckling to herself.

The next morning, only the top of Kit's head showed above the sheets as she began to move, sigh, and then yawn loudly. When she peeked above the covers, Nathan was sitting cross-legged on the bed, looking down at her. She smiled.

"Say, you're kind of a frisky little fella yourself," she said. She furrowed her eyebrows and said in a deep, somber voice, "I've always admired that quality in a man."

"I'm falling in love with you, Kit."

Her eyes softened and her mouth closed. She looked at him strangely, solemnly, almost as if he'd said something wrong. Then, quietly, she said, "Is that okay?"

"Oh, yeah."

She smiled and sat up. They held each other, then kissed. "I thought you might be, but I wasn't sure you wanted to be," she said. "It's wonderful to hear you say it, Nathan. I love you too."

They held each other. "So you knew," he said after they kissed again. "Why doesn't that surprise me? Why are women so much smarter about these things?"

She fell back down on the bed, yawned, and stretched the sleep from her body. He loved how slowly her breasts moved.

"Well," she said, finishing her yawn, "I'm not sure I could explain it in a way a man could understand."

She grinned, then turned serious. "I'm kidding, you know," she said in her concerned voice, not his favorite. "You're so smart, Nathan; you know so much more than I do, like, about the music and things."

He thought about teasing her back but he didn't. In the old days, he would have needed to do something like that, to push some distance into the intimate swell of the moment. Why was it different now? Later. He held her again, kissed her neck, and simply soaked her in.

Then, with a suddenness that startled him, she reared back and sprang from the bed, straight into the air, landing on the balls of her feet, fists balled up in front of her. "Let's *eat*!" she bellowed.

Nathan's eyes moved to the spot on the bed where she'd been just a second before, as if he might find some sort of launching mechanism to explain how she'd moved so fast. He had no idea where she found the traction to jump like that. Remarkable woman.

The last of summer lingered through September, lazily yawning into a thick and gentle autumn that felt like it would never go away. Leaves turned on the trees, but never seemed to make it to their final, brittle brown. For weeks they stayed in dusky yellows, deep oranges, and burnished reds. The slow decay made the air smell pungent and sweet, like wood smoke. The air felt thicker, too, full of other things. Like spring, Nathan thought, except somehow, this felt more like the end of life than its budding.

The dry musk of autumn is certainly a different scent than the honeyed wetness of spring, which seems so alive with fertile things and the coming warmth. The birds sound different, too. In spring, they seem so high-strung and busy. In autumn, they sound hushed, worried: time to go, time to go, bad things coming. But maybe that's just the way sounds carry in the different air, the dead, hard sediment of fall muffling sounds that are amplified by the juicy pollen of spring. Or maybe it's just him: he's put his own meaning to these sounds, because he knows what each season brings.

The melodies to the old traditional songs are like that. Nathan always marveled at how the music could tell him how the lyrics feel. Or do they? Again, maybe that's him, putting meanings to certain melodic changes, because he's learned that they're used for sad songs, romantic songs, or lonesome songs. But it's the same with the old airs, instrumentals that capture life's quieter moments. He always knew how they felt, too, if they were grieving or homesick, heartbroken or merely wistful.

But was that the melody's memory or our own? Were these the emotions the first player felt, permanently encoded into the music, like an ancient insect frozen in mid-flight within a piece of amber? Or was it just that we learn to recognize which sounds represent which emotions, the way we know a soldier from a farmer by the clothes they wear?

No way to know. An imponderable. But Nathan thought imponderable questions were often the ones most worth asking. It's not the answer you want; it's what you figure out along the way. If nothing else, asking them was a good excuse to stuff your hands in your pockets, crunch through the fallen leaves, and let your senses fill with the sights and sounds and smells of another year, gently decaying, turning slowly by, until it is gone, and you are that much older.

Kit's renewed interest in traditional music sparked a creative frenzy. She continued to pore through Nathan's records and songbooks, experimenting with fiddle lines and guitar chords but always translating what she found into the modern language of her own music. She seemed to innately understand that these old folk songs were a common possession, an inheritance—not merely to be preserved in some arch, old-fashioned setting, but used to express how life feels today. Maybe she got that from her childhood, playing old fiddle tunes, and mischievously jazzing them up with her friends when the teacher wasn't around. Tradition was a playground to Kit, a playground and a toolbox.

Occasionally, she would wrinkle her nose doubtfully at Nathan, wondering if he would disapprove of how she'd snatched a line from an old ballad or a fiddle trill from an ancient reel and used it to color her own songs. But he always approved, because he also believed that traditional music was a shared legacy, a common playground, everyone's toolbox.

He also approved because he noticed, more than she did, how much it was changing her music. Her sound was becoming at once more spacious and more economical. As she used the fiddle in her songwriting, her arrangements grew less cluttered and more purposeful. Every note carried an emotional message, emulating the feelings in the lyrics. And as her music became more purposeful, her lyrics became more spare. She didn't need to explain everything; the melodies told you how the songs felt.

She began performing "Deportee," and the response was so good that she learned a few old folk ballads and a couple of Nathan's songs from his first album. She said they didn't sound old to her at all, and they didn't, the way she sang them. But they still felt old to him, relics of a wasted past.

Kit's best new song was a wrenching, stark portrait of a love affair slowly dying. The first time she sang it for Nathan, she was so comically intent about reassuring him that it was not *about* them, but about *what-if* something bad happened, that he got the giggles. Kit had to wait impatiently while he regained himself enough to listen. Even then, her first few starts were halted by him muttering: "It's just what-if, just what-if, just what-if," and then dissolving into laughter.

After a few stern looks from her and solemn promises to behave from him, she sang the song. It was devastating in its unadorned landscape of love decaying from inattention: both lovers busy with their own lives, passing each other like silent ships in darkening seas. But that was never stated; it was all implied in quiet lines describing mundane details, as the lovers prepared for a coming winter: two good people lost in their own day-to-days, walking numbly past each other and past everything they shared.

In her earlier songs, Kit had often used artful, obscure metaphors that were more like poetic one-liners than parts of a larger story. Now, she used winter itself as her emblem of emotional numbness, along with ordinary details like woodpiles by the door, trees growing bare, curtains covering once-open windows, and heavy blankets on beds that once had no need of them.

The final image was crushingly simple, a set of house keys tossed silently into a freezing pond, sinking slowly out of view, and with it the home, the life, the love—everything the couple had made together. The hands of the other lover reach helplessly for the keys, realizing too late what was happening, unable to stop their love from falling into the freezing darkness.

Incredibly, when she finished singing the song, Kit reassured Nathan one more time that it was only a *what-if* song. Her empathy let her write songs like that; it could also be an awful nuisance. He smiled.

"Girls do that when we're happy, you know," she said brightly. "It's, like, kind of a sport with us, thinking up sad endings."

Nathan laughed. "Boys do it, too. Only we're usually mapping out escape routes."

Turning serious, he said, "The images are so simple; everybody can pull them up from their own memories. Everybody knows what woodpiles look like, bare trees, blankets. And when people use their own memories instead of yours, I think they take a song deeper inside them. It becomes more about them."

She half-smiled, not particularly wanting a lesson from him. She'd just written a song.

"It's a great song, Kit," he said. "The keys are the perfect metaphor; how did you come up with that?"

She smiled broadly, arching an eyebrow, like she was preparing to share a secret. She said she'd gotten the idea of winter while she was staring out the window, watching it get dark. She felt a chill and realized that she had, in fact, been cold for a while. It struck her that this was how it felt when people first realized they were falling out of love. They're suddenly aware of the cold; then they realize they have been cold for a long time.

"You'll like this," she said, explaining how she thought about Woody Guthrie as she wrote the lyrics. His songs were easy to understand because the images were of things people saw in their own lives. So she tried to write that way.

When she came to that final image, something to symbolize the irrevocable end of the relationship, she actually made a list. What can represent a life shared? A bed? Too sexual. A house? Too vague and at the same time too easy. A garden? *Yeww.* It needed to be something specific and ordinary—not a big picture, but a miniature, something intimate, personal. A detail of a life. Detail of a bed, a house, a garden.

She smiled at Nathan. "Then I remembered when you showed me that key under the stone in the yard," she said. "I was so surprised by that, and it made me feel so welcome and comfortable with you. And I was, like, that's it! Keys."

He felt an uneasy pang when she told him how much the gesture meant to her, an echo of his old, safe distances, but he batted it away. He suggested that she call the song "Keys," to signal the importance of that image when it comes around.

She looked at him uncertainly, then smiled. "Oh. Okay," she said. "Good idea."

"You have another idea?"

"No, not really."

"Most of the time, a song names itself. You know what it wants to be called. But sometimes, you can help people follow it by highlighting the important moment."

Kit nodded passively. Was she annoyed at hearing another lecture or doubtful about the title?

"You don't have to call it that," he said. "Just an idea off the top of my head."

She shrugged. "No, it's a good idea," she said. "You've been writing songs a lot longer than I have."

"That has nothing to do with anything."

They looked at each other, smiling.

"No, 'Keys' is good," she said finally. Then she put her guitar down, slapped her knees and said, "'Keys' it is."

A few days later, he asked her to record the new song, along with "Deportee" and a couple of her older songs. He didn't mention that he planned to send a copy of the recording to Joyce.

Nathan enjoyed being around Kit's creativity, but it inspired no reawakening of his own muse. A few times he tried to will himself to write, sitting in the bedroom, listening outside his door to the sounds of Kit's productivity. But nothing came, and every time he tried, it made him feel that much more barren and lifeless. And that brought back the old, painful thought—*such a long way down*—mocking him for thinking he could ever feel those artistic fires again, ever feel anything but the memory of fire, the memory of wood.

Watching Kit devour his old folk records, however, inspired him in a different way. Somewhere along the line he'd gotten the idea that young people didn't care about the past. But Kit had such a hunger to know what came before her, not so much ancient history, but the recent story of the folk movement and how it became the cultural underground that she was eager to join. She wanted to hear the stories, the lore—the secret knowledge—that made people like Nathan and Ferguson seem like insiders.

"Ah, the forbidden verses," she'd said about Woody Guthrie's song. She wanted to dig to the bone, the source, the secrets she'd never been told in school.

To Kit, traditional music was as fresh and hip as her latest favorite songwriter. At Dooley's, Nathan had noticed the same eagerness from many of the young people who came to the jam. He began to wonder why they were so open to the idea that something old could be cool. Pop culture today seemed to be all about being new.

But when he thought about it, nothing about pop culture was really all that new, was it? It was just *now*. The next rock band wasn't that different from the last one, nor was the next mini-diva, talent-show winner, or sullen rapper. The new video game, the new sitcom, the new cop show, the new running shoes: how new was any of it?

Growing up in the goo of all that phony newness, what a revelation it must be to suddenly hear the stark, ageless beauty of skin on string, with no electronic screech or squawk. The guitar did not become louder because an amplifier was turned up, but through the muscle of the person playing it. How startling it must be to suddenly hear a lone human voice howling about careless love and cruel murder, killing floods and hard times in the mill, boys, hard times in the mill. That was *new*: raw human passion, unprocessed, unfiltered, naked.

As Nathan saw how easily Kit was drawn to the old songs, he grew more comfortable talking about his own love for them on stage. He started designing some of his Dooley's sets around particular themes: Woody Guthrie's legacy; how you can hear the beginnings of rock-and-roll in the sinewy lines of the Delta blues; how real cowboy songs show the difference between the Hollywood West and the real West, between pop reality and *real* reality.

It gave Nathan a whole new reason to work up songs, or snatches of songs—just enough to make a point. He was surprised at how much open-mikers and jammers enjoyed his new sets. He'd always thought they just wanted him to finish so they could have their turn. But maybe they seemed that way because he thought he had no reason to be singing for them.

As the autumn deepened, news spread of Kit's triumph at the Home Baked. She was soon regularly doing opening acts and headlining at smaller venues. Her nerves still betrayed her from time to time, but she knew how to recover now, and always turned the stage fright into a moment that drew the crowd even closer.

As she became more confident, her music and her stage presence improved dramatically. Nathan had never seen a performer make such quick strides. Her fiddle playing added a compelling dynamic to her sets, and whenever things started to drag, she would tear off a high-gear fiddle tune.

Nathan often went along as her sideman, which gave her shows an extra sparkle. It wasn't just that this up-and-comer already had her own sideman; it was also that it was Nathan Warren. Wasn't that the same guy who was married to Joyce Warren before she got famous? Maybe he's on to something here too. It was a thoroughly stupid notion, of course; but if it helped Kit, Nathan was all for it. Somebody might as well get some use out of that sorry chapter in his life; God knows, he never did.

Ryder finally made his move. For weeks, he'd been coming to Dooley's but not signing up to play. He would just huddle with his pack of squirrels, muttering importantly that he was working stuff out.

Now, on a crisp autumn Tuesday, he strode into the open mike, hips snapping, boot heels clicking, wearing a frayed denim jacket over a fire-engine red flannel shirt. And on his head—could it be? Lord help us, it was: a blue-and-white-striped railroad engineer's cap. Good grief, the Casey Jones of Wellesley. Toot, toot, all aboard.

When Ryder swaggered on stage, Ferguson was already there. He'd started coming in earlier on Tuesdays to catch Nathan's expanded sets. Ferguson stared at Ryder, shaking his head, grinning and chuckling. Ryder smiled back, pointing an index finger and winking. He took Ferguson's grin as a sign of approval. It was not.

"God, Nathan," Ferguson said, "do you think this is his reaction to my little sermon about his songs?"

"Could be," Nathan said. "He hasn't signed up to play since then."

Kit was sitting next to Nathan. She smiled but didn't join in the laughter between Nathan and Ferguson. Instead, she waved at Ryder and made a guitar-playing motion with her hand, mouthing that she was glad he was going to sing. He nodded back curtly.

It soon became obvious that Ryder's new persona was indeed a response to Ferguson's criticisms. He came on like a latter-day Bob Dylan, or at least what he imagined that to be. He mumbled "Howdy" almost inaudibly, then sang one of his older songs that Nathan actually liked. Nothing special, but it said what it wanted to say, and had a nice bridge.

Ryder had rearranged it, though. He used to accompany it with little finger-picked patterns. Now he strummed in short, chunky strokes, and almost spoke the lyrics. And there was something strange about his diction. He wasn't exactly affecting a Southern accent, but his phrasing was thick and muffled. Was he imitating Dylan? Woody Guthrie? Casey Jones? Ryder probably thought it was rural and authentic, but Nathan thought it made him sound like a dental patient whose Novocain was wearing off.

Ryder always slathered his affectations on too thickly, like a teen who wears too much cologne because he thinks if he can't smell it, nobody else can. After the song, Ryder's voice remained in that thick-tongued drawl. Pushing his cap back on his head, he sighed deeply, smacked his lips, and said, "Ya' know, it's a hard life troubadourin'."

Ferguson began to giggle.

Jutting a hip out and sighing again, Ryder said, "That was an old choon of mine, one of many."

"Choon?" Jackie said, reaching into the beer cooler. "What's a choon?"

"I think he means 'tune,'" Nathan said, beginning to laugh.

"That's a relief," Jackie said, handing a fresh beer to Ferguson. "I thought he had a varmint up there he was a-fixin' to show us."

At that, Ferguson choked on his rum, spitting an ice cube over the bar that Jackie dodged nicely. His laughter grew louder. Ryder shot a startled glance their way. Were they laughing at him?

Kit leaned over, smiling like a mother would at rambunctious children, and put a finger over her lips. Nathan nodded.

Ryder muttered that he had a new song, about "this big ol' mess we call a world," and hit a loud minor chord. The song was called "If I Ran This Place," and it was a surly litany of complaints about modern society that Ryder apparently felt could be corrected by simply putting him in charge. Because of its couplet structure, a lot of the rhyming was forced. To conclude a verse about kids getting their wish, he sang, "And if I ran this place, the sea would swim in fish."

That set Jackie off again. "There's no friggin' fish in the sea?" she whispered loudly. "Jeez Louise, I gotta start watching the news again."

Nathan said, "I'm still trying to figure out how the sea swims in fish. Isn't it supposed to be the other way around?"

That was too much for Ferguson, and his laughter became a loud moan that drew everybody's attention. Heads snapped from Ryder to Ferguson, and Ryder missed a couple of chords. Kit leaned over again, not smiling, and again put a finger over her lips.

Ryder's song was not really bad. It had a nice Dylanesque roll to it, and a dark melody that added a touch of melancholy to the anger. He had a good instinct for how to build a song. If he could just stop showing off.

He recovered nicely from the missed chords, and veered into a bridge that was surprising and powerful. Evoking an old street peddler's cry, he changed into a major key, singing, "Come to the big store, come buy, come buy."

Nathan nodded at the stage. He liked the play on the words *buy* and *by*. But the bridge wasn't over. Jumping back to the minor key, Ryder played a few high, bluesy notes, then picked a tight pattern while he sang, almost chanting: "Nothing is real, everything is for sale." Wow. Talk about a mantra for the times.

After that, Ryder popped back into the final verse, which included another line Nathan liked: "If I ran this place, the squirrels would hunt and the dogs would run." Nice—a reverse image that was simple and really made its point. Nathan wondered if the line was a veiled reference to the nickname Jackie had given the open-mikers. He'd always suspected that Ryder thought there was more of a caste system in the folk scene than there really was, and that he blamed it for his lack of success.

After the last scheduled open-miker performed and the witching hour began, Nathan decided to find out if Ryder was upset about the laughter, and apologize if he was. He invited Ferguson to come along. "I don't think Ryder wants to hear what I thought," Ferguson said.

"The bridge on that new song was nice," Nathan said.

"But if everybody's laughing by then, what's the point?"

"Everybody wasn't laughing," Kit said.

"Where'd you get the cap, Ryder?" Nathan said, being careful not to smile.

"It was my gramp's," Ryder said brightly, then grew somber, as if realizing he'd stepped out of character. "Been in the family for years," he said in that thick-tongued, Novocain voice.

"I haven't seen one of those in a long time," Nathan said. "Folksingers used to wear them a lot. You got kind of a retro thing going there."

"Is that what you guys were laughing about?" Ryder asked.

"Oh, man, we just got the giggles, that's all. One of the reasons I came over was to apologize. We got a little carried away."

"So you *were* laughing at me."

"I really liked the bridge of that new song, Ryder," Nathan said. Maybe a compliment would cheer him up; it usually did.

"But not the rest. So you laughed at me."

"Like I said, we just got the giggles, and I'm sorry. But back to your song. I think a political song should be more than just angry slogans. I liked how you made it personal."

"That's not what he said," Ryder muttered, staring at the table.

"What?"

"Ferguson. That's not what he said. 'Find your rage,' he said. 'Write about that.' Now you're telling me it's not good to be angry. Can't you guys get your stories straight?"

"I'm not telling you not to be angry; I'm just telling you what I liked about your song. There are no rules, Ryder."

Kit had wandered over, and stood quietly next to Nathan. As Nathan and Ryder stared at each other, she blurted out, "I liked your new song, Ryder. It was hot. Totally."

Ryder gave her a hard look but said nothing.

"I said I was sorry," Nathan said.

But of course, sorry wasn't the point. Ryder had put weeks into his new persona, written one song and completely rearranged another, and rummaged through the attic for that ridiculous hat. He'd even worked up a new speaking voice. And then he'd been laughed at by the very people whose advice he thought he was following. That was the point.

"He says write about the world," Ryder said sharply. "You say be more personal. He says be angry; you say don't be angry. You guys keep changing the rules. It's not fair."

Fair? Nathan looked helplessly at Kit, who surprised him by saying, "That is what Ferguson said, Nathan. 'Find your fine young rage.' That's what he said."

She smiled at Ryder. "And it sure was a raging song," she said. "I liked it."

Ryder glared at her, not smiling, not acknowledging the compliment. He looked back at Nathan. "You guys never laugh at her," he said, his voice mean and brittle. "Gee, I wonder why?"

His squirrels started to laugh, but not at Nathan. They were looking at Kit. Her cheeks flashed red, and the laughter grew. She stared at the floor.

Kit started to say something, but Nathan erupted into a cold, sarcastic laugh.

"Sure, muffinhead," he said, pointing at Ryder. "Keep thinking like that. Yeah, the reason she's doing so well, getting all these gigs, is because she's hanging out with me. Right. That's why she's playing at the Home Baked twice this year. Ryder, *I* can't even get a gig there."

Kit tried to interrupt, but Nathan was angry now. His voice rising, he said, "It seems like you've always got some excuse, someone to blame for why you're not doing better. Jesus, why don't you—"

He stopped, feeling a sudden pang of sympathy for Ryder. If only he could get through to this kid.

"There are no bosses in this music," Nathan said, his voice calmer, "no rules, no shortcuts, no system to outsmart. There are only audiences, and whether they like you. Have you listened to Kit lately? Because if you really thought about why she's doing so well, you might start to figure out some things."

Kit was blushing furiously. Shaking her head, she turned and walked quickly to the bar.

Nathan and Ryder glared at each other. Nathan realized there was no point in continuing this and went back to the bar.

Sitting beside Kit, he thought he'd have to help her get over the insult. He put a hand on her shoulder and said softly, "I don't think he meant that about you; he was trying to hurt me by—"

Her look cut him off, and she shrugged his hand off her shoulder. She didn't look hurt; she looked angry.

"Nathan," she said, her voice measured and chill. "What is it about me that makes you think I can't fight my own fights?"

"Whoo-aah," Ferguson said, rising from his stool. "Think I'll go talk to Murph."

Nathan gave him a puzzled look, then turned back to Kit. What the hell was going on?

"You're mad at me?" Nathan asked.

"Answer my question," Kit said. Her voice was impossible to read. "Do you really think I can't take care of myself?"

"What?"

Kit shook her head and looked down at the bar. "Do you have any idea how small and, like, totally dismissible it made me feel that you don't think I can handle someone like Ryder? Do you really feel that way about me? Poor helpless Kit?"

He really hated how she kept putting these things as questions. It wasn't as if there were answers. What did she expect him to say?

"I was sticking up for you," he said. "You couldn't have said those things about yourself."

"No, and I wouldn't have. I don't think they were very helpful. Ryder feels like you and Ferguson tricked him. I don't think that, but he does. He was humiliated, and you got mad and decided to humiliate him more by rubbing me in his face. Were you sticking up for me or just sticking it to him?"

There she went with those questions again. There was no way to answer except to admit she was right. Say, she's good at this.

He looked at her blankly. He hated the thought of her being angry at him.

She sighed, and her voice softened a little. "I suppose you grew up thinking it was, like, chivalrous or something, standing up for your girl. And I like it that you want to take care of me, Nathan. But do you have any idea how embarrassing that was?"

"I'm sorry, sweetie," he said. Would a "sweetie" help? She smiled a little. Ah, it did help. A little.

"It's funny," she said. "Sometimes the things we like the least about people are just mirrors of what we like the most about them."

"Ooh, that's great," Nathan said. "Write that down. That's a killer line. Virtues and faults coming from the same source. Boy, you could—"

"Oh, shut up," she said, laughing sharply. "I'm not done with you yet."

He clapped his mouth shut. He knew enough not to smile, but he wanted to. The storm was passing. All he wanted was to see her smile at him, really smile.

She looked down, collecting her thoughts. "What I'm talking about," she said, "is this way you feel like you have to do everything yourself; like you're the only one holding up the sky. You do all this wonderful stuff for everybody, make this safe place for the music where everybody's treated the same, everybody gets to sing their songs. Because everybody's welcome at Nathan's big table."

She looked at him, and put her hand on top of his. "But you do it all alone. You're always talking about community, community, community, but you do everything by yourself."

"I think I know what you're saying," he said, desperately wanting to agree and get this over with. He didn't understand, though. "And I'm sorry I got between you and Ryder. God, Kit, I don't think for a second that you can't take care of yourself."

She smiled and squeezed his hand. They just looked at each other, silently restating their deeper feelings.

"Doesn't what Ryder said bother you?" Nathan asked. "He's always treated you that way, him and his gang. They've never taken you seriously. Doesn't that piss you off?"

Kit took a sip of her beer. "Sure it does. Why do you think I always used to sit in the back, all by myself?"

She put down her beer and cocked her head.

"But what's wrong with a little pissed off?" she said. "It pushes me the right way, you know? Makes me build some good muscle, a little toughness, and, like you say, I'm going to need that if I want to have a music career. Bullies have a way of making you stronger. And that's all it is: just bullyboys trying to be big wheels by making other people feel like little wheels."

"Did you always feel like that?"

Kit laughed. "God, no. When I started doing open mikes, it really hurt. I've always had trouble getting people to take me seriously, you know, because of how I look and how easy I get nervous. All the time I was in school, even college. I really hoped it would change after I got out of school, but it didn't. When I started coming here, there were some nights I had to run out the door or I knew I'd start crying. Which wouldn't help the toughness thing I was working on."

Nathan laughed and rubbed her shoulder.

She smiled at him and leaned a little closer. "Know what helped me figure it out?"

He shook his head, and she wagged a finger under his nose. "You."

"Me? Because I encouraged you?"

"Well, that was nice, but no. It was, like, when I listened to you play and how you talked about the music. To Ryder and those guys, it was all about kickin' ass, gettin' up there and gettin' it done, dude. It was all about who wanted it more. They talked about why a song didn't work, and it was all about acting cool, working on your *attitude*—as if the song didn't matter."

"But you," she said, poking Nathan's chest, "you were a whole different story, and you obviously knew a lot more about it than they did. You were so in love with the music. To them, it's all about the singer; to you, it's all about the song."

She shrugged. "I thought about all that and—*bing*—my little light went on. I realized it didn't have anything to do with who talked the best game, who wanted it more, all that crap. That's just…well…that's how boys talk."

She smiled at him as he shifted uncomfortably on his bar stool.

Clearing his throat, he said, "You know what Pete Seeger said about all that?"

She laughed warmly. "No, what?"

"Well, he actually said this to Tao Rodriguez, his grandson. He's a folksinger, too, and started performing with Pete when he was teenager. One day after a show, Pete said he wanted to tell Tao a secret. 'If you're a musician,' he said, 'it means you're going to die unfulfilled. It means you'll spend the rest of your life on an upward learning curve, because you'll never be as good as you can be. You'll die an apprentice, a student; and there's nothing better than that.' And then Pete said, 'To have achieved the best you can ever be—that's a tragedy.'"

Kit thought about that, sipping her beer. "Sounds good to me,' she said.

Nathan smiled at her, glad the storm was passing.

"You have that kind of effect on people, you know," Kit said. "I was talking to the guy I'm going to open for at the Home Baked. He was really sweet. He called to say he heard I played the fiddle, and asked if I wanted to play with him on the encore. Isn't that cool?"

"He's a good guy. Used to be a regular here."

"He told me that. He said that the first time you complimented him on a song, he thought he'd died and gone to heaven. That's exactly how he put it. But you also said the song would be even better with a chorus, and that he might want to try finger-picking it, so people could hear the words better. He said you were so encouraging that it took him months before he realized you'd actually been criticizing him. Know what else he said?"

Nathan stared into his root beer. He shook his head.

"He said, 'The music always comes first with Nathan, and he's got the scars to prove it.'"

She rubbed Nathan's arm. "Then he said, 'Nathan keeps us all honest. You don't want to be faking it around a guy who's paid those kinds of dues.'"

Nathan laughed a little, still staring at his root beer. He was quiet for a long time, but Kit waited him out. She leaned her head toward him.

Finally, not looking up, he said softly, "Thanks for telling me that, Kit."

"Well, you're welcome," she said, with that clean, open laugh he liked so much. It held such affection, such intimacy. "You're kind of a hard man to compliment, you know."

He smiled at her, looking suddenly very tired. "I know, Kit. It means a lot that you keep trying. It's just that…well, it's just—" His voice trailed off, and he stared back into his drink.

She squeezed his hand, and they were quiet together.

Kit had a new cause. She was going to get Nathan wired to the world. She set her first trap over Saturday breakfast.

"Why don't you have an e-mail list for Dooley's?" she asked nonchalantly, chewing a muffin, then blowing into her coffee cup.

"Don't know," he said. "Never got around to it, I guess. Don't you need some special software or something?"

She laughed sharply, spitting out a piece of muffin. "You're joking, right?"

He shrugged. "I never wanted to spend the money, I guess."

"Yes, special software," she said in a deep, dramatic voice. "Why, the security clearances alone are daunting. You were never a member of the Communist Party, were you?"

And with that, she exploded into laughter, slapping the table and shaking her head. He stared at her.

After she recovered, she said, "I can't believe you're serious, Nathan. You don't need anything. You just set up a group of e-mail addresses."

He looked at her sadly. "Group?" he said, almost whispering.

"Oh my. My own little caveman. It's the twenty-first century, bub. You gotta get with the program."

She stood up, swallowed her last bite of muffin, slugged his arm playfully, and walked over to his old Mac computer, which sat on a small table in front of the living room window.

"Come, little man," she said, still laughing. "Drag your furry knuckles over here."

He sat down dutifully at the computer, heaving a sigh as he turned it on. But actually he was starting to enjoy this. She was always on the receiving end of his stories and lectures. Now she was the teacher, and he liked watching her take charge.

She pulled up a kitchen chair and placed it next to him. "I'm serious about this, Nathan," she said as she walked back in the kitchen to get their coffee cups. "You're the one who's always talking about owning your own art, not letting the industry tell you how to run your career. The computer helps you do all that stuff. Everything you need for the do-it-yourself career, right on your desktop."

"*Your* desktop maybe," Nathan said.

"Yours, too," she said, putting down the coffee mugs and sitting beside him. "This is really basic stuff. Nuts and bolts. Mailing lists, posters, press kits. You can even make CDs on computers. Probably not on this old steam engine, though."

"I like my old steam engine."

"Of course you do. You live in a carriage house. But you've still got everything you need. I know you do, because you send me e-mail. A computer and an IP. That's all you need."

He looked at her placidly and cocked his head.

"IP. Internet provider," she said. "How you get on the Internet."

He nodded gratefully and looked back at his computer. He'd always just thought of it as his e-mail company.

"It's really easy," Kit said, sipping her coffee.

"For you, maybe," he said, bringing up his e-mail. "I'm just not a wired kind of guy. Computer stuff confuses me. I've never been able to get the hang of it. It's complicated."

"Not for mailing lists, it isn't," she said, watching his e-mail come up on the screen.

Nathan knew this somehow connected to their argument at Dooley's, but he wasn't sure how a mailing list became his punishment. Let's see, he stuck up for her with Ryder, which led to her accusing him of being too much of a loner, for which he was now being forced to set up an e-mail list. Okay. Well, let the punishment fit the crime. But somehow it did make sense. The loner was getting connected.

He logged on and heard that annoying voice say "You've got mail!" It always sounded so surprised, as if it really meant, "Even *you've* got mail."

She commandeered his mouse, leaning in front of him. He smelled her hair and kissed the back of her head. She leaned her shoulder back in response and clicked "Address Book" on the top of the tool bar. It was empty.

"Where's all your addresses?" She said.

He riffled through a big pile of papers beside the computer and pulled out a few typed sheets of e-mail addresses, with scribbled additions in the margins and along the tops of the pages. "Here," he said, beaming. He handed her the papers.

"Good lord, you're joking," she said. "But no, you're not, are you?"

Nathan pointed to the top of the first page, where Kit's e-mail address was written in especially large letters. "Look, you got top billing," he said.

She laughed and shook her head, leafing through the pages, then putting them down. "Why don't you just use the address book that comes with your e-mail?" she asked.

"Don't know how to."

"There's no 'know how' to it, Nathan. You never even clicked it to see how it worked, did you?"

"I'm not comfortable with computers, Kit," he said. "I'm afraid I'll hit the wrong button and everything will get screwed up. Crash. Boom."

Sighing sarcastically but clearly enjoying herself, Kit said, "Here, watch." She went to his mail and brought up the last e-mail she'd sent him. She clicked ADD ADDRESS and an entry came up, with her e-mail address at the bottom. She filled in her name, hit SAVE, and then went back to the address book. She clicked it and it came up with her name and e-mail.

Oh, damn. That *was* easy. She's right; he just never tried. She leaned back, rubbing her chin. "I think it looks good that way," she said slyly. "That's all the addresses my little caveman needs."

"Yes, dear," he said. "God, do I feel like a dope. But I'm terrified of these things, Kit. I'm always afraid it's going to crash if I hit a button I don't understand."

"Ever happen?"

"No, but it's like, whenever I call Mac support, I always say, 'Don't give me the theory, just tell me what to do. Talk to me like I'm a particularly bright chimp.' They always seem to know what I mean."

"I'm sure they do. They probably have a special set of instructions for people like you: 'How to talk to customers born during the age of sail.'"

She started to laugh again, but it was a warm laugh, full of fondness. She poked his chest with her finger.

"You're enjoying this, aren't you?" he said. She nodded happily.

"Why didn't you ever set up your address book?" she asked. "Really."

"I told you, I just never—"

"Bullshit."

"I was worried that—"

"Bullshit. You just never tried, did you?"

"I thought I'd screw up something. Look, I don't like to do things I don't know how to do. I'm set in my ways, you know? Crusty. Rustic. I thought you found that endearing."

He looked at her and blinked his eyes.

"Of course I do," she said. "I find everything about you endearing. Even the annoying things. Like this."

"So how do you set up a mailing list?" he asked, hoping to move the conversation along.

Now that she'd revealed the wonders of the address book, the rest was easy. She showed him how to set up a group of addresses, named it "Dooley's List," and put in her address to get it started.

"There," she said. "You're all set. Now you put a sign-up sheet at Dooley's and you can send out mailings whenever something cool is happening. Like one of your special sets. And you can tell them about your own gigs, too."

"I don't know," Nathan said. "They're just signing up for Dooley's, aren't they?"

"Why wouldn't they want to know if the host was playing a show somewhere? Don't be such a priss. And then you can tell venues how many names you have on your list. That's really important; it's usually, like, the first thing they ask me."

He looked at her doubtfully.

"It's not cheating," she said. "You actually do sing there every week."

"I suppose," he said, then nodded. "No, you're right."

"One other thing. Do it, okay? I mean, this is the kind of stuff you're talking about all the time, ways to bring the community together, bypass the industry, blah, blah, blah."

"Blah, blah, blah?"

"I don't mean that it's blah, blah, blah, when you talk about it. But it kind of is, if you don't, like actually *do* it, you know? It's all there, on your rustic computer. And it's free. So if I may suggest…"

"Yes?" he said absently, staring at the computer screen. She moved close to his ear, kissed it, then shouted, "*Do it!*"

He jumped in his chair, rubbed his ear, and said, "Okay, okay. Yes, ma'am, yes, ma'am."

He smiled at her while she laughed. He was enjoying this. He liked that his ego didn't feel threatened by how far ahead of him she was with this stuff. A good sign, he thought.

"What else can this puppy do?" he asked, wheeling the mouse idly around the pad.

She asked to change seats and began browsing the Web. She showed him a site that offered electronic press kits for performers that could be downloaded by venues or media people. She said they only charged a small service fee, and then you put the link on your website so anyone looking for your press stuff could find it for free.

Then she explained to him what a link was.

"There's lots of sites like that," she said, "places that help you do things for yourself."

He'd heard about Internet companies like this but seeing how they worked, he recognized exactly what it meant. Professional press kits, without needing a publicist, agent, manager, or label. Then she showed him CDBaby, an online record store. She showed him a list of artists it offered, and he was surprised at how many well-known names were there.

"How do they pick their artists?" he asked.

"Huh?" Kit gave him that caveman look again.

"How does CDBaby decide if they want to sell your stuff? Do you send in an audition tape?"

"It's not like that at all, Nathan. That's what's so cool. You just fill out an application, send them your CD, and they put up a site for you where people can buy it online. The whole point is to eliminate the middleman. They call it the gatekeeper mentality—that old idea that somebody in power gets to decide whose music gets heard."

"So nobody's in charge of deciding if your music is good enough." He stared at the screen and felt the old sadness come. If only it had been that way when he was…

After a moment, he said, "It must cost a fortune to put your album up there."

She laughed. "Just a setup fee, thirty, forty bucks, something like that."

"You're joking."

"No. That's it. Plus they take a few bucks from every sale, you know, like a commission. But they also have deals with all kinds of sites like iTunes, where people can buy music to download. So your stuff is automatically available there, too."

He raised an index finger. "Download," he said. "I've heard of that."

She laughed. "And now for the pièce de résistance," she said dramatically. She typed in woodyguthrie.org. "I found this after our little behavioral experiment, you know, when we were listening to Woody's music." She rubbed his arm. "Remember?"

"Of course," he said, putting his arm around her shoulder and squeezing. He was feeling close to her right now, and wanted her to know it. He was starting to see how carefully she'd planned all this.

"Just gaze at that, my little caveman," she said, waving her hand at the home page of a site devoted to Woody Guthrie. There was an index with buttons for a biography, books and records, archives, and lyrics. He asked her to hit the lyrics. It showed song titles for all of Guthrie's songs, listed alphabetically. Near the top was one called "Aginst Th' Law." Nathan asked her to click it.

> *It's aginst th' law to gamble, it's aginst the law to roam.*
> *It's aginst th' law to organize or try to build a home.*
> *It's aginst th' law to sing, it's aginst th' law to dance.*
> *It's aginst th' law to tell you th' trouble on my hands.*

"Wow," Nathan said. "I've never heard that song."

He turned to Kit and kissed her on the cheek. "Thanks," he said. "For the lesson and the pep talk. You're right; I figured it was all beyond me, a brave new world. I just got in the habit of never clicking anything I didn't already understand. Food for thought, sweetie."

They both stared at the old lyric, then Nathan asked how she found the Guthrie site.

"Google," she said. She Googled Guthrie's name and woodyguthrie.org was the first site listed. The link said, "Welcome to the official Woody Guthrie website."

Nathan stared at it, shaking his head. So easy to find. Why hadn't he ever done that? But he knew why. Always a reason to not do something.

Ramblin' Randy was in full bellow, belting out an old sea chantey, head tossed back, arm thrumming away in large circles, pounding out a quick guitar beat.

Ohhhhh, Jimmy Long Jack's a Yankee sailor
Blow, boys, blow.
Jimmy Long Jack's a South Sea whaler.
Blow, me bully boys, blow.

Randy was having a ball, and as a result, so was everybody else. Simple enthusiasm counts for a lot at an open mike.

Kit was sitting next to Nathan at the bar, bobbing playfully in her seat, hollering an occasional "*Whooo!*" and laughing, but good-naturedly, supportively. Randy even looked her way and grinned after one particularly loud "*Whooo.*"

It was a different scene at Ryder's table. He and his pals were laughing, too, but not good-naturedly. Ever since Ryder's railroad-cap disaster, he and his adoring squirrel pack had gotten even surlier.

Randy wildly stretched out the word "blow," which came around at least four times a verse, throwing him off beat, and making it impossible to listen without laughing. Did he know that? Nathan smiled. That's always the question with Randy.

Now blow us out and blow us homeward.
Blow, boys, blow.
Blow us in to Boston Harbor.
Blow, me bully boys, blow.

Randy got an enthusiastic ovation. Kit, still laughing, tossed off one more shrill "*Whooo-eeee!*"

"Oh, that was fun," she gasped. "My sides hurt."

"Well, you're next," Nathan said. "Ready?"

"To follow that?"

"Don't worry. They're ready to slow down a little. Do the new one."

"After *that?*"

"One of the great secrets," Nathan said with a conspiratorial wink. "Don't compete with energy, change it. Try it, you'll be surprised."

She got on stage and quietly told the crowd that she wanted to try out a brand-new song. Whispering into the mike, she said, "You'll be the first ones to hear it, okay?" The room immediately hushed. A few people leaned forward in their seats. She glanced at Nathan, arching an eyebrow. How about that?

But it wasn't just that she softened the mood; she was also sharing a secret, a brand-new song. She'd turned her set into a special moment, a sharing of trust.

Kit lowered her head, absently strumming a few soft minor chords. She peeked over at Nathan, then lowered her head again. "It's called…um…'Winter,'" she said, almost whispering.

As she began to sing, he closed his eyes to listen. Like his suggestion, "Keys," her title focused on a central metaphor. But "Winter" created a visual and emotional landscape. His title pointed to the pivotal moment, hers to the bleak mood of the song. He wasn't sure if he liked her title better, but he was glad she'd changed it.

When it was over, he smiled at her, mouthed "Winter," and nodded. She smiled, then bowed her head to the applause. He realized he'd have to be careful about the advice he gave her. She accepted his title by saying, "You've been writing songs a lot longer than I have." But it wasn't his song, it was hers. Tread gently; she trusts you. The point is for her to trust herself.

Around midnight, an overweight, unkempt young woman with drab clothes and mousey brown hair nervously approached Nathan. Could she sing a song, just one, just by herself? Her face was very pale, and there was a faintly medicinal odor around her.

"You bet," Nathan said brightly. "This is the witching hour. That means all the open-mikers who signed up have already played. So anybody's welcome to just hop up and do their thing. Don't need to sign up or anything. The crowd can be a little noisy, though."

She gave him a wary nod, then climbed clumsily on the stage, and stood sheepishly in front of the microphone for an embarrassingly long moment.

"This is, you know, um, just how I've been feeling a lot lately," she mumbled, then began to sing, unaccompanied, eyes looking down or up at the ceiling—anywhere but at the audience.

What came out did not remotely resemble good music; it was barely music at all. Her voice was a low mumble, chanting in a singsongy way about cold walls, windows that see out to nothing, halls that lead nowhere, crowds without faces, feelings that hide under the bed, and feet that move without going anywhere. Nathan suspected it was really a poem, and that she was just singing it because she thought that's what you did at an open mike. He also guessed she'd recently been in some kind of hospital or mental institution.

But as she continued, the poem's painful honesty overcame her musical crudeness. It was horribly believable, a harrowing expression of whatever private hell she was trying to fight her way out of. And in that, Nathan thought, it was supremely artistic.

She seemed quite intelligent but still very much in the hold of whatever illness she was battling. Nathan couldn't imagine the courage it took to mount the stage and share those kinds of feelings. Good for her, good for her.

As the song ended, the crowd stirred from its uncomfortable quiet and began to applaud softly but steadily, in a way that showed genuine respect. What they had heard was difficult but real. Unpleasant or not, moments like that were rewarded at Dooley's.

Just as the woman began to break into an uneasy smile, one of Ryder's squirrels loudly whispered, "Fat chick's got the blues," and the entire table started laughing. The young woman jumped heavily off the stage, almost falling over, and ran out the door to even louder laughter from Ryder's table.

Nathan tried to reach out to her, but she shook her head fiercely and lurched out the door. He turned toward the heckler, a small, skinny, pimpled kid with stringy black hair and an upper lip full of fuzz that looked more like cat whiskers than a mustache.

Ferguson grabbed Nathan by the shoulder. "No, no, this one's on me," he said.

Ferguson was one of those people who get very quiet when they're angry. His voice becomes measured, dead of emotion, and he is even more articulate. He uses logic the way a bully uses a club. As he walked slowly toward Ryder's table, Ryder pointed a finger toward the heckler. What he was actually saying, of course, was, "It wasn't me."

"What *could* you have been thinking?" Ferguson said to the heckler, whose face was now bright red, eyes wide and frantic. The fact that Ryder had given him up left him lost. Without his hero's support, he didn't know how to feel, much less react.

Ferguson stared unblinkingly into the heckler's eyes "Couldn't you see how difficult it was for that woman to get up there?" he said. "Didn't that matter to you?"

Ferguson's voice grew softer, even and colorless, like shaved ice. "That woman— that fat chick, as you called her—wasn't singing for money, to get a gig, to impress anyone. She simply felt something deep down and wanted to share it. Now, what I'd like *you* to tell me is what you've ever done in your scrawny little life that's hipper than that."

Then, brutally, Ferguson waited, folding his arms across his chest and tapping his foot. After a few painful moments, he raised an eyebrow and said, "*Hmmm?*"

When the heckler said nothing, Ferguson nodded his head once and said, "I thought not."

Without moving his head, his eyes turned to Ryder. "While I'm over here, Ryder," he said, "I'd like to apologize for laughing during your set a while back. It was rude and I'm sorry."

Ryder nodded eagerly, and began to ask, "Did you like my—" But Ferguson turned on his heels and sauntered back to the bar.

Nathan grinned at him as he sat down. "Feel better now?" he said.

Ferguson cleared his throat, smiled, and spread his hands wide on the bar. "I do, lad, I do," he said.

Ferguson nodded, then looked sheepishly at Kit. "While I was over there, I apologized to Ryder for laughing at his stupid song."

Kit grinned. "That's a good boy," she said, affecting a maternal tone. "All right, perfesser, now you may have your pie."

"Thank you," he said, "I think I shall." And he waved at Jackie.

Awhile later, Kit told Ferguson how she showed Nathan "the great wonders of the computer age."

Nathan was happy to be her foil, and she was much kinder than she could have been. She told Ferguson her "furry knuckles" remark, but spared Nathan the embarrassment of repeating his question about needing special software for a mailing list. In a gesture that sent a shiver through Nathan, she winked privately at him when the story got to that point, then skipped over it. Our little secret.

By the end, Ferguson was wheezing and drying his eyes with a napkin.

"It's, like, with computers, you can do so much career stuff on your own," Kit said. "You don't even need the music industry anymore."

That prompted Ferguson to ask Kit if she knew about the late folksinger, Utah Phillips. She shook her head.

Ferguson told her Phillips had made it his life's work to show folkies how to sustain the music outside the mainstream. In the seventies and eighties, most folk venues were isolated, struggling to survive after the collapse of the commercial folk revival. During the worst of those years, he was one of the very few performers who could fill folk clubs. He would travel from gig to gig, asking how clubs were dealing with the lack of media attention, ways they'd found to keep their little venues going.

After shows, he often held town hall meetings with local folk communities, listening to their problems and telling them how other communities were solving them. Most of all, he told them they weren't as alone as they thought, that there were little folk communities just like them, all over the country. He helped them see that they weren't these tiny Alamos, holding out by themselves. They were part of a rising tide, a grassroots, national movement to remake the business of folk music outside the mainstream.

"Tell Kit about the puppy poop," Nathan said, already laughing.

"Ah, yes," Ferguson said, straightening on his stool and clearing his throat dramatically. "The Great Puppy Poop Conundrum. Still spoken of at the paper in hushed and reverent terms. Well, some years ago I wrote a story in which Utah referred to, and I quote, 'this sockful of puppy poop we have the audacity to call a culture.'"

"Hah!" Kit shouted, slapping her hands together.

"Indeed," Ferguson said. "The copy editors had a hell of a time with it. They all took a stab at modifying it; but Utah had phrased it so precisely that any attempt to clean it up made it sound dirtier. What else could they bracket in there? Puppy droppings? Canine feces? Dog shit? Even 'sockful of expletive deleted' was worse. God knows what the reader would think he'd said."

Ferguson grinned. "So it ran the way he said it," he said. "The whole copy desk was in awe of how edit-proof Utah was. I called to tell him, and he said he'd actually thought about that when he said it. The man was a genius with words."

While everyone laughed, Ferguson took a long pull of his beer. He looked at Kit and smiled.

"I think you'll appreciate this, Kit," he said. "It ties in to what you were saying about the computer. I once asked Utah why he never signed with a major label. He could have; he had some good offers over the years. He said, 'If I believe the mainstream is polluted—and I do—why would I ever want to wind up a turd floating down the middle of it?' Ah, now, tell me that's not poetry."

Ferguson beamed at Nathan, grinning and stroking his beard excitedly, as Kit pulled out her journal to write the quote down. She made him repeat it slowly, word by word, shaking her head and cackling darkly as she wrote. Nathan smiled and nodded at Ferguson. *I know just how you feel.*

A light rain was falling, barely more than mist, visible only under the streetlights. Nathan looked out the window and traced how the soft rain muted the yellow lamp glow on the black street. He absently rubbed Kit's back as she continued to write in her journal. *These are somebody's good old days, that's for sure.*

Five

"Oh, pu-leeeeze, Nathan? C'mon. Pu-leeeeze?"

Kit was really enjoying herself, waving her arms, tilting her head back, and shouting "please" the way a cheesy pop diva hits her money note. She wanted Nathan to go with her to her first radio interview at the local folk station, WUMB. Nathan was sitting at the kitchen table, shaking his head and looking out the window at the chilly autumn sky. Such a strange kind of blue this time of year. Less shiny, somehow.

Kit was worried about her nerves again, though you'd never guess it by how much fun she was having. She was never quite so cocky as she was when she knew she was going to get her way. Nathan smiled, but shook his head uncertainly. He just didn't like the idea of being part of her on-air interview. She was the guest, not him.

"There's no reason for me to be there," he said. "None. Zero. Zip. They invited you, to promote your gig, which you are doing by yourself. People will think I'm butting in."

She narrowed her eyes, as if planning her next move, and sat down next to him.

"It's just that it's the first time," she said, in that earnest voice that he didn't like. It was the only time Kit sounded the least affected. It was as if she thought it was not enough to be sincere, she had to sound sincere. But she always seemed sincere, so any attempt to emphasize it had the opposite effect. He wondered if she knew that.

"I've never done a radio interview before," she said, furrowing her brow. "And Nathan, it's going to be live. I'm afraid I'll spook myself and there won't be an audience to help me. But if you're there, I won't get spooked because I'll know you're there to pick up the slack if I do get spooked. You know?"

"I think I followed most of that. You need me there so you won't need me there."

She slumped her shoulders in exasperation, then cocked her head thoughtfully. "Actually," she said, "that's exactly what I mean. I won't get nervous because I'll know you're there to cover for me if I *do* get nervous. And if I do, you know, you could do some of those little solo things on the guitar. See? It really does make sense."

He looked at her and nodded slowly. She had a point. It was the fear of stage fright that worried her. And if she did falter, he could play guitar fills until she regained herself. Plus, they were starting to sound good together; it would add some sparkle to her first live radio appearance.

So he'd go. He wanted to play this out a little, though, so he shook his head again, and she sighed. It's always useful to get a reading on how a woman practices the fine art of wheedling.

Of course, a certain level of manipulation between lovers is the natural order of things. He'd never known a woman who didn't see the man in her life as something of a fixer-upper opportunity. And he knew that had been especially true with him. However else women saw him, he was sure that he always looked like he could use a little paint, some new eaves, and a lot of interior decorating.

Joyce was, by far, the best wheedler he'd ever known. She made an art form out of it. She was so blatant, so grand, theatrical, and blissfully full of herself that people looked forward to having her connive things from them. With her, it was a form of seduction.

With Kit, it was more of a game played between friends. But she shared the most important quality with Joyce: it was all out in the open. No sneak attack, no subterfuge. You knew exactly what she wanted.

Nathan, on the other hand, had no aptitude for wheedling. It had once been a source of pride, but he also knew it was a fatal flaw in anyone trying to be a star in the music business. It's a harsh forest out there. Timid creatures aren't rewarded; they're lunch.

He remembered when he would call his old record label and try to pry something out of them about his album. They would duck the subject, chatting with him about this or that, very friendly, while he waited. Finally, he would have to bring it up, as if they had no idea why he was calling.

And then they would make him feel like a selfish child. "Oh, is that why you're calling?" they'd say. Or, "Don't you think we'd let you know if we knew anything?" And he would feel so oily, conniving, and nakedly ambitious. They might have been lousy at keeping their word, but they were experts at making their artists feel like ungrateful pets.

Nathan understood now that it was his reticence, not his ambition, that set him up for that kind of shaming, and that it was they who were hustling him, not the other way around. For a second, he felt the old ache again, but he looked at Kit and it stopped.

He smiled at her. She'd never have to go through that kind of shame. She'd be too strong, too open. Yes or no, she'd say, yes or no. Because beneath the shyness, beneath the nerves, he saw a confidence in her made of sureness and steel. She wrapped it in soft things, but it was steel, nonetheless. Good for her.

"Oh, please," Kit shouted again, almost singing, her voice a high squeak. "Please, Nathan, *Pu-leeeee-e-e-ze!*"

He sighed deeply, as if he was somehow obligated to react that way, and said, "All right, I'll go—if you promise to never, ever do that again."

"What?"

"Say 'please' the way a cat would ask you to stop stepping on its tail."

She cleared her throat daintily and touched her chest with a finger. *Who, me?* Her voice again full of that honeyed sincerity, she said, "Seriously, thank you, Nathan." She leaned over and rubbed his knee.

"You bet, sweetie. So, when is this interview?"

She sat up straight and looked at her watch. "About an hour and a half. I'm supposed to be there in an hour."

"Today? It's *today?*"

She smiled, nodded her head, and popped to her feet. "Come on, we gotta hurry," she said.

The WUMB *Live at Noon* interviews were a Boston folk tradition. The host was an attractive middle-aged woman with twinkly blue eyes, very large glasses, and a perpetually chirpy voice. Nathan found her on-air manner equal parts flirtatious, matronly, and reminiscent of everybody's favorite homeroom teacher. She was particularly solicitous with young performers, and had rescued many first-time interviews from disaster.

Folk radio existed almost entirely on small public stations. Many, like WUMB, were college stations that wanted a local flavor to their format. During his touring days, Nathan was always surprised by how much radio mattered. In towns that had even one folk show, audiences had a pretty good grasp of the national circuit, and knew the names of its headliners. In towns with no folk radio, fans tended to know only those performers who played locally. But Boston was a folk town, the only place in the country with a full-time folk station like WUMB.

The studio was tucked away in the basement of a library at UMass/Boston, a small, mall-like campus in Dorchester, just south of downtown Boston. As Nathan walked into the cramped offices and saw the little studio with its large glass windows, he worried how his unexpected appearance would be received. He didn't want to seem like he was horning in on Kit's act.

The noontime host hugged him as they walked in, then turned to Kit, eyes wide, as if someone had thrown her a surprise party. "Well, look who you've brought along, Kit!" She said, almost shouting. She fluttered her arms excitedly by her sides, in an almost birdlike way. "What a treat! So Nathan's going to play with you? Wonderful, wonderful!"

Winking at Nathan, she said, "I heard you two were an item. How delicious."

Nathan got out his guitar, wondering why he always thought the worst about people like that, or, rather, that they would think the worst of him. In the host's place, would he have thought he was horning in? Of course not. He was there to back up Kit. He shook his head and sighed.

"What's wrong?" said Kit. She sounded a little nervous.

"Nothing, nothing. Come on, let's tune up."

Transcript: *Live at Noon*, guests Kit Palmer and Nathan Warren

Host: We have a very special treat today, with a newcomer to the scene and a surprise guest, who's no stranger to anybody around here. Kit Palmer is an exciting new songwriter, getting lots of buzz from fans and musicians. I've seen her myself, and I tell you, she's really got something going. Joining her is someone we've all known for a long time, one of the Boston folk scene's best friends, Nathan Warren. What a surprise, Nathan; we didn't know you were going to be here.

Nathan: I'm just here to accompany Kit.

Kit: Yeah, he's my band.

Nathan: And roadie. The pay is actually better as roadie. Haven't quite figured that out yet.

Kit: Sidemen are a dime a dozen, but a good roadie…[*laughter*]

Nathan: True enough.

Host: Well, welcome to our studio, Kit Palmer. This is your first time here, isn't it?

Kit: My first time anywhere. Like, on the radio, I mean. And I want to say, if it's not too corny, that I just love this station. It's so cool to have folk music on the radio all the time. Nothing like that where I grew up.

Host: And where was that, Kit?

Kit: Connecticut. We only had one little show, on Sunday nights. So naturally I had to move to Boston.

Host: [*laughing*] Because of us? We're very flattered.

Kit: Well, I really came here to go to college. But I had no idea there was so much happening with folk music. I mean, I always liked it when I heard it, but that was mostly on records. Then I got here, and *whoosh*! There's people singing on street corners and all these cool open mikes and coffeehouses. You know, it's one thing to hear it on records; but when it's, like, happening all around you, it's different. Until I came to Boston, folk music just seemed, I don't know, it never seemed real. Like something from another time. You know?

Host: You bet we do. Kit Palmer is our live guest today on Live at Noon, right here on WUMB. She will be appearing at Jo-Joe's coffeehouse in Jamaica Plain Saturday night. What are you going to play for us, Kit?

Kit: This is a new one of mine, called "Winter." Seems apropos on a chilly day like this.

Host: [*Laughter. More laughter. More laughter*]

Kit: Um. Yup. Okay, here we go.

[*Song:* "Winter."]

Host: That's a song from Kit Palmer, our guest today on Live at Noon. Just wonderful, Kit. So vivid. I love the image of the keys falling in the water. And that was some lovely guitar accompaniment from our old friend, Nathan Warren. I've always enjoyed the way you play.

Nathan: Thanks. It's a great song.

Host: So, Kit, tell us, is Nathan Warren here having an influence on you? So many songwriters around here say he's influenced them over the years.

Nathan: [*Audible sigh*]

Kit: Oh, absolutely. He's showing me all kinds of things. I think he's—

Nathan: Yes, I'm trying to mold her to my will, shape her in my image. Lately I've been trying to get her to think about having a little bald spot on the back of her head.

Kit: [*Laughing*] You don't have a bald spot!

Nathan: In the back of the skull, you know, very dignified. Like a monk.

Host: I wonder if I could—

Kit: You do *not* have a bald spot!

Host: [*Laughing*] Well, I don't know what to say about—

Kit: Where did that even come from? Bald spot! Honestly, Nathan.

Host: At the risk of sounding pushy, would you mind if I asked another question? My listeners sort of expect it of me.

Kit: Fire away.

Host: Actually, Kit Palmer, our *Live at Noon* guest today, why don't we hear another song?

Kit: Oh. Sure.

Nathan: [*Whispering*] Why don't you do "Deportee?"

Kit: [*Whispering*] Left my fiddle outside.

Host: Hello?

Nathan: [*Whispering*] I put it right there, by your feet.

Kit: [*Whispering*] Oh. Whew. Thanks.

Host: Hello?

Kit: Sorry. Nathan needed to mold me to his will long enough to show me where he put my fiddle. Live radio, huh? [*Laughter*] This is a Woody Guthrie song.

[*Song*: "Deportee."]

Host: That was beautiful, Kit. Kit Palmer is our guest today on WUMB's *Live at Noon*. I would never have thought of using the fiddle that way. So sad.

Kit: Thank you. It's such a pretty song. Still timely, too.

Host: Yes, we still take advantage of people like that, don't we? They were deportees back then; now we call them illegals.

Kit: The whole idea of a person being illegal. You know? Something wrong with that.

Host: Once again, Kit Palmer will be performing at Jo-Joe's Coffeehouse this Saturday night at eight p.m. For more information, check out our online events calendar. Kit, it's been lovely having you here; and Nathan, it's always a treat to hear you play. We'd love to have you as our guest sometime.

Kit: Then I can come and tease him, for a change. Bald spot. Really, Nathan.

Nathan: Just a tiny one. Like a monk.

Kit: [*Sighing loudly*] I really don't know what's wrong with him. He's usually so well behaved this time of day.

Host: [*Laughing*] Maybe he needs a nap.

Kit: Or a snack. I keep some graham crackers for him in my purse.

Nathan: Okay, okay, I get it.

Host: [*Laughing*] We might have some apple juice. Would he like some nice juice?

Nathan: Okay, I'll be good.

Host: [*Still laughing*] Thank you again, Kit Palmer and Nathan Warren, for coming in today. Next up, we have some Dar Williams for you, right here on WUMB.

As Nathan drove Kit to one of her waitressing jobs, she was still feeling the adrenaline, talking excitedly about how the WUMB interview had gone. Then she changed the subject to one of the Harvard folk music classes she was auditing. She'd gotten to know the professor a bit. And, she said slowly, as if it carried great meaning, he used to be a *big* Nathan Warren fan. She paused, grinning at him.

He looked at her. "Does it really surprise you that much?"

"Of course not. That's not the point. He asked me if *Mister* Warren would ever consider coming to talk to the class. Like, *Mister* Warren—he said it just like that."

"Is it grammatically correct to call a folksinger 'mister?'"

Kit laughed, a little too much for the joke. Something was up.

"No, really, Nathan, he'd love for you to talk to his class."

"A folklore class? Kit, I'm not quite that old. What, my salad days writing the Robin Hood ballads?"

"It's not like that at all. It's more about the music now, and how it got to be that way. Professor Kahn talks about folk music more like a social movement: how it changed from what it used to be into what it is today. And how it's all connected."

She cleared her throat and leaned closer to him. "He told us that in the 1600s, they made chamber music out of traditional Scottish music; and he said that's exactly the same as the folk-rock bands in the sixties: adapting the old music to what's popular at the time. Cool, huh?"

Nathan nodded, "Wow. That is cool."

Kit smiled. "Yeah. So?"

"So, what? The class? I don't know, Kit. What would I have to say to a class like that?"

"Oh, come on. You're kidding, right? This is, like, *so* right up your alley. You're telling me this kind of stuff all the time."

"I don't know. What could I—"

"It would be fun. I mean, I wouldn't have brought it up if it wasn't—"

"*You* brought it up?" Nathan said, his voice sharp. "Was this your idea?"

"No, no," Kit said quickly. "I didn't mean it that way. I mean I wouldn't bring it up with *you* if I didn't think it was something you'd want to do. They'd love you at the class; I know they would. Or I wouldn't ask. That's what I meant."

He wasn't sure that was exactly the truth; but if she was fibbing a little, she was only thinking of him. He liked the idea that she wanted to show him off. Been a long time since he felt anything like that. But Jesus, a class? At Harvard?

He concentrated on the road as the expressway turned into the big tunnel running under downtown Boston. The bowels of the Big Dig. Maybe not worth the gazillions it cost, but it sure made it easier to get from south to north.

It used to be that everyone had to go on one road through downtown Boston. Even if you were going east or west, you had to take this one congested expressway.

But calling it an expressway didn't make it one. One slow truck could cause a major traffic jam. Now it was a big tunnel with exits whizzing by every eighth of a mile, giving people lots of chances to get off and go where they wanted. But with all those exits coming up all the time, the tunnel reminded Nathan of a bumper-car track. Cars whirred around, changing lanes, veering over for quick exits, or veering away to avoid them. Everybody knew the tunnel was like that, so it was actually pretty safe. It just didn't seem like a good idea to have drivers buzzing around each other like that. Not in this town.

Nathan wheeled onto the Storrow Drive exit. "Shit," he muttered. This was the exit for his house.

"Don't you want to do it?" Kit said. "You're not mad, are you?"

"No, it's not that. I took the wrong exit. It'll take a few more minutes to get you to work. Is that okay?"

"Me? Late for work? Of course it's okay." She smiled at him. "So you do want to do it? The class?"

"Yeah, I dunno. I suppose. Don't you think it would—"

"Great! I'll tell the professor. He'll be wicked psyched."

Nathan shrugged, feeling as though his role in this discussion, as in the earlier one about the radio show, had been more ceremonial than functional. He looked out his side window as they passed through Harvard Square, bustling as usual. Kit drummed her fingers on the dashboard, talking again about how well the radio show had gone.

He looked over at her, still riding her post-show high. She was getting used to that adrenaline now, wasn't she? He smiled. She stared out her window, chattering away so excitedly that she left visible little breaths on the window. Nathan turned his eyes back to the road. He wished he could feel that excited again. About anything.

Kit came over unexpectedly one evening, while Nathan was washing his dinner dishes. She announced solemnly that she and Ferguson had spent the afternoon together, mostly talking about Nathan. She said she wanted him to know because she didn't like the idea of keeping secrets, even, you know, like, perfectly innocent ones. She didn't like that "creepy behind-your-back feeling."

She looked at him so earnestly that it was hard not to laugh. Good lord, you'd think she was revealing an affair. He looked at her, slowly took the dish towel off his shoulder, and put it by the sink

"You didn't…ah…didn't…*kiss* him, did you?"

She sat bolt upright at the kitchen table and gulped. Then he laughed. She relaxed, swore under her breath, and joined his laughter.

At the next open mike, Ferguson also confessed to the meeting. He and Nathan were, as usual, huddled around the bend of the bar. Kit was at her apartment, working on a song and trying out some new apps she'd loaded on her iPhone.

When Ferguson told him about the meeting with Kit, Nathan laughed.

"What?" Ferguson said. "I just don't want you to—"

"I know," Nathan said. "No, it's fine. It's just that Kit came over right afterward and told me about it."

Ferguson laughed. "I should have known. Hey, you'll appreciate this. She really nailed me when we got together. I was ranting about something, the paper, or politics, or corporate swine in general. And she said, 'You just do that to tease people.'"

"Do what?" Nathan said. "Rant?"

"That's what I thought she meant, but she said she meant using all those—how did she put it?—'big flowery words.' She said I only talk that way to see how people will react. So I said, 'Well, little girl, how do you know that?' And she said, 'Because you don't write that way. That's how I know. You don't use all those big words when you write.'"

"Ha! I never thought about that. She's right, isn't she?"

Ferguson nodded, grinning. "Yup, she nailed me. When I write, it's all about being clear and simple. When I get to rattling away, though, well, she's right. I guess I'm showing off a little."

"I enjoy it, though. You get into a real groove. It feels like music sometimes."

Ferguson smiled at the unexpected compliment. Nathan straightened his back and gazed out the window. Very softly, he said, "She's something else, isn't she?"

"You mean the way she nailed me?"

"No, no. Hell, she does that to me all the time. No, it's that she didn't tell me about it. Most people would have, you know? Nailing the big critic? She didn't say a word. That's the way she is."

Nathan told Ferguson the parts of the mailing list story that Kit had skipped over: how he thought you needed special software, didn't know what an IP was, asked if you had to audition for CDBaby.

"An IP? You didn't know what an IP was?"

"Well, I know I've got one. I just never knew they were called IP's. Anyway, Kit really wanted to tell you that story but didn't want to embarrass me more than she had to. I'm sure that's why she didn't tell me about nailing you. She really likes you, you know."

Ferguson smiled. "I like her, too. You know, I'll bet that's why she waited until we were alone to tease me about being a blowhard. So she wouldn't embarrass me in front of my friends. She's very kind, isn't she?"

They stared at their drinks.

"It's not kindness, not exactly," Nathan said. "It's more personal, more internal. Empathy. Kit feels what other people are feeling, sometimes more intensely than they do. That's why she got upset when we laughed at Ryder. Even Ryder, for god's sake—I mean, who else would bother to walk in that guy's shoes? But I think that's why she can write the way she does, get so deep inside everything. Even her fiddling is like that; it's like she feels the emotions beneath the surface of the music. It must be hard for her sometimes, like people with that disease that makes your skin too sensitive."

Ferguson nodded and stared into his beer. He laughed and said, "So you don't need special software for a mailing list?"

"Apparently not. Hey, since we're sharing confessions, can I ask you something?"

"Sure."

"In strictest confidence?"

"Jesus, sure. What?"

Nathan cleared his throat. "What the hell is an app?"

"Application. App is short for application."

"Oh, thanks heaps. That's very helpful. Now I understand everything."

Ferguson laughed. "It's not complicated. App is a word for any of those doodads they put on their phones. You know what a doodad is, right?"

"Sure, it's any kind of doohickey I don't understand."

"See? I told you it wasn't complicated."

Nathan shook his head, laughing. "It's amazing, isn't it? I only understand about ten percent of the stuff Kit says she can do with that phone of hers. She has a dictionary on it, reads the news, listens to music. It gives her directions, maps. It's like she can do everything with it but tune her guitar."

Ferguson stared at him, blinking his eyes.

Nathan sighed. "She can tune her guitar with it?"

"If she has the right app, yes."

Nathan felt like a damn fool. He'd been queasy all week, picturing himself standing behind a bloody lectern, in front of an entire classroom full of bright young Harvard students, spouting about his grand life in folk music. "From Star to Open-Miker," a lecture by Nathan Warren. You pompous old fool.

He should have known that when Kit asked him to speak at Professor Kahn's folk music class, she didn't mean next month or next year. He was expected tonight, seven o'clock sharp.

He told himself he was just doing this as a favor for Kit, lovely Kit. Lovely, conniving Kit. He thought that would relax him, but it had the opposite effect. He wanted to do well because she wanted him to do well. And when he thought that, the nerves came again. Damn fool.

Kit wanted others to take him as seriously as she did. She was so excited about him, the way she was about everything in her exciting, excited life. She wanted to show him off, and that pleased him on some deep level, far beyond vanity. He had always cared about his work, but for his own reasons. He hadn't felt this way for a long, long time. Ever? He wanted someone else to be proud of him.

Then he saw that picture in his mind, babbling away in front of a classroom—at *Harvard*, for Chrissakes! For some evil reason, his imagination placed a pointer in his hand, and he saw himself waving it around stupidly while students snickered and giggled. Pompous fool.

So he was relieved to arrive at the class, and find it wasn't in a classroom at all. Folklore classes were held at Warren House, a billowy 1833 home that had once belonged to a professor of Sanskrit named Henry Clarke Warren.

Professor Kahn met Nathan and Kit at the door. He was a tall, lanky, middle-aged man with an unruly shock of salt-and-pepper hair and horn-rimmed glasses that failed to obscure a pair of thick and flaring eyebrows. He wore gray corduroy pants and a charcoal tweed coat with worn leather elbow pads. He looked every inch the erudite Harvard professor. Nathan glanced down at his own white linen shirt and black jeans. Basic black and white had seemed somehow, well, scholarly. Damn fool.

As they shook hands, Kahn asked if Nathan was any relation to old Professor Warren. Nathan said, "If he's anybody respectable, I doubt it."

The professor laughed, then led Nathan and Kit up the grand stairway to the second floor, where the class was held. They walked in to a long, white-walled and wood-trimmed room dominated by an oval table. About 25 students were already seated there, dressed casually, chatting comfortably, pulling out notebooks and pens. They didn't look at all like the imperious and skeptical students Nathan's mind had conjured. They did, however, look very smart.

Nathan sat in a chair by the back wall, which he chose because it was as far away as he could sit and still be inside the room. Kahn only had to clear his throat softly and the room hushed. Students poised their pens over their notebooks.

Kahn nodded at Nathan. "Before we meet our very special guest," he said, "I would like to illuminate a few points from last week's discussion." *Very* special guest. Good grief.

Kahn began rattling off ways that traditional music had changed over the years, and the many factors that changed it: new environs, new instruments, new neighbors, new ways of life. He was darting over centuries and cultures so quickly that some students never looked up at him; all they saw were their notebooks and their scribbling pens. He talked about accordions replacing fiddles in zydeco music. Then he was in seventeenth-century Ireland, chuckling about how purists predicted the doom of Irish music if that Italian monstrosity, the violin, became popular. Then it was the Old West, telling them that the piano, not the guitar, was the dominant folk instrument until very late in the nineteenth century. Then he was on an old sailing ship, lamenting the end of the sea-chantey tradition as work became mechanized and sailors no longer needed to sing in rhythm while heaving and hauling. Then he was off to 1920s Mississippi, and how quickly the blues turned from a folk form into a commercial fad, thanks to the recent inventions of radio and recordings. *Whoosh, whoosh, whoosh.*

Nathan's head felt like the ball in a brisk tennis match. *Thwack!* Ancient Ireland. *Thwack!* Wild West saloons. *Thwack!* And now, Kahn was describing how quickly the electric guitar was embraced by roadhouse musicians in the thirties and forties, because it could be heard over the crowds; and the blues began to morph into rock. *Thwack!*

Nathan studied the students in the room, to see if he was the only one who felt overwhelmed. Some were writing furiously; others stared at the ceiling or down at the floor, trying to soak it all in.

He looked at Kit, and she was listening the way she did to music, mouth half open, eyes shut then opening wide, moving forward in her seat, then back: the idle motions of intense concentration. She didn't take notes but she was auditing the class. No tests for her.

Nathan looked back at Kahn, who was now in colonial America, talking excitedly about how quickly the banjo caught on after being invented by slaves, who patterned it after the African oud.

Kahn stopped suddenly and smiled. "Don't worry," he said. "You don't need to remember all the details." At that, one young woman threw down her pen in irritation. Now he tells us.

"Here's the point I want to make," Kahn said. Nathan leaned forward in his seat and rested his elbows on his legs.

Kahn spread his arms wide. "Tradition is a bully," he said. "Does that sound harsh? We've talked a lot about what a wonderful thing it is, and it is. But it's an agent of change, and change is always a bully. Industrial revolutions bring new comforts, create new jobs; but they also displace populations, destroy cherished ways of life. In traditional music, new neighbors introduce a new instrument and the old ways are changed forever. A workplace is modernized and a whole tradition of work songs vanishes. With any kind of change, there are casualties. We like to think of tradition as a pure place where old ways are honored and preserved. Nonsense. Tradition is always changing; and change is always a bully."

Nathan suddenly saw how all Kahn's tangents wove together into a single story; it was like music, he thought.

The professor studied the students' faces and smiled uncertainly. Then he looked at Nathan, who was making an applauding gesture with his hands. Hoisting his furry eyebrows, Kahn invited him to the head of the table. Oh, no, Nathan thought, not now, not after that. A little more about the blues, professor? The polka—say, I'll bet *that's* an interesting story.

But Kahn was already introducing him. Through a fog, Nathan heard the words "before your time" and "big star in my day" and "the one Kit's been talking about." Oh, damn. Not now, not yet.

Nathan slowly got up from his chair in the back, where he would have happily spent the rest of his life, and moved to the head of the class. He stood next to Kahn and saw Kit smiling at him. Damn, damn, damn. He had absolutely no idea what to say.

Kahn had been standing as he talked, but Nathan immediately sat down and leaned over the table, folding his hands as if in prayer. Kahn moved to a nearby chair.

After clearing his throat several times, Nathan began to talk, but so quietly that several students asked him to speak up. He mumbled about being a folksinger, about Dooley's; and that he didn't know how Kit had roped him into this. He said he enjoyed the professor's remarks, especially about change being a bully. Then his voice trailed off, and he stared at the table. He had no idea what to say. He smiled weakly at the professor. This was not going well.

Kahn leaned back in his chair and wrapped his hands behind his head. "Well, Nathan, tell us this," he said. "How do you think these young songwriters today connect to the old traditional music, to the old folk songs that were passed on from generation to generation?"

The professor grinned and cocked his head. "Or *do* you see a connection? A lot of people don't, you know. But you're close to it; you hear new songwriters all the time, down at your open mike. And I happen to know that you write your own songs, but also sing the old traditional songs. I've always enjoyed that mix."

"Thank you," Nathan said softly. The professor's eyes were curious, not challenging. Nathan nodded earnestly, but his mind was a blank.

"So tell us," Kahn said, "is there still such a thing as folk music? Or has it all morphed into something else?" Glancing at Kit, he said, "We've had some, uh, *spirited* debates about that down here."

The class laughed, and the girl sitting next to Kit poked her playfully. Kit rolled her eyes. "Spirited," Nathan said, looking at Kit and smiling. "Yes, I can imagine." The class laughed louder and Kit stared at the ceiling, with that mock-innocent look she did so well.

"You know," Nathan said, his voice a little louder, "I used to get flak from purists for writing my own songs and flak from songwriters because I sang the old songs. I never understood the difference. I mean, who wrote those old songs in the first place? Wasn't it songwriters who sang: singer-songwriters? Personally, I think what's happening today carries on that old tradition of making up songs about your life, as it's happening to you. That's how it seems to me, anyway."

The words came more easily. Nathan thought less about where he was and more about how he felt. He cared so much about these things.

"I've thought a lot about this," he said, "and I think it boils down to one thing: authenticity. We may not write about cowboys or maids a-milking anymore, but the people who wrote those songs weren't writing about olden times, you know? They were writing modern songs, about the things they saw outside their windows every day."

He pointed at Kit. "And I think that's just what songwriters like Kit are doing. They're writing about life as it's happening to them; as they see it outside their windows every day. The authenticity they share with the people who wrote those old songs isn't a historical one or a stylistic one. It's an emotional one. The people who wrote those old songs wanted to express their lives authentically, personally, to sing about how their lives *felt* to them. And I think that's what draws people like Kit to folk music today. Right?"

He looked at Kit, and she nodded. "Totally," she said. She seemed to want to say more, but didn't.

Nathan looked around the room and was surprised to see a few students taking notes. What did he say? He eyed the room warily, but again his thoughts overtook his self-consciousness.

"I think it's that ability to share intimate emotions that makes the old songs powerful," he said. "We may not be sailors or sharecroppers, but we all know about missing someone, falling in love, fearing death. I think that's still what drives folk music today. Songwriters like Kit want their music to be about how people really live, and how those lives feel. And that's why the old songs still get to us, I think. Not because they're old—because they're real."

Nathan closed his mouth and shrugged at the professor. Did any of that make sense? Kahn smiled, rubbing a finger over his upper lip.

A young man with short brown hair and the faint beginnings of a goatee said, "But isn't folk music today just another kind of pop? It's a career, just like rock or jazz or any other commercial music: professional entertainers who play concerts, sell CDs, promote themselves. It's not a bunch of farmers making up songs for their neighbors anymore. It's a business."

A few students rolled their eyes. Kit shook her head, and Nathan suspected he now knew who was on the other side of her "spirited debates."

"Good point, and you're right," Nathan said to the student, who seemed startled by the answer. "I mean, folk music is still played socially, the way it used to be—you should check out the Wednesday jam at Dooley's—but mostly it's just another part of the music business. It used to be easy to tell the difference. Like you said, it was folks making music for themselves, for their neighbors. Still, I think what people like Kit are doing is folk music, but the reasons are more subjective now. So let me answer for myself."

Nathan closed his eyes and measured every word. "What the old folk songs taught me," he said, "is that we don't need to have extraordinary things happen to make our lives interesting. That's what we get from movies and TV all the time. It's all about extraordinary people and extraordinary events. But folk songs show us that our ordinary lives are romantic and heroic and interesting. And I think that still sums up the mission statement for folk songwriters: to make our lives, as we really live them, something worth singing about."

He opened his eyes and shrugged. Simple as that.

Kahn said, "You've obviously given this a lot of thought, Nathan. So you don't see any distinctions between the traditional songs and what's being written today? None at all?"

"Oh, things have changed," Nathan said. "But like you said, folk music is always changing."

"How is it changing?" Kahn asked forcefully. "How?"

"Well, I guess the biggest change is that the songs *don't* change anymore," Nathan said. Kahn sat back upright. "Ahh," he said.

"Before records and radio," Nathan said, "people mostly learned songs from each other. The songs got passed around; and after a while, nobody could remember who wrote them. There was no original version, so a song was always changing. People added their own feelings, changed the story, the melody. Everybody felt like they could make it their own song."

Kahn raised a finger. "If I can interject here," he said, "Francis James Child, the great nineteenth-century ballad collector—who was a professor right here at Harvard—compared that process, which is sometimes called 'the folk process,' to a stone that's in a brook for centuries, with water passing over it, rubbing all its rough edges smooth. That's what Nathan is describing, the way songs changed over time, as they passed from singer to singer, generation to generation. Correct, Nathan?"

Nathan nodded. "Like a stone in a brook. Yeah, I like that. But that doesn't happen anymore. It's just gone, man, it's over. A song may still travel from singer to singer, but if it gets too far from the original version, somebody's going to say, 'Hey, you're not singing it right.' Or somebody's going to sue you. The original versions are protected now, by copyright laws, publishing, recording."

He pointed at Kahn. "It's a tradeoff, just like you were saying earlier. The bad news is, you can't change songs now; they don't get to spend all that time in the brook, getting better. But the good news is, you get to know who wrote them. I like it that I know who Bob Dylan is, and Bruce Springsteen, and Ani DiFranco. I'd give anything to know who wrote 'Water Is Wide' or 'Pretty Saro.' I'd love to know if there really was a Barbara Allen. But you can't know that. So it's a tradeoff, just like everything."

Nathan was quiet again. He looked down at the table, then up at the ceiling. He was lost in it all now, wondering to himself, the way he did when he was alone.

"That's what makes the old folk songs, the traditional ones, unlike any other art we have," he said softly. "Maybe you can find something different in a van Gogh painting every time you see it, but the painting never changes. Folk songs do."

He took a deep breath but didn't move. The room was so quiet he forgot where he was.

"A folk song is never finished," he said quietly, as if talking to himself. "It exists in a constant state of being created, always evolving, changing, soaking in the lives around it and reflecting them back. All the places it's been are still in it, all the people who've ever sung it still live inside it. Its borders are always moving, the mood, the colors, changing every time they're sung. Paintings, sculptures, movies, novels, poems: they reach a final destination. Those old songs never do. A folk song never stops being written."

His eyes were still fixed on the ceiling, darting back and forth, lost in the wonder of that, the mystery. Suddenly, hotly, he remembered where he was and looked around the room. How long had he been spouting off? What did he say? Blood rushed to his face, and he felt a shiver down his back. These were his private thoughts, from years of talking to himself about the things he cared about. How foolish to say these things out loud. He cleared his throat, shook his head, and began to apologize.

He was cut short by a smattering of hands and pens rapping on the table. He glanced at Professor Kahn, who was smiling and nodding his head. Nathan grinned sheepishly and looked at Kit. She was beaming at him—absolutely beaming—and he felt his chest swell.

After the class, Kahn asked Nathan to stay behind a moment. Kit said she'd wait outside. She strolled past him, grinning and whistling under her breath. She was so pleased with how this had worked out. Nathan watched her and smiled.

"Nathan, I want to thank you so much for coming to our class," Kahn said, and Nathan's head snapped back to him. "You've thought this out so well, in such a personal way. Not academic. You have a real gift for explaining the old traditions, and how they connect to music today. That's important for young people to hear. Too often, old pedants like me make it seem like ancient history, as if it doesn't have anything to do with them."

"Boy, that's not what I got from you tonight," Nathan said. "I loved what you said about change being a bully. So true. I thought the students related to that."

"Oh well, thank you," Kahn said, looking away. "But not the way they related to you. I can never quite seem to…"

He looked back at Nathan. "Have you ever thought about teaching?"

"Not really. I teach guitar a little, but…you know, I never even went to college."

"Well, it wouldn't have to be in college. Passim has an evening school, and it's not just music instruction. I did a seminar on the blues last spring. You'd be perfect for something like that, because you're a musician yourself, and—"

Nathan laughed. "I can't even get a gig down there, professor."

"Oh, please, call me Maury."

"Maury. Class is out, huh?"

"Forgive me, I should have said it before we began." Kahn looked around the stately old classroom. "Harvard. It gets to you. As much as you swear it won't, it gets to you."

He looked at Nathan, and his face turned serious. "Passim is a different place than it used to be, more of a community center. Very friendly. I mean, if they'd let in a dotty Harvard professor like me, who knows what old walls might come tumbling down. I think you have a real gift for this; I really do."

"Well, so do you, Prof—I mean, Maury. You sure made it easy for me. I wanted to thank you for those questions. I had no idea what to say. Felt like a damn fool, to tell the truth."

"My pleasure. I hope you'll think about doing this more, about teaching. And you're always welcome back here."

Nathan smiled. "Sure. Drop down to Dooley's sometime. I think you'd have fun. The folk jam is really hot these days."

"That's what I hear. If I brought down your old album, would you sign it? I bought it when it first came out."

"Ah, so you're the one," Nathan said, and Kahn laughed.

"Too bad that second one never came out," Kahn said. Nathan smiled but said nothing.

After an awkward silence, Kahn said, "Well, thanks again. And tell Kit I said thanks, too."

They shook hands. "Thanks for what?" Nathan said. They looked at each other, then laughed.

"Ah," Nathan said. "For roping me into this."

Kahn nodded, rubbed his chin and lifted one of his vast eyebrows. "She's a force of nature, that one," he said.

Nathan laughed. "Tell me about it."

Six

The first nor'easter came in on Thursday, just before dusk. It strengthened as dark fell, hitting its wild, fat glory around ten o'clock. Nathan was home alone, with nothing to do, and savored every lonesome moment. It was intoxicating, this sudden and violent coming of winter. He could feel his blood begin to thicken and slow, like cold honey.

He opened the shades, pulled his easy chair close to the largest window, and listened to Corelli. There was something very wintry about the baroque music of Arcangelo Corelli, those plaintive chords and wistful melodies. He preferred classical albums when he wanted his mind to wander; folk music made him think about work.

He watched as the wind grew, tossing large streaks of snow against his windows, so hard he could sometimes hear it slap the glass. By midnight, the snow was coming almost horizontally, piling up against the old oak tree in the yard. The streetlights groaned and swayed from the sudden gusts. Snow would blow fiercely across the yard; then suddenly dance upward and around, as if it was fighting to go back the way it came. Nathan made herbal tea and gazed out the window, blowing rhythmically on the steaming cup to the elegiac cadences of Corelli.

He didn't think about much of anything, just stared, his eyes growing wider and wider as his mind grew cloudier and cloudier. When he went to bed, he left Corelli on the stereo, barely above a whisper, insinuating its alluring melancholy into his sleep.

He awoke the next morning in a warm, woolly funk, which he looked forward to indulging. Just a brood, he thought, a fine, wintry brood. He made tea, not coffee—don't want to get too perky, spoil the exquisite grayness.

While the water boiled, he looked outside. Wet smacks of snow still clung to the windows and lined the frames like creamy icing. The yard was high with snow, well over a foot, piling toward the far fence, like it was trying to climb over. It remained cloudy, with occasional, fierce gusts that blew the snow as if it was still falling. It was white everywhere, except for the granite gray of the sky, the walls of the grand old houses down the street, and the stark black of the bare trees.

He got his tea and, softly blowing on it, returned to the window. The snow was piled on the panes, always more to the left than the right. He wondered why. Taking his first sip of hot tea, he looked into the yard, at the big oak in the sloping yard, and beyond, to the back fence. The branches on the farther trees looked hazy, almost blurry in the drifting air, but the big oak, the nearest tree, seemed sharply in focus. The effect was like a photograph with the background in soft focus, leading the eye to the foreground.

So Nathan looked back at the big oak. The branches seemed lower today, sagging under the weight of the snow. Maybe they just looked that way, because only the bottoms of the branches showed under the snow. That's a strong old tree, he thought, nodding and sipping his tea; it's used to wearing a little snow.

He saw one small bird on a high branch, huddled close into himself, head darting this way and that. Nowhere else to go, nowhere warmer, safer, happier. Boy, he knew that feeling, didn't he? The storm is everywhere, the same miserable chill. So there's no sense moving; there's nowhere warmer, safer, happier. Just hunker down, crawl into yourself, wait it out. Wait it out. Wait it out.

No running today. Later he would shovel. The landlords had a blower, but always left his walkway alone, because he liked to shovel himself out. There was something satisfying about shoveling your way back into the world, scraping a winding little path from his stoop out to Craigie Street.

He waited till nearly dusk, after the streetlights came on, then shoveled to the street, and walked slowly into Harvard Square. The lights shone differently somehow, more yellow than white, making the grand houses look older, more quaint, more out of place and time as the shadows crept over them, blacker and more sharply defined than usual. He wondered why.

After a winter storm, images in the night air always seem sharper, the silhouettes more distinct. Did the cold do that? The earlier darkness? Maybe it was the contrast with the whiteness of the snow; but no, it must be something else, because it was the same with the shadows cast by the bare trees on the walls of the old homes. He stuffed his hands deep in his coat pockets, twirled his wool scarf tighter around his neck, and walked slowly, hearing the new snow crunch beneath his boots.

It was so much quieter in the wake of the storm. It wasn't just the lack of traffic, though it was certainly light for rush hour. Even the human sounds were softer, more muffled. It was like something else. What? He stopped as he rounded Mass. Ave., where it tumbled crookedly into the square. What was it? He looked up at the sky, almost black above the lights of the city. Yes, that's it; it's the same way the air sounds on the hottest days, that same eerie, muted quiet. Odd. Perhaps it's the birds falling silent, becoming sullen in the worst weather, cold or hot. Not many birds now, though. The quiet was broken by the distant metal screech of plows on the jagged old streets.

Not a good sound. He hunched his shoulders into the wind, and walked over to Brattle Street. Nice to have nothing to do.

The second nor'easter, even stronger, blew in sudden and furious, early Saturday night. Rare to have two so close together, but there were lots of *rare* things happening with the weather these days, weren't there? Good lord, have we actually managed to break the weather?

Kit was spending a few days in Connecticut, so once again, Nathan had nothing to do but savor the storm. He repeated everything he'd done before. He pushed his easy chair to the window, sipped tea, and listened to Corelli. Thought about nothing, deeply.

Around ten, he got a big box out of the bedroom closet, marked *Winter Duds*. He pulled out a pair of too-big sweatpants, a ridiculously oversized hooded sweatshirt, thick wool socks, and his furry slipper socks. The first feel of the huge clothes and the first sounds of those idiot slipper socks—*pluf, pluf, pluf*—always made him feel sublimely ridiculous, almost childlike. But they kept his body heat in, surrounding him with warmth that soaked deep into his bones, since it was actually his warmth, kept close in by the thick, loose clothes.

A little after two in the morning, with the storm still slapping hard against the windows and walls, he took a hot bath, now listening to the droning sixteenth-century choral music of Giovanni Palestrina. All about God, at least that's what the lyrics say; but so sad, full of knowable human yearning and the long fear that is always there.

He unfurled his old comforter and turned the thermostat down. The chillier the apartment was, the more acutely he felt the captured heat within his baggy clothes. He put Palestrina on so low that it felt more like he was remembering it than hearing it, and went to bed. He slept like he was dead.

He awoke heavily. The comforter, full of his own heat, drowned him with a delicious lethargy. Overnight, his solitude had deepened. As he slowly got out of bed, the aloneness filled him, made his ears seem clotted and his eyes cloudy, as if all his senses had thickened and slowed, like almost frozen water. It felt like there was a coat of down inside his head, blanketing his brain with an almost liquid warmth. It was delightful, sensuous, and, he knew, deep down, it was dangerous.

And that's when he started avoiding Kit.

"Nice dy 4 styg wrm ;)"

Nathan stared at the e-mail, shook his head, and stared some more. It was like hieroglyphics, utter nonsense. What did it say? Did it *say* anything? Why was it there, staring at him, bothering him, if it didn't have anything to *say*?

It was from Kit, so he shook his head again and tried to focus. Have to answer this. But what does it *mean*? It was written in that e-mail shorthand so many people use now, as if we're all in too big a hurry for entire words. What's the hurry? What's the hurry? What's the hurry?

He sighed and looked out the window. The sky was still slate gray, but distant portions appeared a little brighter, as if the sun might peek out later. He hoped not; gray was good. He looked back at the computer screen.

"Ah," he whispered, suddenly seeing it: "Nice day for staying warm." And then she'd ended with a semicolon wink. It was the first time he'd heard from Kit since sinking into the delicious comfort of his old dark world, and she was asking about getting together. What could he say? He would say no, of course, not now, not yet. But how could he say that? How could he explain that to her?

He couldn't actually lie, but what was the truth? That he wanted to court his old gray mistress today, tomorrow, a little longer, a little more, alone, a little more alone? How could he tell her that?

He couldn't. Hitting the reply button, he wrote, in his old-school complete words: "Can't. Stuff to do." It seemed brittle, so he added "Sorry," then sent it. Almost immediately she replied "cool. later, k." He turned off the computer. It can't bother him if it's not on.

He put Corelli on the stereo, then quickly replaced it with the darker ache of Palestrina. He sat in the big chair by the window, set his padded feet on the sill, sipped his tea, and stared out into the silence of the storm's wake. He thought little, just felt the old sadness, swelling and ebbing, almost throbbing in that strange way it did. And he welcomed it.

As he sank into the gray, Nathan felt the familiar longing to retreat completely into his solitude. The darkness crept around him, flannel-warm, friendly, and forbidden. It was bad stuff, hugging him, fooling him; making him believe that aloneness was actually a form of feeling, and not numbness. He knew, though, that he needed to go down there, down into the dark, to confront the part of him that still wanted to live there. Or was that his way of making this retreat feel like something else?

Kit was doing a suburban open mike on Tuesday and had told him before the storms that she had to waitress the next few Wednesday nights. She wouldn't be at the jam, either.

Was this about her? He shook his head stupidly. How *much* of this was about her? Were the old mumbles coming back, the old fears about loving someone? Or was this just his craving for a life alone, a life apart, the sad safety of believing there's nothing worth doing, worth even trying to do? He shook his head again, and cranked up the stereo. Later.

What he did know was that he had some time. Time to work into this, burrow into it, see how he felt before he had to face her again. Face her? Jesus, it sounded like he was stepping out on her. Was he? Later.

He didn't do much, puttered around the house, shoveled his walkway, hung all his winter clothes in the closet, and put his T-shirts and shorts in the *Winter Duds* box for spring. Mostly, he stared, out the window, at the walls, at pictures in old magazines, and thought about nothing, deeply.

He played his guitar, always huddled near the windows, looking out at the dead white winter. He sang every wintry song he knew but dwelled on "Frankie On the Sheepscot," by Maine songwriter Gordon Bok. It was about two hardscrabble fishermen trying to work the Sheepscot River in winter. But mostly, it was just about winter.

> *He's never got a hat on, and the snow is all about him,*
> *And it packs around his head like his own skin.*

Nathan was hypnotized by the rhythm he played on the guitar, a quick 3/4 roll of treble notes, slapping against the slower drone of the bass strings. It was like a slow boat bobbing in a fast river, the high strings lapping like waves and the driving bass notes like the rushing current.

And yet most of the lyrics tumbled out in 4/4 time, as if struggling against the relentless cadence of the river. It felt tense and unbalanced, like a body lurching this way and that, trying to stay steady on a swaying surface.

> *"Don't I hate this foolish river!" Frankie cries,*
> *"Up and down her like a yo-yo on a string.*
> *Go out in the morning and tear up,*
> *Mend all your afternoon,*
> *And all this dirty river staving by."*

But Nathan wasn't hearing the words, just feeling the winter cold in them. It was the motion and the winter images that entranced him. He would only play the guitar sometimes, waiting for the most vivid winter lines, and singing them.

> *There's nothing out there but hard times,*
> *And time and the flying snow.*

He would stop singing, and play that hard, rolling guitar rhythm—the quick-rushing trebles notes against the slow slap of the bass strings, waiting, waiting. Then he'd sing:

> *And time and the flying snow.*
> *And time and the flying snow.*

Again, he would close his mouth, shut his eyes, and feel the unbalance between the 3/4 guitar and 4/4 verses, like a life lived out of time, careening to and fro, struggling to stay upright against a world with its own cadence, its own purpose.

And time and the flying snow,
And all that pretty river rolling by.

By Tuesday, Nathan found it difficult to talk, even to sing. He had prepared a set exploring different types of work songs, but that was out of the question. Sea chanteys and field hollers? "Haul away, Joe," and, "Whoa, back, buck?" Not a chance.

Hunched in front of the Dooley's microphones, head down, he opened with a quiet instrumental, daring the audience to give him their attention. Then he sang "Frankie On the Sheepscot," barely above a whisper. He finished with what was, to him, the most wintry of the old British ballads, "Unquiet Grave," with its desolate introduction:

The wind blows cold on my true love,
And a few small drops of rain.
I never had but one true love;
And in greenwood she lies slain.

Afterwards, Ferguson muttered, "Either lighten up, or give me a toke of what you've been smoking, hoss. You okay?"

Nathan shrugged, said, "Winter," and walked away. Even Ferguson was too much company right now.

On Wednesday, Kit e-mailed, writing only, "RUOK?" After a few bleary moments deciphering it, he wondered if she was beginning to worry. But that seemed ridiculous: why would she? Worry about him? Someone like Kit?

Still, he couldn't keep ignoring her. He wrote back, "I'm taking a little time by myself." That was true, wasn't it? She wrote back immediately, saying, "gd 4 u. xxx K."

On Thursday, she e-mailed again: "still ok?" He replied, "Yes, fine." Then, feeling utterly foolish, but hoping it might send the right message, he added three x's at the end. She did not reply.

By Sunday, Nathan knew he was in trouble.

He thought about all the years he had spent this way, not just alone but dug in, entrenched in his aloneness. You don't realize how passive you get; you just start whittling away at your life. You tell yourself you're prioritizing: you don't need this, don't need that. But how can you prioritize when nothing seems important? Because life is no longer something you're doing; it's something that's happening to you, a storm hitting you from all sides. What can you do? People, places, things, events: they have nothing to do with you. And you have nothing to do with them.

It's the little details you start to ignore first, the everyday things; and you say you're focusing on the necessary things. But you're not getting to them either. This errand can wait until tomorrow; you don't need to do that chore right now. Instead, you look out the window, and ponder how little you have to do with anything in your life. The storm is everywhere; there's no sense moving, nowhere safer, warmer, happier. Hunker down, wait it out. Wait it out. Wait it out.

Nathan looked out the window, remembering what it was like back then, when nothing seemed like it was worth doing.

"God, but I was deep in," he whispered and got up to make some coffee.

He returned to the window, sipping his coffee; and for some reason remembered the day, several years ago, when he first went out to buy a plant. Something alive in the house, he thought. He couldn't even conceive of it as something *else* alive in the house. Not yet. But it was a first swing of the hammer against the great gray wall he'd built around himself; and it let in a small, but crucial, shard of light. Had he known that at the time? No. Well, maybe a little. Dimly.

Now he saw it with such clarity: his first convincing blow against the comforting dark. Those weak, early blows accomplish so much more than they seem to at the time. They are the mortal wounds to the darkness you are fighting your way out of. The rest simply widen the crack through which your life can pour back in. Those first blows win the war; only battles follow.

His first blow began so innocently. The winter after he quit drinking, he picked up a little Christmas tree at the nearby Whole Foods market. It was perched ridiculously on the meat counter, a tiny fir about two feet high, bedecked in dorky ornaments. He looked sympathetically at it, thinking it would probably be grateful to get out of the public eye with all those stupid things on its boughs. It looked embarrassed, at least to Nathan, like a dog dressed up cutely, pleasing only its owner.

He brought the little tree home, took off its dorky ornaments and let it just be a tree. What's wrong with that? But he also lined up the ornaments on the kitchen counter, because Christmas was a time for dorkiness.

After the holidays, the damn thing just wouldn't shrivel up and die, like the card it came with said it would. Some spreading green thing was now growing out of its soil, all heathery and delicate; and the tree's boughs seemed to be spreading. He wasn't sure it was really growing; it wasn't supposed to. Maybe it was just his imagination. But one morning in late January, it was unmistakable: the larger boughs were beginning to bend toward the morning light in the window.

Well, he couldn't throw it out now; it was getting acclimated. It seemed happy, and it certainly wasn't bothering him. A little water now and then wasn't such a big chore. And when it goes all brown in a week or two, that'll be that.

Six months later, it was getting a little brown around the bough tops, but still happily stretching toward the window. When it finally died in late July, its needles brown and falling, Nathan felt a little lonesome for it.

That's when he decided to go buy a plant. Such a thing had been unthinkable in his traveling days, when he'd be away for months at a time. Much of his austere lifestyle had been a stubborn refusal to give up those old road priorities. It had also gotten easy to not do things.

Still, it was nice having that little tree around; nice knowing he was making something happy by giving it a gurgle of water, sliding it closer to the window that it liked so much. Nice to be connected to something living.

But as usual he hesitated a day, two, a week. Something wriggling inside him back then, however, made him want to follow through. Not because having a plant was so important, he told himself, but isn't it time you started following through on some of these things? You can do anything you want. You're sober now; the world is your oyster. Lord, what a revolting image. What moron dreamed up that one?

And so, one blustery summer Saturday, he drove to a nearby nursery with a large sign that said *Live Organic Plants*. He wasn't sure what kind of live plant one could buy other than an organic one; but it had always looked like a friendly place, and he'd always wished it had something he wanted to buy so he could find out if it was.

This was that day.

He didn't know what he wanted, except that he didn't care much for flowers. He liked things that looked wild, or at least a little weedy. He'd loved the heathery little thing that sprouted out of the tree's soil: something like that, perhaps. Something wild, not cultivated, bred, and hybridized. Maybe that's what they meant by organic plants. He hoped so. A little patch of outdoors for the house, that's all; a bit of meadow by the window.

He found a sprawling, low plant that looked very much like a tiny meadow. It grew this way and that, thick in some places, thin in others. The clerk told him it needed little care, just some water and window light.

But as he asked questions, he made the mistake of saying he'd never had a plant before, and the woman helping him decided to help this poor man join the green world. By the time she was through, Nathan had bought a huge box of organic plant food, a water spritzer for the leaves, a bag of organic soil (organic *dirt?*), and three sizes of pots to accommodate the plant as it grew. Wandering out to the parking lot in a daze, he was surprised she hadn't made him sign adoption papers.

He remembered all that now, years later, gazing out at the snowy yard from his kitchen window. He was surprised at how much more clearly he saw it today than he did back then; how much he understood about how important it had been. Too bad about that; he should have thought better of himself back then. Prouder.

They were hard, those first few steps, very hard. Always the most painful. And yet, he took them; small and clumsy though they were. He took them.

He looked out at the inviting shadows of the gathering dusk. No, he thought. Just that single word. No.

Once, and then twice, he said it out loud.

No. No.

Nathan wasn't sure what he had to think about, as he pulled on his old leather coat the next afternoon. He didn't know where the day's brood would take him, just that it was time to *think this through*. He was beginning to bore himself, always a good sign; and he was worried about Kit. What must she be thinking?

Enough! Get a handle on this, damn it; brood to your heart's content, but figure this out. Those were the marching orders, and where else but Harvard Square, God's own brooding ground?

Everybody surrenders a little as they get older, he thought as he wandered into the square. The sidewalks were more narrowly shoveled since the second storm, only a thin footpath between shoulder-high banks of snow. People turned sideways to pass each other, most smiling and whispering "excuse me" as they squeezed by. Not being in the mood for that much conversation, Nathan walked into the street. Large pools of icy, dirty water lined the streets, forcing him too often into traffic. He walked toward the roomier spaces on the far side of the square.

Maybe you simply get tired, he thought. Restful. You begin to like things being uneventful. Events aren't all they're cracked up to be, you realize as you get older. You don't want more grand failures, and if the price for that is giving up hope of grand success, well, that seems reasonable. How many grand successes were there?

Maybe that's why he enjoyed Kit's ambition, when he had, most decidedly, not enjoyed Joyce's. He still had ambition then: fire rubbing against fire. Was that it?

He stopped in the heart of the square, where Mass. Ave. meets quirky Brattle Street, watching the first rush-hour cars plod slowly by. Was that it? Was he lamenting his lost ambition?

Dusk was beginning to fall. It comes so early this time of year. Car lights came on but didn't brighten the road. The sky over the university was no longer blue and not yet gray, and stark shadows crept up the redbrick walls. Lost ambition. Was that it?

He strolled down JFK Street, hands stuffed in his coat pockets, past where a storied music bar once was, now a pizza place; past where another famous nightclub had been. It became a comedy club, then a Buck a Book, and then a fast-food sandwich joint. There's progress for you.

Had he given up? Was that it? Surrendered? What did he want from his music anymore? Was he still lusting after another try at the brass ring? Ridiculous. At his age? He knew he couldn't compete with the likes of Kit. That was still a game for the young.

And if he could—even if he could—did he still want to? Touring? Where's the motel tonight? Giving up his little lair for months at a time? He remembered something Joyce had told him when she was on top of the pop charts. They were getting a bit drunk backstage after her first sold-out show at Symphony Hall, Boston's most prestigious venue. Her triumphant return.

"There's a bad moment," she whispered, as though sharing a secret, "when you realize that a tour bus is just a bus. You're living on a bus—that's your dream come true. A bus."

At the time, he'd thought she was gloating, in her typically self-serving way—only Joyce could pout and boast in the same breath. But she was also trying to warn him, wasn't she? Or perhaps to comfort him. Maybe she always knew he wasn't going where she went.

Now, wandering across JFK Street in the winter twilight, Nathan thought about how much he enjoyed his ordinary mornings. Coffee or tea? Running or yard work? Corelli or Woody Guthrie? He loved that, especially after all the hard, empty years of cheap motels and strangers' sofas. These domestic rituals gave him pleasure so disproportionate to the small comforts they provided. It was as close to contentment as his train wreck of a life had ever let him get. But there was a certain surrender to it, too. Lie down, you've fought long enough. Take it easy. There, there, now.

Well, then, what *did* he want? Did he want *anything* anymore? The question sounded bad and he tried to bat it away. Later, later. But he knew; instantly, he knew.

A narrow cobbled sidewalk lined with wooden benches cut across a tiny common called Winthrop Square. Nathan walked to the bench in front of Grendel's Den, once his favorite Harvard Square watering hole. He brushed off the snow and sat down. So what *did* he want?

But before he asked, he knew. Even as he brushed the snow, he knew. The answer had come in one small, simple word: useful. He wanted to pick up his guitar and feel like it mattered to someone besides pitying old friends, hopeless students, and hungry open-mikers.

As soon as he thought that, however, he knew it wasn't true. He would have believed it a few years ago. He would have ignored the fact that he wasn't being fair to his students, who took such delight in being able to learn their favorite songs; and that most of his open-mikers welcomed his praise and advice. They no longer bristled impatiently while he did his little sets. Hell, some of them took notes. Kit took notes.

So today, with the winter darkness falling around him, the thought of his music being useful—at least a little bit useful—brightened his mood and quickened his breath. It didn't remind him of all the things he had once wanted so much, but of what he had now, today. It made him think of the set he'd drawn up on work songs, and how excited he'd been to try it. Before the storm; before the return of the welcoming gray, the comfortable cold.

And it made him think of Kit.

He was of some use to her, wasn't he? She would get where she was going with or without him, but that wasn't the point. He was helping her. He loved that about their relationship. Around her, somehow, he didn't feel like such a failure, even as he watched her career surpass his, in such simple easy hops. He didn't mind it a bit; in fact, it was great fun rooting for her. Why? Well, here you are again, right back where you started.

He looked around at little Winthrop Square, with its snowy lawn and neatly lined benches. Near the curb, there was a curious stone marker, old and broken, saying *Newtowne Market*. It was from the early seventeenth-century, bearing the city's original name; before it became a college town in 1637 and decided "Cambridge" was a more erudite moniker. Nathan grinned. There's actually a date certain for when this town first aspired to pretentiousness.

Snow lay in the jagged, stone edges of the broken marker, and Nathan wondered how long it had lain like that. It had obviously belonged to something grander once.

He sighed loudly, and got back to the topic at hand. Where was I? Ah, yes, Kit, lovely Kit. She was the only thing in his life that didn't feel complicated to him.

What? How could that be? She's a woman, for god's sakes, and she's in love with you. And you find that uncomplicated? *You*? His feelings toward her certainly seemed complicated: lover, mentor, compadre, peer, teacher, to name a few. But they all somehow resolved into the single, imponderable sensation of love. She filled him in so many different ways, and he loved them all. So why was he avoiding her? Ah, well, that's easy: because Nathan Warren complicates everything, and nothing so thoroughly as the uncomplicated.

Oh, screw that. Not fair. He needed to think this through, to face the old longings, the solitary life he'd lived for so long. And he needed to do that alone.

So. Is that it? Are we done? His mood was brightening; but nothing much got settled, did it? Yes, it did. You asked yourself a Big Question; and you got an answer. Sort of. But then, most of the Big Questions have only sort-of answers. He'd learned that much.

He thought about the lure of the solitude, how quickly it had seduced him in the dusk of that first storm. Kit is not the problem; your feelings for her are not the problem. But she's not the answer, either. The great emptiness you've worn around you like a favorite old blanket, the emptiness that was almost a lover to you, is neither ended by her nor deepened by her. Funny, you'd think it would be one or the other.

But it is lifting, he realized. That great empty space is lifting. A little. Let it. Don't push it, but let it. It's still there, that's for sure; maybe it always will be. Does a fog like that ever lift completely? Probably not; the aloneness would always be part of him. He'd have to try to explain that to her; she needed to know, deserved to know. And he'd think more about that notion of being useful.

So yes, I guess we're done now. Nathan slapped his thighs, straightened up on the bench, and said, "Well, okay then." Was that out loud? He glanced around, but nobody seemed to notice. Yeah, like talking to yourself in Harvard Square is going to draw attention. Peeing on the monuments, maybe; but then again, this is rush hour. He got up, laughing to himself, and walked home.

Before he called Kit, he wrote a note to himself on a small piece of paper, folded it neatly, and put it in his wallet. It was a trick he used for remembering things, but he'd never used it quite this way. It didn't say "Buy strings" or "Only two drinks an hour." It said, "Don't be so fond of safety."

The large moments of our lives, the crossroads moments where the choices we make really matter, are rarely kind enough to come to us boldly, announcing their importance. Nathan had just traveled through one of those moments, though he wouldn't know that for some time. And when he finally did, he would realize it had been a very different moment than he thought at the time.

But what was important then, and always in these moments, is that he faced it as honestly as he could. So how he passed through that moment, although he didn't understand it yet, set him on the better path. Even now, he thanked Kit for that. What would take him more time to figure out was what he was thanking her for.

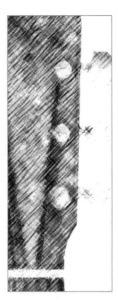

Seven

Kit was distant over the phone. Nathan tried to read her mood. Wary? Cold? Angry? Or was she making an effort to sound casual? He couldn't tell, and that frightened him.

He said he was calling to ask if she'd be coming to Dooley's Tuesday. But he was really calling to ask her back into his tangled life. She said she had to go back to a suburban open mike she'd performed a few weeks before. The host liked her and wanted the owner of the bistro to hear her. Then she might get a weekend gig.

"Great," Nathan said. "That gig can be a tough nut to crack. Impressive."

"Yeah. Um, yeah. Thanks."

"Are you okay?" he asked.

"Sure, why wouldn't I be?"

Nathan didn't want to have the conversation they needed to have, not over the phone. "Well, I've been kind of squirreled away the last couple of weeks, and—"

"You said you needed some time to yourself. That's cool. I understand that. I'm not—" She cut herself short.

What was that tone in her voice? He couldn't read it, but it sure as hell wasn't "Gee, I miss you, honey." There was a distance he'd never felt from her. What was it?

"I'm glad you understand," he said. "It really wasn't—"

"What's not to understand?" she said sharply. Then he heard her clear her throat, muffled and far away, as if she'd moved the phone away from her mouth.

"I'd like to see you, Kit," he said.

"Um. I...I'm waitressing all week. Filling in for someone and doing my own shifts. But I—" Again, she cut herself short. He wished he could read her mood.

After another awkward silence, Nathan said, "Hey, I've got an idea. I'm playing a house concert on the North Shore Saturday. It's hosted by the same couple who run a coffeehouse up there."

"Mmm-hmm," she said. Jesus, she's not even making vowel sounds now.

"Anyway, when I couldn't draw a big enough crowd for the coffeehouse, they started hiring me for these little house concerts. Because they still like me, you know?"

Another pause filled the air. He heard her clear her throat.

"How would you like to come up there with me?" he said. "We could do the show together. You know, swapping songs."

"I'd like that," she said. Her voice sounded a little brighter. Not excited, but a bit more animated. Like it was coming from somebody with a pulse.

"They'll really love you up there, I think, and they enjoy surprises."

"I'd like that."

"Not a big crowd, very informal." He was rambling now, but he couldn't help it. "It's more like a party than a concert, you know? A lot of folks from other coffeehouses come. I'll bet you get some gigs out of it."

"I'd like that, Nathan." And finally, she laughed. Nathan closed his eyes, savoring the sound.

But then there was more silence. Finally, Kit said, "Nathan?"

"Yes, Kit?" It came out sounding more formal than he intended, but for some reason he wanted to say her name.

"House concert. I've never done one before. Is it like a coffeehouse? I mean, what should I wear? Should I dress up?"

"A little more casual than a coffeehouse. It's in a big living room. No sound system. But it's still a show."

"Makeup?"

"Well, I think you look really pretty when you wear a little."

She laughed again, but softly. "Well, I'll wear a little, then. See you Saturday."

"I'll swing by your place around six, okay?" He'd hoped it would be sooner than the weekend, but he didn't want to push her.

"Okay," she said.

He paused a moment. "I love you, Kit," he said. "I—"

"That's nice to hear," she said. He could barely hear her. And then she hung up. He still couldn't read her.

Kit carefully put her guitar and fiddle in the back seat of the car, on top of Nathan's guitar, and slid into the front seat. She was wearing a short, fluffy white parka with fur-like fuzz around the hood that billowed when she moved. Eyeliner enhanced the contrast of her dark eyes against the whiteness of her skin and winter pink of her cheeks. For a moment, seeing her again left Nathan speechless. Could he have actually forgotten how pretty she was? Or did she do this to him every time he saw her?

"I wanted to hook up early," Nathan said, "because I thought we should talk a little about the last couple of weeks."

"Before the gig?" she asked, staring ahead through the windshield.

"Yeah, clear the air."

She nodded solemnly. "Clear the air," she said. She still didn't look at him.

He reached over and turned her head toward him. Then he kissed her. "The first thing I want to say is that I love you, Kit," he said.

"Love you, too," she said quietly. He noticed that her arms started to raise as he kissed her, then fell back into her lap. Uncertain? Nervous? Angry? He still couldn't read her.

Nathan smiled, but she again turned to look out the windshield. "Look," he said, "when those nor'easters hit, I really fell back into myself. I was alone for a long time before we met. Years. And I don't mean just not having anyone in my life. I mean alone. Solitary. You get used to it."

"Used to it," she repeated, almost whispering. Was she hurt? Confused? Trying not to be angry? She puffed one of those little nervous breaths, the way she had when they first met. God, had he pushed them that far back?

"When you've been alone that long," he said, "it gets comfortable, very…intoxicating, I guess."

"Intoxicating," she said, nodding her head. She turned her head to look at him.

"It's not just that you're on your own," he said. "It's something deep down, a solitude that feels sort of warm, safe, comfortable. It gets easy to stay there, wrap it all around you."

"Comfortable, yes. Well, I can see that." She was bobbing her head, then seemed to catch herself. She straightened her back, looked out the windshield, and cleared her throat. "And I was pushing you too much," she said.

"What? No, I—"

"Pushing you, pushing you, pushing you. Being my usual nosy, busybody self. Do my radio show, do my class, do this, do that. *Please*, Nathan; oh, *please*, Nathan. Busybody, busybody."

"No, Kit, no. That wasn't…not at all…I—"

But she wasn't listening. It was as if something she'd been holding in suddenly burst out. She started bumping her head on the dashboard, muttering "Busybody, busybody, busybody!"

"No, Kit, it wasn't like that at all. I just—"

"*Busy*-body, you *busy*-body!"

"Stop that! You'll hurt yourself."

"So what?" she said and whispered another hot "*Busybody.*" Then she straightened up and looked out the side window, her gloved hand over her mouth.

Oh no, Nathan thought, Kit blamed herself for all this. That's why he couldn't read her before; that possibility never occurred to him. He pushed her away, so she assumed she'd done something wrong, then tried to figure out what it was. Wheedling him into doing the radio interview, and then, the same day, roping him into the folk music class.

So she'd spent the last two weeks worrying that *she'd* pushed *him* away. And why? Because she was proud of him. Because she tried to let a little honest sunshine into his dank life. You prick, you utter prick. Hiding away in the great fat universe of yourself. You prick.

"I'm so sorry, Kit," he said softly, his voice trembling a little. "So sorry. No, this was all on me, all on me."

She looked over at him, her eyes now unmistakably wary. How could he have not anticipated that Kit would find some way to blame herself? Perhaps it was simply inconceivable to him: a woman like her, fretting over the affections of someone like him. Jesus, get *over* yourself! She loves you, you brooding prick. She loves you.

"Kit, it didn't have anything to do with that stuff," he said, reaching over to stroke her cheek with the back of his fingers. "I love that about you, that you like to, you know, show me off a little. And I like it that you push me, get me off my tired, old butt, doing new things."

She leaned her head into his hand and said, "Really? But I thought—"

"Really. Count on it." He took a deep breath, then put his hands back on the wheel and looked out the windshield. "This was all about me and the funk I've been in so much of my life. Those storms knocked me back into all that, and I felt like I had to indulge it a little, go back in there, figure out how I felt now. Aloneness like that—"

"I know," she said. "I mean, I think I do, a little. I was like that when I was in college, you know, my depression. My black-clothes period. All I wanted was to get back to my room. So I do know, kind of. It's almost like it's your best friend sometimes."

Nathan smiled. "There were a couple of times I almost felt like I was cheating on you. By staying home and staring out the window."

"Were you?" Her voice was different now, a little stronger and quite a bit older. And there was some warmth in it.

He laughed softly. "Maybe. Maybe a little. That's why I couldn't explain it to you. I needed to get down in there, see how much of me still lived there."

"And?"

"And," he said and paused a moment. This would be the hard part. "And the real answer is that some of me is still down there, probably always will be." He turned to her. "I want you to know that. You deserve to know that."

He touched her shoulder. "But more than anything," he said, "I realized how much I want to be with you. But that part of me, that alone part—"

"You like it," she said.

"What? Yes, I guess that's it. I like it."

"Me too."

"Like it? You mean, you like being alone?"

"Well, yes, that, too." She looked at him. "No, what I mean is I like that about you, that solitude. It's one of the first things that attracted me. For some reason, I tend to attract guys who are very, um, needy. I saw that solitude in you, and I thought, 'Well, here's one I'm not gonna have to babysit.' And also, you know, there's something about that lonesome quality that made me want to, like, cheer you up. Everybody feels that way about you, you know. But I also thought this is a guy who'd let me live my own life, give me room to be who I want to be."

She thought for a long time, and he let her. He had no idea what would come next. She could be angry or relieved, contented or betrayed. All valid. He finally realized she was waiting for him.

"Anyway," he said, "I needed to have a good old brood, go where it wanted to take me, see how it felt. Maybe I needed to catch up with how much my life has changed since I met you. Because it's changed a lot. I should have told you, but what would I have said: 'I just want to see if being with you is really better than being alone?'"

She smiled. "Yeah, I can see how a girl might take that the wrong way." He laughed. Then she looked at him, and her face turned serious.

"And?"

He smiled. "And it's all good, Kit, all good. Look, sweetie, I love that you push me; I love it that you want people to see me the way you do. I love that you're trying to coax me out of my hard little shell. Please don't stop; it makes me feel, well, things I haven't felt for a long time, things I thought I'd never feel again. Not just romantic things, but things about my music, my work, who I am."

"And it's okay?"

"More than okay. I love you, Kit. I want you in my life, just the way you are." He leaned over and kissed her, and this time her arms came over his shoulders. They held each other for a long time.

"So that's it?" she said and he nodded. "Nathan, all that stuff's fine with me. I don't want you to feel like you have to be someone different with me. I don't like it that I'm so pushy sometimes, but—"

"Kit, I—"

She raised her hand. She wanted to finish this. "But you can always push back. I need you to know that. Because I will, too. Push back, I mean. I'm a songwriter, just like you. You need to be alone a lot to do that. You have to like being alone. That's why I want my own place."

She looked up at her apartment and heaved an exasperated sigh. "As alone as I can get in that catbox."

She paused, measuring what she was going to say. She was taking charge of the conversation, which Nathan took as a very good sign.

"Look," she said. "Let's just, like, promise we won't worry about that stuff with each other. Let's both, starting now, say we won't tell each other why we don't want to get together. We'll just say it's not a good time. Both of us. No explanations, no excuses. Because you're right; sometimes anything you say is going to sound bad. You just want to be alone."

She smiled at him and laid out her hands palms up. See? See how easy?

"I don't know," he said. "I kind of like being able to check up on *you*." Too early for a joke? She slapped his arm and laughed. Another good sign.

"Seriously, it's a good idea," he said, "I don't know why I expected this to be harder for you to understand."

"Because you keep forgetting how truly remarkable I am?" She batted her eyes. Boy, that felt good. She was teasing, which meant she was feeling comfortable with him again.

"I do forget how smart you are, Kit," he said. "And quick to figure things out." He let out a breath. "And kind. The way you understand people, feel what they're feeling. It's very kind."

She said nothing, but smiled and rubbed his arm.

"So you're not upset?" he said. "You have a right to be, you know."

She looked out the windshield. "Oh, as long as it's honesty time," she said, "I guess I am a little. If I'd known what was going on, maybe I wouldn't have worried so much. But like you said, anything you told me probably would have made it sound like an even bigger crisis."

Even bigger crisis. Man, she really was worried. You prick. Add that to your little list of home improvements: you're not doing this by yourself anymore. Your feelings are not entirely your own business anymore. You hurt her; you scared her.

"I'm so sorry for that, Kit," he said. "I never want you to have to worry about me, about how I feel about you."

She smiled at him, stroked his arm, and kissed him. Then she straightened in her seat, slapped her gloved hands on her thighs, and said, "So tell me about this place we're playing tonight."

The gig! Great leaping Jesus, the gig. Guitar! He looked nervously in the rear-view mirror and saw his guitar case underneath Kit's. Well, let's hope you remembered to put your guitar in it. He looked at his watch. Six-thirty. Still plenty of time. We'll just miss rush hour.

"Onward," he said.

Kit was still a little wary on the drive up to the North Shore. She wanted to know what house concerts were like but hesitated before asking questions, as if she didn't want to pester. Damn. He loved it when she pestered him. It was going to take awhile to get it out of her head that this had been her fault.

He filled the awkward silences with babble about the long, strange history of house concerts. Folk music began in people's homes, not concert halls. It was the music of ordinary people, the self-made soundtrack to their daily lives. As it struggled to become a modern music genre, it often returned home when times got hard.

In the 1950s, a burgeoning commercial folk revival was stamped out by the anticommunist hysteria. Many folk stars, including Woody Guthrie, Lead Belly, Pete Seeger, and his hugely popular group the Weavers, were blacklisted for their leftist politics. Most commercial venues closed their doors to any kind of folk music. The whole notion of singing "people's songs" was likely to get you suspected of communist sympathies. So you like *folk* music, eh, comrade?

So the music returned to its roots. House concerts sprouted up all over the country, helping to keep stars like Seeger working through the worst of the Red Scare.

But house concerts went back even further. The Boston Irish used to host *ceilis*, or dance parties, in their homes. They called them kitchen rackets, because that's where the musicians and dancers tended to gather. Around the turn of the twentieth century, musical rent parties in African American homes gave rise to the jug-band craze, so named because ordinary household objects like cider jugs and washboards were turned into musical instruments.

In the forties, those traditions were picked up by urban intellectuals fomenting the commercial folk revival. Woody Guthrie, who'd moved to New York City by then, used the word *hootenanny* to describe these informal music parties. He said he'd heard the word on his travels, but nobody has been able to document its use before him, and some suspect he made it up. True or not, it's just the kind of whimsical-sounding word Guthrie would have made up: Let's have a hootenanny! Wherever the word came from, it sure sounded like a music party.

In the fifties, hootenannies began to spread to college campuses, embraced by rebellious students who savored the underground luster of folk music. Then as now, the idea of making music for yourself instead of buying it at the record store seemed radically anti-commercial. The birth pangs of the sixties folk revival can be traced to those campus hootenannies, so it's possible to argue that house concerts were the jumper cables that ignited what Utah Phillips liked to call "the great folk scare of the sixties."

Kit listened quietly, letting Nathan babble on, though he suspected she was more interested in the gig they were doing tonight than a blowzy overview of the house concert's impact on Western civilization. Occasionally, he saw that indulgent smile she often wore when he rambled on about folk music. But she didn't tease him the way she usually did, and he was sorry for that.

They followed the winding road through Salem, past the ominous black Witch House, which was actually where one of the 1692 witchcraft trial judges had lived, now converted into a spooky tourist attraction. As they drove into Marblehead, the road narrowed around the harbor, offering peeks of dark water with every hairpin turn.

Snow was piled in high, sugary banks. It was still early winter, before the roadside
snow turned mud brown and grimy. A nice time of year.

The road was little more than a path by the time they passed Marblehead center,
and the smaller the road became, the older the houses were. They were in a virtual
Currier & Ives painting when Nathan turned onto tiny Mugford Street and drove
up a hill, past the coffeehouse where he was once the most popular headliner, and
around another corner to the house where they were playing. The living room where
his career's dust had settled. Almost unconsciously, he sighed.

"What?" Kit asked loudly. Boy, she was skittish.

"Nothing," he said. "I just have good memories of playing that old coffeehouse.
We passed it on the left.

"That little wooden church?"

"Yeah. Lovely place."

While they looked for a parking place, Kit talked about a song she wrote during
the second nor'easter. "Nothing else to do," she said with a shrug. Oh sure, there was.
You could have stared out the window for a week and a half, pondering why the snow
piles more to the left than the right.

As they got out of the car, Nathan took a deep breath, tossing his shoulders back.
It always seemed colder on the North Shore than in town; but the winter air was crisp
and moist, feeling against the skin the way ice water tastes in your mouth. He noticed
the slight musk of wood smoke in the air. Away from the city lights, the sky was ink
black, the stars startlingly white against it.

"Boy," Kit said, taking a breath and exhaling loudly. "Get that air. It's so sweet.
What do they put in it up here?"

"Oxygen, I think."

"Suppose they'd bottle it for us city folks? Cute little roadside stands?"

"Don't give them ideas."

The house was owned by David and Dianne Gretz. He was the minister of the
Unitarian church where the coffeehouse was held. She was an environmental attorney
in Boston, well known in legal circles for a series of lawsuits against chemical companies in the western part of the state.

Dianne Gretz met Nathan and Kit at the door, opening it to the sounds of
chatter and clinking glassware. Just like a party. After a small parlor, the house opened
into a huge living room and off to the left, a long dining room. The performance area
was at the junction of the two rooms, so people could watch from either spot. Two
straight-back chairs sat there for Nathan and Kit, in front of a large fireplace which
was, thankfully, not burning. One year Nathan sang in front of a raging fire, and one
side of his face was noticeably red for days. Ah, show biz.

The living room was lined with folding chairs. Along the wall by the front door
was a long sofa, flanked by easy chairs. Four wooden rocking chairs sat along the side

wall, already wearing the coats of people who'd claimed them. They were the prized seats, with the sofa coming in a close second. Something about watching a folk concert from a rocking chair seemed so, well, folksy.

About twenty people mingled near the dining room table, filled with homemade sweets, appetizers, and a few steaming hot dishes. Like many house concerts, this was also a potluck supper, making it feel even more like a party.

Nathan and Kit put their instruments by the straight-back chairs and followed Dianne to the buffet table. Kit grabbed a glass of cider and gazed hungrily at the food.

"It's all homemade, isn't it?" she asked sadly.

"Oh, yeah," Nathan said. "Great desserts. Chocolate toffee cookies to die for. They're Dianne's specialty."

"I skipped dinner," Kit said. Then she saw a platter full of small, round, yellow pies. Her eyes bugged. "What are those?"

"Baby quiche, I think," Nathan said.

"No, no, they can't be," she said. "I love baby quiche."

"You'll burp through your ballads."

"I baked them," Dianne Gretz said. She was a willowy middle-aged woman with straight blond hair that fell slightly below her ears. "They're made with Gruyere instead of Swiss. Creamier that way."

Kit gave her a pained smile. "Gruyere? They're, like, my favorite. My mom makes them."

"Help yourself."

"No, I can't. But not because Nathan told me not to."

"Why, then?"

"Because I'll burp through my ballads."

"I appreciate the distinction," Dianne said, laughing. She turned to Nathan. "How are you, Nathan? We don't see you enough these days."

"I'm fine," he said. "Good. Fine."

"That's all you'll get," Kit said, still eyeing the quiche platter. "Believe me, I've tried."

Dianne laughed again, then walked off to see to her other guests.

Kit was wearing neatly pressed black jeans and a soft yellow sweater. The look was perfect, casual and dressy at the same time. A house, but still a show.

"You look great tonight," he said.

"Thanks," she said, rubbing his arm.

He started to tell her that he meant she had dressed well for a house concert, but thought better of it. You earned a rub; leave it alone.

Nathan began the show with "One for Winter," a song Gordon Bok had written with another Maine songwriter, Cindy Kallet. When Nathan was pulling out of his funk, he began singing it instead of "Frankie On the Sheepscot." It had that same wintry Maine feel, but with its brisk cadence and promise of spring, it also had a snap-out-of-it vibe that he found helpful.

> *One for winter, two for spring,*
> *Three for the evening sky.*
> *All you need is a little sign,*
> *But spring is a candle in the wind.*
> *Hey-o, say-o, oh for the joy you bring.*

Nathan was thinking about Kit when he decided to open the show this way. This was her first house concert; he wanted to set a comfortable mood for her. Everything about the song had a midrange feel, from its minor-key darkness to its "hey-o, say-o" strut to its melding of winter landscapes and spring ebullience.

> *As I come over the hills of home,*
> *I heard the kestrel cry.*
> *And all the hills gave on the song,*
> *And the world was full of sky-o.*

Kit picked up on the easygoing mood Nathan had set and was soon chatting with the crowd as if they were all having a slumber party.

Midway through their second set, she sang her new song. It was set to a minor-key melody in the "Wayfaring Stranger" mode, stark and traditional-sounding, yet unmistakably her own, with an oddly accentuated backbeat that made it feel simultaneously ancient and modern.

It began with a simple thought we all have: How do birds know when it's time to migrate? But the way she asked the question showed that she was thinking about very human things.

> *Is there something in the wind,*
> *Breathes a chill in your heart and life in your wings,*
> *Does it whisper, 'start again,'*
> > *Start again?*

The second verse was a similar question, but more abstract, more allegorical, about where the sun goes in the night. Nature was now unmistakably a metaphor for our own fears and yearnings.

> *Where is your home, restless wind,*
> *Is it there, is it here?*
> *Do you search for a place to belong,*
> *Search in vain, search in fear?*
> *Or is your spirit everywhere,*

Is your voice every tree,
Your soul of the air?
If there's no home, is there no death,
Is there no death?

Like the old spirituals from which Kit modeled the song, the lyrics turned the doubt and sorrow of the human experience into something uplifting and eternal. The feelings were intimate, but she used the natural imagery to turn them outward. These were everybody's doubts, everybody's sorrows, everybody's hopes.

The crowd applauded firmly, not loudly but quickly, showing the intensity of its approval, until Kit burst into a full-face blush, which intensified the ovation. Audiences always felt strangely flattered by that blush of hers, as if they had coaxed something special from her, something unguarded and real.

Nathan stared at Kit, dazed by the quiet power of the song. In that moment, he forgot she was his lover and saw her only as an artist, as only another artist can. And he knew, as an artist, that he could never have written such a song. Where did it come from, this primal understanding of pain and fear? How could she *know* these things? And yet there were only questions in the song. We all know those, if only we close our eyes and listen.

Nathan leaned over and whispered so only she would hear: "It's a great song, Kit, great song." His tone was solemn, showing that he meant this artist to artist, songwriter to songwriter. She held his look, acknowledging its seriousness, then turned back to the crowd, nodding and smiling as the ovation slowly died down.

After the show, the crowd mingled around them as they made their way to the buffet. The attention performers get at house concerts can be disquietingly intense. It's not starshine; it's more personal. Something about the closeness of the environment makes fans feel as if they've genuinely gotten to know the performers, and they want to complete the connection.

A girl of eleven or twelve sheepishly approached Kit with a piece of paper and a pen. Her eyes were glowing the way children that age try to hide but cannot, as she stammered out a request for an autograph.

Kit lowered herself so she could speak to the girl at eye level. Signing the paper, she asked if the girl played music herself. Bouncing her head back and forth apologetically, the girl admitted that she "played the fiddle a little."

Kit smiled. "That's just what I do," she said. "Play the fiddle a liddle."

"Oh, no, you're really *good*," the girl said, louder than she intended. She looked quickly around the room and said, almost whispering, "I'm, like, just starting out."

Kit smiled and asked what kind of music the girl liked, nodding in approval at all her answers. Clearing her throat nervously, the girl asked Kit what music *she* liked. First, Kit said she liked everybody the girl had mentioned, especially the songwriter

Antje Duvekot, who she said had influenced her, too. The little girl absolutely puffed up. Then Kit said she'd been listening a lot to the Wailin' Jennies lately, a female string band from Canada.

"They've got a wicked good fiddler," Kit whispered into the girl's ear, "and they're all girls, so they know how to do it right, you know?"

The girl twinkled and nodded her head excitedly. Just between us girls. Kit shook her hand and said she looked forward to hearing her play sometime.

As the girl walked away, Nathan smiled at Kit. "You were great with that kid," he said.

"She was sweet," Kit shrugged, then smiled at David and Dianne Gretz. Dianne gave her a small paper bag. "Baby quiche," she said. "I saved you some for the ride home." She winked at Nathan, handing him a bag, too. "A special batch of my chocolate toffee cookies, just for you. If I remember right, you like them." Nathan nodded and smiled.

"Oh, you shouldn't have," Kit said, fondling the bag in her hands. "You really—"

"Made with Gruyere," Dianne said.

Kit looked at the bag. "Okay, you should have. Baby quiche. It's, like, one of my secret passions."

David Gretz laughed. He looked every inch a Unitarian minister, lanky, with kinky gray hair and eyes that always seemed to be smiling behind round wire-rimmed glasses.

"You're a little young for that, aren't you?" he said.

Kit gulped. "You mean for secret passions?"

He smiled beatifically. "No, for them to be food. That's more for folks our age." He put his arm around his wife's shoulder.

"Speak for yourself," Dianne said.

"I am speaking for myself," he said innocently. "I'm a Unitarian minister; that's all I'm allowed to do."

Then he asked if he could speak to Kit alone. Nathan knew immediately that they wanted to offer her a gig at the coffeehouse, but didn't want to offend him by doing it in his presence.

Their coffeehouse was another of the many venues he'd played once too often, with one too many drinks in him. Like the music itself, these places have long memories. Even if the Gretzes wanted him back, the regulars would remember shoddy performances, slurred patter, and the sad stench of rum coming from his coffee cup. That's the drawback to how personal these gigs are: When you're in that kind of trouble, you wear those troubles on your sleeve. Everybody sees them, everybody knows. Everybody remembers.

Getting into the car, with the Gretzes waving at them from the front steps, Nathan warned Kit he had never been able to find his way out of Marblehead without getting lost.

"It was a straight shot coming in," she said.

"That's to fool the tourists. The trouble is, the road we took became a one-way at the end, so we have to circle around to get back. And this is not a circling-around kind of town."

Twenty minutes later, as they drove past a small white gazebo for the fourth time, Kit said, "Is that the same gazebo, or are there, like, a bunch of gazebos that all look the same?"

Nathan drummed his fingers on the wheel. "Same gazebo."

"Just asking. It's a pretty gazebo. Certainly worth a second look." She cleared her throat daintily. "Or a third. Or a…"

After another pass by Mugford Street, he took a sharp right turn and saw the old movie theater. That was the landmark he was looking for. The problem was that you couldn't see it until you made what seems like a wrong turn. When would he figure that out?

"Aha!" he said. "We're on our way now."

"No more gazebos?"

"I'm cautiously optimistic."

They drove for awhile, then both shouted "Aha!" at an old wooden sign that said *128-Boston-Gloucester*.

"You were great with that kid tonight," Nathan said again.

"She was sweet," Kit said, also again.

"Your first autograph?"

"Yeah, it was, actually. Cool, huh?"

"Your first star moment. Because that's what you were to her. And you used it to make her feel special." He looked at Kit. "That was important, y'know?"

"Important?" she said doubtfully. "Because I was nice to her?"

"It was the way you were nice to her. When you're that age, you're always looking for signs about who you are in the world. That kid will probably go to sleep tonight trying to figure out why someone like you—this big cool star she was staring at all night—treated her like *she* was cool. She'll wonder why you cared what music she liked, why you talked to her, fiddler to fiddler. She's so used to being treated like a kid all the time."

Nathan smiled and looked over at Kit, burrowed into her seat, squinting at him.

"I had a star encounter like that when I was her age," he said, "with a local folk-singer at a record store. Man, I thought he was the hippest thing on the planet. I was so nervous about bothering him while he was looking for records; but he made me call him by his first name, shook my hand, asked me all kinds of questions about myself. He even asked me what kind of guitar I had. You know, I'd been playing maybe six months."

"And *what* did you learn from that?" Kit asked with a hint of sarcasm. Oh, please, sir, what is the meaning of your parable? Nathan was so glad to hear it. She was relaxing around him. Soon he'd be wondering if the punches on his arm would leave bruises.

"Well, I shall tell you, my dear," he grumbled, with just enough old-man pomp to meet her sarcasm. Kit laughed. "I figured out that anyone who dug the music was cool to him. The simple fact that I knew who he was meant that I was into folk music, and that made me hip as far as he was concerned. Because it was all about the music."

Nathan looked at Kit. "Plus, I could tell he wasn't talking to me like a kid; you have such sharp radar for that when you're that age. To him, I was just a fellow folkie. I've always thought that was one of the moments that hooked me on folk music."

"Maybe he was just a nice guy," Kit said.

Nathan laughed. "You know, I thought of that, years later. Maybe he was just being nice to a kid. But it didn't matter how he meant it. I walked away believing that, in this scene, anybody who cared about the music was cool. There's no insiders or outsiders beyond that. When I watched you with that kid, I remembered that. Your first real star moment, and you made it about her, not you. You made her feel like she was cool."

Kit looked out her window. Her gloved hand tapped on the dashboard while she thought that over. Then, as if her brain had finally chewed and swallowed, she turned to him and nodded her head once. "Thanks," she said.

"You're welcome."

There was a long silence as they drove onto the highway. When they neared the exit for Storrow Drive and Nathan's house, he looked at her. Quietly, tentatively, he said, "Take you to my place?"

Kit put a fist under his nose. "You'd better, bub," she said. "You'd just better." And then she laughed, that wonderful, wide-open laugh, somehow both little girl and wise old soul.

She rubbed his thigh, and said, "We're okay now, aren't we?"

He nodded but couldn't think of anything to say.

Back at the carriage house, they didn't talk about the cold distance he had put between them. They just wanted to enjoy being together. They stayed up most of the night, eating the quiche and cookies, listening to old folk records. They held each other for long, quiet moments, and laughed about small things.

Strangely, though, they never got around to making love. Until they woke up, in each other's arms. And then they did, fiercely, as though for the first time.

Eight

As December's darkness grew around them, Nathan and Kit seemed closer than ever. The distances he'd cast over their new love, like winter shadows, seemed only to create new warmth between them. Perhaps that was because she had confronted her first reason to worry about this strange, muted man she was still trying to know, and discovered there'd been nothing to worry about. Perhaps it was because he found her so eager to convince him that she did not want to change him, only to make him happier about being who he was. For both reasons, probably, the way he had briefly left her seemed only to strengthen the friendship that was growing beneath their romance.

He was right about her reaction to his winter duds. The first time she saw him plodding around in his huge clothing and padded slipper socks, she laughed until she literally hurt herself, pinching a nerve near her ribs that made it difficult to sing for a couple of days.

But she could only laugh once because she immediately began wearing his winter clothes. She especially liked a faded beige hooded sweatshirt, which she could wear by itself, like a dress, since it hung nearly to her knees.

Of course, it looked quite different on her. It had always made him look like a rather well-dressed bag of potato chips, but when she wore it, he had trouble keeping his eyes off her, particularly the way it rode up and down her thighs when she walked. Kit was simply incapable of looking ridiculous, even in these ridiculous clothes which, after all, fit her even worse than they fit him. It didn't seem fair. Fun to look at but not fair.

On an early December Friday, with a few flakes of snow beginning to fall, Nathan loaned his car to Kit so she could drive to a last-minute opening-act gig in Quincy. He wanted to stay home and work on a little Christmas set for Dooley's.

As the buzz about her music grew, Kit was getting more of these kinds of bookings. That's how careers often happen in the folk world. After a while, a buzz creates its own energy, like a perpetual motion machine. Performers get hot because they're get-ting hot. It's the flip side of Yogi Berra's famous remark: "Nobody goes there anymore; it's too crowded." Everybody wants to go see the performer everybody's going to see.

Venues want to get in on that, too. The reward for running a coffeehouse is not financial, lord knows; most of them are run by volunteers who regard a break-even season as a great success. The fun is being part of the music, getting to know the performers, and having a story to tell. People wanted to hire Kit so they could say, years from now, "We had Kit Palmer here when she was just starting out. She was an opening act; can you believe it? Right on that stage."

The Quincy coffeehouse hadn't booked an opening act for this show. The head-liner was so popular they knew the place would be packed. But they wanted to hire Kit as soon as they could. It was called the Stone Steeple Coffeehouse, because the church that hosted it was made almost entirely of granite, which had been donated by President John Adams, a lifelong parishioner.

Most folkies, however, referred to it as the Crypt or the Adams Family Coffee-house, because John and Abigail Adams, along with their son, President John Quincy Adams, and his wife, Louisa Catherine Adams, were buried in the church's basement.

As Nathan handed Kit his car keys, he said, "Be sure to say hi to John and Abi-gail for me. Especially Abigail. I had kind of a crush on her when I was a kid. Read a lot of her letters. She was a real sweetie."

Kit stopped in her tracks by the kitchen door, her guitar and fiddle cases slung over her white parka. She stared at him, the beginnings of a smile frozen on her face. She shook her head and said, "You are a genuinely odd person, do you know that? Don't get me wrong; I like it. Like it a lot. But you are, you are just…"

She balled her fists in front of her and leaned her head forward, searching for the right word. She closed her eyes, the keys jangling softly in her clenched fist, and said, "*Odd!*"

"Thank you."

"You're welcome," Kit said, laughing, relieved that he'd taken it in the spirit intended.

"Abigail Adams was a lovely woman," Nathan said, as if it might help.

"I'm sure she was. But it doesn't change the fact that you're….you're…you're just…"

"Odd?"

"Yes, that's the word. Odd." Still shaking her head, laughing under her breath, she walked out the door, waving behind her as Nathan wished her luck.

He closed the kitchen door behind her and smiled. She's right, isn't she? A crush on Abigail Adams. And it hadn't even occurred to him that Kit might find that a little, well, odd. He really was an odd duck. Always had been.

He thought about that as he washed the dishes and looked out the window. Twilight comes so early this time of year. A few puffy flakes of snow floated down, making little curlicues as they fell. Because they were so fluffy? Because there was so little wind? The weather report said flurries, which usually meant they had no idea how much snow was coming but probably less than a blizzard.

He'd grown comfortable with his oddness, hadn't he? As a young man, he was particular about who knew what things about him and tried to conform to what others thought was hip or cool. He was always a rebel, but that came with its own set of norms: the conformity of the nonconformist. He was careful to dress in a way that showed he didn't care how he dressed.

Slowly over the years, he stopped thinking about those things. Partly because as his career declined, he stopped caring about his life at all, much less what anyone else thought of it.

But he realized now, staring out his kitchen window, that he'd also accepted his oddness because he'd come to see what an entirely odd world it was. Not just on the surface, but deep down, in the secrets we keep about ourselves. Did he know anyone who was not, in some way, hobbled by oddness?

And that wasn't just in the odd little world he traveled. His parents, who'd tried so hard to be normal, fought bitterly because they were odd in different ways. And so they passed one another, like strangers, unable to recognize how their oddness could have bound them together. As a child, he watched them destroy each other and often thought that things would be fine if only they could let their hair down around each other, relax and be themselves. They were both lovely people at heart, but in such different ways.

As a young man, he decided it had all been much more complicated than that. Now he wasn't sure. That really was the nub of it, wasn't it? His parents couldn't see each other for who they were because they couldn't accept themselves for who they were. Because deep down, they were odd people. And odd people didn't live on their normal block of normal houses and normal families.

Drying his hands and hanging the towel by the sink, Nathan wondered why it had been easier for him to accept his oddness. Perhaps his parents just didn't give themselves enough time. At some point, they gave up on the growing-up part of their lives, stopped thinking about how they fit in to the world around them, and started pretending they did fit in. Pretending they were just like everybody else. Normal.

But if you keep trying to figure out these things, you may, after a long, long time, begin to see yourself as you really are. The question becomes less "Who am I and how do I fix it?" It becomes "This is apparently who I am; how do I understand it?"

Nathan took a deep breath and looked out the window. The snow was steadier but still light. Boy, that's one of the blessings of age, isn't it? Accepting yourself for who you actually are. What a load of baggage you get to leave behind you then. His parents never got there, never got past the need to hide their oddness. A pity.

He got out his guitar and began thinking about his Christmas set for Dooley's. He was having a lot of fun with these little musical essays. He could do brief snatches of traditional songs to illustrate the points he was making, and he thought the crowd was genuinely interested in seeing how these songs had fit into people's everyday lives.

Many of the old Christmas carols began as pagan songs for midwinter, the time around the winter solstice, December 22, the shortest day and longest night of the year. Later, they had Christian messages written into them, but the older lyrics still shone through, with their focus on anything that stayed alive in barren December: evergreens—fir, holly, and ivy—and animals that did not go away or hibernate—deer and wrens.

The old idea was to surround yourself with as much life and light as you could find in the dead, dark world. Fires and candles were kept burning, partly for their warmth, but also as reminders of the vanishing sun and the promise that the world would slowly turn back toward spring, light, and life.

Nathan wanted to show the audience that there used to be carols for all the seasons. The original meaning of the word *carol* was simply a song meant for dancing, used for rituals, especially to mark the passing of the seasons. Once, long ago, carols for spring, summer, and fall were as important as Christmas carols.

He thought it would be fun to sing a snatch of a spring carol, to show how differently the melody affected people. These seasonal songs all had their purposes, which were reflected in the melodies as well as the words. For spring, it was all about shaking off winter, getting the blood pumping, going outside and getting back to work. In midwinter, the softer melodies had just the opposite purpose: "Slow down," they said, "be still. Huddle around the fire, huddle together, remember, reflect."

Nathan pulled his easy chair over to the window and turned off nearly all the lights. He kept on only one small lamp in case he wanted to make some notes. He began to strum his guitar, finding the chill, minor-key chords common to midwinter music.

He also wanted to show the open-mikers how important visiting was during midwinter. Shreds of those traditions still existed, in Christmas caroling, office parties, exchanging cards and gifts. But we don't remember the *why* of the rituals anymore, so they often feel like a burden, a chore.

In ancient times, this merriment was serious business. Midwinter was not just the darkest time; it was also the most dangerous. What food there was had already been harvested, preserved, stored. The earth had little to offer those who did not already have enough.

So people invented fun ways to call on their neighbors. Officially, the visits were rituals to bless the house and those inside, as one year passed into another. But they were also non-nosy ways to check up on everybody.

People would reward their visitors' songs with food and drink. The ritual said they did this to secure the blessing, but they were also showing their neighbors that they had enough food. If the poorest family came to the door with empty hands, if the old widow didn't have enough wood piled by her door, neighbors would return to help them out. Because midwinter was a time to remind everybody they were not alone, even when it turned this dark, this dead. When the long nights made people feel like strangers in the world, the music reminded them that they belonged to each other, to family, friends, and community. We are not alone, the old carols said; we are alone together.

Nathan knew a quiet Welsh carol that fit the bill. The lyrics made it clear what was going on:

> *Our wassail is made of the elderberry bough,*
> *And so, my good neighbors, we'll drink unto thou.*
> *Besides all on earth, you'll have apples in store.*
> *Pray let us come in for it's cold by the door.*
> *And the night is long, and the day it is grey.*
> *And the old year is fading, the new comes our way.*

Perfect. Now he needed a boisterous spring carol for contrast. He leafed through an old songbook, looking for just the right tone of sappiness.

Vim, he thought to himself, I need a song with lots of *vim*. He'd never known quite what vim was, or how it differed from its companion word, *vigor*. But he knew he was looking for vim.

"Just the thing," he said out loud, looking at an English folk song called "Country Life."

> *In the spring we sow, at the harvest mow,*
> *And that is how the seasons 'round they go.*
> *But of all the things if choose I may,*
> *'Twould be rambling through the new mown hay.*

The chorus was even sappier:

> *I like to rise when the sun she rises*
> *Ear-lie in the morning.*
> *I like to hear them small birds singing*
> *Merrily upon their laylums.*
> *And hurrah for the life of a country boy,*
> *And to ramble in the new mown hay.*

It was positively lousy with vim, set to an almost comically rambunctious melody. Major key, bright, blatant changes. Get up! Get crackin'! Time's a-wastin'!

He picked out the melody on the guitar, chuckling at its juicy exuberance. He settled on a key a few steps above his range so he'd have to screech, making it all the more hard to take. And fun. The point was that this was *not* something you wanted to hear in December.

> *In winter when the sky is grey,*
> *We hedge and we ditch our times away.*
> *But in the summer when the sun shines gay,*
> *We go rambling through the new mown hay.*

He sang the chorus again, pounding his guitar until the strings rattled, beginning with a howl: "*Ohhhhh-OHHH*, I like to rise when the sun she rises…"

As he sang, he wondered what laylums were, and why birds found them such merry places to sing. Still thwacking away on his guitar, he gazed out at the thickening snow, white against the black December night. Stopping suddenly, he looked down at his guitar and then back out the frosted window.

"She's absolutely right," he whispered, laughing and shaking his head. "You are just *odd*."

Nathan was sweeping the kitchen floor, humming quietly to the slow swish of the broom. He stopped suddenly, realizing he was remembering the melody to an old, unfinished song. He hadn't thought of it in years but always meant to finish it someday. Why had it come back to him now? He walked into the living room, picked up his guitar, and sang the first two lines.

> *Make me well, someone, break the spell*
> *That's kept me down since first I fell.*

He sang it again and laughed, remembering the self-pitying lament he'd tried to write after that opening couplet. Pompous young twit. He hadn't even liked the girl who inspired it; he just hadn't liked the idea of her dumping him. It had been nothing but vanity, pure, foolish vanity. No wonder he couldn't finish it; it wasn't true.

Maybe that's why it came back to him after all these years. Maybe he'd grown up enough to know what to write after those first two lines. He felt a faint tickle of inspiration, the strange feeling that ideas were forming into words, in that place beneath our conscious thoughts. He'd always liked the melody and felt it had something to say. There must be some reason it returned to him today. But it had been such a long time since he'd written anything.

The old fear flashed through him: What makes you think you can relight the old, dead fires of inspiration? Keep them cold; they're safer that way; they can't burn you. Always a reason to not do something. But then he thought about Kit during those nor'easters, alone and hurt, wondering what she had done to drive him away, and writing that beautiful new song, turning her feelings inward and then outward, to the way we all feel when winter makes us seem so alone in the world.

He tentatively touched the guitar, as if it was something strange and new in his arms. His fingers faltered and fluttered from the strings. He was afraid; it had been so long, so long. But then he realized he was feeling something different, more recent, not the familiar specters of cold ash and dead ember, the memory of wood. It did not bring the familiar pain, but something that tingled excitedly, expectantly, beneath the fear. What was it?

He smiled and caught his breath. Oh, that. He realized that his fingers felt on the strings the way they had at the first touch of Kit's soft skin, the first time they made love; how his hands had fluttered and faltered on her shoulders and along her arms and back. And how she'd smiled at him, warmly, safely, and leaned into his hands until they found their firmness.

He closed his eyes, keeping that smile inside him, and began to play. He pressed his fingers down until the old sureness returned.

Those first two lines were all he remembered of the original. What did they mean to him, now that he knew about falling, about not being well?

He sang the couplet a few times, then nodded and sang:

Guide me clear of my easy fears
Cold company for all these years

Easy fears. He liked that. That's what makes them seductive, isn't it? They get so damn comfortable. Lie back, snuggle into them. They'll keep you safe, explain away all your failures. All you have to do is believe them.

He wanted to broaden the lens, still embarrassed about the myopic vanity of the first two lines. Me, me, me. God, you'd think you were the only guy who ever got jilted by a pretty girl.

So he thought about those times, in his naked youth, when everything seemed possible. They were good times, weren't they? Cocky times. And yet we all wrote songs dripping with anguish and torment. Oh, the poet's lot! How we suffer! He laughed out loud. It was so innocent, so innocent. And yet we thought we were figuring it all out.

When it was spring, everyone would sing,
We can do anything.

Boy, ain't that the truth? We were nothing but muscle, will, and certitude. We had such faith in our energy. And now? He nodded. It would not be an apocalypse that followed, but numbness, ennui.

Now each new door seems I've walked through before.
There's no frontiers anymore.

Good. He'd widened the lens. The song would not be about what he'd gotten wrong; it would be about what we all get wrong. An elegy to the strapping confidence of youth.

He looked up from his guitar and out the window at a strikingly blue winter sky. The brightness made him squint and look away.

The melody should move somewhere else now, perhaps to a bridge, something darker to reflect how the older singer feels now. Nathan counted beats in his head, strumming a gray minor chord. Ask a question here. What made us think it would be so easy? No, not quite. Be so, be so….ah, yes. Tidy. And then it flooded into him; he sang it the way he knew it would be in the finished song.

What made us think it would all be so clean?
Love, the magician, we sang.
What made us think that our hearts would be enough,
All that we ever would need?

Because that's it, isn't it? Powerful new feelings rage in us when we're young. We think we're really on to something with this love stuff, like we've discovered it for the first time. It's powerful, powerful. Surely, this will light our path; believe in it—"Love, the magician"—and everything will turn out fine.

He shook his head as he wrote down the lines:

What made us think that our hearts would be enough?

Had he ever written anything so sad? The bridge needed something to match that sadness, a coda to describe the singer's life now, something bluesy and blatant about how it had all gone wrong.

This was the place for the self-pity that seemed out of place before. He wanted a line full of defeat, a bluesy wail. He needed to show how much trouble this guy is in now. He thought of the phrase "same old song," perhaps because he was rewriting one of his early tragedies.

Every day, it's the same old song.

Song, song, a line that rhymes with song. He thought about how he felt during the worst times, the longest nights.

Everything I do is wrong

Ouch. And yet that's it; that's exactly how it feels.

Every day, it's the same old song,
Everything I do is wrong

Enough for today; let it breathe a while, incubate. It's an amazing thing about songs: you can leave them alone, then return to find that they've made progress on their own. Like they're living things. And then, suddenly, they seem to have their own energy. Nathan used to call it "the Pinocchio moment," when the piece of wood comes to life. From that moment on, a song participates in its own creation. That's when you know you've got a real song, and you know it viscerally. It's euphoric, like the best rush from the best drug in God's own pharmacy.

Kit was spending the week before Christmas at home in Connecticut, the result of an artful negotiation with her parents. Christmas was a Big Deal at the Palmer home. Her parents spent days decorating the place, until every corner of the house contained some annual ritual, from Advent calendars to electric candles in the living room window to pre-Christmas gifts that were opened on particular days.

On Christmas Eve, they had a chocolate hunt, after Kit's father hid candy balls and chocolate Santas all over the house. For years, Kit had thought she was too old for that, but her arguments fell on deaf ears, since her mother eagerly joined the hunt and teased Kit mercilessly if she found the most Santas.

Kit offered to spend the entire holiday week with them if she could take the bus back to Boston on Christmas morning and spend the day with her new boyfriend. They agreed—on the solemn condition that she take some food back for him; they were convinced, given his profession, that he must live in a state of perpetual starvation.

Kit told Nathan that her parents had actually heard of him, though it wasn't clear if that was helpful in terms of how they felt about him as her new boyfriend.

"Good heavens, Kit," her mother said. "I remember him from my college days."

"Killer guitarist," her father said. He always took Kit's side of things.

"Well, that's a *great* comfort, I must say," her mother replied, shooting her husband a "we'll-talk-about-this-later" look.

But that pretty much ended the discussion. Her mother tried to be the stern one, the taskmaster, but she wasn't much better than her husband at standing up to Kit. Who could say no to that one? Especially with your hands full of chocolate Santas.

All month, Kit had been dropping hints to Nathan about the present she was giving him, with increasing frequency and excitement, so he was not entirely unhappy to see her go. He really was getting tired of hearing about it. He also had no idea what she could spring on him that would be such a big deal—he already had a guitar and there was no room for a pony.

Nathan's Christmas set at Dooley's went just as he'd hoped. The crowd had a ball heckling him about his sappy spring carol, howling at him to stop, please stop, for god's sake, stop.

Of course, that was the reaction Nathan wanted. Before he got on stage, he'd primed the pump by asking Ferguson to begin the razzing. If the squirrels saw him leading the charge, they'd feel free to follow.

"You *want* me to heckle you?" Ferguson said with an ominously innocent stare. Stroking his beard thoughtfully, he said, "I'll…I'll…well, I'll do my best, Nathan. I'll give it the old college try."

"You'll do fine," Nathan said. "I have every confidence."

"Why didn't you ask me?" Jackie said, pouting. "You know I'm better at that kind of thing than he is."

Nathan smiled. "That's why."

"Well, thank you," Jackie said. "Just a little credit where credit's due, that's all."

After the spring song, Nathan launched quietly into the dark, old Welsh carol. The crowd got so involved in singing the chorus they continued on their own after Nathan stopped. He listened, eyes closed, through a couple of choruses, then joined them to end it.

> *And the night is long, and the day it is grey.*
> *And the old year is fading, the new comes our way.*

Immediately after Nathan's set, Ramblin' Randy jumped on stage wearing a large Santa hat. He began so solemnly that it took awhile to figure out he was setting up a gag. What gave it away was Randy praising Nathan for his "elucidating disquisition on ancient midwinter rites." Elucidating? Disquisition?

He droned on, fidgeting with the big white ball on the end of his Santa hat, saying that Nathan had neglected to mention one particularly revered winter beast.

"And so, fellow carolers," Randy said, his tone almost scholarly, "in the spirit of the season and to honor those ancient and revered traditions of midwinter, allow me to humbly sing a humble ode to this humble beast of burden."

Pounding a brassy chord that would have sounded like a church bell if he hadn't made all the guitar strings rattle, Randy sang:

> *Rooooooooo-dolph, the Red-Nosed Rein-deeeeeeeeeerrrrrrr*
> *Had a very shiny nozzzzzzze*

The audience got the joke immediately. Once again, Nathan was being razzed. Randy's pedantic introduction to the 1940s pop hit perfectly mocked the folkloric tone of Nathan's explanations of ancient midwinter rituals.

Nathan made a point to grin throughout the song, so everyone would know he was enjoying the spoof. But he was actually happy about something else. Randy had dared to let a little of his real self out on stage, Dr. Randall Cahill, MIT scientist and professor, and it was welcomed by the crowd. Moments like that can be important for guys like Randy, and as far as Nathan was concerned, it's what open mikes were all about.

During a wild ovation, all the more enthusiastic for its sarcasm, Randy bowed dramatically, swished the great white ball on the end of his Santa hat from one shoulder to the other, and swooped off the stage. As he passed Ryder's table, Ryder sneered at him. "Rudolph the damn reindeer. Jesus, what's next? Sesame Street?"

"Dumb bastard," Jackie said. But she was referring to Ryder, not Randy. "You couldn't give that boy a clue if you stapled it to his forehead."

She was right, of course. Ryder had completely missed the joke. Randy lost his comic swagger and walked quietly, head down, back to his table. The applause ended abruptly, as everyone turned to glare at Ryder. This is what comics mean when they talk about a heckler splashing cold water on a crowd.

Nathan was less angry at Ryder than concerned about Randy. This had been a good moment for him until Ryder shot off his mouth. He was really getting tired of this kid.

He walked wordlessly past Ryder—what's the point?—and over to Randy. The other open-mikers at Randy's table were patting him on the back and congratulating him.

"Randy really got you good, huh, Nathan?" one of them said. He was wearing Randy's Santa hat.

"Sure did," Nathan said "That was great, Randy. And you really got the crowd going. I'm sorry Ryder had to spoil it. He just can't stand anyone else doing well. He's—"

"He's an asshole," Randy said with a shrug. He smiled and motioned Nathan to sit down. "The kid's just an asshole, Nathan. Always has been, probably always will be. I think he wants to be a star so bad, and it ain't happening for him. I see the way he glares at Kit, because she's doing so well, and I want to go over and slap him."

Randy took a sip of beer, then shook his head. "But I can't let stuff like that bother me. I'm just here to have some fun." His voice was voice soft, measured, and intelligent. Once again, this was not Ramblin' Randy but Dr. Randall Cahill.

"I know I'm not very good, you know," he said. "C'mon, you think I don't know I'm a nerd?"

"I wouldn't call you a nerd," Nathan said.

"Nathan, I was planning to do 'Rudolph the Red Nosed Reindeer' anyway. That's why I wore the hat."

Nathan just blinked at him. Even his egalitarianism had its limits. "Well," he said haltingly, "I always liked the way Gene Autry sang it."

"Nice try," Randy said, sipping his beer. "I am a nerd. Nerdy. Nerdish. Nerd-like. Nerd-acious. If it's any comfort to you—and it certainly is to me—I'm an obscenely well-paid nerd."

"That's us," said one of Randy's friends, "just a bunch of folksinger geeks."

Randy laughed and slapped his hands on the table. "Folksinger geeks. Perfect! We should start a union. Folksinger Geeks, Local 101."

Nathan stood up and winked at Randy. "I'll be shop steward," he said.

Amazing, he thought as he walked back toward the bar. Randy knows exactly what he is and how everybody sees him. How about that?

The evening ended with Nathan and Ferguson huddled around the bend of the bar, Jackie strolling over whenever she wasn't needed elsewhere. After Nathan's set, she'd started drinking a syrupy mix of brandy and peppermint schnapps called Snowshoe Grog, and was positively merry by the witching hour.

By midnight, Ferguson was also tipsier than usual. Leaning awkwardly into Nathan, he said, "So you and Kit are doing okay?"

"Never better. It's been kind of an adjustment. You know, I've been alone for such a long time."

"But you're okay now? I mean, you two. You're okay?"

"Yeah, fine. Never better."

"Good," Ferguson said bluntly, lifting his beer. "Then I won't have to kill you."

Nathan stared at him. "You knew about that? About me pulling away from her?"

Ferguson nodded. "She called me late one night. Said she was sorry, but she had to talk to someone who knew you. Did I know what was wrong? Had you said anything? What had she done wrong? She kept asking that. What did she do? What did she do? I'm pretty sure she'd been crying."

"Shit."

"Indeed. Be careful with her, man."

"I didn't know it was that bad."

"Of course not. She doesn't want you to see her that way." Ferguson leaned his face close, and Nathan could smell the alcohol on his breath. For a flashing moment, he wanted a drink.

"Look," Ferguson said, "I think you two are a match made in heaven. But you gotta remember that part of her is still kind of a kid. She thinks everything that goes wrong is her fault."

"Sounds more like me, actually," Nathan said, picking at the bar with his fingers.

"Like I said, a match made in heaven. You have to be careful with her, that's all. She's strong in so many ways, smart, confident. But she feels everything so goddamn intensely. I think she's more vulnerable than she'll ever let you know."

"It'd kill me if I really hurt her."

"Then you won't," Ferguson said with a firm nod. Nathan felt a strange surge of comfort, just from the way he'd said it. He seemed so certain.

Nathan popped out of bed on Christmas morning like, well, a kid on Christmas morning. He'd been looking forward to this all month, planning it, almost rehearsing it. For one thing, he'd let the house become unusually messy so he could spend the morning listening to carols and tidying up for Kit's arrival in the afternoon. That's what this holiday used to be all about, after all: sweeping out the old year to make room for the new.

He stopped at Whole Foods almost every day. He knew he was overdoing it, but it was fun wandering the aisles, thinking, "Wonder if she'd like this? That looks like fun. Do I have enough of this?" That was strange for him; he almost never stocked up on food, preferring to wait until he got hungry, then decide which nearby market or café to visit. He'd picked up another of those little trees, again liberating it from its dorky ornaments and again placing the ornaments carefully along the windowsill.

Why was this so exciting? He thought about that as he fixed his morning coffee. Probably because he'd spent so many Christmases alone. His mother died when he was in his twenties, mostly from drinking but also from sadness, if such a thing is possible. His father passed away a decade ago. But honestly, it had been hard to miss him; he'd been a distant figure for so long. Always, really. The landlords would invite Nathan over for Christmas dinner, but he always made excuses. Sometimes loneliness is less acute when you're alone.

Now, drinking his coffee, he happily checked his holiday supplies. Cookies? Enough for a small elementary school. Enough cheese? Hoo boy, can you freeze cheese? There was only one small turkey but enough fixings to feed the neighborhood.

He stared at his overstuffed refrigerator. Good lord, you really have overdone it. Had he ever seen it that full? Then he smiled, thinking about how Kit would react. First she'd tease him about all the food. Then she'd realize he spent the whole week thinking about her, making lists, running errands, stocking up for their first Christmas together. No harm in that.

He pulled out a couple of brownies, grabbed his morning coffee, and wandered through the old carriage house. He told himself he was forming a battle plan for cleaning but he was actually remembering what the place had been like before he quit drinking. It wasn't simply messy back then, he realized. Every corner had been crowded with the unfinished, the postponed, the important things he meant to get to, but not today.

There had been a huge pile of newspapers and magazines by the stereo. These were not to throw away, but things he meant to read. It began with an editorial he got halfway through; at its worst, the pile was as high as his shoulders.

When he quit drinking, he saw the place as filthy, the debris of a destructive and meaningless life. He saw it differently now. It was actually the debris of a life delayed. His entire life had been in that mess: something he meant to get to, but not today.

He looked around. Despite the messiness here and there, his home was a trim, ordered place. And every corner had a story to tell about Nathan growing tired of the old disarray and creating a new solution. He hadn't simply been getting tidier, as he thought at the time. He'd been learning to live deliberately, pile by pile, dish rack by dish rack, coat hook by coat hook.

He remembered when he put up those shelves, when he bought that CD rack, when he hung the landscape prints on the wall, when he finally got drapes for the windows. It was the little things, wasn't it? There had never been an epic moment; he'd mended his life piece by broken piece.

It really began that wonderful summer he spent fixing up the carriage house and discovered the testosterone-enhancing glories of the hardware store. He began to take great pleasure in figuring out how to solve little domestic problems. He would often laugh at himself because the pleasure seemed so disproportionate to the task. But after years of letting life hit him like high breakers in a cold sea, he found it intensely satisfying to become annoyed at a small problem and be able to fix it.

An early triumph was figuring out how to get the kitchen faucet to stop spritzing water all over the sink. After weeks of swearing at it, one night he peered closely at the tip, trying to figure out what was wrong. Hey, this little thing at the end looks like a separate piece. Why yes, it's a cap, isn't it? And it unscrews. And inside, this looks like some sort of filtering device. Hmm. Filters filter things, so maybe they need to be cleaned of the things they filter. Ah, like all this crud here. You're probably supposed to do that every once in a while, or else why would it unscrew? And when his little repairs worked, he felt like thumping his chest and snorting at the moon.

Sometimes he would wander through a hardware store, feeling manly and considering the possibilities. You can get lampshades without buying the whole lamp? Gee, plungers are cheap, aren't they? Hey, a few hooks on the door would solve the problem of having to shove your coat off the bed every night.

A welcome mat. How homey.

He'd spent so many years in cheap motels and crashing in other people's homes that he got in the habit of accepting discomfort. As the darkness of his life grew around him, it reinforced his belief in his own helplessness. That may have been hard comfort; but back then, he desperately needed to believe that he was not to blame for what his life had become. So when he began to attack these little problems, it meant more than it would have for most people. It was a way of taking back some ownership of his life. It is the small steps we take after the storm; they are always the ones that matter the most.

Now, on this Christmas morning, Nathan could not see a single space in his small house that didn't remind him how he'd slowly pulled his life together. He was a bit in awe of himself. So much work. He could see them all now, a hundred little battles, a hundred little victories. Why hadn't he seen them at the time?

It took less than an hour to clean the place, since it really wasn't dirty, just messy. He got the turkey roasting, following the recipe in an old cookbook his mother had given him.

He poured another cup of coffee, cranked up the carols on the classical radio station, and walked slowly into the bedroom. The bed was made, but there was another holiday ritual, something he did every year and dreaded every year.

From the back of the closet he pulled an old shoebox of family photographs and sat on the bed. He looked at the old pictures of his family at Christmas and saw what he always saw. Nobody seemed to be having any fun. It all seemed labored, posed. But maybe that was because he also remembered the sounds: the raised voices, the anger with things not being merry and bright, the slammed doors, the broken plates. Somebody always managed to break a plate.

He stared at a shot of his parents, arm in arm, smiling in front of the tree they'd argued about the night before. He was guessing at that, but it was a good guess. They always argued about the tree.

"You poor, poor bastards," he whispered at the picture. "If only you hadn't fallen in love with—"

He started to say "each other," but stopped, shook his head, and put the old pictures back in the box. He didn't know his parents that well, or at least not that way. They'd been together a long time before he started showing up in the photographs; whatever good times there had been were over before he was born. He never knew why; even at the end of their lives, neither would tell him. Maybe they had been in love once; maybe it had been worth it. He doubted it, but maybe. And hey, it's Christmas. Even memories get the benefit of the doubt.

He closed the lid of the shoebox and put it back in its place, far back on the farthest shelf of the closet. He heaved a yawning sigh, spreading his arms and arching his back. How's the turkey coming? There must be more to basting than what he was doing.

He poured the juice over the turkey, and over again, and once more, like the book said, and then brushed more butter on it. He felt like he was missing something, so he stood over the turkey, moving it this way and that with the butter brush. Then he folded his arms and considered the turkey. Then he moved it again. Finally, feeling completely foolish, he closed the oven. Standing over something with your arms folded does not make you look like you know what you're doing. At least not with turkeys. With car engines, maybe.

He went into the living room, intending to play his guitar, but walked back into the bedroom. Something was nagging at him. He sat again on the bed and looked up at the shoebox in the closet. He could barely see it.

One of Nathan's greatest strengths was his capacity for unhappiness. He'd always known that about himself. It was the tough gift his parents gave him, tough but useful.

Coming out of the numbing unhappiness of his childhood, he had no real under-standing of happiness, the way most people understand it.

It wasn't just that his family life was bad; it was the almost total absence of good times. Doing things as a family seemed like an awful chore for everybody, met with groans, complaints, recriminations, and, inevitably, fights. Even before he knew why, he learned to groan whenever the family prepared for an outing or a holiday. He also learned to brace for the worst, because it always came.

Family became an unhappy place, because that's what it seemed to be for his par-ents. They often soothed their guilt by telling him what a burden it was being a parent. They endured it, they told him, only because they loved him. He understood now that they were talking to themselves, making themselves feel better about the cold home they had made for him. But no child can know that.

He stared angrily at the shoebox. How can an adult not know better, not see the scars that will leave? What does that tell a child about love?

He was a smart kid, though; he knew it wasn't that way for most people. Some-thing was just broken in his home, and in him.

But his hard childhood gave him one advantage: he didn't mind being unhappy, which gave him strength to endure things others could not, or would not. It allowed him to keep afloat his sinking career, despite all the odds, and slowly convert it into the low-grade but reliable thing it was now. His career might not have amounted to much, but he was still a musician, by trade and by passion. Not many of his contemporaries could say that. That was the tough gift his parents gave him.

It also made him pursue pleasure, which is what people who don't understand happiness often think happiness is. He drank and sought casual, loveless sex that, like the drinking, made him feel full for a moment, but emptied him of important things. The sour moments afterward, when two people who did not know each other withdrew from an intimacy they did not share. The clumsy silences and, even worse, the mild conversation. It was awkwardness that cut like a knife, as strangers recovered from love to become strangers again.

When he could take no more of that, he settled for being alone, years of being alone. He chose large unhappiness over small happinesses that were not real. That had always felt like a surrender, one of so many in the great retreat of his life. But it wasn't, was it? By making that choice, without knowing it, he had begun to set the table for Kit to enter his life.

Perhaps the things that he thought were changing in him now actually began changing long ago. As he tamed his fondness for pleasure, he became attuned to the quieter, more abiding contentments of life. Could that be why he didn't run from Kit, as he surely would have run before, from such a challenging and fulfilling lover? Or was it Kit, lovely, irresistible Kit? He smiled. Hmm. Those two questions answer each other, don't they?

Nathan looked away from the shoebox, a small act of forgiveness, and walked into the living room. He checked the clock to see if it was time to get Kit at the bus station. He'd be early if he left now, but so what? He wanted to get out of the house—enough of this winter brooding, enough! Time for Kit.

He was idling in the taxi turnaround when she came out of the bus depot, wearing an oversized stocking cap and a backpack over that lovely white parka. He honked and she waved, then sauntered toward the car, grinning. She seemed to be having a good day. He smiled and waved back.

She tossed her backpack in the backseat and shuffled into the front. Peeling off her cap, she said, "I told the folks all about you. But they let me come back, anyway."

"Rented out your room, have they?"

"Oh, nice. You know they dote on me. Wait till you see all the food they made me take home."

He kissed her and pulled the car out of the turnaround. The sky had clouded over, casting long shadows over the city streets. A nice wintry mood.

"I told you they were fans of yours, right?" Kit said.

"You told me they'd heard of me. There's a difference."

"That's my Nathan, always finding the gloomy side."

He started to say it had served him well but stopped. It hadn't. Instead, he asked how her Christmas had been so far.

By the time they got to the house, one thing was clear: presents would have to come first. Kit couldn't wait another minute to show Nathan what she had for him.

"So? Where is it?" he said.

"Is your computer turned on?"

"No. Why, is it some computer game? Kill the open-mikers? That would be fun. How many points do you get for Ryder?"

She smiled but didn't laugh. This was no time for repartee. He'd never seen her like this, excited almost to the point of anger.

"Just start the damn computer," she said as she tore off her parka.

"Okay, okay," he said, turning on his old Mac.

She stood beside him, moving up and down on the balls of her feet. "God, that piece of junk," she sighed. "It takes, like, a *year* to boot up."

"Patience, patience. It's a good old horse."

"Horsepower. That's the speed, all right."

"Oh, you young people, always in such a hurry."

She rubbed his arm. "I want to show you your present, that's all."

The computer finally opened up, smiling its geeky Apple smile. She told him to go online, which took another couple of minutes, during which Kit groaned impatiently.

"Okay," Nathan said. "I am wired to the world."

"Google your name."

"What?"

"Google-it-Google-it-Google-it!"

"Okay, okay!"

He Googled Nathan Warren, which he'd done a few weeks before to depressing results. You'd think he'd been dead for twenty years, the stuff that came up. This time, however, the first thing he saw was, "Nathan Warren, Boston songwriting legend, is one of the finest guitarists anywhere in the modern folk realm…" He was starting to get it.

He looked below the little quote. The link was to Nathanwarren.com. His own website.

"Lord. Kit, have you—"

"Click it, click it, click it!"

He did, and a light green page came up. His latest publicity picture, only seven years old, had been turned into a gauzy graphic, forming the backdrop for the home page. Along the left side there was a wide row of button bars: Biography, Press Quotes, Appearances, Mailing List. The look was austere, dignified, and a bit mysterious. It had kind of a mythic aura to it, perfect for an aging folk legend.

"What do you think?" Kit asked, pulling up a chair next to him.

"Very cool. You did this?"

"Most of it. I got some help. Click the biography."

It was instantly clear that Ferguson had written it. Who else could make obscurity sound like such an accomplishment?

"Ask the pundits or the chart-watchers about the most important stars to emerge from the Boston folk scene," it began, "and they will cite artists who are now household names. Ask the musicians who actually haunt that storied scene, however, from major star to open-miker, and a name little known outside Boston will always rank among the top: Nathan Warren."

It went on to recount his career as if he had done it all on purpose. It glanced over his major-label disaster and described his retreat to open-mike hosting as "a step inward, back to his roots." No kidding, so that's what it was. Everything was dignified, dramatic—and almost true.

"Wow," Nathan said. He was overwhelmed.

"Click the press quotes," Kit said. "It's kinda funny."

"Just what you want from a press quotes page."

"You'll see what I mean."

The quotes were almost all from Ferguson but they'd been artfully identified to hide that. The top one was attributed to him, the next few merely to the newspaper.

Another was from National Public Radio, because Ferguson had praised Nathan in an interview about the Boston folk scene.

"You've got to be kidding," Nathan said, as he saw one quote that was not from Ferguson, set apart in its own box. It was from Joyce. And it was new.

"When I was coming up in the Boston scene," she'd written, "Nathan Warren was my Bob Dylan, Woody Guthrie, and Pete Seeger, all rolled into one. The fact that we were momentarily married doesn't change my feeling that he's the best damn folksinger I ever heard."

"Joyce?" He said, shaking his head and reading the quote again. She could be so classy when she wanted to be.

"Cool, huh?" Kit said. "I really like her music, you know. She was a big influence on me."

"On a lot of people," Nathan said. "I always liked her stuff, too." He knew this had to be Ferguson's doing. No one else would have the clout—or the balls—to ask Joyce for a quote about her ex-husband. Even now, as successful as she was, she wouldn't want to cross Ferguson on something like this. Oh, that's not fair. She would have been happy to give that quote to anyone. Music was never a problem between them. Careers, yes, music, no.

Nathan grinned mischievously. "Um, did you get this quote from Joyce?" he asked.

"No!" Kit gulped, then got the joke and slugged his arm. "Ferguson did it. He called her and got it over the phone. He helped me with all the content. And a friend I know from college helped me set it up. She does it for a living."

"Your design, though. It looks great."

"Thanks. Yeah, it was. I wanted it to feel like you. Do you like it?"

"It's beautiful. Makes me look like some kind of legend. Very classy. It's…it's…I mean, I…" He nodded at the screen.

"Good," she said, leaning into him. "I think it'll really help you get gigs. People will be able to find you now."

"It means a lot to me, Kit," he said, staring at the screen. "Not just because of how good it looks. But all the time, all the work." He looked at her, wanting her to see how serious he was. "It shows that you believe in me, in my music," he said quietly.

Kit froze, mouth half-open. There was a long silence. "And I do," she managed finally. "I really do."

"Thanks. For that, most of all."

They held each other, then Nathan eyed the small, wrapped box on the kitchen table. Now he had another reason to be glad he'd given her something special.

"Well, how about a present for you?"

"Yes, my turn. Whad'ja get me?"

"It's in the kitchen."

As she went to get it, he looked at his website. He clicked the button for the mailing list. All the names from his Dooley's list were already there, and many more. He remembered a night a few weeks ago when Kit had been doing something on his computer. He'd wondered why, when her laptop was right next to her. Now he knew: she was getting the Dooley's list to put on his website. The new list was considerably longer, though; he suspected she'd salted it with names from her own mailing list, which was much larger than his.

"What does it mean?" Kit said, walking out of the kitchen. She'd opened the box to find only a small card inside. It read, "Kit Palmer's First Album."

"Just what it says," he said as he put the computer to sleep. "Your first CD. An old student of mine runs a recording studio in his basement, out in Concord. He told me once that if I ever wanted to record, he'd let me use the place at night, for free. I called him and it's still okay. We'll go out in the evenings and make you an album. Kit Palmer, recording artist."

She shook her head slowly, but there was no other reaction. She sat back down, her eyes never leaving the card in her hand. "Tell me more," she said, her voice tense and tight.

"Well, I'll produce it for you, get it mixed and sounding right. I think it should be pretty simple; a first album is mostly to let people know what you sound like on stage."

"But you'll play on it, yes?"

"Sure, if you want me to. I can do some second guitar stuff, throw on a little harmony. But a first album is like a showcase. It should feel like you."

"You really think I'm ready?"

"Absolutely."

She was staring at the floor now, tapping the card on her leg. This was not the reaction he'd expected. Then it struck him: she was scared, a touch of the old stage fright.

"You sure?" She asked doubtfully. "I mean, that I'm ready?" She puffed one of her nervous little breaths. Yup, definitely stage fright.

"Absolutely, sweetie," he said, putting his hands on her shoulders. "Your sound has been coming together so fast. I wouldn't want you to do it, otherwise. A lot of beginners make the mistake of releasing a record before they really know what they sound like. But you're ready for this, Kit."

She looked up at him, a pleased but uncertain look on her face.

"I'll be there every step of the way," he said. "I'll make sure you sound great. It's recording, you know, not performing. You get to keep doing it until it's just how you want it."

That seemed to brighten her mood. She smiled and looked back at the little card in her hand. Nathan took a breath. Now came the hard part, the part he hadn't figured out yet.

"As to getting it pressed," he said awkwardly, "maybe we can go halvsies on that or something. I'm still working out that part."

"You mean the money?" She looked at him and he nodded.

"Oh, that'll be easy," she said. "I can take care of that. Well, I mean my parents can. They really want to help. They love it that I'm trying to be a songwriter. I think I told you that they always wanted me to be the black sheep of the family, the artsy one."

"You sure?" Nathan asked. He hated that he didn't have the money, and he also hated that he felt macho about it. It's only money. But it was a gift; he wanted to be able to do it all for her.

"Absolutely," she said. "Really, my folks asked me today if they could pitch in. They want to be part of it, you know? They've always been like that."

"They sound like cool people," he said.

"Yeah, they are. We've always been more like buddies than parents and kid. No, they'll be happy to pay for it; they'd be hurt if I didn't ask."

She turned serious, speaking in that earnest tone he sometimes distrusted. "What's important is that you'll be there, helping me through it. I'll be so nervous; I know I will."

It wasn't that he doubted what she said in that tone; it was that she wanted him to *know* she meant it. It felt superfluous; Kit always meant what she said. He smiled, stroking her hair. "You bet I'll be there," he said. "Every step of the way. And you are ready for this, Kit; keep telling yourself that."

After a quiet moment, he said, "Hey, we should put on some Christmas music."

"Mmm," she said, leaning over to kiss him. As they parted, she sat bolt upright. "Turkey smells great," she said, slapped her thighs and stood up.

They got dinner ready and listened to carols, alternating between folk albums and the syrupy stuff on the classical radio station: big choirs, orchestras, and *rum, pum, pum* brass bands. No such thing as sappy on Christmas Day.

She teased him about the small mountain of food he'd bought, but not much, because she took it just the way he thought, realizing he'd spent the week fussing about their first Christmas together. By the time she'd put in the food her parents made her stuff into her backpack, they could barely close the door.

They spent a wonderfully quiet evening together. He looked at his website a few more times, and they made a preliminary list of songs for her to record. He played her the carol he sang at Dooley's, and they found a good harmony for the chorus. They listened to music in the winter dark.

Around midnight, they were lying on Nathan's bed, both dressed in his old winter duds, listening to his favorite holiday album, *To Warm the Winter's Night*, by a local Irish harpist named Aine Minogue. It was more midwinter than Christmas, not only in what the songs were about, but in its liquid warmth. It sounded the way a thick quilt made your body feel on a cold night.

They were quiet for a long time after the music ended. He'd never known anyone like this, with whom he could be so quiet and share his solitude. Or was that, perhaps, something new in him, the gray clouds of his life parting enough to let someone else in?

"There's chocolate," Kit said after a while. "In my backpack. I forgot about it. My parents gave it to me at the bus station." She turned her head on the pillow and whispered reverently, "It's organic."

"I think there's a few hundred cookies left, too."

Kit shook her head and sighed. Poor man, doesn't understand anything. "I'm not talking about food, Nathan. I'm talking about *chocolate*."

"Indeed," he said. They rose together and walked into the living room. While he turned on the radio, she riffled through her backpack.

They sat on the sofa, in the darkness, wordlessly passing the chocolate between them, listening to the last of the carols.

Book Two

Wherever I go

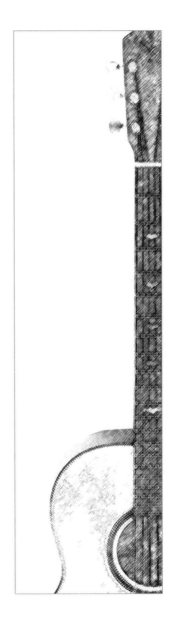

One

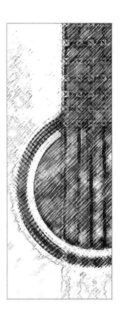

Nothing was going well.

Kit stood before the studio microphone, adjusting her headphones, readjusting them, grinning apologetically at Nathan, shrugging, fussing with her guitar strap, moving her guitar back and forth—a little to the left, no, to the right, no, more in the middle. Anything to put off trying another take.

"Just let me get comfortable," she said, as she had a dozen times throughout the evening. But she never got comfortable. As soon as she began to sing, Nathan saw the red flash on her cheeks and heard her voice falter. She would stop, sigh, shrug, move a foot this way or that, take a few breaths, tap her headphones to make sure they were on, strum her guitar doubtfully, and ask Nathan if he was *sure* it was in tune.

It was mid-February, and this was Kit's first recording session. They'd been in the Concord studio for nearly three hours without a single usable take to show for it. He thought he'd prepared her better and was angry with himself for letting this happen.

Shortly after Christmas, they settled on twelve songs for her first album. He told her to practice them, and only them, until she could do them in her sleep.

"You need to have them down cold," he said, "so they feel easy and relaxed. But you don't want to over-practice; you don't want to get tired of them. They should feel fresh when you sing them."

Kit squinted at him and said, "You know that those two pieces of advice, like, totally contradict each other."

Nathan thought about that. "They do, don't they? Well, you're smart; you'll figure it out."

"Oh, thanks," she said with an exasperated sigh. It was not the usual teasing sigh that led to a playful slug on his arm. She'd gotten irritable as she became more anxious about going in the studio. None of his reassurances helped; she simply did not think she was ready. Something about the permanence of recording bothered her. Until now, everything about her music had been fluid, malleable, a work in progress. She said it was like not wanting to pose for a picture while you're on a diet: you always think you'll look better tomorrow.

Still, Nathan's paradoxical advice worked perfectly. She told him she used the contradictions like the ends of a yardstick, to measure what she was doing. Did she want to stop because something in a song was frustrating her, something that needed more work? Or did she want to stop because she was playing it the same way, over and over, and beginning to lose her edge?

But when they got into the studio, none of that kept her from clenching up like a kid in her first school play. The moment Nathan pulled open the padded door of the studio, he felt her tighten.

"Ho!" he shouted as they walked inside, and Kit almost jumped off the floor.

"Sorry," he said. "I just wanted to hear the acoustics. Notice the way the sound fades? It's perfect for us. Just enough resonance to be lively, but no echo, no boom."

She nodded absently, staring at the walls as if deciding where to dig the escape tunnel.

It was a strange setup for a recording studio, down in the basement of a nine-teenth-century farmhouse about a mile outside Concord. The entrance to the studio was an old storm-cellar door. The control room, however, was on the main floor, just above the studio, in what appeared to have been a walk-in pantry. On the far wall there was a huge mixing board, a control panel full of knobs and dials and buttons next to a large window at floor level, built at an outward angle, so you could see the entire studio below. There was a small microphone on top of the mixing board, with a button Nathan could push to talk to Kit down in the studio.

She was so nervous at first that he suggested they record together. Maybe it would calm her down to see him there, and she could follow his rhythm. But she kept staring at his guitar and forgetting her cues.

"I'm following you, Kit," he said with a reassuring smile. "Just get into your groove and I'll be there."

But she couldn't, and it was ridiculous to think they could record anything that way, without anybody manning the controls upstairs. He would dub in his guitar parts later. So he went up to the control room and tried to use the microphone to tease her into relaxing.

"Ignore that man behind the curtain!" He hollered down to her. "I am the great and terrible Oz." She laughed and then got the nervous giggles, cackling away until he worried that she'd get hoarse. He went downstairs and gave her a shoulder rub. That made her want to neck. She threw her arms around him, kissed him, wiggled her eyebrows, and suggested they "initiate the place." Anything to keep from recording.

"I'm sure it's been initiated," he said, peeling her arms from around his neck. "The guy who owns the studio has three kids."

Then she said that maybe it would help if she could watch him record something. He resisted, saying the producer head and the performer head were entirely different. "I need to focus on what you're doing," he said, but Kit was juiced up about the idea. It took the spotlight off her.

"No, no, no," she said, waving her arms, "let's make it a song swap, like we do at home. Let's have us a real hootenanny!"

He refused a few more times, insisting he needed to man the mixing board. Before he went back to the control room, he tried tickling her to loosen her up. She was still laughing when he got upstairs. He gave her the thumbs up through the window, meaning the tape was rolling. Her smile fell, and she stared mournfully at the microphone, heaving a tense sigh that sounded more like a sob. She looked like she was about to cry.

She finally bucked herself up and timidly sang her way through a few takes. Her guitar playing was ragged and her voice barely audible. He praised her to the high heavens, but they both knew she was nowhere near her usual self. Finally, he said they should consider tonight a dry run and call it a night.

Kit was nearly in tears on the ride home, and nothing Nathan said cheered her up. She would stare at him when he spoke, then slowly turn her head and look out the window, tapping her fingers against her mouth. Very quietly, she asked if she could just go back to her apartment. Driving to his house alone, Nathan cursed himself for not being able to help her.

The next night, Kit got into the car and saw her favorite chair in the back seat, the padded kitchen chair she always sat in when they played together—the one she always joked about stealing. She smiled as she put her guitar and fiddle beside it, immediately getting the point. Relax, have fun. Like in the kitchen.

As bad as the first session had been, the second one was great. It wasn't simply the chair, of course. Kit had obviously had it out with her nerves. She was animated, focused, and bubbling with adrenaline between takes.

Nathan was having a grand time, manning the mixing board, teasing her and praising her through the microphone. Ignoring the man behind the curtain became a running gag. When he said something unexpectedly, she would go searching for the source of his disembodied voice. "Nathan? Are you in the piano? Under the piano? Where are you?" They knew it was dumb, but it broke the tension. You can often chart the quality of a recording session by how bad the jokes become: the worse the humor, the better the music.

Over the next couple of weeks, they got most of the album recorded. Whenever Kit needed a break, he would add a guitar part or harmony to what she'd already recorded.

Once Kit got comfortable, she had no trouble taking control and spelling out exactly what she wanted. He'd never seen her take charge so completely, and he enjoyed it. Funny, he'd never enjoyed that quality in Joyce. But Kit had a knack for being a boss without being bossy.

She gave instructions the way she wrote lyrics, in vivid but indirect images. But music is not something you can easily describe in words. As Ferguson said, it was another language, invented to communicate things words could not. Kit's chief directions for Nathan's guitar were to be either more "sparkly" or more "scary"; and he always knew what that meant, in the context of the music. It was a code for being brighter or darker, but with an emotional connotation that changed with each song's mood.

Once, she asked him to play "more like a tree but bluer." Even she laughed at how stupid that sounded, but he knew exactly what she meant. In this case, "bluer" meant more open, spacious, like a blue sky, not sadder, as in "play the blues." And "like a tree" meant solid, rooted, anchoring her guitar part.

She told him she had spoken that way all her life, and people often thought she was trying to be cute. Maybe it was just the musician in her, she wondered now, and he agreed. Because he knew that language, too.

Someone else might think she was being cute by asking him to play "skinnier." But he knew it meant fewer chords, more single-note riffs. He also knew that "fatter" meant just the opposite, unless it meant "bassier." And he knew when it meant which thing. Because these were musicians, speaking a wordless language they knew fluently.

And she was almost always right. He expected to have to rein her in a bit: most young musicians want to gussy up their arrangements once they see the possibilities of the studio. Not Kit. She was always looking for melodic space, letting rests remain rests, making sure every note had a purpose.

As she took over, Nathan often had little more to do than listen, watch the dials, and make sure nothing got too loud or soft. He had lots of time to think about what he was hearing.

Kit's sound was gelling quickly, becoming so distinctive and individual. She always sounded exactly like Kit Palmer.

Over the years, watching the long parade of up-and-comers at Dooley's, Nathan realized that imitation is a crucial step in an artist's growth. He disliked it when he heard young performers criticized for sounding too much like Bob Dylan, or Ani DiFranco, or the latest folk star to come down the pike. How can you find your own voice if you don't allow other voices into your music?

Imitation is as necessary to creative growth as old branches are to new buds. That's a common mistake older people make about young musicians: they hear any kind of imitation and think it's an affect, a sign of falseness. When young painters copy the old masters, brushstroke by brushstroke, their teachers pat them on the head and put gold stars next to their names. In music, the same process is too often scolded.

You don't learn the scales by rewriting them; you just play them. And the scales of songwriting lie embedded in the songs of all the great songwriters who came before. How do you immerse yourself in the voices of others without being willing to imitate?

Somehow Kit was able to skip that step. When she listened to Woody Guthrie, it didn't inspire her to sound more like him. She immediately recognized his real secret: Woody was always being Woody. So when Kit sang his songs, or learned a lick from an old fiddle tune, she did exactly what he would have done: she made the music utterly her own.

But then Kit grew up imitating traditional music, competing in fiddle contests where she was expected to copy the old tunes note for note and nuance for nuance. Those were the roots of her musical voice, even though she'd moved away from them as she got older.

So when she rediscovered traditional music, she was able to absorb the deeper lessons that tradition can teach. Her music became simpler and more distinctive at the same time, her lyrics more accessible, essential, and honest. Every influence she absorbed made her sound more like Kit Palmer

Maybe that's why Ryder's music never seemed to grow, Nathan thought, manning the studio dials as Kit recorded a fiddle track to one of her songs. Ryder didn't know the difference between imitation and impersonation. When Kit studied Woody, she imitated his individualism, melodic simplicity, and crafty use of repetition. Ryder just changed hats.

Nathan stared at the mixing board, bobbing his head, deep in thought, until he heard a tapping. He looked up and then down into the studio, where he saw Kit smiling at him and tapping the microphone with her fingernail. Hello? He shook himself and picked up the microphone. "Sorry," he said. "Got a little signal drift there. What's up?"

She said she was getting tired, but as long as they were set up for the fiddle, she wanted to try another take of "Deportee." Nathan told her to hop around a little, shake her arms, wake herself up. While she did that, he adjusted a few knobs on the mixing board, then pushed the talk button on the microphone. "Ready?"

"Ready, skipper," she said, a little too brightly, waving her fiddle in front of her. "Ahoy there. Right as rain. Steady as she goes, flibber the mainsail, jimmy the mizzen."

"You're babbling, you know."

"I think I'm channeling Ramblin' Randy."

"'*Remember the Alamooooooooooooo,*'" Nathan sang and Kit erupted into laughter, almost tripping over a mike chord. Nerves. She was getting punchy.

"Maybe we've done all we're going to do tonight," he said. "I'll do that second guitar part for the last song, and we'll call it a night. Sound good?"

She smiled gratefully at him, slumping her shoulders, and suddenly looking tired. It was as if he'd given her permission to be as exhausted as she really was. There may be no more useful skill for a producer than to know when musicians are about to lose it—and stopping them before they do.

Ferguson was about to make a point at the open mike, back arched on his bar stool, finger raised dramatically, when Kit's cell phone began to ring: *Plingle-lickle-ling*! The ringtone was an electric guitar riff from an Ani DiFranco song, but coming through that tiny speaker, it sounded like Tinker Bell playing punk rock.

"What in the weary hell is that?" Ferguson said, darting his eyes around the room.

Kit stuffed her hand into her white parka, shutting off the phone, while her eyes followed Ferguson's glances, as if she too was trying to locate the sound. When she pulled her hand out of her pocket, however, Ferguson saw it and glowered dramatically.

"Busted," Nathan whispered to Kit.

"Indeed," Ferguson barked, pointing an accusing finger. "Our cell phone, I presume?"

Kit nodded sheepishly. "Sorry, perfesser," she said. "Forgot I had it on."

"What was that awful whining? It sounded like a mosquito dying."

"I was thinking more like a yodeling bee," Nathan said. Kit glared at him. He cleared his throat. "If, you know, bees could yodel."

He sat up straight on his bar stool and nodded emphatically. "Which, of course, they can't," he said, in a tone that suggested this might be a helpful thing to say.

Kit shrugged at Ferguson. "It's the beginning of an Ani DiFranco song I really like," she said.

"Was she on helium when she recorded it?"

Kit sighed and slumped down on her bar stool.

An old drunk was sitting sleepily next to Ferguson. He'd been working on the same beer for more than an hour, lifting it up, heaving a breath, then putting it down. Nathan wondered if the drunk was aware that he was forgetting to drink it. Maybe he thought it was a magic beer that kept refilling itself.

The recent commotion roused the old guy, however. He appeared perplexed at first, then began smiling foolishly at Kit. When Ferguson's voice rose, he looked sternly at him, even wagging an admonishing finger. He seemed to think that Ferguson was genuinely angry at Kit. Finally, he tapped Ferguson on the shoulder.

"I beg your pardon?" Ferguson said, rearing back from the drunk.

"Shun't talk to the purdy girl like that. Shu'be nice, sush a purdy girl." The drunk grinned at Kit. "Sush a purdy girl, you."

Kit smiled back, waving her fingers at him. The old drunk glanced down at his beer, again looking perplexed. He turned his watery eyes toward Ferguson, leaning into him as he spoke. "Shun't talk to her like that, no, huh?"

Ferguson pushed him back with a finger. "Do you mind?"

Kit smiled at the drunk again and he grinned back, wrinkling his nose. Jackie quietly picked up his beer, poured it out, and put it back in front of him.

The old drunk looked down at the empty beer mug, nodded emphatically, and buttoned up his faded Patriots jacket. He climbed slowly off his stool as if it was a high and unsteady ladder. He attempted a bow in Kit's direction, again said "Sush a purdy girl, you," pulled his stocking cap low on his head, and pushed himself away from the bar, uttering a loud "Whoo-*ufff*" as he lurched forward.

Ferguson watched the drunk totter off, and Nathan said, "Rough crowd tonight, eh, hoss?"

"Indignity. Disrespect," Ferguson said with a hilariously world-weary whimper. "I'm accustomed to the burden. I shall soldier on."

"That's what we're all afraid of," Jackie said.

"Where was I?" Ferguson said, shooting Jackie a sideward glance. "I've lost my train of thought."

"I could turn my cell phone back on, if it'd help," Kit said, beginning to push her hand into her pocket. Ferguson tried to glower at her, but it quickly became a grin.

"Cell phones," he said. "Yes, let's talk about cell phones. I hate the things. I've never gotten a decent interview on one of those evil contraptions. People always talk like they're in a hurry."

He said he'd recently tried to do an interview with a musician who was using a cell phone while driving to a gig. The conversation was interrupted by dropped words and disconnections. The musician was distracted by the bad reception, and by his driving. Ferguson never had his full attention.

"The cell phone is to conversation what texting is to literature," Ferguson said. "It is e-mail for the mouth. Something about cell phones—maybe it's how clumsy they are—makes people talk in shorthand. And they're distracted. It's not just the signal that drifts, the people do, too."

Jackie told a story about throwing out "some simple-minded suit" whose cell phone rang repeatedly during a show by the weekend rockabilly band. When he refused to turn it off, she told him to leave.

"You're throwing me out for making noise in a rock bar?" the suit complained.

"You're just not up to our usual clientele, sir," she had told him.

Wiping the bar with her towel, she said, "I hate it when suits like that come in after work. It's obvious they think they're slumming—and it's like they *want* me to know that's how they feel. Like this place is beneath them."

Ramblin' Randy had wandered over for a beer. "Boy," he said, "I'm glad I didn't wear my MIT suit tonight."

Jackie slid him a beer. "Dearie," she said, "wearing a suit and *being* a suit are two different things."

"Thank you," Randy said, blushing a little. From Jackie, this was high praise.

"Y'welcome," she said, and sealed the compliment with a wink.

Nights are numb.

Nathan was running errands when the words exploded into his head. They had nothing to do with what he'd been thinking.

Nights are numb. The phrase hit him so hard that it almost hurt, like a sharp knock on the inside of his skull. He immediately knew that it was a line for the song he began to write before Christmas, and that somehow, in that part of the mind that lies beneath our thoughts, he'd been working on it for a long time.

It was nearly two months since he'd gotten off to such a promising start on the song, but he'd been unable to write any more. He knew that he needed to draw the song back inward, after widening the lens with a second verse about the cocky innocence of youth—"When it was spring, everyone would sing, we can do anything"—and a refrain lamenting what happens when that youth learns the hard lessons—"What made us think that our hearts would be enough?"

A big part of Nathan's problem was simple mechanics. Thanks to the surviving line from the original version—"Make me well, someone, break the spell"—he was stuck with a tight internal rhyme to begin each verse. The good news was that the remaining scheme was fairly casual. But he had to avoid any forced rhymes—no moon, june, spooning. This song was happening deep inside the singer, almost a meditation. It had to sound natural, even as it conformed to the strict rhyme scheme and spare structure.

He wanted to turn inward with the next verse, but he also didn't want to get too specific. This was not a song about Nathan's troubles; it was a song about being in trouble. Everybody knows about that.

He pulled into a vacant taxi stand on Mass. Ave. Had he ever seen an actual cab there? Focus, focus.

Nights are numb. Nice, because this was not a song about feeling bad. It was about losing the ability to feel anything.

Nights are numb. They certainly are, when you're in that kind of trouble. What were those nights like for him, during his worst years? He remembered staring at the ceiling, fists clenched at his sides, wondering why he couldn't sleep and thinking how unfair that was. He'd put his whole damn life to sleep.

Nights are numb, but sleep won't come.

Close. He liked the simplicity but something was wrong. He sang it to himself a couple of times, then laughed and said, "Oops." A less experienced singer wouldn't have noticed it, at least not for a long time. But Nathan knew the difficult art of hearing songs the way a listener would, and there was a definite *oops* in the middle of the verse: "numb-butt." Apt perhaps, he thought with a smile, but kind of a mood killer.

Nights are numb, still sleep won't come.

Good. Now, a word that works with "come." He sighed, leaning against the car window, idly turning the steering wheel. What did he think about on all those numb, sleepless nights? He thought about what had gone wrong and why. Wondered what he could have done differently and why he didn't.

And the hollow, awful answer that came was everything and nothing. He'd done everything wrong and yet somehow none of it was his doing. He'd merely been a passenger, along for the ride. His whole life had happened to him while he wasn't looking. That's how it felt then, in the darkness he'd made for himself.

Nights are numb, still sleep won't come
Wondering what have I done?

That's it. Very general, a place everyone has been. He nodded his head and pulled back into the light afternoon traffic. Enough for now. He was a great believer in letting songs rest, so he tried not to think about it anymore. But the song wasn't done with him yet. Everything and nothing, everything and nothing. By the time he pulled into the parking lot of the convenience store, he had the next line.

Things I said but never meant.

The reply came immediately.

Things I meant but never said.

Where the hell did *that* come from? Did he think of that? It had struck him so quickly that it seemed like it must have come from somewhere else. Perhaps from the song itself, as it slowly came to life, beneath his thoughts, and began to take control of its creation. He sang the couplet:

Things I said but never meant
Things I meant but never said

A perfect reversal and yet so simple, a summary of the nature of regret. The things we said and did not say. And isn't it the things we do *not* say that we end up regretting the most.

The couplet came so easily, it felt like a revelation. How had he known that? How had the poetry come so suddenly, so fully formed?

These are the moments that make songwriters say they don't write their songs, the songs merely pass through them. Nathan shook his head slowly, savoring the wonder of it. Did he actually write that? But he knew from years of these strange and beautiful epiphanies that he would never know. All he could do was say thank you to wherever those bursts of creativity originated. It's what the ancients called "the muse," because they didn't know what the hell it was, either.

He sang the new verse through:

Nights are numb, still sleep won't come
Wondering what have I done?
Things I said but never meant
Things I meant but never said

Boy, if that ain't the weary little Nathan Warren saga in a nutshell. Everybody's weary little saga, though, everybody's. At least on those nights when sleep won't come.

He felt his body sag, physically drained from the power of the muse passing through him. It's a lot like the feeling after a strong electrical shock, that strange mix of ache and elation. He really did feel as if something had physically passed through him.

But as he got out his car, he knew he was stumped again, and badly. He didn't even know what kind of song this was anymore.

Nathan sent Kit right down into the studio, telling her to tune up, vocalize a little, open up the throat, and relax while he booted everything up. When she was nervous, like she was tonight, she would watch him set up the soundboard the way a patient watches a dentist turn on the drill.

There was only one song left to record, but it was the one she'd tightened up on during the last session. Now she'd had lots of time to think about getting nervous. He could tell she was spooked, and angry with herself for it.

Maybe it was the song she was recording, "Deportee." It was so far from her actual experience. More likely, it was her raw arrangement, just fiddle and voice. Displaying rawness on stage is one thing, but in the antiseptic quiet of a studio, it can seem phony. And the last thing any true-blue folksinger wants is to get caught faking it on a Woody Guthrie song.

Nathan needed one more trick, something to force her to stop worrying about her nerves.

"Why don't you run through it once while I finish setting up the board?" he said through the studio microphone. "Just for yourself, loosen up. Pretend you're at a little coffeehouse."

"Good idea," she mumbled, took two deep breaths, and began to play the fiddle intro. She immediately fell under the spell of the song. Her eyes closed, seeing the dirty-shirt immigrants filing sadly onto the airplane, unwanted strangers again, now that their work was done. It was all there in the way Kit sang, her fiddle sobbing along, as if hearing the story for the first time.

> *Goodbye to my Juan, goodbye, Rosalita*
> *Adios, mis amigos, Jesus y Maria.*
> *You won't have your names when you ride the big airplane.*
> *All they will call you will be "deportees."*

Nathan smiled as he listened. It was a good old trick but it only worked once. He was glad he'd saved it for now.

When she finished, she looked up suddenly, as if shaken awake, then stared mournfully at her fiddle: Why won't you play like that when it matters?

"Okay," she said, clenching up again. "Wanna try one?"

"I don't think we need to, Kit. You nailed it."

Her eyes bugged. "You were *recording* that?"

"But of course," he said, grinning at her through the studio window. "Come on up; let's listen."

"You sneak!" She shouted. But she was smiling; she knew she'd nailed it, too.

They listened, and it was obvious from the first note. She'd never sung it better or meant it more. Her voice was a little frail at first, because she thought she was just warming up, but that fit the uncertain emotions of the song, creating a swelling crescendo of both music and mood.

"So you're done, kiddo," Nathan said, folding his hands behind his head. "You can relax. Your parole has come through."

"Done?"

"Well, you wanted to double the fiddle part on this one, and you've got a few little harmony and fiddle parts to do. But it's all overdubs. All the songs are done. No more need to get spooked."

"I thought I was over all that," she said, shaking her head and staring at the floor.

"You'll never get over it completely; you just find different ways to beat it. First time in the studio, first-time jitters. Perfectly natural. You know, all the great actors say they throw up before opening night. And the day they don't is the day they retire."

"Isn't that a lot of fun to look forward to."

"The price of giving a shit, sweetie," Nathan said, turning in his chair and adjusting the levels for Kit's fiddle overdubs.

"Isn't that a little easy?" she said. "It's not like I haven't figured this out, over and over and over. So you'd think I'd get past it, but *noooo*. Now I get nervous about being nervous about getting nervous. I mean, who makes things complicated like that?"

"You're kidding, right?" Nathan said. "Look who you're talking to."

Kit laughed and patted his knee, then looked back down at the floor. She was mad at herself. "I should be over all this shit," she said.

"Ferguson's Law."

"What?" She looked up and smiled.

"Ferguson's Law of Surplus Intelligence. He never told you?"

She straightened in her chair and shook her head, grinning in anticipation. A word from the perfesser, just the thing.

Nathan cleared his throat pompously. "Ferguson's Law of Surplus Intelligence," he said, "states that it requires an absolute maximum of one hundred IQ points to function as *homo sapiens*. Therefore, any surplus IQ automatically divides itself into two equal parts, one of which creates problems for the other to solve. This is Ferguson's Law of Surplus Intelligence."

Kit burst out laughing, pounding his knee with her fist. "Omigod, omigod, omigod!" she shouted, "That's totally true. God, that's, like, *everybody* I know."

She let out a sharp "Hah!" and twirled all the way around in her swivel chair. "That's totally how I got through college," she said. "My roommate was always saying, 'Isn't college hard enough? Why do you have to make everything so complicated?'"

"Ferguson's Law in action," Nathan said serenely. "And do you know who inspired the formulation of Ferguson's Law?"

Kit cackled and rubbed her chin. "Oh, let me guess."

"You got it. You are looking at the original lab rat for Ferguson's Law of Surplus Intelligence."

Kit hunched over the soundboard, laying her head in her arms and laughing harder. "Of course you are," she said, the words muffled by her arms.

"Ferguson actually put it to me just that way. 'Lab rat.' He said some rats get through the maze and eat the cheese and some don't."

Her head popped up. "And you?"

"He said I'd get right through the maze, lickety-split," Nathan said, then pointed to his head. "Because I'm smart, you see. But then I'd starve to death worrying about whether it was okay to eat the cheese."

Nathan had to stop a moment. He was laughing, too.

"I'd wonder how long the cheese had been there," he said. "Will it make me sick? Does it have a bunch of preservatives I shouldn't eat? Whose cheese is it? Is the cheese mine, simply because I found it? What are the ethical implications of living in a world like that? What about the rats who haven't found the cheese yet? Shouldn't I save some for them? In a world of cheeses and cheese-nots, shouldn't I be siding with the cheese-nots?"

"Oh stop, you're killing me!" Kit said, pounding her hands on the soundboard. "The cheeses and cheese-nots?"

"That's exactly how Ferguson put it. The cheeses and the cheese-nots. I'd sit there, wondering if I should just eat some of the cheese and save the rest. But save it for who? For me, for later, or for the other rats? Finally, I'd start worrying about what was wrong with me that I didn't know the Cheese Rules."

"And starve to death."

"Yup. That's the one that would kill me: wondering why I didn't know the Cheese Rules."

"Oh, it would, Nathan, it totally would. Being the first one to find the cheese would make you *so* unhappy."

Kit looked at the soundboard, trying to catch her breath. "It really all comes down to that, doesn't it?"

"What?"

"The cheeses and the cheese-nots. It's a cheese and cheese-not world."

They laughed awhile longer, then listened to "Deportee" again. Nathan went in the studio to overdub a guitar part to fill the middle between Kit's fiddle and voice. Then he decided it was better with just Kit.

"It's really a soliloquy, the way you do it," he said. "I don't want to gunk it up."

Kit smiled gratefully at him. He realized she'd already figured that out but didn't want to tell him.

They took turns overdubbing a few fiddle and guitar parts, and he added harmonies to a few of her vocals. Then they were done. Kit Palmer had recorded her first album.

Nathan and Kit staggered out of the studio a little after midnight. He said they should wait a few weeks, "to clear the notes out of our heads," before mixing the album: the grueling, repetitive process of setting the volume levels and the effects, like bass, treble, and reverb. Kit nodded absently, but clearly didn't want to think about all that right now.

As Nathan started the car, she said, "I think you should make a CD, too. I mean, as long as we're doing all this, why not? While we're waiting to mix mine."

He shook his head and said again that this project was enough for right now. He wondered why the idea didn't interest him. Something about it didn't feel right. It was different from the old ennui, though. Maybe he needed to finish that new song first. He shrugged and turned the car onto Route 2, back to Cambridge.

Kit talked about the night's session, and they laughed more about Ferguson's Law of Surplus Intelligence. Then she fell quiet, looking out the car window, tapping the armrest with her gloved hand and smiling to herself. He knew exactly how she felt, the excitement, the exhaustion, and the satisfaction, laced together with the tired glow that comes when the adrenaline wears off. You can almost feel the last of it trickling out through your toes.

He loved being around her at moments like this, vicariously soaking in the feeling. He let her be quiet, recalling how he felt when his career was beginning. Then he remembered those bad final years on the road, trying to stoke himself up for one more show, night after night after night. One more show.

That was the worst part, wasn't it? He almost lost his music. He started to hate it and, even worse, to be bored by it. Same old songs, same old jokes, traveling longer and longer for less and less, the crowds spotty, the pay short. There were days he couldn't bring himself to take out his guitar, warm up the same tired arrangements of the same tired songs, write a set list, knowing that tonight didn't matter any more than last night. What's the point? Can there be a worse question for a musician to ask about his own music?

That may have been what made him stop touring, more than the bad gigs and the drinking. Music was the only light left in his dark life, the only thing he still loved; and only through it would he ever be able to love anything else. Lose that and he would go into the dark room finally and completely, shutting the door behind him.

So he'd gotten off the road and started looking for other ways to be a musician. Suddenly, driving back to town with Kit sitting beside him, he realized that this final retreat had been, in fact, a step back toward life. He would not let the darkness have his music. It had taken everything else, but it could not have that. He finally refused to give the darkness something it wanted.

He looked at Kit, gazing out the side window, smiling to herself. She had asked to be dropped off at her place because she had an early shift at her waitressing job. Maybe she wanted to be alone with the crackle of finishing her first album, to put her feet up, eat ice cream until dawn, and be as full of herself as she deserved to be.

He pulled up in front of her apartment. They kissed and held each other. He wanted to tell her what he'd been thinking and how glad he was to have her in his life. But this was her night, so he just held her closer. The embrace filled him with her, the look and feel of her in his arms, the smell of her, the sound of her moving against him, the taste of her on his tongue.

He wanted to ask her to come home with him, and offer to drive her to work in the morning. Nathan was still Nathan, though; he could always find a reason to not do something. As they held each other, he worried about imposing on her if she wanted to be alone. Then again, it never hurt to let a woman know her company was desired. But it might make her uncomfortable to say no. Always a reason. So he kissed her again, said congratulations again, urged her to do something foolishly indulgent, and to feel very good about herself.

She said thanks, rubbed his arm, and spent a long moment looking at him. Then she got out of the car. Before she could close the door, he said he loved her. She lowered her head back into the car and whispered the same back to him.

He pulled away from the curb, still feeling her all around him. He should have asked her. At least asked her.

Nathan woke up thickly, dreamily. Even though he had slept alone, he felt Kit all around him, filling all his senses. A sensual fog surrounded him, thoughts and feelings wetly mingled. He knew he'd been dreaming about her. And somehow, in that place beneath words, he also knew the dream was about the song he was writing.

Dreams were often where work got done in his songs, work that his wakeful self could not do. He rose slowly, careful not to shake the mood. He sat on the corner of the bed, not thinking, only feeling, opening his mind to what that deeper self had to say. The dream was already disappearing, but not its warm, fleshy mood. He could feel Kit on his skin, taste her in his mouth. He licked his lips. So vivid. How could she not have been here?

Instinctively, his eyes moved to where he would always find her, asleep beneath his covers. How could she not have been here? The room was full of her.

What did the dream want to tell him? He knew from experience how fragile these unformed thoughts were, how easily displaced by the stirring of his day-mind, his practical self. He closed his eyes, sitting motionless on the side of the bed. It was a strange process, not quite dreaming, not yet thinking, just opening, opening. He didn't know how he did it, only that he could. The trick was not waking up, the trick was not thinking.

He imagined the fog of sleep like a cloak he was keeping around him. He fought off mundane thoughts about coffee, getting dressed, the day ahead. What was he feeling? What wanted to come? It had not been a troubled dream nor a happy one. Warm, thick, full of Kit. Kit and something else. Music. Yes, music and Kit.

He lay back down, surrounding himself with the remembered sense of her. He wished she was there, but then the song would not get written. He smiled. Shoo! No thinking, no thinking, just feel, feel. He pulled the covers up over his head, like she did, and rolled himself into a little ball, like she did, keeping the imagined softness of her inside and near. The warm liquid of sleep poured back into his mind, but he didn't let himself doze off. Just stay here, in sleep's twilight, feel, remember, open, open.

Wrapped around himself, holding a pillow where he felt she still was, a single thought began to form, so slowly he could almost feel its atoms gather into molecules, then into solid form, then color, shape, random letters, and then a single word: *home.*

The song was about home; the song was about Kit. About finding a way back home, home to you.

She was the home he had sought without seeking, all those dry, dumb years; the home he had wanted so long ago, before everything went wrong. Before he knew her, before he lost his way.

This song, more than any he had written, needed to resolve intimately, push him to the edge of what he knew about himself. It needed to be as brave as every one of Kit's songs. He needed to put his old, sad self on display. The important thing was *what* he had lost, not why, not whose fault. And what that loss did to him, leaving him with regret as his only reliable companion: "Things I said but never meant; things I meant but never said."

Then another thought came, cleaner, brighter, but still from deep within his dreaming mind. For all the song's loneliness and melancholy, its acknowledgment of mortal failure— "Everything I do is wrong"—this was not a sad song. Because it was not simply about being alone and empty. It was about the moment we realize we're lost, and, by realizing, begin to turn toward home. It was not a song about being lost; it was a song about finding your way back, out of your own darkness. And that there is a way back; there is always a way back.

It was a song about the possibility of redemption that always lies waiting, felt more than known, ready to take you home the moment you know that you are lost, the moment you know what home is, and want it enough to look for it.

Because it's always there, isn't it? Home. Patiently waiting for us to simply see it, recognize it, want it, whatever that home is for us. And in that moment of recognition and of wanting, we slowly begin to turn our life away from the dark and back toward home.

Nathan sat up slowly, letting the covers fall away around him. Was that it? He lingered a moment, respecting the muse, listening in case it had more to say. But he knew that it had told him what it wanted to. Home.

He felt the dream begin to lift, like fog clearing, making everything around him seem suddenly wide-eyed and wakeful. That was it. He took a deep breath that became a yawn and shook the sleep from his body. The scent and feel of Kit were gone, replaced by an almost painful desire to feel guitar strings beneath his fingers. But first, coffee.

With the buoyant rush of caffeine kicking in, he hunched over the kitchen table, still naked, guitar in lap, and began to write. He already knew this would be the final verse, the completion. It was a mechanical task now, after what the dream had brought him. He knew what he wanted to say; it was just a matter of condensing it into the tight structure of the song. Simple words, simple phrases, and that damned internal rhyme. Whittle, whittle, whittle.

He moved his chair closer to the window. The sun, partially obscured by fat winter clouds, cast short shadows from the trees onto the hard ground. All the snow was gone now; everything that had been crystalline and white was now dirt brown and dead black.

He took a drink of coffee, forgot to taste it, and began to write. He occasionally strummed a chord or sang a phrase, searching out the structure that the verse needed. Whittle, whittle, whittle. Home, the way back home.

After an hour, he had it, chiseled and buffed. He sang softly:

Day on day lived the same old way
Never motion, never change.
All that is true and the only way through,
Is to find my way back home to you.

He sang the whole song, then sang it again. That was it. Finished. He looked out the window and saw a small sparrow pecking away on a bare tree branch. Wood for breakfast again? Nathan smiled and looked back down at his guitar.

"So it's a love song," he said softly. "How about that?"

Two

Nathan insisted they wait at least six weeks before mixing Kit's new CD, which was driving her absolutely nuts. The wisdom of waiting was not a zen she had mastered.

But mixing required listening to songs, and tiny moments of songs, over and over, setting volume levels, treble, and bass, deciding on the amount and type of reverb. You had to make sure everything blended together, deal with notes that suddenly got too loud or too soft.

All the instruments needed to be set just right: which is the dominant instrument, which are secondary? How secondary should the secondary instruments be? Should they be the same volume as the dominant instrument or heard only in the background? And that can change several times within a single song: a fiddle part that should hide in the background during the vocals and be turned up between verses.

Almost unnoticeable sounds—a finger sliding on a string, a breath, a guitar brushing against a mike stand, a chair squeak—have to be isolated and cut out. It is a grueling, tedious, and numbingly unmusical process. Nathan had been through it enough to know that hearing everything with fresh ears was essential to making the right decisions.

For Kit, it was all much simpler. They could make their ears fresh if they really wanted to. She had an album completely recorded, sitting in a studio in Concord. Thirty minutes away. There had to be some way to get it finished and out into the world. Now.

"Maybe my ears are fresher than yours," she said. "Ever think of that?"

"I'm sure they are," he said, "but you can't mix it by yourself. You have to wait for my tired old ears."

Once, she argued that three weeks was more than enough time for even the weariest ears to freshen up.

"You'll be glad you waited," he said. "That's all I can say. When you see what mixing is like, you'll know why we need to let it breathe a little."

"It can't breathe in the record stores?"

"You know what I mean," he said.

And she did, which made it worse. Nothing about the way Kit walked through life counseled that putting on the brakes could be the best way to move forward. Nothing in her experience kept her from believing they could do what they wanted now, if they really tried. Her first album was sitting in a small black digital recorder on top of a mixing board in Concord. Thirty minutes away. If they really tried.

He wouldn't even let her listen to it. He'd burned a CD master as a backup copy, but he wouldn't let her near it. She tried several strategies to get around the no-listening rule. Maybe they should make a copy for her parents, let them hear what they were paying for.

No.

Maybe they should let her roommates hear it before mixing. Talk about fresh ears; they never listen to folk music. They would have really different opinions. Very, very fresh.

No.

Late one night, she suggested they could put it on really low, like background music, and see how it felt to them that way. It might help with the mixing. Because that's how a lot of people listen to music, you know.

No.

"Okay, okay," she would say. But it wasn't. This was a new kind of frustration, being unable to push herself forward. It made her cranky, annoyed at small things. It wasn't the album; it was not being able to *do* anything.

Nathan had learned to be good at waiting; she had not, and he hoped she never would. He loved her passion, admired it, envied it. And frankly, he was having a grand time watching her pop her cork.

Sometimes he would catch her staring at him, lips tight, eyes squinted, thinking, thinking. Must be some way to get this moving, some way, some way. Then she'd heave a sigh, swear under her breath, and begin complaining about politics or the environment or something she'd read in the paper.

Fortunately—for both of them, probably—she was doing gigs almost every weekend. He would often join her, playing backup guitar, laying on some harmonies. After recording, their arrangements of her songs were tight and elegant.

She often talked about booking shows together, as a duo. But he resisted; it was Kit's appeal that was making this happen, her fans, her gigs. He was delighted to be part of that but happier in the shadows. The idea that her fans might think he was shoving himself into her spotlight gave him a cold ache in his stomach. He still had some self-respect.

"Damn this thing!"

Nathan was having a bad morning. He was struggling with the coffeemaker, and all the grounds had spilled on the counter. It hadn't begun there, however. He'd stubbed his toe getting out of bed, always a bad sign, and for some evil reason, his toothpaste decided to belch when he squeezed it, spitting a big splash of goo on the bathroom mirror. Cleaning toothpaste off a mirror takes much longer than it should.

Nathan rarely lost his temper but it was most likely to flare when a succession of random things went wrong. That somehow tapped into his general anger at a world that had not kept its end of the bargain, that had not really cared about the things it said it cared about. When a bad day put him in a mood like that, he began sensing some mystical conspiracy that confirmed his lingering, unspoken suspicion that the universe held a particular grudge against him.

"Why are you getting so upset?" Kit asked, looking up from her iPhone, where she was checking her e-mail. He tried to explain that it wasn't just the coffeemaker; the toaster had behaved the same way. And don't let me even get started on the damn toothpaste. How can toothpaste burp?

"You think they're working together?" She said. There was no trace of humor in her voice. Did she really expect him to answer that? Boy, she'd been grouchy lately.

He frowned at her. "Don't take sides," he said and turned back to the coffee-maker. He was trying to remain good-natured, but the adrenaline was feeding his temper now. At a certain point, a mood like this becomes something to savor. He really wanted that coffee.

"I just don't think your stuff is misbehaving," Kit said in a patronizing tone. "I mean, why get mad at a coffeemaker? It's not like you're hurting its feelings."

She smiled at him but not a happy smile. "Maybe you should punish it. Unplug it and make it go outside until it says it's sorry."

He turned away, sensing that anything he said would add fuel to whatever strange fire was building. He put the top back on the coffeemaker, and it immediately slid over, spilling more coffee on the counter.

"Shit," he muttered, as peacefully as he could manage.

"Jesus!" Kit said sharply.

That got him mad. "Look, I'm just having a bad day, okay?"

"Well, *duh!*" She walked into the living room. Plopping down heavily on the couch, she said "What-*ever*," and looked down at her phone.

He stayed in the kitchen, cleaning up the spilled grounds, and finally got a pot brewing. He walked over to Kit with a cup of coffee, hoping to put things right, but she never looked up from her phone. He went over to the stereo, saying as cheerfully as he could, "How about some nice baroque music? I love a little Scarlatti in the morning."

"It's *your* stereo," she said.

My stereo? Where did that come from? He put in a CD and his bad day continued. The CD player made the annoying little series of beeps—*beep, beep, beep*—that it made when it didn't think it had a CD in it. "NO DISC," it flashed at him.

"You do too have a disc in you," Nathan said softly, trying not to lose his temper again. He opened the CD drawer, closed it—*beep, beep, beep*—opened it, closed it—*beep, beep, beep*—opened it, closed it—*beep, beep, beep*—and gave up, blowing out a hard breath.

"Well," he said through clenched teeth, "quiet is nice, too."

He turned to see Kit staring at him. "It won't tell you," she said in that same patronizing tone. You'd think she was talking to a seven year-old.

"Tell me what?"

"If it's in cahoots with the coffeemaker."

He stared at the stereo, waving an index finger. "Don't think you're fooling anyone," he said.

The CD player suddenly made its happy beep and began to play. Perfect. Kit laughed coldly. He turned to see her head still buried in that damn phone. No wonder so many women think about divorce while watching their husbands read the morning paper.

What's going on here? He was having a fine morning tantrum, blowing off some harmless steam. And all of a sudden, it's about Kit being mad at the world. Or at him. Ah, yes. Him.

Kit was very direct about expressing most emotions, but not anger. Nathan had learned that one way she displayed anger was to become detached and logical, then home in on some inconsistency she observed. He would have preferred it if she just threw things at him. When you're mad at your coffeemaker, the last thing you want is someone coolly explaining the wisdom of coffeemakers or why it's stupid to get mad at them. He knew that. Well, maybe not the wisdom of coffeemakers, but he certainly knew it wasn't smart to get angry at them. It was occasionally necessary, however, in order to prove that we are, if not smarter, at least more emotionally complex than our appliances.

So Kit was mad at him. Hmm. About what, he wondered? Not letting her finish the CD? Well, that was certainly part of it. She'd been generally cranky lately, impatient with him and the whole world. This felt different, though.

Nathan had also learned that Kit's anger rarely flared at the moment she got upset. It usually festered for a while, looking for a soft place to land. Sometime later he'd do something she found annoying—and then she'd pounce. Mad at his coffeemaker. That is *so* like him.

They occasionally had these surly moments, the inevitable brushfires of an intimate relationship. Just clearing off old debris, keeping the soil fresh. The moments usually burned themselves off pretty quickly, and whatever really sparked them was calmly discussed later.

What was it this time, Nathan wondered. She usually left him a clue somewhere. What was out of context? "It's your stereo," she'd said.

Oh. That. This probably began last night, when he made her listen to two albums by the late Texas songwriter Townes Van Zandt, then said his ears were too tired when she tried to play him one of her favorite songwriters. That wasn't fair, was it? It was just that he got so excited about sharing his world with her.

He winced because of the thought that inevitably followed: but not so excited when she's doing the sharing. Damn. That's really not fair. And it wasn't true, at least not entirely. He did want to wait so he could appreciate the new music. Listening to the same artist for a long time put him into a groove that was hard to shake. He went to sleep with Van Zandt's easy Texas gait loping through his brain.

There was also no avoiding the fact that he wasn't as excited about her new songwriters as she was about his old favorites. Maybe that was just him being set in his ways, but it was also the modern techno-pop sound with its synthesized smoothness. It kept him at a distance, as if it was more about the machinery than the people.

They both knew it; they'd even talked about it. But did that make it more important or less important to give her favorites a fair hearing? Ouch. Sometimes you answer questions by asking them.

He hadn't explained any of that to Kit last night, so she probably didn't go to bed with an easy Texas gait loping through her brain. As a result, his small tantrum wasn't met with her usual teasing and sympathy. It ignited something left over from before, something small but brittle and combustible, lying old and useless at their feet. Burn it off.

Kit was still looking at her iPhone, in a posture that unmistakably said she was angry. Nathan found the album she'd wanted to play for him, stuck it in the CD player, and sat down on the floor, looking at the lyric booklet.

After a few seconds, he heard her put the phone on the table beside the sofa. "Cool voice, huh?" she said quietly.

He looked up at her and nodded. "Nice lyrics, too," he said, then looked back down at the CD booklet. They listened together. After the album was over, they'd talk it all out. Maybe he'd say again that he found it hard to get into some of her favorites, so she could say again that that was okay with her. But later, after the music. Burn it off.

One night in the recording studio, Nathan had suggested that Kit stop performing at his open mike. He said she was getting too many paid gigs to continue being seen as an open-miker. He might hate the idea that there was a caste system in the folk scene, but that didn't mean it wasn't real. For Kit to keep doing open mikes, even his, could diminish her stature in some people's eyes.

He expected her to put up an argument, but she immediately agreed, adding softly, "If that's what you think is best, Nathan." He'd learned to be a bit suspicious when she seemed pliant. She always listened to his advice and often took it, but she usually put up some resistance, if only to reinforce that these were her decisions to make. Which, of course, they were.

Thinking it over later, Nathan figured she'd probably already reached that conclusion—she wasn't doing any other open mikes—but didn't want to be the one to bring it up. That could be an awkward moment, explaining to your boyfriend that you're too big and important to play his gig anymore.

Or maybe she simply agreed with him. There was a very practical side to her ambition, a business side free of ego or insecurity. She knew how fast her mailing list of fans was growing; it had more than a thousand names on it. People would often write in more than one name, saying, "I have to sign up my friend too; she'll love you." Kit had to be aware of how popular she was becoming.

She still dropped by on Tuesdays, but usually late enough to miss most of the music. She would wave hi to everybody, then join Nathan, Ferguson, and Jackie at the bend of the bar. Sometimes Nathan would see Ryder scowling at her from his perch among the hungry squirrels.

The jam was a different story, however. Kit loved having a place where she could play socially, with none of the pressures of performing. And she still preferred the smaller back room jams, just sitting around a table, playing whatever came to mind.

One drab March Wednesday—is there any other kind of Wednesday in March?—Nathan turned the sound system over to the jammers and walked to the back room. He wanted to make sure Kit was coming over to the house. He was finally ready to sing his new song for her, after weeks of fussing with the guitar arrangement.

Kit only brought her fiddle to the jams, but she was playing somebody's guitar when Nathan walked in. She was singing "One of These Days," an Earl Montgomery song she'd learned from one of Nathan's old Emmylou Harris records. Kit had made it a very different song, though. Emmylou sang it as a fragile hymn of resilience; Kit made its hopefulness sound doubtful, the unreachable dream of someone not ready for the big changes she is promising herself:

> *One of these days, it will soon be all over, cut and dried,*
> *And I won't have this urge to go all bottled up inside.*

It wasn't better—nobody sings anything *better* than Emmylou. But it was radically different, as full of uncertainty as Emmylou's version was of grit. The way Kit sang it, this was someone wary, frightened, muttering to herself all the things she could not say to an uncaring world.

Nathan stood behind her, listening with his eyes closed. Like Emmylou, Kit was a much trickier vocalist than people realized. Nathan always smiled when he heard people talk about what a natural singer Emmylou was. Honest, yes, but natural? She had an endless array of vocal tricks, an encyclopedia of sobs, catches, trills, and cracks. You thought they were natural because that's what she wanted you to think.

Kit was becoming like that. As she sang "One of These Days," her voice sounded at once whispery and clenched, insinuating the anger beneath the hurt. It didn't seem like an inflection, though; it seemed like this was simply how she felt. Because that's what she wanted you to think.

> *One of these days I'll look back, and I'll say I left in time.*
> *Because somewhere for me I know, there's peace of mind,*
> *There's gonna be peace of mind for me, one of these days.*

The shyness that had plagued Kit was becoming a powerful tool in her musical vocabulary. Even her nervous puffs of breath had been turned into a truncated, breathy sustain that always seemed raw and unexpected, whether she used it to suggest sorrow, anger, or uncertainty. Like so many of Emmylou's tricks, it sounded accidental, a moment of sudden, unfiltered emotion. But also like Emmylou, Kit knew exactly what she was doing.

Kit finished the song and handed the guitar back to the guy from whom she'd borrowed it. Everybody started chatting, sipping their beers, and laughing, in that ancient ritual of the jam. Kit saw Nathan and waved. He smiled back. A fiddler across the table from Kit began to play a quick French-Canadian reel, and one by one, everyone joined in. Kit picked up her fiddle, let out a little "Whoo-*yup!*" and joined the tune.

Nathan felt a tug on his sleeve and turned to see Professor Kahn, whose Harvard class he had visited. "Deep in thought?" Kahn said.

Nathan smiled. "Just listening to the music. Nice to see you, professor."

"Please, call me Maury."

Nathan noticed something different about Kahn. Had he lost weight? Dyed his hair? No, still the same salt-and-pepper tousle. Then he spotted it. Kahn had trimmed his great speckled eyebrows. The difference was stunning. It made his face look thinner and at least ten years younger. But it also made him seem a bit less, well, professorial.

Kahn pulled an old CD out of the pocket of his corduroy blazer. "Would you mind signing this?" he said. It was Nathan's first album, the local one. He remembered that Kahn had mentioned it at the end of the folk music class.

"Boy, you are an archivist," Nathan said. "Talk about ancient folk history. Sure, I'd be proud to." He wrote on the cover, "To Maury, one fan to another, Nathan Warren."

Kahn read it and smiled. "I'll treasure this," he said and tucked the CD back into his pocket. "I've got someone here I'd like you to meet, Nathan,"

He pointed to a young woman standing beside him. "This is Betsy Stotts," he said. "She runs the folk music school at Club Passim."

Nathan shook her outstretched hand. She was a small, slim woman with straight brown hair, almost mousy, and the kind of dusky skin the old ballads used to describe as "berry-brown." She was dressed in baggy blue jeans and a pinstriped men's dress shirt that hung nearly to her knees. The plainness of her appearance was belied by her startlingly light blue eyes and fleshy, upturned mouth.

"Folk music school," Nathan said, nodding thoughtfully. "Sounds like one of those classic oxymorons, like 'military intelligence' and 'liberal consensus.'"

Stotts laughed politely, and Nathan realized she probably heard cracks like that all the time, like a dentist being told he's looking down in the mouth.

"Sorry," he said. "You probably get that a lot, huh?"

"Well, a little bit," she said. "The 'liberal consensus' one is new. I like that; it reminds me of board meetings at the coffeehouse."

Nathan folded his arms and smiled at her. She was one of those plain women who could be very pretty if she wanted. Sometimes women who work at being plain don't know that about themselves; they're too shy to believe it. Others do know and theirs can be a sadder story. For some reason they've had a bellyful of being pretty and everything that comes with it.

"What's up?" Nathan asked, eyeing them both.

"Well, why don't you tell him, Betsy?" Kahn said in his helpful-teacher tone. He grimaced after saying it, and Nathan smiled at him. Harvard, it gets to you.

Stotts eyed Kahn doubtfully, then looked toward the floor. "Well," she said softly. "I was wondering—that is, we were wondering at Passim—if you'd consider teaching a class for us."

She glanced up at him without raising her head. "Maury told me what a great job you did at his folk music class. And Kit's told me some of the stories you tell her. We'd love to get you down to Passim. I mean, if you'd like to teach, you know...." Her voice trailed off.

"Well, I teach guitar," Nathan said. "But I really don't like to teach it in groups. I prefer one on one, because—"

"No," said Kahn. "That's not what they're thinking about. Something more general, about how folk music got to be the way it is. Along the lines of what you talked about in our class."

"I wouldn't have any idea how to do that," Nathan said.

"Wasn't that what you told Kit about doing our class?" Kahn said, wagging his eyebrows. The effect wasn't the same without all the foliage.

"But a whole class, Maury?" Nathan said. "A whole semester?"

"Eight weeks, actually," Stotts said, raising her head and meeting his gaze. "Maury told me some of the things you said, you know, like about how Kit's songs are like the old folk songs because they're about real life. I thought that was awesome."

Awesome? Nathan smiled uncertainly.

She continued, her voice stronger. "And what you said about how the old songs keep changing, and never really stop, I mean, how they always…they never…" She glanced over at Kahn. Help.

"A folk song never stops being written," Kahn said. "That was wonderfully put."

Stotts nodded and smiled. Awesome.

Nathan stared at Kahn. Good lord, he was actually being quoted by a professor. From Harvard. A man so erudite he has to trim his eyebrows.

"That's the kind of stuff I was looking for," Stotts said. "I mean, you can do whatever you want. But we have lots of guitar teachers; it seems like everybody wants to teach that or songwriting. We don't have anybody to just sort of explain what folk music is."

"I don't know," Nathan said. "It's not like I've studied this, really."

Kahn burst into laughter. "Sorry for laughing, Nathan, but *really*. Not studied it? Lord, man, you've lived it. Your whole life. That's what they want. Somebody who knows it because he's lived it."

"Really?" Nathan shook his head slowly, tentative as always. He uncrossed his arms and stuffed his hands into his pockets.

"I want to have something down there besides music lessons," Stotts said. "Sort of a music appreciation class for folkies, you know? I just didn't know who to ask, until Maury told me about you."

"I don't know," Nathan muttered, continuing to shake his head doubtfully. Finally he said, "I'm flattered you'd ask. Let me think about it, okay?"

Stotts shrugged and gave him her card. Kahn thanked Nathan for his time, with a formality that suggested he was a bit annoyed, and the pair walked over to Kit's table. Nathan wondered if they'd all hatched this up together. Stotts said she'd talked with Kit about it. He watched them for a while, thinking what a ridiculous idea it was. A whole class? Me? But he'd promised to think about it and he would.

Before heading back to the bar, he asked Kit if she wanted to come over after the jam. He had a surprise for her, he said, and she nodded.

He smiled again at Stotts and Kahn. A whole class? Me?

Nathan and Kit were on opposite ends of the sofa. He sang his new song, eyes closed, while she sat cross-legged, arms folded in her lap.

> *Make me well, someone, break the spell*
> *That's kept me down since first I fell.*
> *Guide me clear of my easy fears,*
> *Cold company for all these years.*
>> *Every day, it's the same old song,*
>> *Everything I do is wrong.*

> *When it was spring, everyone would sing,*
> *We can do anything.*
> *Now each new door seems I've walked through before.*
> *There's no frontiers anymore.*
>> *And every day, it's the same old song,*
>> *Everything I do is wrong.*

> Refrain:
> *What made us think it would all be so clean?*
> *Love, the magician, we sang.*
> *What made us think that our hearts would be enough,*
> *All that we ever would need?*

> *Nights are numb, still sleep won't come,*
> *Wondering what have I done?*
> *Things I said but never meant,*
> *Things I meant but never said.*
>> *Every day, it's the same old song,*
>> *Everything I do is wrong.*

> *Day on day lived the same old way,*
> *Never motion, never change.*
> *All that is true and the only way through,*
> *Is to find my way back home to you.*
>> *Every day, it's the same old song*
>> *Everything I do is wrong.*
> *All that is true and the only way through,*
> *Is to find my way back home to you.*

Kit gazed at Nathan's guitar, her head nodding slightly. At first, he took that as a good sign. Just as he was beginning to worry, she said, "Play it again?"

"Now?"

Kit laughed softly. "Of course now. Please?"

He played it again, a little slower, and she kept her eyes closed all the way through, leaning toward the sound hole of the guitar.

When it was over, she said, "My first reaction was that it was the saddest song you ever wrote. But it really isn't, is it? Because he's, like, figuring it all out."

"His way back home."

She nodded. "Back home. That's beautiful. I love it, Nathan, really. The sadness drew me in, but then you took me somewhere better."

"It's about you," Nathan said, almost interrupting her.

"It is?"

"Who else would it be about?"

"I wasn't even sure it was about a person."

"Well, I left the home part vague, so people could figure out what it means for them. But for me, it's about you."

They looked at each other and Kit, of course, began to blush. He realized he'd been looking forward to those red cheeks for weeks.

"Nobody ever wrote a song about me before," she said.

"You were never stupid enough to fall in love with a songwriter before."

"Good point."

They were quiet, then Kit smiled.

"Play it again," she said.

Kit's head pounded rhythmically against the padded armrest of the studio mixing board. She'd fallen into a pattern of bumping the armrest a few times with her forehead, then grinding her head back and forth. For the past hour, her chief mixing instruction had been, "Whatever."

"Maybe we could just bring in another singer," she groaned. "This chick is like, *sooooo* depressing,"

"We're almost done, sweetie," Nathan said, in a chipper tone that made Kit audibly grind her teeth. He was having a ball; she was suffering death by a thousand cuts.

They'd been working on mixing the first song for four hours, much of it setup time. They had to get the instruments panned, which meant deciding whether sounds came out of the left speaker, the right, or equally out of both. Nathan wanted Kit's voice to be centered—coming equally out of both speakers—with everything else behind and to the sides. They also had to select the right reverb from an assortment of nearly two-dozen preset possibilities, ranging from "grand concert hall" to "small living room." After an hour of sampling the menu, Kit mumbled, "Is there one for 'under the bed'?"

For the past twenty minutes, Nathan had been deciding whether one loud note Kit had sung was distorting or just peaking nicely. The levels on the board told him it was distorting but they were digital—what did they know? Eyes closed, he kept listening to the line leading up to the note, pausing a moment, then rewinding it—*pleeble-eeble-eeble-eep*—and listening to it again.

He was in a zone, working the dials, listening, listening. When it came to the computer, he was barely emerging from the Stone Age, but digital audio technology came naturally. He didn't know why, but guessed it was because this was music. He was always in his element there.

Pleeble-eeble-eeble-eep. Does it distort or just peak? It was a striking note, almost startling, but that suited the lyric. It felt jagged, but Nathan liked that. The one thing he didn't like about digital recording was that it reduced everything to sound waves. Everything was fixable, which made it tempting to fix everything. But music isn't perfect; it's human.

When they were recording, Kit would sometimes ask if a wavering note or out-of-synch chord could be fixed. Almost always, he'd say, "It's what you did. I like it." He wanted the emotion of the moment, the idiomatic, imperfect vibe of performance.

Digital equipment cannot calculate such things, and something gets lost in cleaning up everything until it's shiny and perfect. A little clumsiness often makes music more powerful, just as it does in life: a man fumbling to put the ring on her finger; a child stumbling in her hurry to hug a parent.

The magical moments in music are often runts, missteps, even mistakes, that make everything sound suddenly real. Human. In a digital world where everything can be made perfect, the majesty of the beautiful mistake can be lost. It just gets fixed.

Pleeble-eeble-eeble-eep. Nathan closed his eyes and listened. One more time to be sure. *Pleeble-eeble-eeble-eep.* "No, I like it," he said slowly. "It feels real."

"Does it distort?" Kit said in a hoarse whisper, her head still buried in the armrest.

"A little, but that line is supposed to leap off the page. I like it."

Pleeble-eeble-eeble-eep. Kit swore under her breath.

"What do you think?" he asked, playing it again.

"I think we should put that poor girl out of her misery," she said, grinding her forehead back and forth. "No jury would convict us." Then she said, "I like it, too. Let's leave it."

"Voilà!" Nathan said, slapping his hands together so loudly it made Kit jump. "Then we're done."

She sat up straight and looked at him. Her eyes were pained and tired. "Done? But that's only one song."

"Yeah, but it's our template. I'm sorry, I should have explained. We won't have to go through this with every song. Now we know what kind of reverb we want, how we want things panned, volume levels, bass, treble, all that stuff. We know where we want your guitar and the other instruments, the harmonies. Everything. From here on, we refer back to this mix. That's why I wrote down all the levels."

She stared at the controls, band after band of knobs, buttons, dials, and small monitor screens with sound waves streaking across them.

"So we won't have to go through this for every song?"

"Nope. The rest will go much faster. We know what we want now."

"What we want is for that stupid singer to, like, get over herself and shut up."

"You're probably not going to believe this, but the way you sing is making the mix go a lot easier. You have a great sense of dynamics; you almost mix yourself."

He nodded absently at the board, suddenly spacing out. The concentration is so intense in a studio that sometimes the brain shuts down, like a computer freezing. His eyes glazed over and he let out several breaths in an odd, irregular rhythm.

Distantly, he heard Kit say, "Yoo-hoo, brood-boy. I was asking what you meant by dynamics."

He shook his head. "Sorry. Picked up a little signal drift, I guess. Happens when I'm mixing."

"Happens when you're awake. You are such an airhead."

"Thank you," he said brightly. "Dynamics. Well, I guess the essence of dynamics is not doing everything the same way. You have a good sense of space and you're not afraid of silence. You know when to be loud and when to be soft, when to be busy and when to be spare."

"Thanks. I guess I don't want to be a hotshot."

Nathan laughed, which startled her. "I didn't say you weren't a hotshot, sweetie," he said. "I said you had good dynamics. You're just smart enough to know when simple is better than fancy. But not a hotshot? *Pu-leeze.*"

Still chuckling, he began to set the levels for the next track. Kit smiled a little but said nothing. Nerves a little raw? Be careful here. Musicians listening to their own mixing can feel exposed. Everything sounds like you're finding fault. Is that note too loud? Is the voice off-pitch? What's that noise in your guitar? Is the timing off? Just seeing your voice reduced to quivering waves on a screen can be bruising.

The mix going "much quicker" meant two more days and nights in the studio. Nathan had picked this March weekend because the guy who owned the studio was out of town and said they could stay in the house, get everything done in one marathon session.

They slept in a guest room upstairs, under a fat patchwork quilt and thick flannel sheets that were delicious to make love under and almost impossible to get Kit out of. Especially to go back to mixing.

After a final fourteen-hour session, they staggered out of the studio late Sunday night. Nathan had never seen Kit so tired, with gray, puffy circles under her eyes. He told her they'd "live with the mix" for a while, then tweak anything that needed tweaking. Kit assured him that unless they heard a loud fart somewhere, she had tweaked her last tweak.

As she slid into the car, she said, "What a horrible thing to do to a singer. I never want to go through that again. I mean, *yuck*!"

"You will," Nathan said, turning on the ignition. "Many, many times." He was tired, too, but elated. This was a very good album; he was sure of that.

"Somebody else can mix it next time," Kit said.

"The only thing harder than mixing your own music is letting someone else do it."

She tilted her head back and gave him an aloof look. "You may overestimate how self-absorbed I really am," she said.

Pulling the car out the gravel driveway, he stared at her, arching a single eyebrow.

Kit settled into her seat and cleared her throat daintily. "Maybe not," she said.

Three

All the talk at the open mike was about Ferguson's review of Kit's CD, which had run in the Sunday paper. A few weeks before the CDs arrived, Ferguson asked Nathan to burn off an advance copy. He wanted to be the first to go on record predicting big things for Kit Palmer.

"Not personal, Sonny, just business," Ferguson said in his best Michael Corleone impression. "A critic makes his bones by being ahead of the pack."

Everything about the review was like an anointment. Ferguson called the album "the most convincing debut by a local songwriter since…"—then rattled off the names of several national stars, including Joyce Warren, that it was widely known he had helped discover. It simultaneously put Kit in their league and reminded readers that Ferguson had a terrific reputation for picking future stars.

Then he got to the music. He praised her mix of traditional and modern influences, saying it made her melodies "strikingly original yet strangely familiar, even on first hearing. She draws us in and then, always, surprises us."

About her songs, he wrote, "This is youth darkly reflected: the isolation, the need to hide from a peering, unkind world, the fear that nobody else knows how we feel. But she has a rare gift for finding some flicker of redemption in even the most frightened, lonely corners of our lives; something that tells us we are not as alone as we think. In this, Palmer proves herself to be not only a promising new voice but an important one."

He ended the review with what folk aficionados knew was his signature way of predicting stardom: "Keep an eye on this one." When he'd written that about Joyce, her phone rang off the hook for days. Nathan knew; he had to answer it.

When Ferguson walked into Dooley's, Jackie immediately gave him a beer and a stiff shot of top-shelf rum, rapping her knuckle on the bar to signify that it was on the house.

"Nice review Sunday," she said. The past few weeks she'd been almost as excited as Kit about the new album.

"Thank you, Jackie," Ferguson said, sniffing the rum, then sipping it elegantly. "This is first-rate stuff."

"You deserve it, binky. That was a proper piece of work. Proper piece of work."

Ferguson froze in mid-sip, mouth open, staring at Jackie. This was Jackie's highest praise, and she said it very seldom. Jackie nodded firmly, as if punctuating the compliment, tossed her towel over her shoulder, and strolled down the bar.

Nathan nudged Ferguson with his elbow. "I thought it was a proper piece of work, too," he said. "You have no idea what this means to Kit."

Ferguson harrumphed, then gulped his drink. "Sure I do," he said. "But like I said, it was strictly business. That's how I got the paper to run it so quickly. I said we needed to be the first to cover this new kid; and they know I don't say that often. As much as I grouse about what's happening down there, it's still a newspaper. Being first matters."

"That's not what I mean," Nathan said. "I'm talking about what you wrote. Those other songwriters you mentioned—they're all heroes of Kit's. Even Joyce. You made her part of that. That's what meant so much to her."

Ferguson coughed sharply and tried to shake the compliment off with a long pull of his beer. It didn't work. Wiping his mouth, he grinned awkwardly, as if trying not to, and muttered, "Aw, hell."

Nathan was in such a good mood that he actually winked when he saw Ryder. He responded with a manly nod. He was doing kind of a street-punk thing these days, wearing a baseball cap with the visor jutting off to the side, baggy pants hanging low, and an oversized black canvas jacket. When he talked between songs, he was even making those exaggerated hand gestures that rappers do. Truth up, from the Wellesley 'hood.

Nathan wondered if Ryder had gotten one of those barbed wire tattoos around his arm. Can you get tattoos in Wellesley? Probably, but just the kind that wash off.

A hard, freezing rain had begun to fall, almost slush, splashing and clotting when it hit the streets. Yuck. This is April? Nonetheless, Ramblin' Randy sang a couple of sprightly spring songs because, he said, it was "almost spring."

Nathan looked out the window while Randy sang about bobbing robins and blooming heather. You could tell by the way cars swiveled and slowed that the slush was freezing on the road. Calling this "almost spring" was like calling someone who just died "almost alive." Accurate, perhaps, but not particularly helpful.

Kit sailed in a little before ten. Her white parka glistened with icy rain drops. She had a big beret flopped cutely over one ear, and her dark eyes burned with excitement. God, she was pretty.

She immediately grinned at Ferguson, waving at him as she peeled off her cap and gloves. Her eyes were about twice their normal size, and she was smiling wide and toothy. Nathan could see she was absolutely inflated with herself. Oh, this was going to be fun.

As she started to walk to the bar, the crowd interrupted a shaggy, barely audible ukulele player with a rousing ovation for Kit, many shouting, "Whoo, Kit!" and "You go, girl!"

Kit gave the crowd a slight bow and turned to the hapless ukulele player to mouth an apology. She turned again to the crowd, waving for them to stop. Oh no, really, stop, stop. Please, oh no, really? For me? Nathan laughed, ducking his head so Kit wouldn't see.

She rushed over to Ferguson. "You sweetie!" she hollered, throwing her arms over his shoulders with such force that he almost spilled his beer. "I...I...loved every word you wrote. And you know what? The album isn't even out yet, and I've sold over two hundred copies on my website. Almost all of them since your review came out. So thank you, thank you, thank you."

She kissed his cheek and pulled away, continuing to pat his shoulder with her hand. Ferguson tried to tell her what he'd said to Nathan about it not being personal, but it was no use. She was cranked, her head darting around the bar like a bobblehead toy on steroids.

"I'll tell her later," Nathan said to Ferguson. "Not personal, just business. I don't think it would process right now."

Kit's head snapped over to Nathan. "What?" she said, and he started to explain, but she said, "Did you sing your new song again tonight?"

"Yeah, I thought it—"

But she was gone again, grinning at Ferguson. "Have you heard it? Nathan's new song? Isn't it just the best? I think it's, like, the best song he ever wrote. Totally. Don't you?"

Ferguson got as far as drawing a thoughtful breath but made the mistake of nodding his head, which gave Kit all the information she needed. Her head snapped over to Jackie, who was covering her mouth with a bar towel to hide her laughter.

"Jackie," Kit said, sitting down between Nathan and Ferguson, "did you, uh, happen to see the paper Sunday?" They talked while Jackie poured her a congratulatory drink. Kit asked for a rum and Coke, but Jackie refused to give her anything with caffeine in it and made her a rum tonic instead.

"I was filling orders on my website, like, all day," Kit said, twirling a lime slice around the rim of her glass. "Nothing like that's ever happened to me." She winked at Ferguson. "Somebody must be reading that paper, huh?"

She turned serious then. "But it wasn't just that you were nice; you totally got what I'm trying to do. That line about my songs saying that we're not as alone as we think. I mean, you really understand."

She stopped suddenly, as if she might have said something stupid. Of course he understands; he does this for a living.

But Ferguson was smiling broadly. "Thank you, Kit. That's the nicest thing you could say to me. It's a critic's biggest fear, you know, that you're missing the point."

"Oh, no," Kit said. "You got it. That 'youth darkly reflected' thing, and that they're not just sad songs. Totally. Just totally. Totally."

"You're stammering," Nathan whispered out of the corner of his mouth.

"I don't think so," Ferguson said, raising his glass to her. "I think she's eloquent. Thank you, Kit." And they clinked glasses.

There was laughter coming from Ryder's table as he huddled forward, snickering to his squirrel pack. Just as Kit and Ferguson clinked their glasses, Ryder said something loud enough for the bar to hear—loud enough that he must have wanted everyone to hear:

"She probably slept with *him*, too."

Like a TV clicking off, the bar fell silent. Kit swiveled around on her bar stool and stared at Ryder. Her face had no expression, just an unblinking gaze, right into his eyes. There is something uniquely unnerving to a man about a beautiful woman's steady, emotionless gaze. Ryder could hold it only a few seconds before looking down. Then, perhaps realizing the size of his mistake, he looked at Nathan and then Ferguson.

Ferguson's stare was as cold as a casket and when he was sure he had Ryder's attention, he mouthed one simple, unmistakable word: "*Dumb.*"

Nathan wondered if Ryder would ever figure out how much Ferguson meant with that one small word. Ryder had erected a terrible wall between himself and the only critic in town who might ever write about him. Although Ryder didn't intend it that way, his remark was as insulting to Ferguson as it was to Kit. He had publicly insinuated that a professional critic's coverage could be bought with sexual favors. There may be no more damaging a charge that can be made against a journalist. Ryder had said that Ferguson's judgment was for sale.

Because the remark was made publicly, the prudent, professional thing for Ferguson would be never to write a word about Ryder, either good or bad, since anything could be suspected of being influenced by the accusation. If he panned Ryder, perhaps he was getting even. If he praised him, perhaps he was bribing Ryder to silence him. Dumb.

Nathan began to walk over to Ryder's table, then turned to Kit. "I want you to know this isn't just about what Ryder said to you," he said. "I have a responsibility to everybody who comes in here, you know? So it's not like I'm fighting your battles for you. I know you don't need anyone to do that."

Kit smiled and rubbed his arm. "Thanks for saying that. No, I'm fine." She glanced at Ryder again. "Do what you gotta do."

When he got to Ryder's table, Nathan raised his hand, and Ryder reflexively ducked his head. "Don't hit me," he yelped.

Nathan was simply pointing to the door. He lowered his arm. "You think I'm going to *hit* you?"

Despite his anger, Nathan felt a pang of pity for Ryder. Nobody flinches like that without reason. Something deep inside Ryder, something hurt and angry, made him need to come here every week, far from home, and pretend he was somebody else.

"I'm just pointing you to the door," Nathan said. "I've had it with your sour mouth."

He smiled grimly and waved his arms around the room. "Well, Ryder, this is what you always wanted. It's all about you. Everybody's looking at you. How's it feel?"

Then he leaned forward and said, in a loud whisper, "Now, get out—and don't come back."

It sounded like the applause began at Randy's table, but everyone took it up, along with various shouts of "Bye-bye," "Good riddance," and one loud holler of "See ya', wouldn't wanna *be* ya.'" There was laughter, too; everyone seemed to understand that treating this moment lightly was the best way to devalue what Ryder said.

Showing even less sense than he already had, Ryder rushed to Jackie for help. Jackie?

"He can't do this, can he?" Ryder said in a painfully adolescent whine. "I mean, this is a *public* place!"

Jackie looked down at the bar, waving a finger in his face, the sign she gave customers when she was busy. With an exasperated grunt, Ryder folded his arms over his chest and waited.

Jackie slowly looked up at him, holding the soda nozzle in her hand. She motioned Kit to move over a little to her left, then sprayed Ryder in the face with ginger ale.

Amid gales of laughter, Ryder stormed out of the bar. None of his squirrels left with him, which didn't surprise Nathan. Once your leader has been hosed with ginger ale, he loses a little of his, um, street cred.

Ferguson looked at Jackie. "Ginger ale?"

Wiping the collateral spray off the bar, she said casually, "Gets sticky faster. Very, very sticky." With a world-weary sigh, she shrugged at Kit. "A girl learns these things," Jackie said.

Nathan got on stage to refocus the crowd's attention, and asked for a round of applause for the poor songwriter—one of Ryder's squirrels, actually—whose set had been interrupted. Wanting to show the crowd that this had been only about

Ryder, Nathan asked the kid to do an extra song and patted him on the shoulder. The audience applauded tentatively.

Nodding gratefully at Nathan, the songwriter coughed into the microphone and looked at Kit. "Just so you know," he said to her, "I think what Ryder said sucks. Like, totally." Kit smiled at him, nodding her head.

When Nathan got back to the bar, Ferguson was staring at Kit, a wide-eyed, bewildered look on his face. He cocked his head like a confused terrier.

"What's on your mind, perfesser?" She asked.

"You would have *slept* with me?" he whimpered, then turned to Nathan. "Why doesn't anybody *tell* me these things?"

Jackie and Kit burst into laughter. Jackie shook her head, still laughing, and popped open another beer for Ferguson.

The bad moment had passed.

The evening ended as it usually did, with Nathan, Kit, and Ferguson huddled together at the bend of the bar. Open-mikers approached Kit all evening, congratulating her on the album and asking where they could get one. Nathan promised to bring some the following week. No one mentioned Ryder's remark; that would have given it too much weight. It was treated like a bad fart, to be politely forgotten as soon as the odor vanished.

Kit said she'd just watched a new film version of *Pride and Prejudice* but liked the "really old" one better.

"You mean the Laurence Olivier one?" Ferguson said. "Yeah, I think he was the best—"

"Um, actually, I meant the PBS one. The really long one? With Colin Firth."

Ferguson stared at her. "Oh lord," he groaned. "I am ancient. I am stone. I am a redwood; hear me creak."

"But I *like* old things," Kit said. "I just said—"

"Yeah, old like from *Masterpiece Theater*. Thank you, Kit. You're a comfort and a balm."

Kit slumped in her seat, shaking her head, laughing and swearing under her breath. Then she sat upright and patted Ferguson's shoulder the way a small child might pet a large dog. "There, there, perfesser," she said in a childlike squeak. "You're not old to me. You're more, like, venerable."

"Oh, wonderful. Like a statue, I suppose."

"The Bunker Hill of the Boston folk scene," Kit agreed, nodding. "They looked at the lights in his eyes: one if by banjo, two if by bagpipe."

"That's not Bunker Hill," Nathan said. "That's Old North Church."

To which, of course, Kit said, "Sorry. Before my time."

To which, of course, Ferguson began groaning again about being a redwood.

Nathan suspected that Kit was showing off a little: look, she could still tease the important critic, even after her big review. But as usual with her, there was kindness to it, too, and that obviously registered with Ferguson. As he grumbled and creaked, he was stroking his beard, a sure sign he was tickled with what was going on. By teasing him, Kit was saying that nothing had changed between them. No professional distances would be observed now that she'd seen how much he could help her.

Jackie rang the witching hour bell a little after eleven. The stage remained empty, so Murph put on a Quincy Jones CD, officially ending the open mike. The talk slowly turned from the review to the paper.

Ferguson didn't rant about the evils of corporatism, however. He seemed sad, wistful, and something else. Frightened? Whatever it was, it worried Nathan. When Ferguson was ranting, he was okay. This was different.

"You didn't have any trouble reviewing me," Kit said. "I'm sure they didn't do it because like, oh boy, you mean *the* Kit Palmer? It got published because of you, not me. So they must still respect you, yes?"

Ferguson shrugged. "Well, like I was telling Nathan, they're still a newspaper; being first matters. That's how I pitched it."

"So they trust you," Kit said. Ferguson shrugged.

After a moment, Kit cleared her throat sharply. "I want to tell you something," she said, "but you gotta promise to not start groaning about being a redwood or anything."

They looked at each other until Ferguson realized she expected an answer.

"Yes, okay," he said. "No more being a redwood."

"I mean, I don't want to make you feel all old and wrinkly again."

"I never, for one moment, felt wrinkly. Proceed, child."

"Okay. Well, it's just that I grew up reading you. My parents subscribe to your paper because they think the local paper is too conservative. When I was a kid, learning the fiddle, I'd grab the paper whenever one of my fiddle heroes was in Boston. And if there was anything in there about them, it was always by you. When I started getting into songwriters, it was always you writing about the ones I really liked."

She leaned close to Ferguson. "That's why this review means so much to me. Because it's by you. I called my parents yesterday, and you know what they said? They said, 'Well, it's official now, isn't it? You're really a songwriter.'"

Ferguson looked at Kit, fingering the neck of his beer bottle. "Thank you, Kit," he said finally. "That means a lot to me. It doesn't make me feel old at all. It makes me feel, uh, permanent."

"Not in any sort of treelike way, I hope," Kit said warily. "Because you promised—"

"No, no, no," Ferguson said, chuckling. "But it reminds me why I put up with all the crap at the paper."

"Here's the thing, Kit," he said, leaning closer to her. "You may see me as a big-shot critic; a lot of folk people do. What you don't see is how it works down there. I'm just a freelancer. An awful lot of what I do is groveling, arguing, pleading. Sometimes I feel like such a pest."

He smiled at Kit, a sad, tired smile. Suddenly he did look old.

"How do you put up with that?" Kit said.

"Oh, I've just been around the block. I know the freelancer tricks: meet your deadlines, make sure your copy is clean, make sure they get the artwork they need. The secret is to be low maintenance and high reward. That's even more important these days, because the mother ship reduced the staff so much. Everybody's overworked."

Ferguson was quiet for a moment, as if deciding whether he wanted to say any more. Then, with a shake of his head, he continued. "It's just that I have to keep proving myself, over and over and over. At my age, you want to be past all that, the audition part of your life. Things get okay for a while, then it starts over again. Some new editor takes over or some directive comes down from the mother ship, and I'm back to square one, figuring out what they want, what story angles to pitch, whether to be obsequious or direct. Begging, needling. Being a pest."

"Because it's for the music," Nathan said.

"Because it's for the music," Ferguson replied. "Thank you. Yes, I have to remember that. Now more than ever. For the music."

"It's not fair," Kit said. "You shouldn't have to keep going through all that. I wish you could do something about it. It's just…just…not fair."

"Do something? Like what?"

"I don't know," Kit said, almost under her breath. "Just something."

May. Madrigals.

A drenching rain in early May brought with it a sudden warm front. It was as if the long, numb winter had been a stubborn weather pattern and not the endless February it felt like. Everything seemed to blossom overnight.

Blowing on his first cup of coffee, Nathan looked out at the sloping yard. It was amazing. Tree branches that had been bare and black, barely pimpled with buds, were now noticeably green. The light streaking in through his windows felt warm and full of promises. The sky was baby blue, with wispy streaks of clouds at once softening and brightening the morning. He opened the door to look farther down Craigie Street. It was as if the world had been in black and white when he went to bed and now it was in color.

The scent in the air almost made him dizzy. It smelled of wet earth, budding things, the sting of pollen, even the faint, sweet scent of grass. Life. That's what it was—like the air was full of life.

Which meant it was time to crank up the madrigals on the stereo, a spring ritual for him. The sappier the better:

The spring, clad all in gladness,
Doth laugh at winter's sadness.
Fa-la-lala-lala, fa-lala-la-la-lala

Over the years, Nathan had developed an amateur passion for classical music. It was difficult for him to listen to folk music without working, analyzing guitar lines, or wondering why the singer resolved a phrase a certain way. As he listened, he would often find his fingers moving on invisible strings.

He wanted some music in his life that he could just enjoy, without all that care and worry. Ferguson told him once that his greatest regret about becoming a critic was how it had "professionalized" his ears. His listening became educated, cultivated, studied; he was always analyzing, critiquing.

The reward for this was a deeper and more informed appreciation. But Ferguson said he missed the wide-eyed wonder he once had, that pure, unfiltered connection between ears and emotions.

Nathan knew exactly what he meant. It had made him so sad when as an adult he listened to one of his favorite boyhood blues albums. He instantly realized that the mysterious wetness in the bluesman's voice did not spring from some gritty, mystical wisdom. The old guy was drunk. With all his heart, Nathan wished he'd never figured that out, that he'd left the record in the back stacks of his memory, where mysteries could remain mysteries.

So he promised himself he would never learn enough about classical music to let his ears become clogged with knowledge. And he had kept that promise.

His classical tastes were seasonal. Fall was the time for full-tilt Baroque: Albinoni, Telemann, Scarlatti. Vivaldi felt a bit too scrubbed and tidy for him, as if the composer was doing it all in his head. Much of Mozart struck him that way, too, but he was pretty sure he was wrong about that.

When fall thickened into winter, he liked the glorious melancholy of Corelli, those sad, open chords. As the cold grew, he listened to medieval choral music, to Palestrina, Tallis, and the haunting hush of Hildegard von Bingen.

In bleakest winter, he listened almost obsessively to Ralph Vaughn Williams. Nathan loved the pieces the composer had based on ancient English melodies, especially "Variations On a Theme by Tallis." On the blackest winter nights, Nathan would listen to the Tallis piece over and over, eyes closed, leaning into his sofa, until his body felt like fog.

But now it was high spring, and his bed was warm and full. No Tallis for this puppy. Sap, sap, sap. Much *fa-la-la*-ing, lusty youths, flaxen maids, and the merry, merry month of May-o.

He hadn't revealed his madrigal fetish to Kit, who was still deep beneath his sheets, sleeping as though she had not slept in years. Like she did every night. He still envied that; she seemed to get so much out of everything she did.

He put on the perkiest madrigal album he had. Sap to the nth. And vim. Lots and lots of vim.

> *My bonnie lass, she smileth,*
> *When she my heart begui-i-i-i-leth.*
> *Fa-la-la-lala-lala-la*

Madrigals were really the first pop songs, hugely popular from the thirteenth to seventeenth centuries. They were artfully composed simulations of the music ordinary people sang: faux folk songs dressed up for elite society. And they were sappy. But then, didn't the word sappy come from the silly way we feel in spring, when the sap starts running in the green things? Spring was the sappy season.

> *Now is the month of Maying,*
> *When merry lads are playing.*
> *Fa-la-lala-lala, Fa-lala-la-lala*

He glanced at the bedroom door and wondered how Kit would react. She seemed to enjoy listening to classical music with him, even though it made her remember the unpleasant strictness of her first musical education, before she was allowed to turn her violin into a fiddle.

But madrigals? This was in-your-face sappiness, full-frontal sap. What would she think? Well, as long as she didn't think he'd been around when they were written.

Kit was impeccably tasteful, and as innately hip as anyone he'd known since Joyce. But she lacked Joyce's snootiness, her feeling that certain things—and people—were cool and that other things—and people—were not.

To Kit, it was loving things that was cool, not what sorts of things you loved. She enjoyed sharing Nathan's passions, he thought, simply because she enjoyed sharing passion. He once opened his eyes in the middle of a Corelli sonata to see her looking at him, smiling fondly. He gave her a quizzical look. What? "I just like watching you listen to music," she said softly.

He wasn't sure she bothered to consider how much she liked the things he showed her; she simply enjoyed hearing new things. No wonder he pissed her off sometimes; it was so hard for him to get excited about new things.

But then, not much excited him these days—or not much *used* to excite him. She was changing that, wasn't she? Had he been so happy about the coming of madrigal season last year? No, in fact, it put him into a bit of a funk. Another spring, another year, passing, passing, passing.

He turned up the madrigals some more and looked at the bedroom door. Get up, get up. And then he could hear her stirring, harmonizing a deep "*poom, poom*" to one passage. Just letting him know she got the drift.

The bedroom door flew open and she appeared, tangle-haired and wearing the shirt he'd worn yesterday.

"There's no such thing as corny to you, is there?" She said, yawning widely. "Not in your lexicon at all." She smiled, shot off another "*poom, poom*" and said, "I think that is so hip."

Stretching the sleep from her back and shoulders and taking a few running steps in place, she said, "What's for breakfast? I could eat the whole damn merry greenwood."

Kit was working her new record the way a casino gambler works an inside straight. Nathan told her not to look at her CDs as "product," the way the music industry would, but as "fan-seeds." Every one she got into somebody's hands, whether or not she was paid for it, had the potential to multiply into more fans. And in the folk biz, it was fans, not record sales, that built careers.

She rolled her eyes as he lectured and reminded him, several times, that she was not born yesterday. But she also made a list of ways to spread the album around and she put free tracks for downloading on all the social websites she used.

She always carried a few albums in her backpack and guitar bag, and made sure there were a few boxes in Nathan's car. At Dooley's, she handed one to anyone who made even a passing reference about it. She always refused to take money. "You can give me yours when it comes out, okay?" she'd say. The open-mikers smiled at that, proud that she considered them peers. Nathan noticed they were treating her differently now, the way college athletes might treat a former teammate who'd made the pros.

Kit had a new sureness about herself, a stronger connection to the innate confidence Nathan had always sensed beneath the shyness and stage fright. Ferguson's review, and the CD's success, had made it official: her music was as good as she hoped it was. The rest was hard work and intelligence, and she had no insecurity about those things.

Kit was selling so many albums through her website that she contracted with a service that enabled her to take credit card sales. You really could do anything on the Internet. She sent the album to CDBaby, the online record store. It sold so many copies that it made her one of its daily featured artists. She called Nathan at three o'clock one morning to shout that she'd just sold her first iTunes download. Her music was spreading like kudzu.

Nathan's website was working for him, too, though more personally than professionally. Old fans and friends began e-mailing him through it. They kidded him for taking so long to get his own site, and several asked him about releasing a new album. He guessed they had Googled his name from time to time, but never found a way to contact him before.

One e-mail meant a lot to him. It was from a woman who'd worked at the major label that never released his big album. She said she always wanted to tell him how badly she thought he was treated. She'd loved his album, she wrote, and argued that it should be released. But she still wanted to apologize to him, personally.

"This kind of thing happens too often in the music industry," she wrote, "but it was even worse with you. I always thought it was a shame. Your music deserved better. I want you to know that the way they treated you is one reason I'm no longer in the music business."

At first, the e-mail made him angry, brought back the old frustrations. But it also was reassuring to know that someone from that label saw things the way he did. See, I wasn't paranoid; they really were screwing me. There is a certain comfort in that. He wrote her back, thanking her coolly.

He wondered what his life would have been like if someone back then had apologized, or at least acknowledged how badly he was treated. Just once, during those dull, dead years, when his whole life existed from phone call to phone call. What would it have been like if he had known that someone at the label—just one good soul—saw things the way he did?

Still, it was good to hear it now. He hadn't made it up; that's something, isn't it? So he wrote to her again, more personally and gratefully, revealing some of the pain he felt then and the anger he still felt. She never replied. Some things never change.

In early May, he called Betsy Stotts to say he would teach the Passim course she offered him. Why not?

He needed a better idea of what she was looking for, though. They talked for an hour, laughing as much as they brainstormed. She was bright, with an easy laugh that made him want to say funny things.

She said she was looking for a fan's-eye view of the folk world, a people's history. She was particularly interested in how the old folk songs connected to the work of today's songwriters.

"That's something we're always talking about here," she said. "It'd be cool to have somebody like you talk about it. You know, because you work with young songwriters, and you've been around, well…you know—" She cleared her throat.

"Since the old ballads were written?"

She laughed. "No, no, that's not what I mean. But you know about both worlds, the old songs and the new stuff. People will be interested in what you have to say."

"Honestly, Betsy, that's never been my experience."

There was an awkward silence. Why did he say that? They were interested at Dooley's, at Harvard. Kit was interested.

"I think you'll be surprised," she said. "I know I'm interested."

"Well, that's one," he said, and she laughed. "If nothing else, we'll just have a good chat, you and me."

He asked what they should call it, and she suggested "A People's History of Folk Music." He cringed. It sounded so academic and, well, like it should be taught by someone who knew what he was talking about.

He said he wasn't thinking about a history class but a look at the folk world today and how it got to be that way.

"I've always been more interested in the questions than the answers," he said. "There's so much about the tradition that we don't know, can't know. But it's fun to wonder about it."

"Yeah, the mystery of it. That's a big part of what drew me to folk music."

Nathan started to laugh.

"What?" she asked.

"How about mystery instead of history. 'A Brief Mystery of Folk Music.'"

She liked that a lot. "It lets people know it won't be too scholarly."

"No worries about that with me as the teacher," he said, and she laughed again.

Nathan liked the title because it let him off the hook. All he needed were questions. He had lots of those.

Kit was telling every venue to bill her show as a CD release party. She wanted all her gigs to feel special. She also wanted them to sound like the album, so she asked Nathan to accompany her. He was fine with that, as long as the gigs remained Kit Palmer concerts. The brighter her star shone, the less he wanted to seem like he was basking in it.

She designed posters that said Kit Palmer and Nathan Warren CD Release Party. He made her change them to Kit Palmer CD Release Party, with Nathan Warren, guitar. She resisted at first, arguing that the co-billing made it more special. But he knew he was right about this. "Whose CD is the release party for?" he asked.

Still, she pushed him to do more songs at the shows. Again he said no. A song or two, maybe, but it was her name on the marquee, her fans in the seats. He told her this was just good business. Her mailing list was growing by leaps and bounds, and her new fans expected to see her as the star they thought she was.

She brought up her old idea of working as a duo. It could be a parallel thing, she said, booked separately from her solo shows. They could get pictures together— wouldn't that be fun?—and while they were at it, he could get a new promo picture for himself. They could even come up with a cool name for the duo. People love seeing us on stage together, let's *go for it*! If it was done separately, it would mean more gigs, being seen by more people. Isn't that, like, the whole idea?

He had to think about that one—she did have a point—but he still said no. This was her time, her career that was heating up, her CD that was generating all the excitement.

After a few heated discussions, Kit gave up on the idea, but Nathan could tell she was disappointed and a little hurt. She connected his refusal to the distance he sometimes pushed between them, and to his old passivity. Why couldn't she get him excited about this? About anything?

It didn't feel like that to him, however. Nathan loved accompanying her and serving as her straight man between songs. He delighted in being able to enrich her sound on stage, and he basked in how the between-song teasing of this beautiful woman suggested their romantic closeness. It was actually embarrassing how pleasing that was, how it made him want to thump his chest and make primal snorts at the sky. Dear lord, the uses we find for our testosterone.

Four

There was something about a heavy spring rain that haunted Nathan like a nor'easter. He stared out the window, feeling the gray pull him into himself. It was morning but the sky was dusk dark. The rain came almost straight down, streaming along his windows.

The budding leaves and bushes, with their brightening greens, seemed out of place against the dull gray of the clouds, the wet, autumnal chill in the air. This was like two different days, Nathan thought, both spring and fall, bright and dark, green and gray. Nice.

He turned to make his morning coffee, and remembered that Kit had brought him a bag of cinnamon coffee from her waitressing job. Just the thing. As he got it brewing, he opened the kitchen door to let in the fine morning chill. The rich patter of the rain was almost orchestral, high and staccato against the cement stoop, thicker and lower against the wooden walls, muffled and heavy where the water hit the soft grass. The bass section, Nathan thought with a smile.

He breathed in the different scents of cinnamon and coffee, mingling with the smell of wet grass and clean spring rain. This is perfect; thank you, Kit. She had borrowed his car, and was off in western Massachusetts, making her debut at the Iron Horse, an important songwriter club in Northampton.

He didn't want to accompany her this time. The Iron Horse was another club he'd played during his worst years. He didn't remember if he ever played there drunk, which almost certainly meant that he did. Either way, he had bad memories of the place and was sure they had the same of him. No need for Kit to be seen in that rancid light.

So Nathan had the house to himself. He pushed his old chair up to the window, stared out the window, and let the storm have its way with him. He didn't put any music on the stereo, just left the kitchen door open. The rain was doing fine.

A day like two days, he thought again, putting his feet on the windowsill, blowing on his morning coffee. It's the betweenness that's so haunting, isn't it? He felt his eyes glaze, growing at once wide and blank, his mind becoming cloudy, taking him to that place where he thought so little, so deeply. Was that it? The betweenness, the sense of twilight and morning mingled.

The ancient Celts worshipped states of betweenness, calling them veils between the worlds: twilight and the dusk before dawn, not quite night and not yet day. They believed the world of the gods and the world we knew were closer then, the veils thinner between heaven and earth, spirit and flesh.

There were places like that, and the Celts thought they were holy, too. Shorelines and marshes: not quite land, not yet water. Groves, belonging to both field and forest. The Celts went to those places to talk to their gods.

But when we go to worship, Nathan thought, we gather in great stone buildings with windows that keep us from seeing the world. As if God and the world he gave us were separate things. That had always bothered Nathan. Either God was everywhere and everyday, or religion was just something we made up for our own reasons. And if we had to go to a place that hid us from the real world in order to worship that God, it felt more like the latter: something we made up to pretend we understood things it is not possible for us to understand.

If Nathan was religious at all, and he thought he was, his faith was closer to what those wise old Celts believed. A real-life faith, religion with a little honest dirt under its fingernails. The Celts saw their gods everywhere, in trees and water, animals and fire. He'd never been able to feel that within the forbidding walls and unseeing windows of the church. Perhaps it was the performer in him; even as a child, he saw that as stagey and artificial.

At the Episcopal church his mother dragged him to as a child, the priest would say before the offertory, "Remember our Lord and Savior, Jesus Christ, who said, 'It is more blessed to give than to receive.'" And Nathan would think, "Yeah, but I bet he didn't say it to beg people for money." Then Nathan would shake his head and fold his arms over his chest, with that blissful smugness children feel when they discover irony, and assume they are the first to ever do so.

But that wasn't what finally drove him from the church, was it? That happened later, on a warm spring Sunday when he was twelve or thirteen. Even now, he winced at the memory. In his church, genuflecting, or bowing before the altar as you enter the pews, was an optional obeisance. Nathan found that extremely troubling. Doesn't God care whether we bow or not, he would ask his mother, again and again? And she would answer, again and again, that he should just sit up straight and try listening for a change.

But his mother never tried to defend the fact that genuflecting was optional. Nathan noted this with keen interest, thinking that perhaps she was revealing something of her true self, her real beliefs. And he was starving for that, for any glimmer of how his mother felt beyond "Sit up straight and try listening for a change."

She dutifully took him to church for years, never seeming to be particularly devout about anything but going, until her drinking and the decay of her marriage made it impossible to maintain even the facade of normalcy.

His father never went to church, saying it was the only day of the week he could sleep late, and then complaining, as he so often did, about how hard he worked "to put food on the table for all of you." Years later, Nathan realized that work was his father's place to hide, his ticket out of the horror of his unhappy home and loveless marriage. A morning alone must have been an irresistible luxury.

When Nathan finally figured that out, he liked to imagine his father feigning sleep until he heard the front door close, then springing from his bed, putting his jazz records on the stereo, and dancing around the living room. He probably just slept, but maybe, once in a while…

One Sunday morning in early spring, Nathan's mother finally admitted that she also found it "a little odd" that something like genuflecting would be optional. He basked in the revelation, and in this rare moment of adult conversation between them.

In the sermon that day, the priest lectured the congregation about how stylish all the ladies looked in their new spring hats, sternly reminding them that this was not why we go to church. Nathan frowned and crossed his arms over his chest. Aha! Another irony. Because the priest himself was quite the dandy, as he'd once heard his mother describe him. He always dressed impeccably in fancy tweed coats or blazers with bright gold buttons. At services, he wore elegant, expensive-looking robes, flecked with gold and silver that shimmered when he moved. His longish hair had a carefully cultivated salt-and-pepper shock that he tossed dramatically over his forehead during intense moments of his sermons, then pushed back with a grand sweep of his hand. He always struck Nathan as vain and theatrical, and suspected his mother felt the same way. Quite the dandy.

On the way out of church that day, she paused to shake hands with the priest. To Nathan's surprise and delight, she said very dryly, "I see you have brand new vestments, Reverend. Very stylish; the colors go so nicely with your hair."

The priest acknowledged the dig with a wry smile.

In the car, Nathan raved on and on about his mother's jab, calling it brilliant, cool, very cool, *so* cool, and "just the coolest, Mom." She laughed at first, teasing him about making such a fuss, trying to retain her maternal pose. Finally, she said, "All right, all right, we've had our fun. But don't think for one minute, little man, that this means you get to sleep late next Sunday, like your lazy father."

And with that, fun time was over; the wars had resumed. Nathan clamped his mouth shut and looked out the side window. His mother looked at him with a strained look he later realized was regret. Their moment of closeness was gone.

Now, watching the rain stream down his windows, he understood that what had delighted him was not her mild sarcasm, but her rare display of authenticity: this brief moment in which she allowed the incisive, droll, and laser-bright woman she was to shine through the dull varnish of suburban respectability. She fought that realness all her life, in her torturous quest for normalcy, finally drowning it with drink, in dark rooms with shades drawn, so the respectable world would not see. And along with it went every measure of joy she took from her sad, short life.

That's what all those "cools" had been, Nathan realized now, his child's way of encouraging this rare moment of realness. He had used praise the way a parent would, to coax more of this behavior from his mother. That's also why it had felt like such a hard slap when she pushed him away, back into the cold no-man's-land that lay between her and her husband.

Realness. That's what young people want most from their elders, Nathan thought, nodding and watching the branches on the far tree sway in the coming rain. They don't want us to act young or hip or cool; they want us to be real. How common a mistake that is, to think that young people want us to be more like them. They simply want us to be more like ourselves, to be real, just for a little while, for one true moment.

Nathan looked away from the window and began to stretch the morning dullness from his body. He shook the trance from his head, stood, and stretched more deeply. One true moment. That's really it, isn't it? One true moment.

Nathan spent the rest of the day preparing for his Passim class. He would always remember it as one of his best days. So peaceful, so purposeful.

He used the title of the class, "A Brief Mystery of Folk Music," as a yardstick. It gave him freedom to have fun without having to tie everything into a tidy, authoritative bundle. The title promised adventures, not essays.

Still, he needed some semblance of an outline for each week's ramble. He wanted the course to connect folk's past to the music today. That was important: to explore the history in relation to what students had in their iPods. But there had to be some order to it, didn't there?

For weeks he'd been jotting down his favorite stories about folk music—not necessarily the most important ones, but the fun ones, the odd, mysterious, and revealing ones. The ones that felt like secrets.

There was a story he'd heard about the old Texas blues legend Lightnin' Hopkins. He had a few minor R&B hits in the forties, right around the time rhythm and blues was getting its name. What Hopkins took away from the experience, more than anything, was that he should never trust a white man with a pen in his hand.

And so, the story goes, one fine day Lightnin' found his cupboards bare. It was the dawn of the sixties folk revival, and several small record labels had expressed interest in recording him again. He always said no but now he needed the money. He got in his car and drove to New York, the Big Apple, Gotham, the City So Nice They Named It Twice.

Arriving at one of the labels, he told them he would record for them but he would not sign anything and would not accept a check. Cash only, one payment. And a bottle of gin. Of course, the right thing would have been to say, "Oh no, Mr. Hopkins, that will cost you a lot of money. Think of the royalties, sir!"

But the label would get to keep those royalties, so they scurried to the bank and came back with a few thousand dollars in a big brown envelope. And a bottle of gin. He opened both, put one in his pocket, the other in his mouth, and sang them twelve songs, all in one or two takes.

"Everybody happy?" he said when he was through. Everybody nodded, so he left, got in his car, checked his address book, and drove to the next label that had asked about recording him.

He made them the same proposition, got the same deal and, drinking their gin and stuffing their big envelope in his pocket, sang them the same twelve songs. He repeated this process with five or six other labels over the next few days, then drove home to Houston and restocked his cupboards.

Nathan didn't know if the story was true, but he hoped it was. He did know there were a curious number of Lightnin' Hopkins records from the early sixties that featured different versions of the same songs.

Nathan also wanted to show the students that one way traditional songs differ from modern ones is that they changed as they traveled and were sung by new singers, new generations, new cultures. A traditional song could have dozens, hundreds, even thousands of variations—the folklorists call them variants.

And songs became magically melded over the years. There were bits of an Irish ballad in an American cowboy lament, traces of a German hymn in a Tex-Mex love song, an African American field holler embedded in the chorus of a New England sea chantey.

How did they travel so far? Who changed them, and why? Or could it have happened on its own: the same lonesome couplet created by two different lovelorn lovers, sitting on two different lonely shores, longing for two different distant loves? The same sweaty, hard-luck lyrics imagined by a slave toiling in somebody else's field, and by a poor sailor hauling away on somebody else's bowline? We can never know, and Nathan found the wonder of that intoxicating.

He knew a couple of stories that showed how the old ways carried over into modern times. In the early 1950s, American folklorist Alan Lomax went "field collecting"—searching out traditional music in its natural environs—in England and Scotland. He brought along a young Appalachian singer, Jean Ritchie, who would soon be one of the commercial revival's first big stars.

Ritchie was both a songwriter and a source singer, which is a term folklorists use to describe someone who knows a lot of traditional songs and came to them in traditional ways: through the commonly held repertoire of family, community, faith, or occupation. Ritchie grew up in Viper, Kentucky, listening to her elders sing Appalachian versions of old British ballads and to songs that were uniquely American. But she also wrote her own songs.

One day, Lomax recorded Jeannie Robertson, one of Scotland's most important source singers. She and Ritchie hit it off famously and were soon chatting away and swapping songs like long-lost sisters. Ritchie sang Robertson a love song she'd written, called "One I Love." Robertson immediately learned it, and soon other collectors were recording her version, assuming it was an old Scottish song.

Some forty years later, a lovely Irish singer named Karan Casey recorded "One I Love." She'd learned it from a Dublin source singer named Frank Harte and assumed it was traditional. When she found out it had been written by Ritchie, she tracked her down and soon they were hitting it off famously, chatting away and swapping songs like long-lost sisters.

Nathan thought that would work well with a story about Sarah Makem, the mother of Irish singer Tommy Makem, who became famous with the Clancy Brothers, the hugely popular Irish folk group of the 1960s. Tommy's mother was also a renowned source singer, and young folklore students often came to the Makem door, hoping to record her songs.

Sarah Makem was always happy to sing for people, so she'd invite them in, make them a nice pot of tea and a plate of cookies, then sing them whatever came to mind. More than once, young Tommy would watch a student go bug-eyed and begin to scribble furiously in his notebook, because Mrs. Makem was singing something that didn't appear in any of the traditional collections he'd studied. Could this be a *new* folk song, something no one had collected before? What a rare feather in the student's cap! To a folklorist, this was the equivalent of an astronomer discovering a new star.

The student would thank Mrs. Makem profusely and scurry out the door, eager to get the song documented before anyone else did.

While his mother talked about what a nice young man that was, but in such a hurry—aren't they all these days?—young Tommy would run after him.

"I'm sorry to have to tell you this," he'd say, "but Mum learned that song off the radio last week. Perry Como sang it, I think. See, she doesn't care a damn where they come from. If she likes 'em, she sings 'em."

Nathan loved that story. It showed how futile it is to try to categorize traditional music, to chart its travels or ever-changing sound. It's like trying to pin a butterfly that's still in flight.

Tradition is a living thing; Nathan believed that utterly. It's a force of nature, a river still running, its current denying our attempts to freeze it in time, file it away, fix its origin or destination.

But tradition is something else, too, something Nathan was just starting to figure out. Consciously, at least. Had he always known it, felt it, wanted it to be true? He looked up from his desk.

Tradition is another word for community, isn't it? And sharing the music of people from the past, hearing how they felt about their lives, is a way of experiencing that community. It's a powerful thing, the first time we realize that community can exist not only with people around us, but also with those who came before us.

Nathan felt a chill and looked out the window. Was it getting dark or just raining harder? He checked the clock. Raining harder. He felt the chill again and realized the wind had picked up. He walked to the kitchen door, stared out at the drenching rain, then closed it. The floor was wet. He looked at it vacantly. Tradition is another word for community. Why hadn't he realized that before?

He made himself some tea and returned to his work. Tradition, another word for community. Hmm. He began leafing through his notes.

Fame is a funny duck in the folk world. Folk's notion of fame has always been both larger and smaller than the kind of fame pop culture celebrates. Nathan wanted to explore that in one of the classes, because it showed some essential demarcation points between folk and the mainstream music industry. He knew a couple of stories that fit the bill.

In the 1970s, Pete Seeger was invited to sing in Barcelona, Spain. Francisco Franco's fascist government, the last of the dictatorships that started World War II, was still in power but declining. A pro-democracy movement was gaining strength and to prove it, they invited America's best-known freedom singer to Spain.

More than a hundred thousand people were in the stadium, where rock bands had played all day. But the crowd had come for Seeger.

As Pete prepared to go on, government officials handed him a list of songs he was not allowed to sing. Pete studied it mournfully, saying it looked an awful lot like his set list. But they insisted: he must not sing any of these songs.

Pete took the government's list of banned songs and strolled on stage. He held up the paper and said, "I've been told that I'm not allowed to sing these songs." He grinned at the crowd and said, "So I'll just play the chords; maybe you know the words. They didn't say anything about *you* singing them."

He strummed his banjo to one song after another, and they all sang. A hundred thousand defiant freedom singers breaking the law with Pete Seeger, filling the stadium with words their government did not want them to hear, words they all knew and had sung together, in secret circles, for years. What could the government do?

Arrest a hundred thousand singers? It had been beaten by a few banjo chords and the fame of a man whose songs were on the lips of the whole world.

Folk is thought of as a fringe music, but what rock star has that kind of fame? Which of the world's great pop stars could have done what Pete Seeger did, knowing that a hundred thousand people from another country, speaking another language, would know the words to the songs he came to sing for them? And that they would rise and do it in defiance of their government? That is *fame*.

There was another story about folk fame that Nathan loved. It was about Joe Cormier, a delightful Cape Breton fiddler who lived in Waltham, Massachusetts, working as an electrician and playing his fiddle for dances on the weekends. When he was nearly sixty, he was awarded the prestigious National Heritage Fellowship Award, putting him in the league of past winners such as B.B. King, Bill Monroe, Doc Watson, and Mavis Staples.

Cormier was suddenly an international star, performing at Carnegie Hall, the Kennedy Center, and the Smithsonian. Someone asked him how it felt to become famous at sixty.

"Famous?" Cormier said, his eyes twinkling. "Let me tell you a little about being famous."

He said he'd grown up in a tiny fishing village in Cape Breton. Even as a boy, he'd shown promise as a fiddler. Every Saturday night, the village held a dance in the town hall. At a certain point, the dancers would stop, the band would put down their instruments, and Joe's father would lift him up on a table. Everybody would gather round while Joe played a few tunes.

"Now let me tell you what I mean by 'everybody,'" Cormier said. He said it meant all his neighbors, the parents of the children he went to school with, his teachers, and the shopkeepers in town. Every week, the entire town stood around this little boy, looking up at him and cheering as he played the fiddle. And during the week, everywhere he went, he was told how well he had played. By everyone he knew, by everyone his parents knew.

Smiling coyly, Cormier said, "Hey, I've been famous all my life."

Fame is personal in the folk world. The latest pop superstar might sing before tens of thousands, but they're strangers. How much more intense was the fame Joe Cormier knew in that tiny fishing village. His audiences were the people he saw every day, the men his father worked with, the women his mother talked with over the backyard fence.

Even now, fame was like that in the folk world. In the coffeehouses, people sat a few feet away from the stage. They wanted to experience art that was close, human, authentic in the most intimate ways. It was personal.

Whew. So many stories. Nathan looked down at the piles of paper. They were still piles, weren't they? He'd hoped they would have sorted themselves into something a bit more orderly by now. Still, he was beginning to see how various tales and tunes connected in ways that might incite some good conversation. This was gonna be fun.

He looked out the window, into the solemn darkness of the evening. The rain still pelted against the panes. No wonder he was in such a trance, with that wet drumming against his walls.

He suddenly realized he had no idea how to get things going. He could see some connective tissue, but no beginning. Where do I start?

He stared out the window for a long time then laughed softly, remembering his morning brood over Kit's cinnamon coffee. Start real, start personal, start true. One true moment.

"Exactly," he said, patting the pile on his desk.

A little before midnight, Kit called from the Massachusetts Turnpike, saying she was about a half hour out of Boston. She was still "kinda wiry" from the gig and wondered if he'd mind some company. The original plan was for her to drop the car off in the morning.

"Sure, come on over," Nathan said. "You know, you don't have to call first."

"I didn't want to wake you up."

"Ah. Yes. I see. And the phone wouldn't do that. Well, that's very—"

"Oh, shut up," she said, laughing sharply.

"Drive safe. I'll have some tea waiting for you."

"Chocolate. Must. Have. Chocolate."

"I'll look around."

When she arrived, she put down her guitar and fiddle with a satisfied grunt, then hugged him. He leaned against the stove and asked about the gig.

"Boy, I thought Cambridge was the Cambridge-iest place on earth, but I think Northampton's got it beat. It's—"

"Cantabridgian," Nathan said.

"Huh?"

"The way you say it is 'Cantabridgian,' not 'Cambridgey.' Things or people pertaining to Cambridge are called Cantabridgian. Don't ask me why."

"Is this going to be on the test?"

"Sorry."

"*Any*-way," she continued, "it's kind of snooty, in an earthy-crunchy way. Like some people I know who feel like they have to *correct* people all the time."

"Sorry."

"The crowd was really quiet. I was surprised I got an encore."

"Wow. That's not the easiest place to get an encore."

Kit nodded and looked around the kitchen. "They asked about you. The Iron Horse people. Said to be sure to say hi."

"They did? I am stunned."

"Yeah, I got the feeling they liked you. They said you played there, but just once. Like it was too bad you never came back."

"That's not how I remember it. Let's just say it was a mutual decision."

Kit tilted her head uncertainly. "You know, I think some of these places that you think hate you or have these awful memories of you…" She hesitated.

"Yes?"

"Well, I think some of it's maybe in your head?"

"Is that a question?"

"No, it's, like, my feminine way of not being declarative." She smiled, fluttering her eyelashes. Then she turned serious.

"But really," she said, "I didn't get any of that vibe out there. They all seemed to like you and thought it was cool that we're a couple."

Nathan looked at her awhile, sitting down on a kitchen chair. "Yeah, well, you were playing there, so…"

Kit slumped her shoulders. "Yes, I'm sure that's it. They didn't want to offend their singer by telling her what an evil-hearted slug she was with. Like, you wouldn't want to get your songwriter all moody and sad right before the show. I mean, moody songwriters in a folk club—who ever heard of that?"

Nathan sensed an opportunity to change the subject. "Especially in a sparkly town like Northampton," he said brightly. "It's all sunbeams and rainbows out there, isn't it?"

"Oh, definitely. The whole town is done up in pastels. Like a great big Necco roll. The songwriter I played with rode in on a unicorn."

They laughed and riffed on that for a while, conjuring a town that lay somewhere between the East Village and Candyland.

In the back of the refrigerator, Nathan had found a big bar of chocolate left over from Christmas. Wine and chocolate had become Kit's favorite post-gig snack. Nice buzz.

Her eyes bugged when he told her. "You mean that organic stuff my folks gave me?" she said.

"Now, is that a question, or are you just being feminine again?"

She laughed and slugged his arm. "You really can be a miserable old fart sometimes."

"Yes, but I'm your old fart. And I have chocolate." He grimaced, shaking his head. "Hoo, that didn't sound right. 'And I have candy for you, little girl.'"

"Chocolate is not candy. Chocolate is a drug."

"Yes, well, that's much better, isn't it? 'And I have drugs for you, little girl.'"

The combination of wine and chocolate did not incline Kit toward sleep. They stayed up till dawn, playing records, talking about the biz.

She said the woman she'd shared the gig with was a really good songwriter, and the club invited them both back for a gig in the summer. She'd suggested that Kit enter the songwriting contest held each year by the Falcon Ridge Folk Festival, just over the Massachusetts line in upstate New York. It was the biggest songwriter festival in the Northeast. Kit asked what Nathan thought.

He said he detested the whole idea of treating music competitively, as if one song could be measured against another. It's not like a track meet, he snarled, where everything can be precisely marked and measured. These are songs, for chrissake. Kit quickly agreed.

"Hey, I swapped CDs with that songwriter," Kit said. "Wanna hear? She's kind of a cross between Aimee Mann and Alison Krauss. You know, broody but twangy."

They listened, and Nathan said he liked her too. But between the two of them, the songwriter would be known forevermore as the "Unicorn Chick," because of the joke Kit made about her earlier. The fact that her music made her the furthest thing imaginable from that description just made it funnier to them—like calling Aimee Mann "Bubbles." Private jokes are always funnier when no one else has a chance of getting them.

Nathan left his house in the late afternoon, looking forward to a lazy stroll into Harvard Square for his first Passim folk music class. He was amazed at how little nervousness he felt, compared to the dread before the Harvard class. Perhaps it was because this was happening at a coffeehouse, always his home turf; perhaps because he'd grown comfortable with his Dooley's sets; perhaps because Kit so often made him proud to be an elder in the folk tribe.

As he turned out of the driveway and onto Craigie Street, he was struck by the colors of early summer, the garish greens and reds and yellows.

He looked at the tight row of grand old Colonial homes across the street. It had kind of an impressionist-painting feel, the colors soft and yet distinct. One home was heather green with emerald shutters; another ice-cream white with a playful maraschino roof. A bright yellow house stood beside a slate gray one, almost as if one was in the sun, the other in shadow. His favorite was a ribbon-candy purple with twinkly blue shutters. It looked like it should have a slot for coins in the roof.

As Craigie crept closer to the Square, the houses got smaller and more Victorian. It was a remarkable change, like watching time itself stroll from one era to another.

At the precise moment he passed from Colonial to Victorian, the air was overtaken by the whirring of nearby Mass. Av., Cambridge's main artery. The sound of birds and children playing was displaced by the mechanical din of traffic, automobile horns, and a distant jackhammer.

It's the way New York City sounds all the time, that continuous breath of mechanical motion. At four in the morning, you can open a Manhattan window and hear the same whirring and wheezing, like a low and endless sigh. They call New York the city that never sleeps; it's really just the city that never shuts up.

Nathan turned right, away from the noise and onto tiny Berkeley Street. It was a nice moment, and he always listened for it. Just as the whirr and honk of the city began to disturb the peace of Craigie, he ducked down another quiet, leafy street.

He told himself this was a shortcut, an insider's secret path to the square, but he knew it was roughly the same distance. Its advantage was keeping him tucked away within the quiet backroads of old Cambridge.

He liked the architectural jumble of Berkeley Street, a mix of Colonials, Victorians, and stone-and-ivy homes from the early 1900s. There was something that felt right and proper about things that were of their own times standing unapologetically next to things of other times. Something balanced, settled, real. "We are what we are," their confident shadows seemed to say. Balanced and settled, but in the glorious, mixed-up way that life is balanced.

He stopped and looked up and down the street. He'd never thought about it that way before, but that's why he enjoyed this little street so much, with its cacophony of architecture. It felt like life happening the way it actually does, the way a forest has small new trees sprouting up in the shadows of grand old ones. Life is never all of one time or another.

Never all of one time or another. That's what the old songs tell him, isn't it, as they make him feel what the first singer felt, and what every singer afterward has felt? There is no such thing as a new moment; every moment contains every moment that came before it.

He stood still, head cocked down toward the street, eyes closed, hands stuffed in his pockets, thinking about that.

Nathan was on fire.

Remembering his rainy day preparing for the Passim class, he wanted to start real, start personal, being just who he was. One true moment. So he sang a couple of songs and talked about how he became a folksinger. He explained the wonder he felt about the old songs and the mysteries in them. Then he began asking questions that had no answers—his favorite kinds of questions. Who wrote them? Why? What was in their long-ago hearts?

Sixteen students, mostly in their twenties, sat on folding chairs in a large function room above the cellar coffeehouse. As Nathan sang and told stories, they put down their pens and leaned forward in their seats. It began to feel more like a chatty house concert than a class.

To wrap up, he told a story that is well known in folklore circles. In the early twentieth century, a British folklorist named Cecil Sharp wandered through Appalachia, collecting the music mountain people made for themselves. Like the people who'd settled there, most of the music had its origins in England, Scotland, and Ireland.

One day Sharp listened to an illiterate hillbilly sing "The Death of Queen Jane," an ancient and fairly accurate British ballad about the 1537 death of Jane Seymour, days after giving birth to the male heir that her husband, King Henry VIII, desperately wanted. After the hillbilly stopped singing, Sharp asked if he knew whether the story was true.

"Oh yes, it must be true," the man replied. "It's such a pretty tune." He added that he didn't think it had happened near where he lived, but a few counties over, and a long time ago.

Scholars often use that story in a patronizing way, to show the provincial vistas of the humble folk. But Nathan heard it differently.

"What's amazing to me," he told the class, "is that the hillbilly was right. He couldn't read, couldn't write, had probably never been outside the county where he was born. He'd never heard of Jane Seymour or Henry the VIII, except from that song."

Nathan leaned forward, eyes burning. "But he *knew*. He *knew* that song was true. And he was right. He was also right that it had not happened near his home, and that it happened a long time ago. He knew those things because the song told him and because he knew how to listen to it. He had the right kind of ears."

Nathan sat up straight, searching the faces of the students.

"That's the kind of ears I want us to go looking for," he said. "I think it's the greatest thing folk music can give you. This music wasn't made by fools. Whoever wrote that ballad about Queen Jane was able to put enough information in it—not just in the words, but also in the melody—to tell someone hundreds of years later, in an entirely different world, that the story was true. Man, if that ain't genius...."

Nathan shook his head, looking off into space. Then he shrugged, brushed his hand shyly through his hair, and asked if anybody had a question. People nodded politely and looked at each other, but nobody wanted to go first. It was as if all the excited air had been sucked out of the room.

God, he hated that, the fear people had of showing that they didn't know about music. Where does that come from? They wouldn't feel that way in a class about history or math or plumbing. But when it came to music, something made people afraid of not being *in the know*. It probably had something to do with that ugly notion of being unhip. Nobody worries about being a hip plumber.

Betsy Stotts raised her hand and said, "What do you think is the most important difference between folk and pop? I mean to you, when you listen to it?"

Nathan could have kissed her. Everyone laughed, and he could feel the room relax. The question was so simple that it seemed like Betsy asked it to make everybody feel comfortable. Get the ball rolling.

"Well, for me," Nathan said, measuring his words, "it's that folk music is still life-sized, the way it's always been. We're always being told that some new pop album or movie is larger than life. It's not a concert, it's a larger-than-life concert *event*. I don't even know what that means. Are there concerts that aren't events?"

He paused a moment, gathering his thoughts.

"If folk music taught me anything," he continued, "it's that there's no such thing as larger than life. Life is as large as it gets. If it's not life-sized, it's smaller. That's what I hear in the old folk songs, and in what songwriters are doing today. They want to keep it real, and this has always been real people's music. That's where it got its name: music about real folks, real life. You look inside the songs and you see people just like you, with the same troubles and worries and dreams and fears. Whether the song was written last week or a thousand years ago. It's life-sized."

From that, the class burst into lively conversation, often ignoring Nathan while they talked among themselves about whether certain performers were authentic and folky or poppy and commercial. Sometimes they'd turn to Nathan, as if expecting him to referee. But he said approving things about all the musicians mentioned and told the class, in several different ways, that it was up to them to decide. "Does it move you?" he said. "In the end, that's all that matters."

The class was scheduled to run an hour. After nearly two hours, Stotts said she needed to close up the school. She suggested people go over to the Border, a Mexican restaurant across the street. They gathered around a large table, talking and eating until after midnight.

Over the next few weeks, the Border after-party became a tradition. Word spread about the class, and Stotts told Nathan that more than forty people had signed up for the fall semester. She asked if he'd think about a similar class on songwriting. He agreed immediately.

As they were leaving the Border that first night, Nathan thanked Betsy for asking the first question. It broke the ice, he said, because it was so basic. Coming from the school's director, it gave everybody permission to open up.

As he held the door for her, Betsy swept by, arching an eyebrow and smiling. "Maybe I just wanted to know the answer, huh?" she said with a wink.

Five

Nathan paced the kitchen, a sharp pain pounding in his stomach. Damn, damn, damn. He bounced his shoulder against the refrigerator and slapped the kitchen counter hard with his hand. No, no, no. He was barely aware he was doing these things, pacing and pounding as if the motion might move him toward some way to fix this. But it was too late.

He'd made a mistake, a bad one, the kind he never wanted to make with Kit. It had seemed so innocent at the time, a few glib words, forgotten as soon as they were spoken.

Why couldn't he just keep his sour old opinions to himself? He bounced himself off the refrigerator. Well, because she kept asking for his sour old opinions. His hand slapped the counter top. Well then, why couldn't he think before he spouted off like some senile sperm whale?

He felt a sharp pain in his hand and looked at it. The palm was red, the joints white. He sat down and began drumming his other hand on the table. It had been such a small, careless remark that Kit had to remind him of it. After she returned from the Iron Horse gig, she asked him about the Falcon Ridge Folk Festival songwriting contest.

They'd had a grand giggle over the whole idea. How preposterous, Nathan said. Songwriting contests? You might as well judge the best snowflake in winter or falling leaf in autumn. Dam, damn, damn. Why couldn't he think about it for a minute? Maybe things had changed since he formed his sour old opinions. But there was always a reason to not do something, wasn't there? That was his forte. Now, he'd transferred that virus to Kit, and it had hurt her brightening career, perhaps badly.

The songwriter she'd shared the Iron Horse gig with, the one they nicknamed the Unicorn Chick, had given a copy of Kit's album to one of the contest judges. He called Kit to ask why she hadn't entered. It was too late for this year, he told her, but she should really consider it next year. He thought she'd have been a shoo-in to win, or at least reach the finals. They'd listened to more than four hundred entries this year, he told her, and he thought Kit's album was better than any of them.

He also told her that the four finalists got to play a couple of songs on the main stage and were included in a fifteen-city New Voices tour before the July festival. This year, nearly all the venues would be places Kit had never played, important clubs, career-building clubs.

The Unicorn Chick told Kit she did the tour last year, sold about fifteen hundred albums, and was hired back at almost every club she played. After her two-song set on the festival's main stage, she sold two hundred albums and was returning to Falcon Ridge as a headliner. Between the tour and the festival, she'd added a thousand names to her mailing list. It was a terrific opportunity for a performer with a hot new album.

Nathan had taken all that away from her because he didn't know what he was talking about. And worse—much worse—he took it away because she trusted him.

When that thought hit him, the ache in his stomach became a piercing knot of pain, shame, and something else. Fear? Yes, maybe that was it. Fear that she would never trust him again, never look at him with that wide-eyed pride, the way she did at the Harvard class, or rely on him, the way she did in the recording studio.

Kit was obviously angry, but trying not to be mad at him. Every time he tried to apologize, she interrupted him in ways that felt like slaps, and said it was her fault. She'd never been so blunt, so quick to cut him off, so dismissive of what he had to say. She should have checked the details, she said. But to Nathan, that meant it was her fault for assuming he knew what he was talking about. For trusting him. Damn, damn, damn. He never wanted this to happen. Not this. Not with Kit.

Early in their relationship, he'd worried about exactly this kind of thing and promised himself it would never happen. He would never lead her down his own care-less career path. Now he'd broken that promise, and he didn't even know he was doing it. That's how careless it was. Careless. How could he be careless with her? About anything? Sitting at the table, the knot of pain came again, doubling him over.

Over the next few days, he tried to get Kit to unload on him, scream at him, let out all the things she was bottling up. She was upset, and why shouldn't she be? She could have performed on the main stage of her first folk festival, in front of fifteen-thousand diehard fans. Whole careers are made from moments like that.

The feeling that she'd missed the boat was new to her. She hadn't missed any opportunities yet; she was the kind of person who grabbed at every brass ring, however small or unlikely. She could enter next year but the album wouldn't be new. And for a young singer with a debut album, next year was a century away. It's like the old saying about striking while the iron is hot. Her iron was hot now, today, this summer.

But she told him it was her own stupid fault and that's all there was to it. So she barked at the television, swore at the breakfast dishes, threw a magazine across the living room. Anything to keep from aiming her anger at him. Because it wasn't his fault. Take the word of a fool, you get what you deserve. Damn.

Instead of being at the festival as a performer, she was going as a volunteer. The Unicorn Chick told her it was a must-do; *everybody* would be there. Most people camped at the festival, which was held at a big farm in upstate New York. She'd meet lots of musicians and be able to sing around the campfires at night. That's why so many young songwriters went to Falcon Ridge, to sing at the song swaps that went on all night. That's why a lot of fans went, too, to hear music up close, not merely from the stage.

Kit volunteered for the full load, putting up the tented outdoor stages and laying down the hay for the footpaths and parking lots, setting up everything from sound systems to port-a-potties. She'd be camping there for at least three weeks. On the way back, she had another Iron Horse gig with the Unicorn Chick, so she'd be gone for more than a month.

As she prepared to go away, she was sullen and detached, all the while insisting that she wasn't upset. There's always next year, she'd say with a tight smile. And a few minutes later, like clockwork, she'd throw something across the room.

Nathan didn't mind her being pissed off at him. He didn't even mind her thinking he was a fool. What woman doesn't spend some quality time listing all the foolish things about the man she loves? What he couldn't bear was the idea that she blamed herself for trusting him.

Something could break between them if this continued. But every time he tried to bring it up, he got the same false smile and the same crap about how it was all her fault. Damn, damn, damn. Always a reason to not do something. That was his specialty, not hers. Why couldn't he have kept his sour mouth shut?

In a few days, she would be gone for longer than she'd ever been gone. And he would be alone again. For the first time that he could remember, he was afraid of distances growing, like long shadows, between him and someone he loved. Because for the first time, the shadows were not coming from him.

The Saturday before Kit left for Falcon Ridge, she announced that he was driving her to the big supermarket in Porter Square. It was not phrased as a request or even a question. She needed some things for her trip, she said, and they should pick up some food for the house.

"For the house?" Nathan said. "Why?"

Kit stared at him like he was a seven year old asking why he had to wash his hands before dinner.

"Because, Nathan," she said in a gratingly maternal whisper, "you don't have any decent food around here, and I'm going away for a month."

He started to get angry but simply shrugged and got the car keys. He was so glad she wanted to do anything with him that even a trip to the supermarket was welcome. Lord, she'd been in a foul mood.

When it came to shopping, Nathan had never gotten out of his old road habits: travel light, shop light. He liked to wait until he was hungry, then decide between Whole Foods, a neighborhood market, or a café. What was he in the mood for tonight?

For general shopping, he tended to buy small sizes of things like shampoo and soap. He knew it was stupid and more expensive, but he was set in his ways, he told himself. Always a reason to not do something. Even with shampoo.

They drove silently to the huge supermarket in Porter Square, a few blocks from Dooley's. He hated that store, just hated it. Pulling into the parking lot, he sadly eyed the convenience store across the street. Great deli, cool magazine rack. He looked up at the towering entrance to the mega-mart. All hope abandon, ye who enter here.

While tinkly music played through distant speakers, Kit pushed the cart purposefully through the sparkly aisles. Nathan tagged behind, looking at her. This was not going to be a good day.

The first thing she needed was toothpaste. Kit pondered her choices, idly tapping a finger on her cheek. After peering down to read the prices, she grabbed a three-pack of very large tubes.

"You gonna need that much?" he asked innocently.

She heaved a loud sigh without looking at him and tossed the toothpaste into the cart. As she turned the basket around, she said, "It's on special." Her back was already turned when she said it.

He didn't know how to move around in this mood of hers. She still insisted she wasn't angry with him. That was so obviously untrue that it put something even worse between them: falseness. It frightened him more than the anger. She was leaving in two days, and he was afraid she'd go without resolving any of this. Untended wounds don't heal; he'd learned that much.

She got a few more things for the trip, soap, shampoo, sunscreen. She studied her list to see if she had everything.

"Insect spray?" Nathan said, almost whispering.

"What?" she said sharply.

"Insect spray. Do you have any? It's buggy out there, especially at night."

She started to give him an exasperated look, then realized that was a good idea. "You think I'll need it?"

"It can get buggy."

She nodded and went to pick some up. Eyeing the basket, she nodded and said, "Now let's get some things for you."

"I'm good."

She looked at him the way a tired mother looks at a child she should have left at home. "There's no decent food at the house," she said.

Nathan shrugged. "I'm kind of a one-day shopper."

"You're kind of a one-day everything," she snapped, wheeling the cart around and walking quickly up the aisle, again forcing him to tag after her.

He walked behind her as she tossed oranges, apples, and bananas into the basket. Fresh fruit, that's nice. He always liked having fruit in the house but rarely picked it up. It either wasn't ready to eat or looked like it might spoil before he got around to it. She was right, wasn't she? A one-day everything.

At the dairy section, she picked up his favorite cheddar and Swiss cheese. Given her mood, he felt almost flattered by that. At least she still cared enough to pick his favorite cheese.

"Don't want me to be a cheese-not, huh?" he said, recalling their laughter over Ferguson's Law of Surplus Intelligence. She flashed a brief smile but said nothing.

Things started to ignite at the tea aisle. She was holding up a ridiculously large box with a bright red cover that said One Hundred Twin Flow Tea Bags.

"If you buy something like this," she said, "you won't keep running out all the time. It's cheaper, too."

Despite himself, Nathan was starting to get angry. And deep down, he thought that might be good. He gave her a funny look. Was she picking a fight with him?

"I don't like that tea," he said.

Again, she gave him that exasperated-parent look. "It's the generic brand. You don't even know what kind it is."

"But I know what kind I do like."

"So do I, but that's not what you have at the house, is it? Because you ran out of it and had to get the only kind they have at the little store up the street."

"Okay. Point made. But why would I buy a bigger box of tea I don't like?"

She slapped the big red tea back on the shelf, shaking her head. "What-*ever*," she said.

This was getting weird. Nathan wondered whether he should stoke the growing fire. The last thing they needed right now was a big fight over nothing.

On the other hand, this was how Kit often dealt with her anger. She would take an indirect route, focusing on something unimportant, like his morning tantrum over the coffeemaker. It was odd, because she was so direct about her other emotions.

Nathan walked beside her as she wheeled the cart over to the produce aisle. Did she know she was picking a fight? Was she picking a fight? Should he risk it? She was going away, and there was so much they needed to say to each other.

She finally exploded at the produce department, holding up a giant stalk of broccoli while he tried to explain that broccoli made him fart even when it was on special at what he agreed was a very sensible price.

"Jesus," she snapped, her voice rising. "You always got a reason, don't you?"

"To not eat broccoli? But it—"

"This is not about broccoli."

"No."

"This is *not* about goddamn broccoli."

"No."

He tried desperately not to smile, but the broccoli was a bit past its prime and wiggled limply as she waved it under his nose. When wagging something sternly under someone's nose, it's best if what is being wagged doesn't wiggle. She followed his eyes to the wiggling broccoli and chucked it over her shoulder in one swift motion. It landed back on the shelf, almost perfectly in its row.

"Wow," he said, looking over her shoulder. "Nice toss."

"Oh, shut up," she said, smiling but just for a second. Then she frowned at him, her eyes glaring coldly.

"Don't you see what I'm getting at?" she said. "If you thought ahead a little, you could always have what you want. Do what you want. I'm talking about control, Nathan, taking a little control over your life. That's what you're always preaching to me about, right?"

"Oh God, Kit, can we talk about something else?" He knew it was the wrong thing to say but he wanted to ignite this fire, let it burn. Burn it off.

"Please, please, please," he said, waving his arms. "Can we talk about something else? Anything. The weather. Sports. Why sports sucks. Your favorite feminine hygiene products. The lighter side of the Bush family. Or you can just stick little pins in my eyes. Anything you want but please, can we stop talking about shopping?"

"We're not talking about shopping. We're talking about you, the big preacher, always telling us little squirrels how we're supposed to care about our lives, take control, and—"

"But tea, Kit? Broccoli?"

That hit the motherlode. Her eyes grew wide and she stomped her foot as she screamed, "Everything!"

She noticed a few startled shoppers staring at her and looked down at the floor. But she was mad now, really mad. Her cheeks flashed red and then went pale. He'd never seen her like this.

"Damn it, Nathan," she said in a harsh whisper, "you don't get to choose. Life isn't a big aisle in a supermarket you can wander through, picking what you want to care about and leaving the rest. Life is…*life*. You care or you don't. Right? Right?"

He nodded at her, cocking his head angrily. But deep down, he welcomed this, wherever it was going. It was real; it was Kit, back from the dead.

"It's just so disappointing," she said. "You're always getting everybody excited about how we're supposed to care about everything. But it's like you don't even care about your own life."

"But Kit, I mean, really. Shopping?"

"Right, exactly. Little unimportant things like actually living day to day. No, you're, like, all in the clouds, up there with the big *important* stuff. Life, but only in theory. Love songs about dead people. Traditions, but from long ago. Things that move you, but that already happened. It's all so far away, Nathan. You know?"

His mouth opened and then closed.

"But your own life?" she said. "Today? Tomorrow? Nothing. You've got nothing. Like living is something for other people. You care about life, just not your own particular life. And it doesn't work that way. You don't get to make that choice. You just don't. You *don't!*"

He had to say something. Maybe it would provoke the rest of what needed to be said. "Kit, I just don't think buying the right vegetables is such a precious life experience."

"It is too!" she said sharply. "Everything is! That's what I learned from *you*, damn it. Life's not just important when big, special things happen to us. Life is every day and it's all important, all worth singing about. That's your goddamn mantra, Nathan."

There was some tenderness in her voice now, but also pain. She didn't like being disappointed in him, which hurt Nathan more than the disappointment itself. But the wound was open to the air now, where they could examine it, tend it, heal it.

"It's life, Nathan," she said. "You're either on the bus or watching it drive by. Those are the only choices."

Nathan looked down the produce aisle and stuffed his hands in his pockets. He looked back at her, his eyes soft and curious.

"I just love you so much, Nathan," she said, "and I'm tired of watching you give up. Watching you beat yourself up about things that happened years ago."

She put her hand on his cheek. "Before I was there to help you, before I could do anything about it."

Her eyes filled and she kept her hand on his cheek. "You need to look around you. You're the only one hurting you now. The only one. You're the only one around you who doesn't love you."

It was all coming out now, flowing together in the imponderable logic of love. The songwriting contest, the tea, the broccoli, the awful things that happened to him so long ago, and the abiding wounds they left. Always a reason to not do something, to not care. That was his curse and now it had reached out to hurt her.

He shook his head and brushed her cheek with the backs of his fingers. But there were no words yet. Could it all be true? All of it? He got the part about not getting to pick and choose. She was dead right about that. But the rest? The only one around him who doesn't…?

"Let me think about all of this," he said quietly. "Do we have everything we need? For your trip?"

She looked into the basket, checked her list, and they went through the checkout line. When they got in the car, he turned on the radio but not the engine. Celtic Sojourn was on WGBH. Jigs, reels, and old ballads. Just the thing. Love songs about dead people. He sighed.

They both sat there, saying nothing, peering through the windshield as if they were going somewhere.

"I don't know where to start," Nathan said finally. "I know what you're getting at, but I also feel like I've dived into the deep end more with you than I have in a long time. More than I ever have. And…and…I feel so much more connected to the world, to my life, than I did before I met you. No one's ever been so good to me. Like my website. Nobody's ever—"

She let out a sharp laugh. Not the reaction he was expecting. She turned in her seat and looked at him.

"Oh, Nathan," she said. "I mean, thank you, but Jesus, people do things like that for you all the time. All the time. Because they respect you, like you, believe in you, just like I do."

"No, they don't, Kit. Nobody's ever—"

"What about Ferguson? All that great stuff he wrote on your website?"

"Well, Ferguson. We're old friends; he was just—"

"Damn it!" Kit shouted. She was mad again. "How dare you? I mean, how *dare* you? You think Ferguson wrote those things because he's your pal? He didn't send you a bill for it because he's your pal. But you think he'd write something and put it up in public, just because you're old friends? A writer like him? He wrote it because he believes it. The first time I talked to him he said you were the best he ever saw. And you should have seen him; his eyes were just burning. 'I've written that in the paper,' he said, 'and they don't pay me to be anybody's friend down there.' It was so important to him that I knew that."

She looked out the windshield. "Don't you see what you're doing? First you say that nobody's nice to you the way I am and the next minute you're using the fact that Ferguson loves you to dismiss everything he wrote about you. Can't you see how unfair that is? To him and to you?"

He'd never thought of it that way. And she was right. He'd dismissed Ferguson's praise as a favor from an old friend.

"You probably think Murph keeps you at Dooley's because you're, like, a charity case or something," she said.

"Well, he sure doesn't make money on—"

"Jesus, you do! How many Porter Square bars are as full as Dooley's on Tuesday and Wednesday? That place up the street isn't even open on Tuesday."

Her voice softened. "Murph keeps you there because he respects how you do your work. He's told me that. He said you're more professional than just about any musician he's worked with. You take care of everything; you get there early to answer the phone. Murph thinks you do it so that if some local star calls, you can get them to drop down."

She smiled. "But I don't think that's why. I think you want to be there in case some scared kid calls. You want to be able to answer their questions, encourage them, get them to take that first big step. Because you know how hard that first step is, and how easy it is to get discouraged if somebody treats you like…well, like you're some kid who's never been on stage before."

She leaned her head closer to him. "That's how you made me feel the first time I came in with my guitar. You probably don't remember, but you went over to sign me up and said all the right, sweet things. You told me you'd seen me coming in for a while, and you were glad I brought my guitar. 'I had you pegged for a musician,' you said, and then you winked. It made me so proud, even though I knew you were just saying it to be nice."

She looked down at her lap and smiled. "I was so scared, Nathan. One hard little word, the way so many open-mike hosts are with newcomers, and I'd have been off to shiver in my little corner again. The only way I got up the nerve to bring my guitar was that I decided I could say it wasn't mine if anything got weird. I'd say I was carrying it for a friend. But you seemed so happy I was going to sing. All of a sudden, I felt like I couldn't let *you* down. You didn't know that, did you?"

He shook his head. She rested her head against the car seat. "You made me feel so welcome, so special. I already had a crush on you, but after that, whew! I was a goner."

"Lucky me," he said. They were quiet, looking at each other, smiling. He felt himself grow warmer, like something cold hit suddenly by the sun. It was going to be all right between them.

He wasn't sure if it was the right time to ask, but he wanted to make sure everything got said. Get it out. Now. Before she went away. Burn it off.

"Is this about the songwriting contest?" he said.

She swore under her breath, looking away from him. "No," she said sharply. "This is not about the damn contest; this is not about me. It's about…" She paused, looking out the window.

"Well, maybe it is a little," she said. "That's how it started, anyway. But then all those other things connected to it. You're always saying you should own your life, own your art, take control. But it's like you just want me to do that; you never want it for yourself. And you never want to do it with me."

She rested her hand on the dashboard, tapping along as she spoke. "You want to do gigs with me, but only if they're my gigs. You don't want us to be a duo, even if it's just once in awhile. It would be so cool to do some gigs like that."

She looked at him. "You produced my album, and I love it that you want to help me. But you wouldn't record any tracks of your own. Even when it was free, and you could do it as easy as me. Even when I asked. It had to be all about me."

She put her hand back in her lap. "And I want it to be about us," she whispered, head down. There, she'd said it.

She looked back out the windshield. They were quiet for awhile, then he reached over and they held each other. He knew he would have to think about all of this. But he couldn't do that now. All he could think, as she settled into his arms, was that they were going to be all right. They were going to be all right. They were going to be all right.

After the supermarket fight, things seemed to snap back to normal between them. She'd let it out; he'd listened. A few times he tried to assure her he was working on what she'd said, but she just smiled. She wasn't trying to change him, she said; she simply wanted him to care about himself as much as she cared about him. He liked hearing that, but when he tried to think it through, something nagged at him, like an itch under the skin. He agreed with her about almost everything, but something didn't gel. What was it?

Despite how quickly they patched things up, Nathan knew that some kind of atonement was coming. It always did, after they argued. No matter how the fight turned out, or who apologized to whom, she would ask him to do something, just for her.

He could always see it coming, too. Her voice took on an airy, singsongy tone that she never used at other times. She wasn't looking for punishment or retribution; it was more an act of fealty, the way a knight who'd slighted his lady would be sent errant, to prove his love by slaying some evil beast or dragon.

The latest act of fealty came the morning she was leaving for Falcon Ridge. In that unmistakable chirp, Kit said "You'll never guess who called me last week. Ryder."

She wants me to slay Ryder?

"He called to apologize, can you believe it?" she said, picking up her breakfast muffin as if that was the end of it. He waited. She chewed thoughtfully and looked out the window. After a moment, he realized she was waiting for him.

"Ryder?" he said, sipping his coffee. "Really?"

She nodded, still acting almost comically casual. Kit was many things; casual was not one of them. "He called to apologize, you know, for saying I was sleeping with Ferguson."

"Ryder?"

"And that he was happy for all the things that were happening with my music."

"Ryder?"

"Stop saying that," she said, laughing. "Yes, Ryder. He actually said he was mean to me because he was a little jealous."

"Yeah, like water is a little wet."

She laughed again and gazed at the ceiling. "I think you should invite him back to Dooley's," she said.

So that was it. You may keep your sword sheathed, Sir Knight; milady merely wants you to make peace with Ye Great Worm of Wellesley.

"You do?" he said, doing his best to match her casualness. Actually, he was beaming. This was so much like her, to pick an act of atonement this generous. Like when she got mad at him for intervening between her and Ryder and then made him set up an e-mail list for himself.

"Are you sure about this?" he asked.

She nodded. "You should have heard him on the phone. He was so sad. He really misses being part of the scene. He asked me if I thought you were still mad at him. And I told him I didn't think you were mad; you were thinking about the open mike."

"No, I'm pretty sure I was mad."

"Yeah, but you know what I mean, right?"

"I do," he said. She was smiling coyly at him. Can I actually make him do this? Just for me? He smiled back. Of course you can.

"Do you really want me to invite him back?" he said.

"I really do. I think he needs Dooley's, Nathan. And I never thought he meant what he said."

"But does that make it better or worse that he said it?"

She thought about that. "I guess it makes it worse," she said. "But it also means he probably won't do it again, yes?"

Nathan shrugged. Then he remembered how Ryder had squealed "Don't hit me" when Nathan pointed to the door. That was pure reflex; nobody reacts like that without a reason. Kit was right; he needed some place to go where nobody knew him, to pretend he was a big shot. To pretend he was somebody else. It must have taken a lot for him to call Kit.

"You sure about this?" Nathan said, looking doubtfully at Kit. But he was just letting her have her way with him. "Because I'll only do this for you. Not for him. For you."

She smiled broadly. "Yeah. Definitely. I want you to."

A van pulled up in the driveway a little before noon. It was Kit's ride to Falcon Ridge, along with several other volunteers. She took her guitar and fiddle out to the van while Nathan carried her backpack and a tent she'd borrowed from Ferguson.

As the van pulled away, Nathan thought about their fight at the supermarket. He walked into the yard and sat down against the big tree. He picked a long piece of grass and chewed it, listening to the busy summer air.

He closed his eyes and leaned his head against the craggy bark. He moved to the left and right, until his head slipped into a comfortable nook. He heard a bee— or was it several bees?—amid the crowded chatter of birds and insects. He spit out the blade of grass and picked another.

Kit was right about *what* she said at the supermarket, but he wasn't sure about the *why*. At least not all the whys. She was certainly right about life, that you're either on the bus or watching it drive by.

And she was right that his shopping habits were impractical. But careless? He loved his little shopping rituals, picking between the markets he liked, knowing what each had to offer. But that's what she was getting at, wasn't it? She wanted him to pay attention to what he was doing. To care.

He realized the tree was making his back numb and shifted around until he slipped into another notch of the curving trunk. It pushed his back up straighter, and he immediately felt the pleasant rush of clenched muscles relaxing. He took a deep breath and looked around. When you're not sweating all the time, July's a pretty good month.

What Kit had said about becoming a duo didn't feel right. Working with him, or in any kind of group, would confuse the issue for her new fans. Kit was a songwriter. Sure, she was a great fiddler and singer, too, but that was icing on the cake. This wasn't carelessness, his old passivity. This was business.

Something else bothered him, but the thoughts weren't near enough to grab. He didn't think he was letting his music languish. He was having so much fun backing her up and doing his little sets at Dooley's. The Passim class. He just couldn't muster the energy for things like albums and press kits and promo pictures. Was he still afraid? He had every right to be. But it didn't feel like fear; it didn't feel *bad*. What was it? Something else, something else.

He realized he'd thought about this as much as he could for one day. Spitting out his latest blade of grass, he slapped his thighs, grunted pleasantly, and stood up.

Pulling a soda out of the refrigerator, he thought of Kit, then slumped his shoulders. Oh, damn. Slowly, penitently, he walked to the phone and called Ryder.

"Hey Ryder, it's Nathan. I was wondering if we could get together next week. Kit told me you called her. Actually, she was the one who suggested I call."

"She did?" Ryder said. His voice was frail and wary.

"Yes. This was her idea." Nathan wanted him to know that.

There was an uncomfortable silence. Then Ryder said, "Nathan, I've been meaning to…I mean, trying to, I mean, I didn't mean what I said. I'm really not—"

"I know, Ryder, and so does Kit. She told me you apologized. Your heart's in the right place; it's just that your mouth can't always keep up with it. So let's work something out. We miss you at the open mike."

"We do?"

"Sure, the whole gang. It's not the same old clubhouse without you and your hats."

"Well, I haven't really been wearing hats lately. Do you think I—"

"This isn't about your hats, Ryder. How about Tuesday around six, at the diner up the street from Dooley's? The all-day breakfast one, you know?"

"Yeah. And…Nathan?"

"Yes?"

Barely above a whisper, Ryder said, "Thanks."

"You bet. Bring your guitar. You can stick around for the open mike."

On Tuesday, they had a brief meeting, sitting at the counter of the diner. Ryder apologized so many times that Nathan asked him to stop. Nathan explained that the open mike was not about who was good and who wasn't; it was about everybody getting a chance to share and being accepted for it. Ryder promised to behave, so Nathan invited him back.

"Nathan, um, one more thing?" Ryder said.

"Sure. What?"

"I mean, it's not a big deal, but…" Ryder hesitated, squirming uncomfortably on his stool.

"What?" If he asks about his damn hats…

"Well, it's just this," Ryder said, squirming again and looking away. "It's, um, Jackie. I mean, if she doesn't know—"

Nathan laughed and patted Ryder's shoulder. "Don't worry, ace, I'll tell her you're cleared for landing. She will keep her ginger ale nozzle sheathed."

Ryder slumped his shoulders and smiled. "Thanks. It stunk for days. Especially my hair. And it smells really different after it dries."

"Jackie is a cunning and resourceful woman."

After Ryder left, Nathan ordered a cup of tea. He wanted a little time to think before going to Dooley's. He called Jackie, in case Ryder showed up before he did.

"Okay," she said. "We're kinda low on ginger ale, anyway. You sure about this?"

He told her Kit had asked him to do it, which was all Jackie needed to hear.

Sipping his tea, it struck Nathan that Ryder was not a serious musician. Ambitious, yes, but serious? Not the way Kit was. Ryder wasn't getting gigs yet and he'd been a Dooley's regular for at least a year longer than Kit. But it wasn't because others were unfairly stepping over him, as Ryder thought. It was because he wasn't putting himself on the market. He hadn't even put together an audition recording.

As terrified as Kit was when Nathan met her, she was always pushing herself forward. She didn't know if she had the nerve to play at Dooley's, so she forced herself to at least bring her guitar, inventing a cover story in case her courage failed. But that *was* courage, wasn't it? Find out what you can do and make yourself do it. If you can't finish, at least start.

Kit's talent wasn't the only thing that pushed her career forward. It was also her will. Even with that awful stage fright, she got right up in the world's face and made it say yes or no to her.

Nathan had known a lot of poseurs like Ryder, but he'd never seen one build a decent career. Some were talented enough, but they didn't have Kit's will or courage. Swagger only takes you so far.

Artists like that sometimes get ahead in rock or pop, where confidence can be manufactured from smoke machines and lighting effects. Where there's enough money at stake to attract managers with the toughness their clients lack and who see that lack of toughness the way a hungry wolf sees a limping deer. Fortunately, predators like that rarely track the low brush, where the folkies live. What's the point?

Nathan had once asked Kit how she was able to keep getting on stage before she got control of her stage fright, knowing it was likely she'd make a fool of herself.

She'd said, "There was no way to get from where I was to where I wanted to be except to not mind being a fool. But there's a bit of the fool in all art, you know? Especially something like folk music, where you really have to be yourself. You have to put yourself out there, risk spontaneity. How can you do that without being willing to play the fool?"

Then she'd smiled and said, "The secret I discovered is that audiences love it when you risk being a fool. Whether you make it to the next trapeze or fall on your face, they like that you tried. You took that chance for them, and they love you for it."

Ryder would never take those risks. At some point, maybe he'd learned the wrong lessons about taking risks, about getting up after being beaten down. There was a great fear in him; there always is with guys like that.

But folk music still had a place for Ryder, Nathan thought as he finished his tea and savored the late-day caffeine buzz. So many venues, record labels, and other folk businesses were run by people who had tried to be stars but lacked the crucial ingredients.

What was it Kit said when she got angry at Nathan for trying to protect her from Ryder? What we love most about people is often a mirror of what we like least about them. Things that seem like flaws can become useful tools if we figure out our real place in the world.

That's the great thing about community, Nathan thought, idly tapping his spoon on the counter. Everybody gets to serve according to who they really are. Whatever you have to offer is welcome and helpful. Everybody can find a job that suits them, and it all helps to keep the big wheel moving. When you think about it that way, folk music's neediness is one of its chief virtues, isn't it? There's always work that needs doing. And that's how community is supposed to work.

He looked up to see the waitress leaning against the back wall, arms crossed, eyeing him ruefully. He gave her a questioning look. What? Her head pointed toward the counter, where he was still tapping his spoon – *whap, whap, whap* – like Thumper the rabbit in Bambi. Oh. He put the spoon down and mouthed *sorry* to the waitress.

That would be another talk to have with Ryder. Not yet, though. Let him figure some of this out for himself. Then, late some night, he would sit Ryder down and say, "You know, there's lots of ways to be part of this music. You don't have to play to be a player."

Nathan was stir crazy. Kit had been gone nearly two weeks, and he sat in the kitchen, refusing—absolutely refusing—to clean the sink again. Like he did this morning. And the night before. He put away the dishes stacked in the drainer, ignoring the times he'd decided that was a waste of time, since they ended up right back in the drainer.

He thought about playing the guitar but was too fidgety. It was funny, because he and Kit would often go days without seeing each other. Something about knowing he couldn't see her, though, made him unable to sit still. He was amazed at how acclimated he was to having her in his life.

Last night, bored out of his skull, he used an Internet travel site to look up places where he used to play. It wasn't the nostalgic fun he thought it would be. He clicked "Sites of Interest" and "Nearby Attractions" for towns he'd traveled through and saw museums, scenic views, parks, historical homes. Damn. All he remembered were the coffeehouses and the bars. He'd missed so much.

Some good times, though. He Googled a few of the old bars and was delighted when he found them still open. He looked at the pictures and remembered each bar's special charm, along with the local pickers, the coffeehouse volunteers, the women. There were some good times.

Now, on a sweltering late-July Thursday, Nathan called Ferguson to ask if he wanted to get together for dinner.

"Have we ever done this before?" Ferguson asked.

"Had dinner?"

"Made a plan to have dinner."

"I don't think so. We usually just bump into each other."

"That's what I thought. Why do you suppose we've never done this before?"

"Kit's never been gone this long before."

"She's having a strange effect on you, hoss."

"No kidding."

They met at Chez Henri, a Franco-Cuban bistro, one of Ferguson's favorite haunts. If he wanted to get pie-eyed, its rum drinks were a great way to start. When he first became a critic, he liked the Periodistas, because it meant "journalists" and had a kick like Hemingway's shotgun. Now he thought the drink had a bit too much pretension and a lot too much sugar, so he favored the more austere Marilene, with its eight year-old rum, muddled lime, and bitters. Quick to the head, soft on the tummy.

Chez Henri was one of those places it was cool to know about, tucked away on a side street between Harvard and Porter Squares. Nathan found Ferguson at the bar, finishing a Marilene. He'd probably arrived early to get a few drinks down before Nathan arrived. It was an old drinker's trick, one Nathan knew well: get a head start before the nondrinkers show up. He knew immediately that Ferguson had the day off tomorrow.

The place was pricey, but you could get a pretty cheap meal from the bar menu. Of course, you had to sit at the bar, which was fine with Ferguson. He'd staked out a couple of stools by the corner, where Nathan could lean against the wall and look out the windows at quiet Shepard Street.

After joking more about why they'd never done this before, Nathan ordered the cheese and fruit plate. Ferguson had clam fritters, with lemon-chili aïoli, thank you very much. And a half-carafe of wine.

Nathan told him about the fight he and Kit had at the supermarket. Ferguson muttered "Good for her" so many times that Nathan suggested, to save time, he raise an index finger when he wanted to make that point.

Grinning wryly, Ferguson raised his finger and kept it there.

"Okay, okay," Nathan said. "I get your point. Good for her."

It wasn't as if Nathan was trying to tell his side of the story. The way he was telling it, Kit was heroic, though he couldn't resist describing the wiggling broccoli and her impeccable overhead toss back to the produce shelf.

Nathan was soon so down on himself that Ferguson started sticking up for him: you've come a long way, pal; this is tough stuff, bound to take some time.

And Ferguson agreed with him about the idea of forming a duo. "She's in your shadow enough as it is," he said.

"Well, I wouldn't put it that way," Nathan said with a shrug, glancing up the bar. Do Franco-Cubans drink root beer? His club soda tasted an awful lot like, well, club soda.

"Of course you wouldn't," Ferguson said. "You'd disagree if I said that you were in your own shadow. But you're still better known than she is, at least with some people. I don't think it's hurting her, because she can make the sale on her own, and because you've been careful about it. But if you two actually worked as a group, it would get in the way."

Nathan nodded, then said, "How can I be in my own shadow? I mean, isn't the very nature of a shadow—"

"Oh, shut up."

Nathan laughed. "That's just what Kit would say."

Ferguson smiled and raised an index finger.

"Oh, shut up." Nathan said.

As they ate, they talked about how well Kit's career was going and what the next steps should be. Ferguson said she needed to get her music heard beyond Boston. He suggested a publicist in western Massachusetts who could help get her album to folk radio shows around the country. Nathan wrote down the phone number.

"It's nice, isn't it?" Ferguson said, eating some fritter. "Realizing you've learned a few things that can help people. I think that's the biggest perk to my job. It's amazing how much I can do simply because I've been around awhile. I'll say, 'You won't get anywhere talking to that person. Here, call this number, and *only* talk to such-and-such. They'll take care of you.' I mean, it's easy for me, you know? One of the best things about getting older."

"Elder," Nathan said.

"What?"

"Becoming an elder. That's what's happening. We're becoming elders."

"Like elders of the tribe?"

"Exactly like that. The keepers of the lore, the stories, the knowledge about how things work. Somebody passed it to us; now it's our turn. We're the elders."

"I don't know if I'm ready for that."

"Ready has nothing to do with it," Nathan said, laughing. "You're already there; you just said so. You know all this stuff about how things work and you're passing it along. That's what elders do."

"What makes me think this has something to do with Kit?"

Nathan smiled. "It starts with her, that's for sure. I get such a kick out of showing her things, especially things she already sort of knew but forgot or didn't think were important. Like her fiddling. It's not so much that the fiddle put her back in touch with traditional music, it put her back in touch with her own music, the stuff she grew up hearing. It helped her songs sound more distinctive, more like her."

"I've noticed that too."

"It's such a pleasure to realize you've lived long enough to know things that are worth passing along. As soon as Kit told me she grew up fiddling, I knew it would help her find her own sound and be more comfortable playing music. It feels good that I've been around long enough to know things like that."

"Elders," Ferguson said, lifting his glass. "Well, here's to being elders."

Nathan talked about his Passim classes. He'd just done one on political music, showing how it was always part of the tradition. Some of the young students thought that protest music started with the sixties or Woody Guthrie, but he sang them snatches of antiwar ballads from the 1600s and labor songs from the early 1800s.

"They thought it was much cooler that protest was always part of folk music," he said. "I don't think young people see the bright line between old and new, the way we did. It's like our generation wanted to see the distinctions, and this generation wants to see the connections. They're not purists. For people like Kit, it's one big happy jumble."

"All people's music," Ferguson said.

"Exactly. It's authentic because it's real, not because it's old, or Irish, or Appalachian. That is so hip. It took me years to figure that out."

"There's a funny thing about purists," Ferguson said. "I have this weird vantage point because I'll be writing about bluegrass one week, Celtic the next, then maybe the blues. In every kind of music, there are certain artists the purists point to and say, 'That's the yardstick. That's when it was pure, so that's how it should always be played.'"

"But here's what's odd," he whispered, as if he was sharing a great secret. "The artists the purists point to are always people who changed the music. *Always*. Think about it. In bluegrass, it's Bill Monroe and the Stanley Brothers. But man, they invented a whole new way of playing. In Irish music, it's Turloch O'Carolan, the blind harper from the 1600s. But he broke all the rules; I mean, he wrote *chamber* music! The jazz purists point to Louis Armstrong, and he's another guy who changed everything. See what I mean?"

Nathan stared at him, grinning. It was like hearing a beautiful song for the first time. "Wow," was all he could say.

"Interesting paradox, huh?" Ferguson said. "Purists set the rules by exalting people who broke the rules."

Ferguson swiveled to catch the bartender's eye. Nathan looked out the window at the falling dusk. The sky had turned that curious shade of red it sometimes does between the gray and the black. He remembered the old saying "Red sky at night, sailor's delight."

Old sayings…old truths…how can truth become old? Shadows had moved down the walls of the brownstone across Shepard Street, making the latticed fire escapes look like iron ivy crawling along the soft brown brick. Could he actually see the shadows move or was that a trick of the eye?

Eyes glazed, Nathan said, "Every generation departs from the norms of the last one. The new generation's departures seem rootless to their elders, lacking tradition. But then that new generation ages, becomes set in its ways, and its departures become the norms the next generation rebels against."

Nathan let out a long breath, still looking out the window. "And that's how the big river keeps rolling along, isn't it? We spend part of our lives thinking we're rebelling and part of our lives thinking we're resisting rebellion. But we're always doing what the big river wants. What the tradition wants. Taking it up and passing it on. Rolling it along."

As though coming out of a trance, Nathan's head snapped back toward Ferguson, and he straightened on his stool.

Ferguson stared at him, his beer stalled in mid-flight to his mouth. "Where the hell did that come from?" he said.

"I have no idea," he said, and they both laughed.

Nathan looked back out the window. The red had become a dark purple, belonging more to night than dusk. This time of day changes so quickly; maybe he did see the shadows move.

"I suppose I got it from watching Kit," he said. "And remembering. Watching and remembering. It's true though, don't you think?"

"True? Man, it should carved in granite somewhere." Ferguson closed his eyes, the way he did when he was forming his words carefully. "We think revivals are occasional things, happening within one generation or another. But they're not, are they? Revival is always happening; it's the way tradition breathes, inhaling the new, absorbing what's useful and sustaining, exhaling what's fleeting."

"And the breathing never stops," Nathan said. "Like a river never stops."

Ferguson exhaled slowly, then looked down at his beer. Nearly empty. This place was not cheap, and it was time to drink.

"Why don't we stroll across the street to the Lizard Lounge, catch some music?" he asked Nathan.

"Sure. What's there tonight?"

"Um, actually, I think it's an open mike."

"Oh, goody."

"We don't have to—"

"No, it's fine. I could use a Coke. Open mikes and soda pop. Welcome back to Nathan-land."

Ferguson tilted his head uncertainly.

"Don't get me wrong," Nathan said. "I think I'm starting to like Nathan-land."

Grinning, Ferguson grabbed the check with one hand and raised a finger high into the air with the other.

Kit finally rolled in around five in the afternoon, looking excited, exhausted, and very, very pink. She was wearing a Falcon Ridge T-shirt and frayed jean shorts. Her dark eyes were fiery, but ringed with tired gray circles, and her face was bright pink. Boy, she was right about that. Before she left, she'd warned Nathan that she did not sunburn, she sun-*pinked*.

Before he could even say hi, she tossed down her gear and, laughing loudly, threw her arms around his shoulders and her legs around his waist, knocking him back against the counter and almost onto the floor.

He managed to get a kiss, but then she was off, laughing and chattering about what a great time she'd had. She tracked through every room, dropping her things here and there, making the place hers again, and he loved her for it.

She turned and looked at him, framing her bright pink face with her hands. "Well, get it over with," she said, cocking her head.

"Your freckles are bigger," he said helpfully. Actually, he thought she looked adorable, but knew better than to say so. Cute was not what she was after. She'd told him that her family always teased her about how pink she got, so she was expecting the same from him.

"And?" She said, bobbing her head to the left and right within her framed hands. She looked like a kid playing a daisy in the school play. He was trying hard not to laugh.

"Well," he said, "it'll be harder for people to tell if you're blushing."

"No cracks about being a lobster?"

"Not at all. Not the least bit lobsteresque. Lobstericious? Lobstertarian?"

She cleared her throat impatiently.

"Salmon, maybe. Lox."

"Oh, thanks."

"Bubble gum?"

She sighed.

"Very pretty bubble gum."

"Nice save."

"With freckles. Very pretty bubble gum with freckles. It's a bold look, not for everybody. But you *make* it work."

She laughed, walked over to him, and they held each other. "I wouldn't care if you came back with plaid cheeks, Kit," he said. "I'm that glad to see you. I don't know what you've done to me; I used to be so comfortable by myself. But I've been going nuts around here."

"Good," she said into his shoulder. "I missed you too."

"I got so lonely I went out to dinner with Ferguson," he said.

She arched her head back and looked at him. "You did? Really?"

He nodded. "And then we went off to an open mike. On our night off. We were miserable without you."

She smiled. "You're making me forget about the bubble gum."

"Like I said, on you it works."

"Don't push it."

Kit had some chocolate and iced coffee, which did nothing to slow her down. They sat on the sofa, and she talked nonstop for an hour, telling him everything that had happened at Falcon Ridge.

She'd made the rounds of the musical campfires every night and met lots of musicians. She would fiddle at one, sing at the next. After the first night, she started carrying a notebook because so many people wanted to sign up for her mailing list. By the end of the festival, she had more than two hundred names on it. That was astonishing. She also sold around fifty CDs and gave away many more. Without even being on the lineup. Damn, damn. If only he'd kept his big mouth shut about the songwriting contest.

She said she'd had lots of time to think about their fight and decided that missing the contest was her fault. He protested, but she was firm.

"Tell me one thing," she said. "If I had told you about the tour and being able to sing at the festival, what would you have said?"

"I don't know, Kit, but I still—"

"No, answer me. What would you have said? If you'd known about the tour and the other stuff."

He looked down, shaking his head. "I would've told you to do it," he muttered. Why was that so hard to admit?

"Exactamundo. Because it's all about getting on stage, getting the music out there. That's what you tell me all the time. But I didn't find out that stuff before I asked you."

He looked up at her and shrugged. He'd grown so comfortable with this being his fault.

"You were like, 'This is what I think,'" she said. "And that's what I wanted you to do: tell me what you thought. But it's got to be up to me to find out what the deal is before I ask you. It's my life, right? Right?"

"Yes, but that wasn't really what we were fighting about," he said. It was odd how uncomfortable this made him. "And I've been thinking about everything you said. I agree with most of it. Nearly all of it. I just—"

"Good," she said softly, leaning into him. "That's all I want, for you to think about it. I'm not trying to change you or anything. I like you just the way you are." She started rubbing his chest. "I just want *you* to like you, too, because…" She kissed him and her hand moved up over his shoulder.

After dinner, they sat around the stereo, listening to music, talking about small things. It was the middle of August, so of course, the Red Sox were in a slump. Neither of them paid much attention to sports, but it was very Boston to groan about the Red Sox in August, so they did. They were simply enjoying each other's company, doing nothing together. But Kit seemed to have something on her mind.

A little after midnight, she spilled it.

"Oh," she said with a delicate cough. "One other kind of cool thing happened at the festival."

"Yes?"

"Wanna hear?"

"Of course."

"I think maybe I got a manager. At least, a guy who says he wants to be my manager. Says he's got a lot of connections."

Nathan swallowed hard. "Wow," he said, as nonchalantly as he could. "How about that."

Six

Everything about this manager smelled wrong to Nathan, but he'd have to be very careful how he handled it. He'd made a bad mistake about the songwriting contest. As much as Kit insisted that was her fault, she also knew that his opinions could be wrong for her.

Nathan spent days wandering old haunts, taking the same walks he did to brood about his failures. But he thought only about her and the trouble he was sure she was heading toward. Again and again, he saw his young self in her confident, excited face, strutting blithely toward the sounds she wanted to hear: such a bright future, such talent, such promise, star, star, star.

He could tell how much Kit loved to just say "my manager." And why shouldn't she? Get a paid gig and you're a professional; get a manager and, girl, you've got a *career*.

But the more Nathan heard about what this guy was offering, the more his old antenna went ballistic. And when it came to the pond scum of the music industry, he still had a pretty sharp antenna. All his instincts, his hard-learned lessons, told him this guy was either a snake or a fool. Either way, Kit was likely to lose and lose big. The songwriting contest was a missed opportunity; her entire career could be at stake now.

For starters, what the hell did Kit need a manager for? She was only beginning to headline her own shows, and only at small coffeehouses. She had no national presence, no record deal; she had never set foot on a major concert stage. What was there to manage?

Kit knew something was up; but for now, he needed to keep his feelings to himself. She probably thought he felt threatened or jealous, because she kept telling him this guy would only be her manager, strictly professional. And that she thought he was kind of dorky, in a sweet way.

Nathan did feel threatened, but not the way Kit thought. His concerns were less romantic than, well, environmental. He felt like a landlocked seal watching an oil slick move slowly to shore, and thinking, "This does not look good."

This guy was an oil slick, slimy, encroaching, and toxic. When he met Kit, he told her she was the most promising songwriter he'd seen at the festival, and that she could go far "with the right handling." And he said this after hearing two songs at a campfire hootenanny. Nathan's private nickname for the guy became "Slick."

But Nathan couldn't simply tell Kit that Slick was bad news. Not with her suspicion that he was jealous. Not with the mess he'd made of the songwriting contest. Not with the mess he'd made of his own career.

He didn't need to use his own career as a reference point, however. Hell, Joyce didn't sign with a manager until she moved to L.A. She hired one to negotiate her first record deal, and she was very smart about it. She refused to talk about a long-term deal until she saw how he handled the record label. The last Nathan heard, she was still with the guy.

But it wasn't just that Kit didn't need a manager. It was also that Slick wanted to be both her manager and music publisher. That didn't make sense. Those were two completely different jobs. It's like somebody saying he'll fix your teeth and repair your car. The smart money is that he'll screw up one of those jobs; the smarter money is that you'll end up with spark plugs in your mouth and gold fillings in your transmission.

Worst of all was the money. Lots of money. Slick was going to finance a major studio record to be used as a demo for getting a recording contract. They would hire the best studio musicians, maybe even an orchestra. Got to spend money to make money, he told her.

It would cost tens of thousands of dollars. Kit saw that as a sign of how serious Slick was. Nathan saw it as debt. Slick was also going to finance a big tour, with a full band, to show that she was ready for prime time. But who would come? She was still unknown outside the Boston folk scene. Kit thought that showed how much he believed in her.

That's such a common mistake with young artists. They're so hopeful, and the music industry uses that hope the way the oil industry uses oil. It's a cash commodity, and it burns fast. To guys like Slick, it's a renewable resource, but only because there's always another Kit around the corner, another wannabe with stars in her eyes. To the wannabe, it's not so renewable.

In the pop world, the label execs, managers, and agents are usually in on it together. They live off money the artists haven't earned yet, burning it off on budgets for recording, touring, marketing, hotels, and the great catchall, "expenses." But it's all money the artists have to earn back before they see a penny for themselves. Nathan read somewhere that a major-label release had to sell more than half a million copies before the artists made a profit. And less than five-percent of major-label releases sold that well. What kind of business runs that way?

Nathan remembered something Joyce had told him years ago, as her career was beginning to slide. Almost overnight she went from being a hip coquette to an inside joke, thanks to a *Saturday Night Live* skit lampooning her insinuating vocal style and famously bobbed hairdo. The nub of the joke was that she was getting a little old for the sly, girlish sexuality she projected. She was all of twenty-eight.

Joyce and Nathan were getting drunk backstage after a concert. Her tour had been a major disappointment. She still had her diehard fans, but she was losing the fickle mainstream audience.

Joyce brushed a bouquet of flowers in the center of the buffet table. "When I was having all those hits," she said, "I'd always find roses and a big basket of fruit waiting for me in my hotel room."

"That's nice," Nathan said, and Joyce laughed sharply.

"Not so nice," she said. "I never figured out that I was paying for them. They were put on the label's 'Joyce Warren budget.' With their compliments and my money. Silly me, huh?"

It would be even worse for Kit. Before she even had a career, Slick would saddle the "Kit Palmer budget" with tens of thousands in debt.

And that's where this got really dangerous. Kit would be damaged goods before any label got a look at her. She would not come to them free and young and unfettered, they way they liked their budding stars, but laden with debt and a manager who took a big chunk of everything she earned until that debt was paid off.

The only way this deal worked was if Kit got very big, very fast. Only if a label was sure it could burn off that debt in the first flush of success would it even consider investing in her. And for a folk songwriter, in this pop market, that was unthinkable.

So in the end, it didn't matter whether Slick was a snake or a fool. If things didn't work out with Kit, he would move on, keep throwing things against the wall until something stuck. But the things he was throwing were lives, and when they didn't stick, they broke into pieces. Nathan knew all about that.

Kit would spend her life the same way he had, wondering how it all went so wrong, whether it was her fault or simply fate—living forever in a bruised and blackened past. He couldn't let that happen; it would kill him to watch that happen. Not to Kit, lovely Kit.

He had wondered if anything could throw him back into the dark place from which he was beginning to climb, and now he knew. Watching someone he loved descend into the same darkness and not being able to stop it. That would put him back there, and he would never want to see the lying sun again.

Nathan felt as if he was walking on a narrow shard of glass. There was no safe footing. How could he destroy Slick in Kit's eyes without appearing jealous, or like the dundering old fool who convinced her to ignore the songwriting contest? The guy who always had a reason to not do something.

There was only one way. Somehow Nathan had to get Slick to do the job for him. Slick had to be the one to talk Kit out of making this mistake. When that first occurred to Nathan, it seemed impossible, given how good Kit was at reading people. But as he thought about it more, he decided it might be doable. Tricky but doable.

If he was right about Slick, it shouldn't take too much for someone as smart as Kit to see through him—given the proper vantage points. That would be Nathan's job.

The first thing he had to do was make damn sure he was right. After all, he'd been sure about the songwriting contest, too. Maybe, just maybe, the music business has changed, and scooping bright young things from campfire sing-alongs to sign them to lifetime contracts is de rigueur these days. Yes, and maybe the Republicans really are the party of the working man.

First, he called Ferguson, who said he didn't know about Slick but would ask around. Next, Nathan called a few compadres from his touring days, who were now working in the commercial music industry. Was Slick known in publishing or management circles?

When Ferguson called back the next day, he told Nathan, "As near as I can tell, there's only one thing about this guy that should give you the slightest pause."

"What's that?"

"He's an *asshole!*" Ferguson shouted the last word so loud that Nathan jerked the phone away from his ear. As Ferguson bellowed on, Nathan could make out the words *fraud*, *pimp*, and *genetic hiccup*.

It turned out that Kit wasn't Slick's first client. He'd signed a few local songwriters to the same deal, and the debt killed their careers. But there was another problem with Slick's contracts. They also gave Slick a first option on future albums, which meant that a label had to negotiate with him first. That would be a deal-breaker for most labels: they'd have to pay off Slick before they could even talk to Kit.

And Slick had not been able to do anything for his clients. The records he'd made were badly overproduced, full of clumsy rock backing and syrupy string arrangements. They went nowhere.

"He wouldn't be so goddamn dangerous," Ferguson said, "if he didn't have so much money to throw around. Probably a trust-fund baby. I can't imagine anyone doing this with money he had to work for. You're not going to let Kit sign with this guy, right?"

"Not if I can help it," Nathan said. "But it's tricky, very tricky." He explained his dilemma, and his plan to get Slick to destroy himself.

"So the plan is for you to trick Kit into believing you're okay with this guy?"

"Yeah, at first."

"Trick Kit."

"A little. Just at first."

"You're going to trick Kit." Ferguson started to chuckle. "Well, lord love a dreamer, pal. I wish you well." Still laughing, he hung up the phone.

If you wanted to put a picture next to the phrase "nice guy," you could not do better than Slick. He was a slight figure with delicate features, tiny white hands, and fluffy auburn hair. His eyes were light blue, almost incandescent, and he was dressed casually, in jeans and a pastel green sport shirt. Everything looked like it had never been worn before.

Nathan didn't need to do any scheming to set up his encounter with Slick. Kit wanted them to meet; she wanted them to be *very* good friends. She said it several times. *Very good friends, such good friends.* The more she said it, the more he suspected that she thought he was jealous: the male staking his territory, rutting and pawing his cloven hooves into the ground.

That was embarrassing, but it worked in his favor. She would be looking elsewhere for signs about what he was doing, which might give him some extra time. Because Ferguson was right: he wasn't going to trick her for long.

Nathan, Kit, and Slick were sitting at a back table in a quiet bistro in Cambridge's Central Square. The contract she was going to sign was in the middle of the table. Slick had made some minor changes, at Kit's request, after praising her for how carefully she read it. "You sure you weren't a business major at college?" he asked with a smile. Snake.

As soon as they sat down, Slick patted the contract and assured Kit that she didn't have to sign it tonight but he hoped she would. He was ready to get to work, by golly.

Nathan was trying so hard to be pleasant that Kit started giving him looks. There was a cheerfulness to his voice that felt forced, even to him. But it was crucial not to appear hostile to Slick. Not until Slick started doing Nathan's work for him.

Nathan leafed through the pages of the contract. He'd read it already, damn near memorized it. He was well prepared; the trick was to not show it.

Nathan laughed. "You know, I never got around to signing one of these things myself," he said. "I had a pretty big record deal but never got a manager. Probably should have."

"I know," Slick said. His voice was breathy, soft, and sweet. "That story's a legend around here, Nathan. You got such a raw deal. I took a music management course at the Berklee School of Music, and they actually taught that as part of the class."

"How not to have a career. Well, I'm the poster boy for that." He smiled weakly at Kit.

"Nathan really wanted to meet you," Kit said brightly. "He's been looking forward to it. Me too. I want you two to be friends."

"Well, me three," Slick said. He leaned toward Nathan and widened his eyes. "I'm a big fan, you know. I love your music."

Nathan forced a smile. Slick's name was actually Michael David, and Nathan wondered if that was his first two names, without the surname. It sounded phony, like an overpriced hair salon.

Nathan looked at Kit. "It's amazing she's ready for this step so fast," he said. "You really think she needs a manager already?"

Slick beamed at Kit. "Well, she's quite a talent. I think she has 'star' written all over her."

Nathan launched his first attack, more a probe of the enemy's position than a frontal assault. Slick had told Kit he thought he could get her songs recorded by other singers. That meant he would have to work with some major publishing companies.

"So, Michael," Nathan said, "you were telling Kit about getting her songs recorded by some other people. That's exciting. How do you shop songs around like that? I wouldn't know where to start."

"Well," Slick said, leaning back in his chair, "I'm sure I'm not telling you anything you don't know, but this is a who-you-know business."

Nathan nodded. "So which publishing companies do you work with? Which ones do you think would be best for Kit?"

"I'll try them all. That's the way it's done. You gotta make the rounds."

"You sure do. So who's your contact at Bug?"

"Bug?"

Nathan nodded. He'd settled on Bug Music because it was the folk-friendliest publisher in Nashville, handling songwriter gods like John Prine, Kate Wolf, and Townes Van Zandt. He also picked it because he knew somebody there who said he'd never heard of Slick. The final reason was that it published some of Kit's musical heroes. He was pretty sure she'd seen the name on albums.

Nathan glanced at Kit, and she was looking excitedly at Slick. The name definitely put some stars in her eyes. Good, good.

"Bug," Slick said again. "You mean Bug publishing in Nashville?"

"Yeah," Nathan said. "It always seemed like a place Kit might end up. They're really good about the folk end of the songwriter market."

"Well, I see bigger things for Kit than just the folk market," Slick said, trying to change the subject.

"So, do you know people at Bug?" Nathan asked again. "I know a few folks there but I'm sure a lot's changed since I was getting my songs around. Back in the Ice Age, as Kit likes to put it."

"I do not," she said, laughing. "I love your songs, especially the new one."

"New one?" Slick said. "Man, I'd love to hear your new stuff. Maybe we could—"

"So, if you don't know anybody at Bug," Nathan said, "where do you shop songs in Nashville?"

Slick let it pass that he didn't know anybody there. "To tell you the truth," he said, "I don't focus on Nashville a lot, although I do know people there. I see Kit moving in more of a pop direction. You don't see her as a country act, do you?"

Nathan could see the pattern already. Slick wanted to talk in broad, general terms. He was a big-picture guy, not a details guy. Snake.

Slick nodded at Kit. "New York, L.A. I think she'll do much better in places like that."

"Dar Williams is on Bug," Nathan said. "No country crooner, she."

"I adore Dar Williams," Kit said, nibbling a breadstick. "I used to listen to her when I was just getting into my teens. It was like she knew all my secrets. That's so important when you're that age."

Slick smiled at her. "God, I love how sensitive you are," he said quietly.

Nathan smiled at Slick. Do not slap him. Under no circumstances are you allowed to slap. "So what makes you think Kit's songs have pop appeal?" he asked.

"Well, they're great songs," Slick said, holding his arms out wide. Then, as if sharing a great industry secret, he whispered, "They're very fresh."

"Fresh."

"Fresh."

"And that's something they're looking for these days? Fresh?"

"It's all about fresh. That's the new buzzword."

"Fresh is the new 'new,'" Kit said, laughing to herself.

"I'm not kidding," Slick said. "Fresh is the thing. And your songs are very fresh."

"But it's still a who-you-know business," Nathan said.

"It is."

"So who do you know in Los Angeles?"

"Los Angeles?"

"That's where a lot of pop publishers are, isn't it?"

"Some. Also in New York. Gotta work both towns these days. It's a bicoastal business. I log a lot of frequent-flier miles, I can tell you." He laughed.

Again, Slick was broadening the lens, changing the subject. And again, he hadn't mentioned anyone he knew anywhere. Was Kit catching on?

Slick excused himself to go to the bathroom. Kit leaned over to Nathan. "What's up with you?" She asked.

"What do you mean?"

"You're so…so…bubbly. If I didn't know better, I'd think you've been drinking."

"I'm excited, that's all. Big night." He shrugged

She eyed him suspiciously. "Okay. It's just, like, you and bubbly; it's a strange combination."

She knew something was up; he wasn't going to fool her much longer. But if Slick kept cooperating this well, it wouldn't matter. What an amateur. The important thing was to keep getting him to do the heavy lifting.

Slick sat back down. "This is a cool place, isn't it?" he said. "Nice and quiet."

"You've never been here before?" Nathan asked.

"No. I've been by it a few times, always wondered if it was as nice as it looked. You guys want to eat anything? On me."

Kit and Nathan looked at each other, then shook their heads. "I would like some wine," Kit said.

Slick ordered a carafe of red wine. There was no root beer, so Nathan had a Coke. Watch the caffeine, though. No slapping, no slapping.

"Can I ask a little about this manager-publisher thing?" Nathan asked. "That's a big chew for one person to bite off, a lot of work."

"Well, I'm kind of a workaholic," Slick said. Once again, he'd changed the subject, hopping over the specifics. Boy, he was slick.

"Well, you'd need to be," Nathan said. "But I've never heard of anyone doing both those things for the same client."

"Oh, it happens," Slick said, nodding knowingly.

"Really? Who else is managed that way? Anyone we've heard of?"

Slick smiled at Kit, but she was staring evenly at him, tapping a finger on her wineglass.

"No one off the top of my head," he said, sounding a little nervous. "But it happens. Believe me, it's more common than you think."

"I'm sure you're right," Nathan said. "I'm pretty out of date when it comes to the music industry."

"Tell you the truth," Kit said, "I thought that part was a little odd, too."

"It allows *focus*," Slick said, as if that was a technical term only a few people knew. "I can put all my *focus* on you."

"Here's what confuses me about the manger-publisher deal," Nathan said. "It seems like there could be times when you'd be in conflict with yourself; when the manager's interest wouldn't be the same as the publisher's."

"Really? I can't see how—"

"Let me give you a hypothetical, okay?" Nathan said. He was surprised at how calm he felt. But when the bunny just lies there, you don't need to pounce.

"A hypothetical?" Slick said.

"Sure. Let's say you get an offer from a big star who wants to record one of Kit's songs. But this star wants an exclusive on the song, doesn't want Kit or anybody else to record it. That happens sometimes. The star wants the song to be associated with him completely."

"Yes?"

"Well, a deal like that comes with a lot of upfront money. The star pays a huge advance for exclusive rights to the song. It can be thousands, even tens of thousands of dollars."

"What's the problem with that?" Slick winked at Kit. "You're not one of those artists who's afraid of making money, are you?" He laughed, but Kit only smiled.

"Nothing wrong with money at all," Nathan said. "The point is that it might be better for Kit's career to keep that song for herself. Less money right now, but better in the long term. Let that song work for her as a performer, you know?"

"I'm still not sure where you're going with this."

"Of course not," Nathan said. Oops. Easy, boy. "It's just that I can imagine a man-ager and a publisher having an honest disagreement about that, because their interests would not be the same. The publisher's job is to represent the song and giving it to a big star is a major coup. And not just for that song: it increases the value of the writer's whole catalog. The manager, on the other hand, has Kit's whole career to consider. Sacrificing the big money now could be better for her over the next ten, twenty years. See what I mean? Different priorities."

"Not for me," Slick said, smiling fondly at Kit. "My interests would always be her interests."

"That's a lot of money to turn down," Nathan said.

"Not if it wasn't in Kit's best interest."

"Her publishing-career interest or her performing-career interest?"

"Not if...not unless...well, whichever. Whatever is in Kit's best interest."

"I'm sorry for pushing this," Nathan said, leaning forward, "but I'm still not clear. See, after you start representing her, Kit's going to owe you an awful lot of money. The record, the touring. You're financing it all. Obviously, you want to get that debt paid back."

"I prefer to call it an investment." Slick said serenely.

"Of course you do. But it's still money. And there it is, being offered to you all in one big chunk, all her debt and then some. And Kit gets a big payday, too. But you'd turn it down if you thought it wasn't in her best interest?"

"Of course."

Nathan nodded. "Very impressive."

"Not a tough call at all," Slick said firmly. He smiled at Kit, but she was staring into her wineglass.

"Hmm," Nathan said, leafing through the contract. "That in here anywhere?" Kit looked up at Nathan.

"What?" said Slick.

"You know, that you would always act in her career's best interest, even when it was in conflict with your interest as her publisher."

"In the contract?" Slick's voice had a little edge in it now.

"Yeah, to get everything off on the right foot, you know. Spell everything out. Trust but verify; good fences make good neighbors; no secrets among friends, all that good shit." Nathan looked up from the contract, squarely into Slick's eyes. "The best surprise is no surprise?"

Kit was still looking into her wineglass. She said, "I didn't see anything like that in the contract."

"Well, by golly, we can put it in there!" Slick said, slapping his hand on the table. "We can put anything in there that we want. I want you to be happy about this, Kit. It's your career we're talking about. Nathan's right. Spell it out up front. By golly, he's right; leave it to an old pro like Nathan. That's the way to do things."

He smiled beatifically at Nathan, then at Kit, then back and forth again. For a moment he thought he was okay. But Nathan saw the opening, wide and inviting. Time to pounce.

"So Kit gets final approval on publishing decisions," he said.

"I'd consult Kit on something like that. Certainly. On everything."

"Consult. That's not the same as approval." Nathan looked down at the contract. "That in here anywhere? A consulting clause?"

"Say, am I under oath here or something?" Slick laughed nervously, but his voice was turning cold. There had to be a mean side to a guy like this, devouring one young songwriter after another, never getting a return on his investment.

"Seems like a reasonable question, Michael," Kit said quietly.

Nathan looked at her. There was sadness in her eyes. She was figuring it out, but Nathan hadn't expected this. He thought she might be angry, but this was something else. Nowhere to go but onward, though.

He pushed the contract toward Kit. She began leafing through it, shaking her head slowly.

"Let me tell you why this concerns me," Nathan said. There was no emotion in his voice. "She'd be into you for a lot of money, thousands. Hell, tens of thousands by then. It would be tempting to get that money back."

"Not if it wasn't in her best interest," Slick said, his voice higher, almost whining, like a child trying to win an argument by saying the same thing over and over.

Nathan smiled. "But it's funny how a pile of money can change your priorities. Somebody could convince himself that a big payday was in everybody's interests. Kit would make a lot on that deal, too. That's why I wondered if Kit would have final approval."

"I would never do anything without consulting Kit."

"Consulting," Nathan said. "Not the same as approval."

"We could work out *something*," Slick said sharply, then took a quick breath. He realized he'd let his anger flare and looked at Kit. "I want Kit to be happy with the contract," he said, his voice false and squishy, like velveteen.

Kit picked up her wineglass and emptied it in one swallow. She looked down at the contract, all thirty pages. Without a single word about what rights and powers she would have. She pushed the contract to the middle of the table.

"I don't know, Michael," she said slowly. "This is a very big step for me. I'm going to have to think about it for awhile. Very big step."

"Kit," Slick said, sensing it slipping away. There was desperation in his voice, which he tried to cover with a whispery softness. "I think we can do big things. Great things. I don't want you to miss out on—"

"I have to think about it some more," she said bluntly. It was not a tone that invited a response. "I'll get back to you."

"You'll get back to *me*?" Slick said with a sarcasm he immediately tried to reign in. "Kit, really, I—"

"Sound decision," Nathan said, putting a little of that cheerfulness back in his voice. "For both of you, I think. Haste makes waste. Stitch in time saves nine. Hmm. They don't mean the same thing, do they? Still, care and caution, care and caution. You don't want to go tumbling down the same nasty hill I did."

Slick glared at Nathan. There was no fondness in his eyes. Guess he wasn't such a big fan, after all. Slick turned to Kit, widened his eyes and tried one more time.

"Hey, why don't we get some more wine?" He said. "Lighten things up a little. Nothing's written in stone here. Nothing we can't figure out. I still think that—"

"Tumbling down the same hill," Kit said, almost to herself, as she got up from the table. "No, we all have to find our own hills, don't we?"

She looked at Nathan. So sad, so sad. He didn't expect this. "Can we go now?" she said, her voice tight. "I really think we should go now."

"Kit, I—" Slick said, grabbing her arm as she stood up.

"I have to think about this, Michael," she said, pulling her arm away. "I'm very grateful that you want to help me. But I have to think about this." She left the contract on the table.

Slick stood up and looked harshly at Nathan.

"She'll get back to you," Nathan said. And then he winked.

As soon as they got outside, Kit turned to Nathan, almost in tears, rubbed his arm and tried to smile.

"You knew from the beginning, didn't you?" She said.

Ferguson was right; he didn't trick her for long. Whatever you do, don't trick her now. She's had enough trust broken.

"Yes. At least, I was pretty sure."

"How? I mean, it sounded like such a good deal."

"The first thing was that I don't think you need a manager. Not yet. If a reputable manager was interested in you, maybe he'd help you out, give you advice, try to build a relationship. But I think he'd also tell you that you don't need a manager."

He looked back through the darkened windows of the restaurant. "This guy wanted to own you before there was anything to own."

"He seemed like such a nice guy."

"He probably is," Nathan said, which seemed to startle her. "I mean, he doesn't make any money unless you do, so I'm sure he means well. But meaning well isn't the point. Knowing what he's doing is the point. And giving you some control, some choices. That's the point."

Kit stared at the sidewalk, shaking her head slowly back and forth. He let her think. She raised her head and looked up and down Mass. Ave. She turned to him and smiled. "I don't know how to even begin thanking you," she said.

"That smile will do fine. I was afraid you'd be mad at me."

"Why?"

"Maybe you'd think I was trying to meddle, micromanage your life, or something like that. I didn't want you to think I was being, you know, possessive."

Kit's eyes widened and her lips clenched. She stared at him, her lips growing tighter and her eyes bugging wider. Then she laughed. The first shriek was so loud it made him flinch.

"You?" she said through the laughter. "Po…po…possessive? Oh dear, oh dear, oh dear." She laughed so hard she doubled over. "Oh, oh," she said, wheezing for breath. "I'm sorry, but like…I'm sorry, but…"

When she calmed down enough to straighten back up, she looked up at him, laughing and wheezing for breath, holding her stomach.

Finally, she said, "Oh, Nathan, honestly, sometimes you're just too cute for words. Worried that I'd think you're too possessive. Whoo."

She patted his cheek and said, "Don't worry, tiger, I like my men kinda clutchy. Lets me know they love me." And with that, she was off again, laughing and doubling over. This time, he joined her. Indeed. Nathan Warren, Mr. Clutchy.

When she settled down, the sadness returned to her eyes. "I need a drink," she said. "Do you mind?"

"Not at all." They walked around the corner to an Irish pub on Prospect Street.

They sat at the far corner of the bar. She ordered a rum and Coke and drank half of it in one gulp. She let out a small cough after she swallowed, shaking her head slowly.

"You seem sad," Nathan said, sipping a Coke. "Disappointed?"

She took another long swallow and raised her glass to the bartender.

"Not like you think," she said. "With Michael, of course. Certainly not with you. You're my hero, bub, my knight in shining armor. I didn't even know I was tied to the tree, didn't even know Michael was the dragon."

She looked down at the bar and her eyes filled. "I just feel so dumb and young and helpless. How could I be so naive? So naive and stupid." She looked at Nathan, and a tear spilled down her cheek. He wiped it away with his finger.

"You would have figured it out," he said. "You sure figured out what I was doing. You were way ahead of him on that."

"I read that contract over and over. There was nothing in it that protected me, not one word. But I never noticed. Not until you pointed it out."

"Actually, Slick pointed it out."

"Who?"

"Oh, sorry. Michael. That's been my private name for him. Slick."

"Well, if the Vaseline fits."

They were quiet a moment.

"Slick," Kit said, picking up her second drink. "And I didn't see it at all. It's so obvious now. But he just rolled over me. All that flattery, and I'm all, like, gooey and stupid. Flattery and pipe dreams. Shit, shit, shit."

Putting her head down, she said, "Dumb, dumb, dumb. I should have seen him a mile off. Slick. Discovering me at a campfire. Jesus, I should've known better."

She took another swallow of her drink. "I thought I was really starting to get around, you know? Hanging with you and Ferguson, talking about the biz, soaking it in. Got my record, got gigs, got my own website. Hey, look at me. But I'm still an idiot kid from Connecticut, loose in the big city."

She slurred "city" a little. The rum was starting to kick in. Good. She could use some anesthetic.

"That's not fair, Kit," Nathan said. "And it's not true. Michael was slick, very slick."

"He didn't fool you. Not for a second. I should've seen it from that first night around the campfire. The way he talked."

"What do you mean?"

She smiled at him, the same sad smile he'd seen at the restaurant. "It was all about me, how good I was, how much people like me. How pretty I was."

"So?" Nathan said, waving the bartender over for another round. Time to finish the job. He needed to make sure she didn't come away from this doubting herself, her ability to run her own life, her art, her career.

"That's how this business works," he said, leaning close to her. "Guys like Slick, they're good at what they do. They don't just flatter you. They listen to you and figure out what you want to hear. It's more than flattery, more insidious. They make you believe they're telling you the facts about yourself. The facts you want to hear."

"That's not what I mean," she said. "It was all about me, Nathan. Me. Not my music. It was never about why my songs were good, why people liked them. It was how cool I was, how smart I was, how pretty. That's, like, a total red flag, and he was waving it in my face the whole time. Damn it, I should've seen through that."

"I didn't," Nathan said.

"What do you mean? You saw through him right away."

"I don't mean this time," he said softly. He looked past her, at the wood walls behind the bar. "I mean last time. When it happened to me. A guy just like him, at my record label."

Nathan was quiet. Then he turned to Kit, who was looking at him, waiting. And for the first time in his gray little life he was glad—actually glad—for what had happened to him so long ago. How else could he know the things he knew, the things he needed to know, so he could help her now?

He leaned over and looked straight into her eyes. His voice was strong and sure. "What you need to remember is that you didn't sign that contract. Not until you put him in front of me. You found the person who had the most experience with this kind of thing, and you made Slick get past him. You made him go through me first."

He put his hand on her arm. "You did that, Kit. All by yourself. You put him in front of me. Before you signed anything."

She looked at him and blinked. "I did, didn't I?"

He nodded. "And if it wasn't me, you would've gotten somebody else. Ferguson, maybe. Sure it all sounded rosy. But you made sure somebody was walking down the garden path with you, somebody who'd been there before. So you already know the most important thing you need to know, to go where your music's taking you."

"What's that?"

"You know what you don't know. You can never know everything and the minute you think you do, they'll eat you for lunch. You know that—and you know what to do about it."

She peered at him and put her glass down. "I never thought about it like that," she said, shaking her head the way you do when you're feeling the liquor and notice that shaking your head feels good. She looked at the bar as she thought about what he'd just said.

"Well, anyway," she said, smiling and picking up her glass. "Thanks."

"Always happy to be your knight in shining armor, sweetie. Any time."

They huddled at the bar, Kit getting a little drunker as they recounted the blow-by-blows of Slick dismantling himself. They laughed about Nathan's scheme and how Ferguson had reacted when he heard the part about trying to trick her. Now, more than ever, was the time to tell her everything.

A few weeks later, as a sultry September began to feel a bit like autumn, Kit walked into the open mike. Nathan didn't see her; he had his eyes closed, listening to Ramblin' Randy sing an Appalachian lament. Despite the clumsy vocals, the old love song was transporting.

Joyce used to sing that song, back in her Cambridge days. Now, as Randy sang of lone pines, blue mountains, and whitetail deer, Nathan saw lamplit, cobbled streets and the tiny Harvard Square club where he first heard Joyce sing.

It's funny how that happens, how the images in our favorite songs take us into our own memories, and not to the places they describe. Rushing rivers become narrow city streets, and a forest becomes a dark-lit little coffeehouse. A sad-eyed mountain girl named Polly becomes Joyce, when she, and the whole world, seemed new and ripe and full of promises.

Nathan opened his eyes to see Kit smiling at him on the stool he'd saved for her. "Welcome back to the world," she said. "Please watch your step while deplaning."

"I love that old song," he said. He gave Randy a thumbs up as he climbed off the stage.

It was taking awhile for Kit to get over Slick. Beyond the embarrassment, it made her unsure of herself. Nathan knew what a raw wound that was, painful to the touch until the scar tissue hardens.

After saying hi to everybody, Kit said, "I suppose you all heard about that slimeball manager I almost signed with."

Ferguson raised his eyebrows and Jackie shrugged. She heard so many stories at the bar, she said, it's hard to keep them straight.

Kit smiled and began teasing herself in a way that showed she was getting over it. Admitting you've been stupid is the first sign you're getting smart again.

"You know what he called me at Falcon Ridge?" she asked.

Jackie, cleaning a glass, leaned in expectantly.

"He said I was like some wild mountain flower."

Jackie flinched, waving her bar towel in front of her face, as if she'd been hit with a bad odor. "Oooh," she said with a sour face.

"Exactly," Kit said. "Wild mountain flower. Jesus, if that didn't tell me to put on the bug spray—"

"D-Con, honey," Jackie said. "D-Con."

Kit rubbed Nathan's arm with one hand and pointed to Ferguson with the other. "Lucky thing I had good buddies looking out for me," she said. It was the first time she'd acknowledged Ferguson's help. She followed it with a solemn "Thank you," to which he wriggled uncomfortably on his stool and stroked his beard.

As the witching hour began, Ferguson was again grousing about the paper. An editor had said Ferguson needed to be careful about "seeming too much like a teacher."

"What's wrong with being a teacher?" Kit said. "I think you're a great teacher, perfesser. I'll polish your apple any day."

"I hope that's not a double entendre," Nathan said.

Kit pursed her lips and shut her eyes. "I...don't see...how...it...could be," she said, as if trying to imagine it. Then she turned to Nathan, with that sarcastically innocent look she did so well. "What would the apple be?"

"I'd rather not think about it."

Kit looked back at Ferguson. "Sorry, perfesser. You were saying?"

"Well, he told me the stories should be light and fun. Frothy."

"Frothy?" Nathan said.

"Frothy. Somebody must have gotten a memo with the word *frothy* in it. So it's all about *frothy* now."

Jackie stared at Ferguson. "Frothy," she said. "I don't even know what that means." She looked at Nathan. "Can you think of *anything* about this friggin' town that makes you think frothy?"

"The harbor before they cleaned it up?"

"I don't think that's the kind of frothy they mean." Ferguson said.

"No."

"No," Jackie agreed, shaking her head solemnly. Then they all laughed. All except Kit. She was staring at Ferguson, almost scowling. Either she was angry or thinking very hard. Nathan could never tell with that look.

Several minutes later, while everybody else was talking about politics, Kit straightened up on her stool and cleared her throat, as if she wanted to say something important. Everybody looked at her.

"I've been thinking a lot about this, Ferguson," Kit said tentatively, apparently unaware that the subject had changed. "And you know what?" She looked at Ferguson, and her cheeks flashed pink. He waited.

"You know what?" She said again, puffing one of her nervous little breaths. What was she nervous about?

Ferguson smiled, realizing she was waiting for a response. "No, Kit, I don't. What?"

She looked at him, nodding her head. Again, Ferguson said, "What?"

"Well, it's just that I think you should do something." Kit's face reddened more and she stammered as she spoke. It was as if she'd scripted this but forgot her lines.

"Do something?" Ferguson said. "About what?"

"The paper. I think I have, like, an idea." She stopped, her eyes moving anxiously from Ferguson to Nathan to Jackie. Everybody was quiet, waiting for her. She looked back at Nathan. Help.

"What's your idea?" Nathan said.

"Oh," she said with another nervous breath. "Well, it's just that I've been thinking about this a lot, and…" She took a deep breath and said very quickly, "I think you should stop being a turd."

She smiled and spread her hands wide, as if everything was clear now. See?

Ferguson sat bolt upright. "Excuse me?" he said.

'No, no, no," Kit said, shaking her head. Her face was now bright red, and she sounded out of breath. "Oh god, that's not what I mean at all. I don't mean that you *are* a turd. I mean, like, of course, I don't mean that. Just that you should stop *being* one."

Ferguson stroked his beard thoughtfully. "Ah, I see," he said. "Well, yes, that's entirely different, isn't it? Stop *being* a turd."

Kit's head was on the bar now, softly thumping. "No, no, no," she muttered in time to the thumps. "That's not what I mean, either. Jesus. It's like Utah Phillips, that thing you told me he said. That thing I wrote down? About the mainstream. Remember?" She turned her head to look at Ferguson, then turned it back down and resumed her thumping.

To the rhythm of the thumps, she said, "He said, 'If I believe the mainstream is polluted…'" She peeked up at Ferguson again.

He nodded, remembering the quote. "'And I do,'" he said, quoting Phillips.

"'And you do,'" Kit repeated, sitting up straight. "'Then why would you want to be a turd floating down the middle of it.'"

They smiled at each other, then Kit rolled her eyes. "God," she said. "Like, ever talk before? I'm so sorry. That came out all wrong. But you know what I mean, don't you?"

"You think I should stop working at the paper?"

"No. I mean, we need you down there, if you can stand it. It may not be the paper it used to be, but, like, that review of my album really helped me. You still do a lot of good down there."

"So what then?"

"Well, maybe you should start your own paper or newsletter or something. I've been thinking about this. A lot. I even talked to some people at Falcon Ridge, and everybody said they'd love it if there was a little folk paper, you know, just for us. And you're sure the guy to start it."

"Just like that?" Ferguson said. "Start a folk paper?"

"Sure, just like that." The red was vanishing from Kit's face now. "Just like Nathan and I put out my CD; just like Nathan got the open mike going; just like you got the paper to cover folk music; just like WUMB started being a folk station. Just like we do everything. Right? Isn't that what you guys are telling us squirrels all the time?"

"All the time," Jackie said, nodding firmly. "All the friggin' time."

Ferguson glared at her. "Isn't there someone down the bar who's in danger of going home sober?" he said.

"Nah, I'm good," Jackie said, grinning and crossing her arms. No way she was missing this.

"Jesus, I don't know, Kit," Ferguson said. "It would be great to have a folk paper around here. I've actually thought about it once or twice. But where would we get the money?"

"Aha!" Kit exclaimed, slapping her hands on the bar. "Now we're getting somewhere."

"We are?"

"Sure. We already know what's number one on our to-do list. Get the money."

Nathan said, "I don't want to be an old grumpy-bear, but isn't that pretty much number one on everybody's to-do list?"

"Great!" Kit shouted, so loud that Ferguson jumped in his seat. "Then we know we're on the right track. Our number-one thing is the same as everybody else's." She smiled slyly at Ferguson. "Nathan said so."

"And in matters of finance," Nathan said, "it's well known that Nathan Warren is the place to go."

"Oh, shut up," Kit said, then looked back at Ferguson. "Off and running, per-fesser. We're off and running."

Nathan shrugged. "She's right, you know. We've been spouting this stuff for years. Grassroots community, do things for ourselves, don't depend on the corporate swine."

Jackie chuckled, looking back and forth between Kit and Ferguson. "Like a rat in a trap," she said.

Of course, Kit knew she was being ridiculously simplistic. But she was making a point, hoisting Ferguson on his own petard. And she was right: this was how things were done in the folk world. Our own folk paper, run by and for folk fans. Just like our own venues, record labels, music stores, management agencies, festivals. Just like the whole folk biz works. Because if it doesn't, then the music is always vulnerable to the whims of the mainstream, the latest memo from the mother ship.

Kit rubbed her hands together. "Boy, you old soldiers are right," she said. "This is fun, huh?"

Ferguson scratched his cheek and smiled weakly. "Wheee," he whispered.

"Okay, then," Kit said, saluting Ferguson. "What do you want us to do first, skipper?"

Ferguson looked at her imploringly. "Why, pray for me, child. Pray for me."

They began to talk seriously about the idea. Ferguson said he'd actually thought about doing something like this when the mother ship bought the newspaper. But he was too busy then. Now, with his workload down, well, maybe he could.

Kit said she'd already talked to some people who were interested in getting involved as writers, layout people, or office volunteers. She even talked to a guy at Falcon Ridge who said he was in advertising and offered to help sell ads. A young woman who was taking pictures at the festival said she'd love to let "a real folk paper" use her photos.

It was so much like Kit to put all this preparation into the idea before springing it on Ferguson. It also explained why she got tongue-tied at first; she'd been planning this ambush for months.

"You've really been thinking about this, haven't you?" Ferguson said.

"I got all their numbers, too," Kit said, nodding. "I told them I'm just thinking out loud, you know. I didn't say you were going to do it or anything. But whenever I mentioned your name, I could tell people took it more seriously."

Nathan looked at Ferguson. "You really are the only one who could get something like this going. If you're behind it, people will know it's for real."

Randy had walked over to get a beer and listened for awhile. He said he might know where there was a printing press they could use for free at MIT, then asked if he could talk to Ferguson privately, when he had a moment.

Ferguson looked off into space. "So many things we could do that I can't do at the paper anymore," he said. "Stories about local coffeehouses—not just the performers but the people who run them. Give them some attention. Lots of album reviews, the local ones along with the national ones."

"And you'd never have to worry about being too teacher-y," Kit said.

"No," Ferguson said with a final smile of surrender, "we wouldn't have to worry about that at all, would we?"

Around midnight, Randy and Ferguson got together in the back of the bar. Ferguson would never say what they discussed, but after that he told people that money shouldn't be a problem, at least not at first.

As long and luxurious as last autumn had been, this fall was sudden and violent. An early-October cold snap brought snow to the northern mountains and frost to the far suburbs. It was a mixed blessing for kids, making for a paltry jack-o'-lantern crop but sparing them from endless weeks of mommy's homegrown zucchini.

In town, the leaves turned from green to brown almost overnight, skipping the dusky yellows and burnished reds that Nathan enjoyed so much. But the early chill had its upside for him, too. The air took on a thick woodsy scent. By mid-October, he could comfortably wear his favorite suede winter coat, and Kit was back in that fluffy white parka he liked. Only she could make a parka look sexy.

Nathan and Kit might as well have been a duo. He was playing at all of her shows, and she was performing every weekend. With the focus on her album last spring, Nathan forgot to call the few local coffeehouses that still hired him, so he was always available.

Rehearsing more seriously, their arrangements tightened until their guitars sounded like one instrument. The tight sound allowed her more freedom in her vocals. Nathan knew her groove so well that he could anticipate when she might slow down to value a particular note. It was as if he knew before she did. The way she looked at him after moments like that, when his guitar crested with her singing, told him she felt the same way that he did. It was a lot like sex.

Knowing that his guitar would be there, she started doing more on the fiddle, which made her shows more dynamic. They did some songs with fiddle and Nathan's guitar; and whenever the crowd needed a pick-me-up, Kit tore into a fiery Celtic fiddle tune, while Nathan pounded out bold percussive chords. Knowing that the strength of his guitar allowed her to explore these frontiers in her music filled him with a pride that was embarrassingly macho. Ah, the wonders of testosterone.

Both of Nathan's classes at Passim were going well. The songwriting class was called A Brief Mystery of Songwriting, to mirror his popular folk music class. He was surprised at how much money he was making; he hadn't given that any thought when he decided to do them. But once the student tuitions were divided between him and the school, he was making nearly five thousand dollars for each eight-week class. Between that, Dooley's, and his private teaching, he started getting the novel feeling that he had an actual job; and he liked how the pieces fit together. It was as if being an elder was his main gig now.

Nathan's newfound prosperity allowed him to refuse Kit's persistent requests to pay him for accompanying her. Without the extra income, he was pretty sure he would have lost that argument. But he was able to say he didn't need the money. As a result, she was able to quit her waitressing jobs. Kit Palmer, full time musician: how about that?

Ferguson was amazed at how fast his folk paper was coming together. The biggest reason was that volunteers signed up in droves. That was partly because they all saw the need for it. But even more, it was because this was the first opportunity the folk community had to do something for Ferguson. All those years he'd been there for them, helping in so many ways, but they'd never had a way to return the favor.

At the big paper, he'd grown accustomed to feeling like an outsider. Now he was surrounded by volunteers, most of them young, all of them folkies. He told Nathan he felt like a stray dog who'd been adopted by a college dorm.

Kit offered to write record reviews, but Ferguson talked her out of it, saying it would put a distance between herself and other performers. "People you're doing gigs with will expect reviews," he said. "You'll never know if they're being nice because they like you or because they want you to write about them. Trust me on this one."

So Kit helped set up the software for a folk events calendar, which would be the centerfold of each monthly issue. She also created a special, folk-friendly spell-check, so a hasty editor would never spell-check John Prine into John Prune, Catie Curtis into Cutie Curtis, or Ani DiFranco into Any Difference.

Nathan wanted to help, but had no idea how. One night at Dooley's he asked Ferguson if he could do anything.

"Write," Ferguson muttered over his beer. Nathan thought he said, "right."

"What?" Nathan said.

"Write," Ferguson said.

"Right about what?" Nathan said.

"Anything."

"You're right about anything?" Nathan was totally confused.

"No, *you* write about anything."

"I am?"

"What?"

"I'm right about what? What the hell are you talking about?"

At the same moment, they realized they were having a "Who's on first?" moment and began to laugh.

"Whoo-eee," Ferguson said. "It's a good thing us geezers are getting lotsa help from the young 'uns."

"So what the hell are you talking about?"

Ferguson explained that he'd been thinking of asking Nathan to write a regular column. Not reviews, just musings, stories about the music, whatever he'd been thinking about. He could model it on Pete Seeger's old Appleseeds column in the national folk magazine *Sing Out!*. Seeger would fill his columns with random thoughts, stories, ruminations, opinions—anything that happened to be running through Pete's ever-running mind.

"Just stuff you're wondering about," Ferguson said.

"Wondering" became the name of the column. As with his Passim classes, the title let Nathan off the hook. Wondering—that he could handle.

Nathan and Kit lay quietly in bed, listening to the November night. It was one of those strange New England evenings with no rain falling, but in all other ways violent and stormy. Fierce gusts sent acorns, twigs, and leaves snapping against the carriage house. Tree branches scratched against the walls and windows, as if begging to come in. This will probably be the end of the leaves, Nathan thought. As brown as they are, they'll never hang on through a night like this. Too bad.

Kit was lying on her back, staring out the rattling window. "Quite the night, huh?" she said and turned toward him. Nathan's eyes moved reflexively to the thick sway of her naked breasts as she moved. She smiled, and he shrugged sheepishly. We're men; we can't help it.

After a quiet moment, she said, "Are you sorry you never had kids?"

His eyes widened. She continued smiling, then her eyes widened, too.

"Omigod!" she said. "I didn't mean it like that. That's like, totally the last thing on my mind."

He nodded and tried to read her look. He wasn't sure he'd seen it before: thoughtful, fond, but very serious.

"So are you?" she asked again. "Sorry you never had kids?"

"Sometimes, sure," he said. "Sometimes it surprises me a lot. Other times, it makes sense."

He described his childhood, how trapped and unhappy his parents had seemed to him. They both treated family as if it was a burden, and seemed to blame it for their unhappiness.

"I'm not so sure I was right about that," he said. "I mean, I know they loved me. But it's what we believe as kids; that's how we start to see the world. Maybe the most important thing parents can do for their kids is just enjoy them. I never got the feeling my parents enjoyed being parents. So family seemed like something to run away from."

Kit searched his face. "That's so different from how I grew up," she said. "Until I was about six, I thought my parents were kids like me. They used to get in the sandbox with me, splash around in the pool. We sometimes had food fights at the dinner table. We still do."

Nathan smiled. "That's exactly what I mean. Just enjoy them. I don't have any memories like that."

He looked past her to the wild sway of the branches outside. Suddenly, the wind fell and the branches were still, as if pausing to catch their breath. The wind blew again, and the branches scratched against the window. Strange night.

He looked back at Kit. "I never decided not to have a family," he said. "But I was so focussed on my career. I didn't want to be one of those parents who felt like they'd given up their big dreams for their kids and made them feel guilty about it."

"Like your parents," she said. He nodded.

They looked at each other. Kit waited. "Then I was alone for so long," he said. "Until it started feeling like that was the way I was supposed to be."

He reached over and brushed her face with his fingers. "Until you came along," he said.

She didn't respond the way she usually did, leaning into his touch. He pulled his hand away.

"I think maybe there's another reason," she said.

"What's that?"

Her eyes narrowed. "Well, this is just stuff I've been thinking about, okay? So I'm not sure how it'll come out."

"Uh-oh."

"No, it's not like that, nothing bad. But it's maybe going to sound really sappy. Okay?"

"Sap away."

"I started thinking about this when I was at the festival. I thought about you a lot. How you are, how we are. The things we talked about before I left. How you've been alone for so long. I know you feel bad about that but I also know you like it. Being alone, I mean."

"And?"

"And just because you've been alone so much and never had kids or anything, I think…well, I think it would be a mistake to think you haven't had lots of love in your life. Because I think you have. Lots."

She paused a moment, then said, "I've never known anybody like you that way. I mean, it's everything you do. Every song you sing, every note you play. Everything about the way you treat people, how you talk to the jammers and open-mikers. There's so much love in it. I know you don't think about it that way, because it's just how you are. But I've never known anybody who puts so much love into everything. Everything you do."

Nathan sensed the power of what she was saying. Everything you do. She was right that he'd certainly never thought about himself that way. Could it be true? He'd always thought of his solitary life as a surrender, full of selfishness, self-absorption, self-pity. Self, self, self.

"But I've been alone so long, Kit," he said. "By myself, for myself. And before you knew me, there was nobody—"

"Different kind of love, Nathan. Maybe you had to leave room in your life for all the love you gave away all those other ways. All the love you have for the music and the people who want to care about it as much as you do. You're so good at helping people do that, and you put so much of yourself into it. Maybe you had to leave room for all the love you were giving away all the time. Just giving away. I think maybe it empties you out more than you think."

He said nothing. He wanted it so badly to be true. Could it be? She seemed to know, she seemed so sure. And who knew him better?

She reached over and stroked his shoulder. "I mean it, Nathan. I've thought about this a lot. Everything you do. Every single thing."

He reached over to brush her face again. This time, she pushed herself softly against his hand and closed her eyes.

Seven

"Nathan? Hi, it's Joyce."

Nathan rolled the telephone cord in his fingers. He looked at it as if it was doing the talking. Who? Huh?

"Nathan?"

"I'm here. Hi, Joyce. Sorry. You surprised me."

She laughed that husky laugh of hers, the one that made you think you'd said something smart and somehow sexy. "Nice to know I can still do that," she said. "Got a minute?"

"Of course."

After a hasty round of how are you's—Joyce was always impatient with the amenities—she got down to business. By then, he'd guessed why she was calling.

It was Kit. More than a year ago, he'd sent Joyce a few of her songs recorded in his kitchen, but he never heard back. When Kit's album came out, he sent that, too, along with a letter singing her praises and explaining that they were a couple. He never heard back.

Now Joyce was telling him she'd listened to both recordings and was convinced that Kit was, as she put it, the real deal.

She said she was starting an independent record label for herself and a small stable of young songwriters. She wanted it to be a real artists label, a way to bypass the mainstream music industry. But she had enough connections to secure a distribution deal with a major label, so the albums would be eligible for commercial radio, which almost never played indie records. She wanted it to be the perfect combination of indie freedom and mainstream muscle: a major label's head and a folk label's heart.

"Wow," Nathan said. "Sounds great." Joyce was exactly the person to pull off something like this. Industry head and folkie heart: that was Joyce Warren to a T.

She was calling the label Choyce Records. That was also vintage Joyce. First, it was a clever superlative—that's a choice record!—with a feminist vibe, as in pro-choice.

And it summed up what she was trying to do: give artists power over their careers. In the music business, as in life, power usually boils down to choices; who gets to make them and who doesn't.

But also, because of the spelling, everyone would know whose label it was and who was doing all these wonderful things. She had a genius for turning the right thing into the smart thing. In Joyce Warren's universe, idealism and ambition were not opposing values.

A few years ago she'd recorded an album of songs by obscure young songwriters. The media portrayed her as a champion for the next wave of folk artists. That's when she let a few gray streaks show in her trademark bangs. She wasn't going to win an argument about whether she was getting older, and pop remained a youth-obsessed business. So she decided to exploit her maturity.

Her last album was a flop, a clumsy mix of mature ballads and adolescent love songs that was heavily remixed by her label, the drums all but drowning out her vocals. They didn't bother to tell her they'd done it, and she was so disgusted that she left the label.

That's when she started thinking about her own record label. And that, she told Nathan, was where Kit Palmer came in. Joyce was looking for a "flagship artist," an unknown for Choyce to introduce to the national spotlight.

"Later, I might sign some established acts," she said. "But for the launch, I want to find, you'll pardon the expression, a virgin." She laughed that husky laugh again; it still made his spine rattle.

"So here's the deal," she said. "In a couple of weeks I'm doing a concert at Sanders Theater. The press version is that I'm coming in a week early to visit old friends before kicking off a national tour. The truth is, I want to see about signing your ingénue."

"Kit," Nathan said. He wasn't sure why.

"Yes, Kit. Of course. Not your ingénue?"

"Very much her own ingénue." He realized that might sound harsh so he added, "Like you were."

"Ah," she said. "Sorry. Didn't mean to sound patronizing. I think the world of her. What a songwriter."

"I think so."

"Anyway, if everything pans out, I'd love to make the announcement at my Sanders show. You know, the old hometown, a couple of local gals, all that sweet shit. So maybe you and I could meet first, go over the deal, make sure everything's right. Obviously there are some things I need to know about her before I move on this. And it would be glorious to see you, my old blue darling. Simply glorious."

How utterly like Joyce that was. This was actually her being polite, observing protocol. She saw Kit as Nathan's find, his ingénue. She didn't want to encroach on his territory by contacting her directly. Like two lions politely negotiating over a wounded antelope: "No, you go ahead with the shank; I'm happy up here, nibbling on the neck." God, what a business.

Or maybe it was because he was the ex-husband and Kit was his new girlfriend. Joyce didn't want to walk over him like he wasn't there. That was a kinder thought; perhaps that was it.

Nathan's first impulse was to tell her to call Kit directly. To tell Joyce that Kit was nobody's fresh kill to carve up into equitable portions.

Then he remembered Slick, and began to think strategically. There could be a real upside here. He would immediately tell Kit, of course, and if she wanted to deal with Joyce, that was fine.

But this could work to Kit's advantage. Nathan meets Joyce first, gets a sense of what she wants and what's in it for Kit, using his trusty old antenna. Then, when Kit meets her, she'll know what's coming. Forewarned is forearmed.

"Nathan?" Joyce said. "Did we lose you again?"

"Just thinking, Joyce. That still takes me more time than most people."

She laughed. "Than it takes me, you mean. Old Joyce: fast on the trigger, slow on the aim."

"My memory is that you hit everything you wanted to hit."

"You're *sweet*," she said and laughed. She'd never been sensitive about being seen as tough. It was a point of pride with her.

"That sounds like a good plan, Joyce. I appreciate how much thought you put into this. And that you're trying to be fair to everybody."

"Maybe you get a little more careful with your aim when you've been the bullseye as much as I have."

"Maybe. But you've always been good about doing things the right way. I admire that about you. Always wanted to tell you that."

There was a silence. "Thank you, Nathan," she said softly. "That means a lot coming from you."

"You're welcome. I mean it."

"You always do."

After an impatient round of goodbyes, she hung up. So that was set. Kit had a gig in New Hampshire in the evening and they were driving up together. He'd tell her about it in the car.

He sat in the chair by the window for the rest of the afternoon, thinking. This was big.

Joyce arrived Thursday and asked to meet with Nathan right away. That woman was always in a hurry. She wanted everything squared away in time for her show the following week. She said that meant getting every detail ironed out before then. But to

Nathan, it meant she had virtually decided to sign Kit. Only some major disappointment would keep this from happening. And Kit would not disappoint.

Joyce was staying at the Charles Hotel in Harvard Square, and asked if they could meet at nearby Grendel's Den. When they were married, the small basement pub was their favorite watering hole. It was one of the few places that still reminded Nathan of the funky old square.

Grendel's opened in 1971, but for reasons no one could remember, the sign on the front said, "Est. 1271." Some people thought it was a reference to the ancient saga of Beowulf, whose antagonist was the monster Grendel. But Beowulf was written centuries before 1271, so theories abounded as to why the painter settled on that date.

Maybe he didn't know Beowulf was older; maybe 1271 sounded old enough. Maybe he screwed up the 9. Harvard Square used to be full of odd little mysteries like that. Most of them were solved by building over them with chain stores, ATMs, and boutiques. A pity. Nothing is allowed to be odd anymore.

Nathan walked into the pub around eight, and everything looked the same: dark wood and gray stone, lamplit and dusky, with a round bar dominating the middle of the room and a large fireplace along the front wall.

He saw Joyce, coiled and prim, sitting by herself at a small wooden table by the back wall. She waved, and he smiled.

From thirty feet, she looked youthful, vital, almost unchanged. In fact, she was even more beautiful: her face more angular, the cheeks deeper, the eyes more credibly wearing the sly, sexy wisdom they once only pretended to know. Her body was still lithe and slim.

Only when he got closer did the age begin to show, and the tiredness beneath the age. It was a startling effect, like a picture coming slowly into focus only to disappoint. And there was something else, something even sadder: a mature beauty underneath it all. You knew she would be lovelier if her face was able to look its age and not forced to squeeze into its vanished self, like a paunchy old man trying to wriggle into his college jeans.

She still wore the exaggerated pageboy that was her trademark. In her youth, it had been brash, sexy, and androgynous, contemptuous of conventional feminine fashion. Like she was so hip she didn't have to look hip. Like she wasn't sexy; she was sex.

Now it made her look like a woman trying to be a child. The bangs were pushed over to the side a bit, the hair carefully flecked with streaks of gray. But not enough gray, and done so deliberately, it just made it more obvious that she dyed her hair.

In fact, everything she did to make her appearance more youthful from a distance made her look older close up. Older and insecure about it—and one thing Joyce had never looked was insecure.

Nathan leaned over and kissed her cheek, surprised at the roughness of its feel. Too much stage makeup for too many years. "You look great, Joyce," he said.

She smiled and patted his hand as he sat down but ignored the compliment. Maybe she heard too many compliments; maybe she knew it wasn't true.

"The old back room is gone," she said with a pout. "Remember? With those mirrors and that winding stairway to the restaurant upstairs? They told me you have to go outside to get upstairs now. Poop."

"The upstairs isn't part of Grendel's anymore. They gave up the lease on it years ago. The pub is all that's left."

"Well, they saved the best part. I used to love this place. It made me feel so smart to hang here, you know? Smart and hip. It was so...so Harvard Square."

She looked around the room, soaking in the memories. She smiled at him. "The fireplace is still there. Remember?"

"Runs on gas now."

"Of course it does," she said, clucking her tongue. "Doesn't everything?"

She was drinking white wine. Lifting her glass, she said, "Oh, that's right. I heard you quit drinking awhile back. Does it bother you if I—"

"Not a bit. If I wanted one, I'd have one. I just got tired of it."

"Good for you. I still enjoy my wine."

"Good for you."

They were quiet for awhile, smiling at each other, remembering. Finally Nathan said, "I've wanted to thank you for that website blurb. It was very kind."

Joyce's eyes widened, then narrowed. "Website blurb," she said uncertainly. "Website. For your website? I'm sorry, Nathan, but I don't...oh, you mean that thing I did for Ferguson?"

He nodded and she smiled. "So that's what it was for," she said. "I don't think I knew. He asked me if I'd give him a quote about you and I chattered away. I've always been a fan, even after...well, you know."

The waitress came over, a short, smiling woman with bright red hair. She obviously knew who Joyce was and kept staring at her while she asked Nathan for his order.

"Do you have root beer?" he said.

The waitress's shoulders sagged and she looked at him.

"Oh, no," she said, "I'm afraid we don't." She looked back at Joyce. "We, no, we...I'm sorry. I'm so sorry."

"It's just root beer," Nathan said. He looked at Joyce. "I got in the habit when I quit real beer. Kind of a placebo."

"You know what?" the waitress said, perking up. "You should try the almond soda. It's kind of root-beery but, you know, like, with almonds."

"Sounds good."

She was delighted. She was not going to disappoint Joyce Warren's table. "Yeah," she said, "it's, like, made from this Italian syrup called orzata. Kind of milky, creamy, you know, like root beer."

"But with almonds."

"Ex-*actly*," the waitress said, as if he'd figured something out in a very clever way.

"Sounds yummy," Joyce said

"Oh, Ms. Warren, would you—"

"No, I'll stick with my Chardonnay, thanks"

Joyce looked at Nathan through narrowed eyes, as if trying to see him the way he used to be. She drew in a long breath, then exhaled it slowly, as if she was smoking a cigarette. She used to smoke like a 1940s movie star, sultry and smart, but he heard she'd quit recently. Apparently, this was her placebo.

"You look terrific," she said as she exhaled. "Really. Exactly like Nathan Warren. Life must be agreeing with you, old boy."

"It's leaving me alone," he said in his old cynical tone. It's funny how we reconnect with people from our past and go back to being who we were when we knew them. He shook his head quickly, as if tossing off the thought.

"I don't know why I said that, Joyce. It's not true. Not anymore. Life is treating me well. Or maybe I'm finally learning how to treat it well."

"Wow. That must have taken some work, if I know my Nathan."

"It did. I got a lot of help, though."

"Kit?"

"Yes, Kit."

"So my old blue darling is finally in love. About bloody time."

"I am. She's a remarkable woman, Joyce; you'll love her too. Can't help it."

The waitress brought the almond soda, waiting while he sipped it. Sweet, thick, good.

"You're right. Like nutty root beer." He nodded his thanks to her, and she looked at Joyce, who was smiling at her. She trotted off happily.

"So tell me about this protégée of yours," Joyce said, her voice suddenly serious.

"Well, I wouldn't call her my protégée. I really haven't—"

"How is she on stage?" she said, cutting him off. This was business. "You know how important that is."

"I do. And she's great. She used to have awful stage fright, the worst I've ever seen. She could totally fall apart up there. But she's turned that into a really charming stage persona. A little shy, but she lets the audience in on that and they love her for it, you know?"

Joyce nodded thoughtfully. Of course she knew.

"She's funny, too," he said. "And her humor is like her songs, full of quirky details and shared secrets. Everything she does with an audience feels like that, like she's taking them into her confidence."

"I know what you mean. Dar Williams is like that."

"Exactly. One of Kit's heroes, actually. You are too, by the way."

"Really?"

"You bet. From when she was, you know—"

"In the cradle? Yeah, I get that a lot these days." Joyce laughed sharply, then leaned forward. "I know you know about these things, Nathan, so I'll just ask you straight out. Is she good enough on stage? Tell me the truth; it won't help anyone if you…" Her face softened. "But you always tell the truth, don't you?"

"I try to. And I know what you're asking. And the answer is yes. Absolutely. Good enough and more. Audiences fall in love with her, Joyce. She always makes the sale."

Joyce leaned back, nodded once, and picked up her wineglass. Exactly what she wanted to hear. Nathan could tell she was making up her mind. Of course, it was Kit's music that really convinced her, but it felt great that Joyce trusted him this much. Something shot through him that felt warm and then hot, the way a shot of brandy hits the stomach. Joyce was going to take his word on Kit's stagecraft; that was enough for her.

This was going to happen.

Kit was going get her break.

Kit was going to be a star.

"Good, good," Joyce said, as if everything was settled. "Here's the plan. If we can make a deal, I'd like to rerelease her first album right away. Just the way it is; you did a wonderful job producing it. Sweet and simple."

"Thank you."

She nodded briskly. "I'd like her to join the tour with me, introduce her to my fans, and then get right to work on a new album when we're back in L.A. More produced, for commercial airplay. You okay with that?"

"Sounds great."

"Good. I need to get the deal done in time to announce everything at my concert, introduce her, have her do a few songs. Get the buzz going. It's a week from Friday. Sound doable?"

"Shouldn't be a problem." He smiled. "Kit's interested. Very excited. Especially about it being your label."

Joyce smiled but only for a second. Clearing her throat, she said, "So, uh, do I negotiate with you?"

Nathan sat back, startled. He blinked at her a moment, trying to understand.

"What?" he said. "No, no. You negotiate with her. I'm just the boyfriend."

Joyce relaxed into her seat and took a drink of wine, smiling to herself. "Of course you are," she said.

She sat up straight. "So when do I get to meet this new phenomenon?"

"Whenever you like. How about tomorrow? I'll set it up for you."

She raised her wineglass, as if to toast. "You do that, boyfriend," she said, clinking his glass and looking for the waitress.

As they waited for another Chardonnay, a young woman walked slowly toward their table. She stopped a few feet away and stared at Joyce, cocking her head down and over, almost like a puppy showing submission. She was very blonde and wore jeans and a blue hooded sweater, several sizes too big. She froze there, eyes wide, approaching only when Joyce smiled and nodded to her.

"Oh, Ms. Warren," she said as she reached the table, "I'm just—"

"Call me Joyce, please." Joyce held out her hand. "And your name is?"

The girl looked almost frightened, shaking Joyce's hand. "Um, Kiki," she said in a hoarse whisper. "My name is Kiki."

"Hello, Kiki. What can I do for you?"

"Well, I was just…I mean, I'm like, such a big fan…I'm sorry to bother you…." She looked uncertainly at Nathan, then back at Joyce.

"Yes?" Joyce said. Her voice was pleasant and kind.

"Well, I'm like, could I have your autograph?" She thrust a bar napkin and a pen onto the table.

"I'd be delighted, Kiki. Should I sign it to you?"

"Yes, please." Kiki stared at Joyce's hand, shaking her head in disbelief. "I totally loved your last album. I totally played it to death. It was, like, totally awesome."

"Thank you for telling me that, Kiki," Joyce said, carefully folding the napkin around the pen and handing them both back to her. "It's one of my favorites, too."

"It *is*?" Kiki said, almost shrieking. "Because it's *my* favorite, too. Totally. That is, like, *so* amazing."

"I'm glad to hear it. Thank you, Kiki. It was nice to meet you."

Kiki nodded and backed away from the table, still staring at Joyce. She shot a glance at Nathan. Is he anyone? She decided not, and scurried back to her friends at the bar.

"I thought you hated that last album," Nathan said.

"Never correct a compliment," Joyce said. "I learned that a long time ago. She loves my album; I'm supposed to argue with her?"

"Of course not. You're a smart cookie, Joyce. I liked that you didn't bring up how young she was."

"She probably knows." Joyce smiled. "I learned that from my son. Young people don't need to be reminded that they're young any more than we need to be reminded that we're not."

"Indeed. You're a grandma now, I hear."

"And loving it, just loving it. No worries. Spoil them rotten, and let the parents clean up the mess. Two of them, you know, a boy and a girl."

Joyce looked off in the distance, taking another of her cigarette breaths, inhaling deeply and exhaling through pursed lips. "I screwed things up with my second husband too," she said softly. "As bad as I did with you."

That took Nathan by surprise. He'd never seen their marriage as anything either of them screwed up. They simply shouldn't have gotten married.

"I was so focused on my career," she said. "With him, I mean; you too, I suppose. I got even worse when things started going downhill. Lost him, and he was a great guy. But I woke up in time to keep from blowing it with my kid. That's when I quit the business for a few years, until he was off to school and didn't need Mom hanging around all the time."

"Good for you."

"Good for him. He's a great kid. Gave me every chance in the world."

"They will, if you let them. I'll bet you're a great mom."

"You think?" She smiled brightly. "Thank you. I try to be, I really do."

She narrowed her eyes again, taking a drink of wine. "So tell me, my old blue darling. Why didn't you come out to L.A. when I invited you? I've always wondered. I was hot then; I could have gotten you a deal just like *that*." She snapped her fingers. "And I wanted to. I told you that."

"I thought I had a deal, remember? I was waiting for my big record to come out."

"How long did you wait?"

"I'm still waiting," he said, laughing coldly. But the moment he said it, he knew it wasn't true. He'd slipped back into the old Nathan, finding the cynical answer for cynical Joyce. Her eyes covered him like caresses, looking up and down his face. He knew that look.

"Wait a minute," he said. "Were you thinking we might get back together out there? Was that why you invited me?"

She laughed and leaned back in her chair. "Now why would I want to do that?" she said, taking another of those cigarette breaths and reaching for her wine.

That had never occurred to him, not once. He'd thought Joyce was just being nice, trying to get his career going again.

"Well," he said, smiling sheepishly, "I'm not very smart about that kind of thing. When it comes to women, I mean. As you probably remember."

"Men never are. But if they gave out prizes, you'd get one."

They talked about the old days, laughing about their brief brawl of a marriage. Nathan told her emphatically that he didn't think any of it was her fault, or anyone's fault, which pleased her. Joyce was so self-centered, of course she would have blamed herself. Everything was about her, so everything that went wrong would be her fault.

But her feelings for him had been deeper than he ever knew. He felt bad about not knowing that.

Nathan couldn't resist telling her about Slick, and how he dismantled him in front of Kit. He was bragging, he knew, but who would get the joke better than Joyce?

By the end of the story she was laughing so hard she choked, and he had to get up and pat her back until she regained herself.

"Well, if you ever run into the little rodent again, do tell him to contact me," she said. "I have a collection of bronzed balls on my mantel, from guys just like him."

"I'm sure you do, Joyce. I'm sure you do." He smiled and whispered, "I'm just glad mine aren't up there."

She looked startled, then grinned. "You? Oh, never; not you, my old blue darling." Chuckling into her wineglass, she whispered, "You're just the boyfriend."

Kit was waiting for him at home, so Nathan hurried back after walking Joyce to her hotel. He figured that Kit would be as nervous as a cat in a kennel show, but he found her asleep on the couch. Remarkable woman. He'd planned to tease her by telling her all about his almond soda instead of getting right to the details of Joyce's offer. But as she rubbed the sleep from her eyes and apologized for dozing off, he thought, what's the point? He was more nervous than she was.

They sat at the kitchen table, going over Joyce's plan: the tour, rereleasing her CD, recording a new one in L.A. Everything about this deal sounded right, he told her. Kit wouldn't be touring by herself, but with an established concert star, so the shows would make money on their own. The CD sales from the tours would help pay off the label's initial investment. She wouldn't be sinking into debt, the way she would have with Slick, and by touring with Joyce, she would reach thousands of new fans.

Joyce had given Nathan a copy of the contract, and he pored over it with Kit. She noticed that it had protections for her, as well as for Choyce Records. Kit would have final approval over song selection, supporting musicians, and, most importantly, the final mix. That meant it couldn't be released without her consent. Joyce reserved the right to pick a producer, but only for the first album they made together. She wanted to make sure it was radio-friendly.

The more Nathan looked at the contract, the more he realized how serious Joyce was about Choyce being an artists label. She was out to prove who knew what about the business of music. Lawyers know law, accountants know accounts, musicians know music. The decisions at Choyce would be made accordingly.

Nathan and Kit talked over the deal late into the night, woke up talking about it, and kept talking about it through two morning walks. They took two walks because the first one was to get coffee, which they came home without.

This was much more than a break for Kit. It was a once-in-a-lifetime opportunity. As Choyce's first discovery, the label would spare nothing to make her a success.

Beyond that, Joyce's interests were entirely different than the typical music mogul. She didn't want to make money from Kit as much she wanted to find fans for her own music. The only strict clauses in the contract were about Kit touring a lot, both solo and with Joyce. As Kit's popularity increased, Joyce wanted access to her young fans. Joyce's ultimate goal, Nathan realized, was to revive her own career. She would be hailed as the guardian angel of the next generation, the grande dame of folk music.

And that was Kit's best protection. If Choyce's premiere artist left the label in anger, bad-mouthing Joyce to the media, it would destroy her new image and alienate the young fans she hoped to attract. So even if Joyce's altruism wavered, her self-interest would continue to ensure that Kit was treated well.

It was clear from the contract, however, that Joyce had other reasons for wanting Choyce to work the right way. She was out to stick it to every executive who'd ever damaged her, and to prove that the business of music didn't have to be run like a slaughterhouse. Music is a soft art; it can be a soft business, too. And if you don't want to play the game that way, well, Joyce had a space reserved on her mantel for your bronzed balls, too.

Nathan loved the idea of Kit beginning her long flight under Joyce's tough wings. He'd never flown in the skies she knew. The dangers were different up there, the air thinner, the predators more cunning.

That afternoon, Kit met with Joyce at her hotel. Nathan stayed home, alternately pacing and doing yard work that didn't need doing. When he found himself putting down his rake to pick up leaves one by one, he realized he needed to relax. No chance that Kit would find him dozing on the couch when she got home.

She came back a little after nine, raving about Joyce. For the first ten minutes, she sounded like Kiki, the very blonde fan at Grendel's. Kit raved about how "totally awesome" Joyce was, and how, "like totally cool" it was that she was so nice. She showed Kit pictures of her son—who was "totally cute"—and talked about how fond she still was of Nathan. Kit wiggled her eyebrows and said Joyce had described him as "quite the catch."

Then Kit told him a story that erased all Nathan's doubts.

"We were looking over the contract together," she said, "and I picked up this pen and started tapping it. Nervous, you know? Well, Joyce grabbed that pen out of my hand and shook her head at me. She said, 'Never have a pen in your hand when you're reading a contract, dear.' Then she said, 'And another thing. Never, *ever* sign anything the first time you read it.' Isn't that cool? She's really been around, huh?"

Nathan nodded and smiled. Kit heaved a sarcastic sigh and said, "She sure doesn't understand business the way Slick does."

Nathan laughed. "That's because they're not in the same business. I don't even think I was in the same business Joyce is. Not really."

"We talked about you, too. About coming with me. On the tour. The record. She likes the idea. She said she'll pay you—well, Choyce will—and she said she was open to the idea of you producing the next record. She wants to talk to you about it, though. She wants it to be right for commercial radio."

Kit's eyes widened. "Know what else she said? She said she'd like it if this opened some doors for you too."

Her eyes looked into his. Her breathing increased. "So you'll come with me, yes?"

Nathan smiled and rubbed her arm. He'd already thought about what to do if she asked. "Of course I will," he said softly.

She was still locked and loaded, nodding her head excitedly. She'd expected more of a fight about this. For a moment, she stared at him, breathing quickly.

"You will?" she said.

"Of course."

"You will, you will, you will," she stammered, and threw her arms around him.

He held her as she burrowed into his shoulder, rubbing her face against the soft flannel of his shirt.

There were a million details as Nathan prepared to go away. Kit signed the contract after having a lawyer friend of her father's go over it, as well as a music attorney that Ferguson knew. They both pronounced it not only fair but extraordinarily so. Two lawyers had actually been Joyce's suggestion. "Always get a second opinion, dear," she said. "Contracts are as risky as surgery."

Joyce had not signed it yet. She was having her lawyers in L.A. go over the changes Kit requested, mostly ensuring that she had enough time off to write songs. Joyce was fine with that; in fact, she apologized for not thinking of it herself.

A million details, Nathan thought, as he sat by his telephone. And not much time. The morning after the Sanders show, they would join Joyce's tour and stay with it for several months, until it ended in L.A. Then they'd record the new album.

He wondered if Joyce would ask him to make a record. Not quite the ingénue talent Choyce was looking for, but she'd always liked his music. Maybe he could start by recording the songs from that unreleased album. That would make a good story line for what Joyce was trying to do: the album the industry wouldn't release. Later, later.

A million details. First, he called Murph.

"Well, pal, Dooley's is gonna miss you," Murph said. "But we'll keep a light burning in the window for you, okay? Got any idea who I could get to fill in while you're gone?"

"I was thinking about Randy," Nathan said. "He's gotten a lot more confident lately, and he's a teacher, so he knows how to ride herd if he needs to. I think it might do him a world of good."

"Would he have to do a whole set every week?"

Nathan laughed. "Up to him, I suppose. I just think—"

"I'm kidding. If that's what you want, the gig's his."

"Thanks, Murph. For that and, you know, for putting up with me all these years."

"My pleasure. The gig's always here for you. This is your open mike, Nathan. Your jam. That's the way I look at it."

Next, Nathan called Randy, who almost prayerfully agreed to fill in as substitute host.

"I'm honored, Nathan," he said. "Honored. I…well, I hope I don't let you down."

"You'll do a great job. That's why you were the first person I called."

"The first?"

"The first."

"The first."

"The first."

"I'll try to live up to that trust, Nathan. I'll…I'll—"

"You'll do fine, Randy. Just have fun and don't let the kids tear up the furniture."

Randy laughed, realizing he might be taking this a little too seriously. "I'll keep it fun, Nathan. I'll try to keep it just the way you left it. And Nathan?"

"Yes?"

"Thanks."

"You're the perfect guy for this. I should be thanking you."

"I don't mean about the hosting. I mean everything. The open mike, the way you've always treated me and my geeky friends. Thanks."

Nathan was quiet for a moment. "You're welcome," he said finally.

Randy laughed gently. "I know. That's what I'm thanking you for."

Nathan felt a wave of satisfaction as he hung up the phone. That's what open mikes are for, to be important places for people like Randy.

A million details. He called one of the regular jammers and explained the situation. The jammer promised that one of the regulars would always be there in time to set things up and get the ball rolling. They usually did that, anyway, he said, so it was no big deal.

They had a brief argument over the money Murph paid Nathan. Nathan wanted whoever showed up early to get it, and the jammer wanted to save it for Nathan. Nathan put his foot down, but something about the way the jammer agreed made him suspect they'd either save it for him or spend it on something for the jam. New mikes, maybe.

A million details. He called Betsy Stotts. She said she was disappointed but also excited about the news. "We'll say we're just postponing the classes, okay?" she said. "I mean, we'd hate to lose you for good."

"You bet. Thanks. I love doing the classes."

A million details. He phoned his landlords, who were just as excited as everyone else. He thought he would be apologizing for not being around to do yardwork, but they promised to look after the place for him. They also said they'd save his mail for him. He hadn't thought of that.

A million details. He called his private students, gave them referrals to other teachers, and promised to let them know when he was resuming lessons.

A million details. He looked at the phone and couldn't think of anyone else to call.

A million details. He looked around his house. Have to empty the refrigerator. And pack. A million details.

But after fifteen minutes gazing out the kitchen window, he couldn't think of any more details. How depressing was that? A half hour of phone calls, one large trash bag, one small suitcase, and Nathan Warren's life was good to go.

Wouldn't Thoreau be impressed? Simplify, simplify. Of course, the old philosopher had done it on purpose; Nathan's life was simple by default.

He looked out at the big tree in the sloping yard. There were still a few blackened leaves clinging stubbornly to the biggest branches, but everything else was winter-bare. A hard fall, might mean a hard winter.

Nathan took a deep breath and felt the tingle of new things coming. One night on TV, he'd heard the late comedian George Carlin say, "An artist has an obligation to be en route." Nathan liked that so much he put it on his wall. Now he was en route again. Or had he always been?

He never thought he'd feel this again, the old wanderlust. But it was different this time; it was for Kit, and that made all the difference. The adventure was being there for her. It would be good to see the road again, wouldn't it, to travel it this way? For someone else.

Eight

Kit was trying to be cool but it wasn't working. She and Nathan stood inside a large function room in the basement of Sanders Theater, casually dressed, with garment bags and instrument cases slung over their shoulders. Kit was staring at a buffet that spread over two long tables at the far end of the room. It was a pretty standard performer buffet—cold cuts, cheese, rolls, a variety of chips, pita bread, hummus, and vegetable sticks—but Kit had never seen the way concert acts are treated backstage. It smacked of importance, laid out just for you, for your convenience, because you're a big, busy entertainer.

She wandered up and down the buffet, finally settling on a carrot stick. Nathan suspected she took it less because she was hungry than because she had to take something from her first performer buffet. Indeed, she took two small nibbles and threw it away. Wouldn't want a whole carrot stick before you sing.

It was three hours until showtime. They'd finished their sound check in the main hall, and Nathan was savoring Kit's big-show buzz. She was nervous, but he thought it was more excited-nervous than stage fright. In a few hours, she would perform for the first time in a big concert hall, introduced to Joyce's fans as Choyce Record's flagship artist. Who wouldn't be excited?

At some point, the novelty of things like buffets would wear off for Kit, just as they had for Joyce, years ago, when she sadly realized that a tour bus was just a bus. One day, when this was simply the way Kit lived, she'd have a moment like that, and realize she was usually eating the kind of food you get at a badly catered office party.

Then, being Kit, she would start bringing her own food, probably some kind of organic nutrition bars. And chocolate. Lots of chocolate.

Nathan doubted she'd become one of those stars who stipulate everything they want backstage, in what are called riders, because they're tacked on to the end of a standard contract. Some riders are reasonable. It's natural for perpetually touring performers to want a certain sameness to their pre-show surroundings. Same food, same beverages, a little privacy.

But for some stars, detailed riders are a conceit, a way of retaining the glow of self-importance Kit was now feeling. An eighties rock band became infamous for its petulant riders, which included having only a certain color of M&M's. Not jelly beans, mind you, for which different colors have different flavors, but M&M's, which taste the same whether they're red or green or brown.

Kit would never be like that. She wouldn't wear her stardom imperiously, the way stars like Joyce did, but—

Nathan stopped in mid-thought and looked at the buffet. Impressive. Joyce must not have any food riders, unless she's a stickler for celery sticks and ripple chips. Maybe she had some special snacks in her dressing room. But she hadn't designed a buffet menu in her contract rider. Good for her; maybe she was finally learning to relax.

"Where do I get dressed?" Kit whispered out of the side of her mouth as she shifted the guitar case awkwardly on her shoulder. She'd decided to leave her fiddle on stage.

"This is the hospitality room," Nathan said. "You and Joyce each have a private dressing room around the corner."

She mouthed the word *private* to herself, shaking her head. Get a load of me.

Joyce's road manager walked briskly around the room with a sheaf of papers, handing them out to everybody. He was a tight little man with spiked orange hair and the darting, too-wide eyes of someone who thinks he doesn't need much sleep but is mistaken. Wired and punchy. He kept his lips in a white line that could be either a smile or a frown.

He zoomed past Kit and Nathan, slapping a sheet of paper into each of their hands. He studied them, trying to compute—do they need these?—then zoomed away, sighing with exasperation, as if they had done something wrong by accepting them.

The paper was Joyce's set list, from beginning to "Ensemble Encore" and "Solo Second Encore (Kit Palmer, fiddle, vocals)." Kit looked at it and said, "Wow, should I have one of these for my set?"

"The crew didn't ask for one at sound check," Nathan said. "You're just doing four songs. Probably not a bad idea, though, once the tour gets rolling. You definitely want to let them know if you change anything."

"Whoo," Kit breathed, studying Joyce's list. This was no coffeehouse gig.

Joyce swept into the room, regal and fierce. Her eyes swept the buffet, and she sighed wearily. Then she noticed a large bucket of iced wine at the end of one table and pointed to it, as if to say, "At least you're here." Below it on the floor were two coolers filled with soda, bottled water, and beer.

She walked over to Kit and gave her cheek a little kiss.

"So glad you're here, Kit," she said quickly. "The crew said you sounded great at your sound check—hi, Nathan—and I know my fans will adore you. Don't worry about a thing, dear, they're gonna eat you up with a spoon. Promise. You all set with everything? Good, good, we'll see you upstairs."

And she was gone, waving an irritated finger at the road manager, who slumped and followed her, head down.

Joyce wore her stardom snugly, like a second skin. Even before she was a star, Nathan thought with a smile. She was probably bossing around the doctor the moment she was born, saying, "I'd think twice before you slap this particular pink ass."

Nathan walked Kit down a carpeted hallway lined with smaller dressing rooms. About fifty feet from the hospitality room was a small gray door with a piece of plain paper taped to it that said "KIT PALMER, PRIVATE," next to a door marked "JOYCE WARREN, PRIVATE." Nathan could hear Joyce inside, lecturing the road manager about something.

Kit stared at her door, even reaching out to touch the sign with her name on it. She smiled at Nathan, mouthing the word *wow*.

He opened the door and bowed curtly. "Milady's dressing chamber?"

She swept in, tilting her head back and laughing. Good, good. Savor the moment but keep your feet on the ground.

It was a small white room with bright overhead lights and a dancer's barre across a mirrored wall on the far side. Adjoining it was a smaller room with a dressing table, a mirror surrounded by light bulbs, and a door leading to a bathroom.

Nathan left her there, suggesting she take a little downtime. She silently put down her bags. Some time alone would be good, time for her to soak this in and deal with the inevitable ego swell. Coax out the adrenaline, then throw a tight lasso around its neck. She closed the door behind her, lost in the power of the moment.

Nathan wandered down the hall. He knew Joyce wouldn't have thought to reserve him a room so he walked into the one marked "BAND, PRIVATE." It was a bigger version of the room Kit was in. Joyce's quartet were already in there, sitting around a long table. Most of them were eating. The guitar player was changing strings.

"I think I'm in here," Nathan said. "Do you mind? I'm Kit Palmer's band."

"Tight little combo she's got," one of them said, waving him in.

"Oh, you're Nathan Warren," the guitarist said. "You used to be married to—"

"Briefly. Very briefly."

"Can we see the scars?"

They all laughed and showed him where to put his gear. Why were professional sidemen always so friendly? Necessity, most likely. They collaborate for a living and have to contend with demanding stars. On this level, conviviality can be a survival mechanism.

Before he dressed for the concert, Nathan took a walk around Sanders. It was a vast stone building built in the 1870s as a memorial to Harvard alumni who died in the Civil War. The concert hall seated about a thousand people, small by pop-star standards but definitely the big time in the folk world. Nathan pulled open the thick padded doors of the main hall and walked in. All the sound checks were done; it was empty, the calm between storms.

The pew seating formed a huge semicircular gallery, winding up the rounded walls, almost encircling the proscenium stage. The walls were ribbed with lightly varnished wood descending in an arc behind the stage to form a natural acoustic amphitheater.

He looked up at the stage, with its tall spruce columns and curved backdrop. Songwriter Cheryl Wheeler joked once that it was like performing inside a big rolltop desk.

Nathan walked onto the stage. Everything was wonderfully close and the slow rise of seating gave everyone a ringside seat. Looking out from the stage, he saw clean lines and warm wood, every corner punctuated with handcarved filigree. Everything felt burnished and cared for. The floor of the stage, however, was a dirty tan, wearing scuff marks from decades of concerts, commencements, and lectures.

Like Carnegie Hall and all the truly important venues he'd seen, Sanders looked very different to performers than it did to the audience. To the crowd, everything was plush and buffed. It wasn't simply scrubbed and shiny, it was given that extra rub to make it *look* scrubbed and shiny.

But to those entering from the wings, Sanders felt purely functional. Backstage, it was comfortably worn, frayed from years of hard use. From the outside, it was a place for art, from the inside, a place for work.

Nathan took a deep breath, soaking in the tense quiet of an empty stage. Nothing smells like a grand concert hall. If excitement had a scent, this would be it. Hmm, so there's a little of the old sawdust left in your veins after all. He looked around the ancient hall, imagining the songs Kit would play, going through the set in his mind. Unconsciously, his hands began to move at his side, the left making chords while the fingers of his right hand plucked on imagined strings.

Nathan went to get Kit a little after nine. It was intermission, after which Joyce was going to introduce her. He knocked on the door. "Ms. Palmer? Ten minutes, Ms. Palmer."

She opened the door immediately, guitar in hand, nodding majestically, "Thank you, boy," she said, "you may go now." Then she laughed that open-throated laugh, both wild and sweet.

She looked him up and down and said, "You look great, Nathan." He was wearing a midnight blue wool shirt with soft gray lines traced in large squares. He'd had it dry-cleaned, so it would look especially pressed. Same with his black jeans, his newest, crispest pair. She eyed him again, arching an eyebrow and clucking her tongue. "Definitely," she said.

Ah, the coveted eyebrow arch of feminine approval. Good wardrobe choice.

No need to worry about upstaging her though. Kit was wearing a sleek black skirt that hung tight to mid-calf, then flared. It was slightly longer in back, giving it a waifish look, a dressy mix of urban and peasant. She had on high burgundy boots, the kind with a million little hooks.

She wore a white satin blouse, open just enough to reveal a trace of cleavage. The blouse was billowy at the shoulders, the sleeves fluffy until they narrowed above the wrists. A black silk scarf with a silver shimmer was tied around her neck, accentuating the contrast between her dark eyes and her ivory skin.

She was wearing eye makeup and a hint of blush on her cheeks. He seldom saw her in makeup, and the effect was startling.

"As for you," he said, "Whoo. Just whoo."

"Yeah?" She said, sparkling.

"Oh, yeah. And on stage, I mean, for performing…up there, it'll look…I mean—"

She laughed. "Well, if my boy's stammering, I must be dressed for company. Ready?"

"Ready." And they walked upstairs to make Kit Palmer a star.

Standing in the wings, Kit softly bounced on the balls of her feet as Joyce introduced her. Joyce was dressed down, though in a way that suggested she'd gone to a Bel Air boutique and said, "I'm thinking dressed down for this tour."

She wore light blue jeans tucked into black-and-turquoise cowboy boots. The jeans were faded but obviously new, the faded streaks following symmetrical lines down her legs. She had on a soft red blouse and a sassy black vest that ended just below her breasts. Around her throat was a thin, long purple silk scarf that accentuated the litheness of her slim body. Nice look for her, Nathan thought. If only she'd let her hair age as gracefully as her wardrobe. That gray-flecked bob was ridiculous.

Kit had written a new song but didn't know if she would sing it. They'd rehearsed an alternative if she decided against it, but Nathan thought she should do it. Even in a big hall, on an important night like this, trusting the audience with a brand-new song would draw them closer to her. Just like it would at a coffeehouse.

But the song worried her; it was the most provocative thing she'd ever written. She wasn't sure about taking such a big chance tonight.

Kit walked to center stage and stood behind Joyce's mikes. Nathan sat on a folding chair that was a little behind her on the right. Smiling tentatively, Kit thanked Joyce for her introduction and began to sing the song she wrote during last winter's nor'easters.

Where do you go, little bird,
When it snows, when it snows,
When this world turned to sleep,
Do you know, do you know?

She chose that as an opener more for its familiar-sounding melody and relaxed groove than for its lyrics. Joyce had told her that, at a big concert, the first song was more about mechanics than meaning. The audience will be thinking about you, taking in your appearance, voice, and style. That first song is also when you define the dynamic arc of your set, so it should be mid-range in tempo and volume, setting the bar from which you move up and down.

Is there something in the wind
Breathes a chill in your heart and life in your wings?
Does it whisper, 'start again,
Start again'?

Kit sang it a little faster than usual, her body swaying to the cadence. Nathan played high, lonesome licks behind her, like the far cries of winter-worried birds, then moved his part closer inside hers, doubling her guitar as her voice rose.

The song received a long round of applause. Nathan guessed that the song's folksy feel came as a relief to Joyce's older fans, who might have worried that this new young writer would seem foreign to their ears and remind them they weren't hip anymore. Kit probably thought of that, too. This was her parents' favorite song.

She stood quietly for a few seconds, scanning the crowd. Then she puffed a quiet breath and leaned into the microphone. "Can I tell you a little secret?" she said.

Nathan looked at the crowd. Some leaned forward in their seats, a few began to nod, even to say, "Yes" and "Go ahead."

Nodding, she leaned closer into the microphone and whispered, "I'm really nervous."

The crowd laughed. A few shouted "Don't worry" and "We like you" and "You sound great." She smiled, said thanks, and shrugged shyly. Then she told them how much she'd always loved Joyce Warren's music, and how much it meant to be on her new record label.

But Nathan knew how to read the signs, and Kit wasn't the least bit nervous. There was no hint of redness in her face, and her voice was calm and confident. She simply wanted to take the audience into her confidence, let them share her big moment. What a pro she'd become.

Next, she surprised everyone by doing a song she hadn't written. She'd thought about doing Woody Guthrie's "Deportees," but wanted to save the fiddle for last. Instead, she sang "One of These Days," the song she'd learned from Nathan's Emmylou

Harris record. Its theme of hopeful self-reliance was perfect for the occasion. She also thought it might be familiar to some of Joyce's fans. She dedicated it to Joyce for "making this song not true for me anymore."

> *One of these days, it will soon be all over, cut and dried,*
> *And I won't have this urge to go all bottled up inside.*
> *One of these days, I'll look back, and I'll say I left in time,*
> *Because somewhere for me, I know, there's peace of mind.*

The applause was stronger. The crowd had wanted to like her for Joyce's sake, but Kit was moving them beyond that. She did not come on like she wanted to impress them, but serenely, with gliding, gentle songs that felt both personal and familiar. She wasn't a new flavor they had to roll around in their mouths and decide if they liked it. She had them in the palm of her hand.

For a quiet moment, she eyed the crowd. Nathan knew she was deciding about the new song. He could almost hear the wheels churn in her mind. Giving it this much time, though, he knew what she was deciding.

"Um," she said a little uneasily, "I wasn't sure if I would do this, because it's, like, my *big night* and everything." She tossed her head at the words "big night," as if it embarrassed her, and the crowd laughed warmly. "But you seem like nice people so can I do a brand-new song for you?"

The crowd cheered the idea, some hollering "Yes" and "Go for it!" One woman shouted "Anything you sing is okay with us." The crowd laughed and Kit smiled. "Well, I guess that means yes," she said.

She paused to quiet the mood, then said, "We all know kids like the one in this song. But we usually don't notice them or think about them until it's too late. That's sort of what this song is about. It's called 'Judas' because he's another guy nobody noticed. Until it was too late."

Nathan put his guitar string-side down on his lap so the audience would know he was not playing on this song. She'd wanted him to accompany her, but he wanted to focus the attention on the lyrics. It was a stark song; let it be stark.

He certainly understood why she had reservations about singing it. It was a wincing portrait of the kind of unattractive kid who huddles by himself in the playground during recess, forced to live in a dark, imaginary world because no other world will welcome him.

> *Judas Iscariot is kicking up seashells and he's cursing.*
> *He's being tortured by the roaring in his mind*
> *That won't surrender the scene,*
> *And even here, alone in the dark,*
> *A thousand eyes are burning*

Holes into his heart,
Holes into his heart.

The melody was almost a chant, a carriage for the lyrics. Kit had told Nathan the idea came when she read about a recent schoolyard shooting. The people who knew the shooter said they weren't surprised; he was such a strange, angry boy.

That got her thinking about the strange, angry kids she'd known growing up, especially one boy who always frightened her, even though he never said a word to her or anyone else. She had such a gift for using her ordinary experiences to fuel these extraordinary displays of empathy and intimacy.

She wanted the song to be provocative, not to make us sympathize with the little monsters who do these things but simply to consider that something makes them become little monsters. Nobody wants to be a loser, nobody wants to be a monster. Not if there are choices. So she contrasted history's most despised villain with a Jesus who:

Was every mother's perfect son,
Not like Judas in the back of the school bus,
Invisible to everyone.

Her voice was a whispery mix of sadness, anger, and sympathy. Nathan remained motionless, looking only at Kit, so the eyes of anyone glancing at him would be led back to her.

He thought about her music as he listened. This was Woody Guthrie's final lesson, and she'd learned it well. Woody told people he was more of a journalist than a poet, and that his beat was the unsung. But that's always been folk music's beat, hasn't it? The humble, the forgotten, the poor, the ordinary, and less than ordinary. The people we never notice.

And that's why Kit's new song was so daring. There was no one in our society who frightened us more than these sulking time bombs ticking away in the back of the school bus. Kit was not asking us to feel sorry for them, only for some grim morsel of understanding. Something makes these kids explode. Nobody is born wanting to explode.

Last night Judas' father threw his son against the wall.
That's how you learn to be invisible.

Despite his efforts to be still, Nathan shook his head in awe. How could Kit know that? How does she *know* these things? Her parents still had food fights with her, for god's sake. Where did it come from, the powerful force that could connect her simple memory of a sullen classmate to this kind of human horror?

Empathy. That was the only answer Nathan could come up with, some kind of empathy beyond most people's understanding of the word. Because he knew that Kit's view of the world began with her keen awareness of how lucky and loved she had been all her life.

> *And it may well have been any day like the rest,*
> *But the tape shows him moving,*
> *And he's standing in the hall.*
> *He's never felt this alone before.*
> *He is walking through the door and it's springtime.*

The song ended by sadly returning to its beginning.

> *Judas Iscariot is kicking up seashells and he is cursing,*
> *And if he stands here long enough,*
> *Maybe he will turn to stone and wash away,*
> *And he won't find the bullets*
> *On that fated morning,*
> *And he will wake up from his dream.*

Is that his wish, or is it ours? Do we, in our silent hearts, wish that all the schoolyard scowlers, all the quiet, bullied, always-frightened, heads-down children in the world would turn to stone and wash away? Kit won't say, won't offer answers to questions that have none. What a song.

It was even more powerful coming from someone as endearing, attractive, and yes, cute, as Kit Palmer. She was the spitting image of everything this Judas could never be. What a generous and brave thing to do with all that sparkle. Especially on a night like this.

There was silence after the song, and it lasted long enough to become uncomfortable. Kit kept her head down, the way it was when the song ended.

Then it began, one pair of hands applauding. Nathan followed the sound off stage: it was Joyce. The ovation immediately spread to the audience, first with a few hands clapping amid the many who weren't ready to shake themselves out of the difficult place Kit had just taken them.

The applause slowly crescendoed, punctuated by shouts of "Wonderful," "You made us cry," and even "Brava" (this was Cambridge, after all). A few stood as the applause grew, and soon the whole crowd was on its feet. A standing ovation for a newcomer's third song. At somebody else's concert.

Nathan looked at the scene, smiling. Only in folk music. This hushed, painful ballad was bringing the house down. No smoke machines, no high-kicking choreography, no "money note," as the music industry calls those show-offy sustains that turn talent show winners into divas du jour.

This starmaking moment, for that's what it was now, came as a sad whisper. The energy came from the radical power of Kit's empathy and craftsmanship. She had made them see, then care about, the least of the least of us—and they loved her for it. Nathan looked out at the crowd: many were stomping their feet as they whooped and whistled and cheered. God, he loved folk music.

Kit unstrapped her guitar. A few people shouted, "No" and "Sing another." But she wasn't done. Grinning slyly, she reached for her fiddle, resting on a small stand behind her. Crooking it under her chin, the audience began to applaud again. She owned this crowd.

"I bet you could use a pick-me-up, huh?" she said, wagging her eyebrows. The audience settled in their seats, a few audibly heaving sighs of agreement. She laughed.

"Well, here's a little set of old Scottish fiddle tunes. But first, give a shout out to my wicked good guitarist and main squeeze, Nathan Warren."

Nathan nodded at the applauding crowd and bowed his head toward Kit. Despite himself, he felt his chest swell. Main squeeze, eh?

Behind the bold pulse of Nathan's guitar, Kit ripped into a rollicking set of reels, each quicker than the last, ending in a wild series of arpeggios. Kit hopped up and down, laughing loudly, then lowered her shoulder toward Nathan's guitar and skidded to a stop with four fast, sliding notes, one fierce arpeggio, and a rich, slamming staccato chord.

The audience went absolutely nuts. From the first notes, they'd been clapping in rhythm, faster and faster as she sped up her playing. When the tempo became too fast for them to accompany, the clapping became a thunderous ovation that continued through her final riffs. She bowed and put the fiddle back on its stand, then bowed again as the audience stood up again, hollering and stomping their feet. Some were chanting "Kit! Kit! Kit!"

Holding hands and bowing one more time, Nathan and Kit started to leave. As they did, Joyce ran on stage, hugging Kit and shouting, "Kit Palmer! She'll be back with me a little later."

With a firm push, she hurried them off stage. She needed to get this crowd back. Nodding her head once, she kicked her band into a Nanci Griffith song she'd had a hit with at the peak of her stardom. It wasn't on the set list, but an old favorite would refocus the audience's energy on the star they'd come to see. And its tempo was close to that of Kit's final tune. In seconds, the crowd were back in their seats, clapping in time and singing along to the familiar chorus. Joyce was very, very good at this.

Nathan led Kit wordlessly down the stairs to the dressing rooms, allowing her to bask in the moment. Her breath came in quick spurts and her cheeks flared red. She stared at her feet as they walked.

They passed a dozing security guard at the entrance to the dressing-room hallway and Nathan said, "I've never seen you better. Every note, every decision, every chance you took. You owned them tonight. You're ready for this, Kit. I mean it. Ready, ready, ready."

"*We're* ready for this," she said, putting her arm around his waist and squeezing. "I couldn't have done any of it without you. I felt so safe that I could fly anywhere."

He knew that wasn't true, and it bothered him to hear her say it; especially now, after what she'd just done on stage. She needed to know that she was the one making this happen. But he just put his arm around her shoulder and squeezed.

Nathan and Kit got back into their street clothes and joined the small after-concert crowd milling around the buffet tables. Joyce came in after signing autographs and walked immediately over to the bucket of wine bottles. Her band was there, beers in hand, hovering around Kit, laughing and chatting like old friends. Was that how it started?

Joyce reached around the bass player to grab a bottle of wine, chuckling dryly. "There's my boys, always find 'em at the bar," she said.

The band laughed nervously, and Joyce turned her attention to Kit. "You were lovely tonight, Kit, just lovely. Didn't I tell you my audience would eat you up?"

As Kit started to answer, Joyce reached around the back of her guitarist to get a plastic tumbler. "Gee, guys," she said, "shouldn't you be, oh, I don't know, off somewhere learning to play these goddamn songs? That second-set opener was sloppy as hell."

"Wasn't on the set list, Joyce," the guitarist said. "We haven't rehearsed that one since L.A., remember? If you give us a little—"

"Oh, *my* fault," Joyce said. "I see. Okay. Never mind."

She turned her back and walked over to the other side of the room, plopping heavily into a large, molded plastic chair. The guitarist started to say something, but the bass player tugged his sleeve. They grabbed a few beers from the cooler and headed to their dressing room.

"I thought you sounded great," Kit said to Joyce. "It was exciting to hear that Nanci Griffith song. I always liked it but I especially like how you sing it."

"Thank you, dear," Joyce said, taking a big drink of her white wine. "You should hear it when…oh, never mind."

The road manager wheeled into the room, saw Joyce, and started to turn around. Too late.

"Oh, James, dear," she said. "If it wouldn't be too much trouble in your busy schedule, do you suppose you might glance at our contract and refresh yourself on the things I need to have in order to do my job?"

Ah, so she did have contract riders.

"Yes, Joyce, absolutely," James said. "I—"

"If it's not *too* much trouble."

"Of course not. That's what I'm here for."

"Is it," she said icily. It was not a question. "And perhaps you could schedule a rehearsal in the not too distant future?"

"You said you didn't want—"

"*Ne*-ver mind," she said in a high-pitched squeak. This was obviously some kind of signal, because he snapped to attention.

"You have a couple of hours after sound check tomorrow, Joyce," he said. "How would that be?"

"If it's not too much trouble."

"That's what we're here for. To get it right. So I'll just—"

"Thank you," she said, the way Queen Victoria might dismiss a prime minister who'd just told her that they lost a war.

Nathan was sitting by one of the buffet tables, sipping a Diet Coke. He smiled reassuringly at Kit. *This too shall pass.*

Kit turned to Joyce. "This was, like, the best night of my life, Joyce."

"I'm so glad," Joyce said, her voice suddenly filled with warmth. She smiled at Kit and finished her wine.

Refilling her tumbler, Joyce said, "You remind me of when I was your age." She winced. "Ooh, I hate to hear myself sound like that. When I was your age, little girl…"

She grinned at Nathan, and said, "Never thought we'd ever say things like that, did we, old salt?"

"Oh, I don't know," Nathan said. "I always wanted to be like one of those old blues guys who gets rediscovered by some young pup. Have him get me gigs, drive me around, buy me wine, listen to all my old-fart stories."

Joyce threw her head back and laughed. "Oh, man, I remember that!" she said. "You used to talk about it on stage. You said that was your only ambition. Ha! That was a great bit."

She looked at Kit. "Help yourself to the wine, Kit. I wouldn't recommend the food."

"Chocolate's good," Kit said brightly. After her set, she'd found a bowl of little Hershey bars.

"Wine's better," Joyce said, burying her nose in her tumbler and giggling to herself.

Kit poured some wine into a tumbler and she and Joyce toasted each other. Nathan watched them down their wine like a pair of old drinking buddies. He did miss those after-show drinks, the conviviality, the sweet collision of adrenaline and alcohol. But that was the only drink he missed. He took a big gulp of Diet Coke. Not the same.

Joyce got up and went to the buffet, where a young woman was beginning to pack up the food. She beamed at Joyce, eyes wide, mouth open.

"Would you mind if I had a nibble at the trough before you take everything away?" Joyce said, her voice cold. "Some of us have been working all night, you know."

The young woman was crestfallen. "Oh please, Ms. Warren, help yourself," she said, backing up a step. "I was just…they told me upstairs—"

"Thank you. You're too kind. Where's the chocolate?"

Joyce grabbed some chocolate and plopped back into her chair. Smiling at Kit, she said, "So hard to get good help these days, isn't it?"

Kit tightened her lips in what Joyce took to be a smile. While Joyce unwrapped a chocolate bar, Kit glanced at the volunteer, who looked like she'd just heard that her cat died. Kit gave her a reassuring smile. The volunteer shrugged and stared down at the buffet table. To pack up or not to pack up? She looked like she was trying not to cry.

"You really have the gift of gab, Kit," Joyce said, swallowing some chocolate and picking up her wineglass. "Nathan told me your patter was like your songs and he was right. That's a great quality; the audience thinks they're getting to know the person behind the songs."

"Well, they are, I guess," Kit said with a shrug. "It's just, you know, how I talk."

"Oh, don't be so coy. You're among friends. I'm just saying it was well done. Well crafted."

"Thanks," Kit said shyly, beginning to blush. But Joyce was eyeing Nathan with a mix of affection and something darker. She drank more wine.

"Why didn't you come out to L.A. when I asked you?" she said. The wine was starting to kick in. It sounded like she said "when I ashed you."

"Oh, that's right," she said. "We went over this already. You were waiting for your album to come out. What a pity. I owned that town back then; I could've gotten you a deal. Easy-peasy."

She buried her face in her wine tumbler. "Woulda, too," she mumbled. She drank and was quiet for a long time. Nathan and Kit looked at each other.

"You wouldn'a liked it there, anyway," she said finally, her speech slurring more. She probably hadn't eaten; the wine was having much more effect than it did at Grendel's. Wine and adrenaline on an empty stomach: that can be a high-octane fuel. Nathan was getting nervous. Where was she going with this?

"No," Joyce said, staring into her wine, "you wouldn'a liked it in La-La Land. Too hot for you." She raised an eye to him, over the rim of her tumbler, and started to laugh. "In more ways than one," she said in singsongy tone.

Kit looked back and forth between Nathan and Joyce, her face darkening.

Joyce laughed loudly and said, "No, no, my dear, you were better off staying right here in lil' ol' Cambridge. Nice lil' ol' Cambridge."

"I'm sure you're right, Joyce," Nathan said, trying to dispel whatever bad cloud was gathering. "I wouldn't have liked it where you went. And I don't think I would have done well. Took me a long time to figure that out. But I'm sure you're right."

"Wouldn'a liked it at all," Joyce said, as if she hadn't heard him. She sprang to her feet and spilled a little wine. Giggling softly, she steered over to the tub where the wine bottles were. She picked up another open bottle and poured it into her tumbler as she returned to her chair.

"You're such a sweet, sweet boy, Nathan," she said. "You always were, you know. Sweet, sweet boy."

She winked at Kit. "Isn't he a sweet boy, Kit?"

"He is," Kit said, smiling uncomfortably. "Try telling him that, though."

"Oh, is he still like that? Gloomy ol' Nathan? The great stone face, the gray man? Are you still the great stone face, Nathan?"

He smiled. She had completely missed what he'd just said, his surrender to her greater strength and success. He didn't like where this was going, and he didn't like the look on Kit's face.

"Sweet, sweet boy," Joyce said, taking another long swallow of wine. "Nope, you're lucky you never got to L.A. You wouldn't be a sweet, sweet boy anymore. Sweet boys don't last long out there. No sweet boys there at all."

She sighed heavily, drank more wine, and crossed her legs.

Nathan eyed her. Was she jealous of how well Kit had done? But she wanted Kit to be that good; it was in her interest. Still, Kit's ovations had jarred her; that was clear from the way she pushed them off stage. Joyce got the crowd right back, though, rolling into that Nanci Griffith song. It was brilliant stagecraft, and Joyce knew it. But she didn't like how the band played it.

Nathan looked at Kit, who was staring at Joyce with an expression he'd never seen before. He looked back at Joyce, whose nose was buried in the wine tumbler. She was chuckling to herself again. What is *up* with her?

Then it hit him. My god, she's not jealous of Kit, she's jealous of him. Maybe because he was so happy with Kit and content with his life. But it was probably more because, in Joyce's most frightened heart, she was still the young upstart she'd been when she first knew him. Still the brassy Cambridge up-and-comer, being measured against the gold standard. And in those days, the gold standard was Nathan Warren.

She'd eclipsed his career a hundred times over. But no matter how far we travel, we never entirely stop being the frightened beginners we once were, wide-eyed and wary, entering a world full of people who seem to belong.

Nathan was not simply her first husband, he was the first mountain she climbed. And in that frightened, forever-young part of her, she still had to measure herself against him, against who he was then. And that's a contest you can never win. If he'd learned anything from his long, dark years, it's that you can never defeat your memories. Poor Joyce. She hadn't figured that out yet.

She was still babbling about what a sweet boy he was and how L.A. would have changed him. She was right, but what's the point? Kit should be her focus tonight, not Nathan, not old, dead memories.

But oh, doesn't the alcohol bring the ghosts out to play. Poor Joyce. This was her big night, too, the beginning of her third act, and it had begun so well. And there she was, huddling with her wine and her ghosts.

"You're very, very lucky you never got where I got," Joyce said, as if talking to herself now. "You're much better off running that cute lil' open mike of yours. Cute, cute, lil' open mike in cute lil' ol' Cambridge. Safe lil' ol' Cambridge. That's where my lil' Nathan belongs. Thank your lucky stars you never had the stones to go to L.A."

Nathan heard Kit gasp.

Stones? Did Joyce say stones? That he wasn't *man* enough to follow her? Oh, damn.

Nathan looked at Kit. Her face was deathly pale, and she still wore that expression he couldn't read. She was obviously mad, but not in any way he'd seen before. This was stronger than anger, both hotter and colder, and it frightened him.

"Speaking of, uh, stones," Kit said, putting down her wine, "you wanna know what made me fall for Nathan?"

Joyce grinned impishly. "Sure, girlfriend. Dish, dish."

"I'd go to Dooley's and sit way in the back. And I just thought he was the coolest. Here was this guy, after all these years, still playing music the way he wanted to, and helping people who were just starting out and didn't know anything. He'd be up on that *cute* little stage and you knew he never sold out. He was so real. That's what really got me."

Joyce smiled at her dreamily.

Kit took a step toward Joyce. "Know what I remember most about you, when I was a kid? You'll think this is really funny." Her voice was like black ice, smooth and dangerous. Joyce completely missed the signs.

"What's that, dear?" Joyce said, waiting demurely for her compliment.

"We thought you were funny; all us kids did."

"Do tell," Joyce said with a viper-like casualness. This wasn't going at all where she thought it would.

"Yeah," Kit said, grinning and nodding. "You were this funny old folkie lady on TV, this old folkie momma talking about her kid and then going all, like, sexy, and singing about men wanting to touch her all over, all flirty-dirty and wah-wah-wah."

"Wah-wah-wah?" Joyce said, trying to smile and look aloof. But her eyes flinched and her mouth involuntarily jerked and tightened. She took one of her cigarette breaths, immediately realizing it was an affect, another of the studied mannerisms for which people Kit's age have infallible radar. It was as if Joyce tried to take the breath back, and the sound that came out was almost a moan.

Nathan glared at Joyce; why did she have to start this? But he also felt a tired sympathy for her. The old Joyce would have been laughing her head off. She would have agreed with Kit, joined in the mockery, then said something snarky and cynical, like, "Yeah, but a girl's gotta make a buck, doesn't she?"

This was getting bad. Nathan tried to lighten the tension. "I think Joyce was just having a little fun, Kit," he said. "I don't think she—"

But the words stopped in his throat as Kit looked sharply at him, then turned back to Joyce. He'd never seen Kit like this, so angry and yet so calm. She moved another step closer to Joyce and her voice was cool, deliberate, full of youth's untested confidence and her own enormous inner strength. This was something beyond anger.

"When I got a little older," she said, "I started really listening to your lyrics. Understanding them. Then you were a completely different person, someone older but who knew how I felt, deep down where I didn't think anybody knew. That made me feel I wasn't as alone and different as I thought. I loved you for that. I still do."

Joyce started to smile then stopped. She didn't know how to react, how to feel.

Kit sighed. "So I don't get it, Joyce, the way you're treating everybody. You're a big star, you're so successful and good at what you do. But you still have to put on all your star grease and go around bullying people. Nathan, your band, your road manager, that poor volunteer who was just trying to clean up our mess. *Your* mess. Just doing her job that she's probably not even getting paid for."

Joyce finally realized how bad this was getting. "Kit," she said, "I certainly didn't mean…" But she sounded patronizing—if the poor child only understood. Kit waved her hand once, and Joyce stopped in mid-sentence.

Her voice rising, Kit said, "Maybe you think Nathan is a failure, because he never, like, got into *Rolling Stone*. But I don't. He didn't stay small; he stayed real. And you didn't."

At that instant, the same thought struck both Nathan and Kit. Their eyes met. He shook his head: don't do this, don't do this.

Joyce had not signed the contract yet. This could end everything, this one hard little moment.

Kit nodded that she understood. But then she made a small shrug of her shoulders. Too late. There was no way to stop now. This had gone beyond defending someone she loved. She was declaring herself, at the most important moment. Now, when it would be the easiest to tuck her principles in her pocket. Now, when there was so much to lose. When do these things matter more?

"I never want to be like that," she said, looking unflinchingly at Joyce. "Somebody who tries to make herself feel big by digging her heels into people she doesn't think are important. That isn't being big to me."

Joyce crossed her legs, uncrossed them, then crossed them again. She brought the wine to her lips, then put it down without drinking.

Eyes filling, Kit said, "I don't want to live in a world where people come in different sizes, and some are big and some are small. I want to live in a world where everybody's important. And that's Nathan's world."

Kit backed toward the door as she spoke. Picking up her parka, she put her hand on the doorknob behind her. Nathan suddenly realized she was going to leave and tried to stop her. Kit shot him a look, shaking her head once. She turned to leave, then looked back at Joyce and said, "I'm glad you like my songs. That means a lot to me. Thanks for—"

Kit closed the door behind her. Nathan could hear her back slam against it. There was a moment of silence, then a muffled but distinct shout of "Shit!" from behind the door. And she was gone.

He opened the door, but she was already out of sight. He knew she would need to be alone, for a while at least. She would have lingered if she wanted him to catch her.

He walked back into the room and everybody was quiet for a long time. The volunteer at the buffet table was frozen in place, mouth open, a garbage bag in one hand and a tub of potato salad in the other. Joyce shuffled uncomfortably in her chair. She put her drink down and again crossed and uncrossed her legs. Her eyes never left the door.

"Remind you of anyone?" Nathan said.

"Oh yes," Joyce breathed, and it was the saddest sound he'd ever heard.

Nathan gathered up Kit's gear; she'd run out without it. Her cell phone was turned off, but he knew it was in her parka pocket so he made sure Joyce had the number, then hurried home.

He put Kit's things down in the kitchen and walked through every room, turning on the lights. He wanted her to know he was there, if and when she showed up. He made some tea—this was going to be a long night—and waited at the kitchen table.

Kit burst in a little after one. They stared at each other at first, saying nothing. Her eyes were wide and her mouth was open. She was panting; she probably ran most of the way.

"I know, I know," Nathan said as she caught her breath.

Her voice wheezy, she said, "She still wants me. Can you believe it? She still wants me!"

"I know."

Kit told him she had walked around and around Harvard Square, examining the apparent self-destruction of her career.

What made her the craziest, she said, was that she didn't know how she felt about what she'd done. How could she have said those things? Should she have said those things? Were they true? Why the hell had she opened her big mouth? What would happen now? How much could someone like Joyce Warren hurt her if she wanted to? Was it worth it? Most of all, she asked herself that. Was it worth it?

Pacing frantically around the square, she wondered why nobody was calling her to talk this over. Then she remembered she'd turned off her cell phone when she got to Sanders. She found it in her pocket and clicked it back on. Almost immediately, Joyce called.

Nathan said, "She felt terrible about the whole thing. And she thought it was her fault. The minute you closed the door and hollered 'shit'—yeah, we all heard that—it was like she woke up. She apologized to me and to the volunteer at the buffet table. That poor kid, I thought we were going to have to get oxygen for her. Joyce gave her the purple scarf she wore on stage, called it an I'm-sorry gift."

Kit nodded impatiently. Back to my story, please. She had to get this out.

Nathan said, "Sorry. Continue."

"She apologized to me, too. She said the wine hit her too hard; she was feeling her age, maybe a little jealous. She said she didn't mean any of it."

Nathan said, "She really didn't, you know. Joyce doesn't like that side of her, the big-star part. I mean, she loves being a star but she wants to wear it well. She's just so damn ambitious and she's had to fight for everything. Maybe she has to throw that weight around sometimes, to convince herself it was worth what it's cost her."

Kit nodded briskly. "*Any*-way," she said. "You won't believe what she said when she called. Even after all those awful things I said. Not about you. I mean, I was glad I said those things. But…"

She rolled her eyes—now she was interrupting herself. "Joyce kept saying she was sorry. And then—you'll never believe this—she said she had the contract in front of her but she'd only sign it if I said it was okay. After all that! She said she wanted it to be my decision, my choice."

Nathan took a sharp breath. "The choice she never had. Kit, that's the Joyce you're signing with. That's who she really is, beneath all the bullshit."

"That's good, because…"

She paused for effect, nodding her head.

"Yes?"

"Because I told her to go ahead and sign it. The contract. So it's official; I am a Choyce recording artist." She threw her arms wide, as if accepting an ovation.

He got up from the table and hugged her. "Congratulations," he said. "It probably doesn't feel like it right now, but you earned this, Kit. You earned it."

They sat down. Kit drummed her fingers on the kitchen table while she tried to come down from the roller coaster she'd been on.

"I can't believe Joyce can forget that whole mess," she said.

"She liked what you said."

"She *what*? You mean the stuff about you?"

"And the stuff you said about her."

"She *liked* that?"

"Well, she didn't like hearing it. But she liked the fact that you said it, that you stood up to her. She said you were tougher than she thought. And that you'll need that where you're going."

"God, she really is tough."

"As nails. She also got it that it wasn't all about her."

"It wasn't?"

"Weren't you saying some things about yourself? About who you are and what kind of career you want?"

Kit thought for a moment. "Oh. Yeah. I guess I was. Maybe that's why I couldn't stop. Once I got started, I had to say it all."

"She respected that. Even more because you did it tonight, your big night, when it would have been so easy to let it slide."

"Wow. She's really something, isn't she?"

"She is. Like I've been telling you, underneath the bluster and the vanity—all the star grease, as you put it—Joyce is all about the music. She's a true believer, just like me, just like you."

Kit looked out the window, nodding and thinking.

"The things she said about me," Nathan said, "they were true, when you think about it. I mean, how she said them was harsh but she wasn't wrong."

She looked at him. "You really think that, don't you? She was wrong about everything; she even told me she was."

"She did?"

"Yes. You know, it wasn't that thing about not having the stones to go to L.A. that made me mad. That was, like, totally juvenile."

"No?"

"No. It was that crack about your *cute* little open mike. I blew a fuse when I heard that. I think what you do there is important, Nathan. It sure was to me."

"Yeah?" he said. It was all he could think of.

"Yeah. You're so good at showing everybody that this music is bigger than we think it is, that it's this big tradition, this community that's lasted forever. And all we have to do to be part of it is to love the music. That's *important*, Nathan. And you do it all the time, all the time."

She smiled at him and shrugged. "Anyway, that's why I blew up on her. God, I was mean, wasn't I? I was so mad. It didn't make you mad at all? Those awful things she said?"

"No, not really. A few years ago it would have cut me to pieces. Because it would have fed into all the things I felt about myself. Why I failed at everything."

Kit leaned toward him. "And now?"

"I didn't take it personally, I guess. I realized that it was about her, not me. Why did she have to say those things to me, the volunteer, her band, that train wreck of a road manager? It didn't have anything to do with me, even the stuff she said about me. She was measuring herself against her old self. Against her memories."

He smiled at Kit. "And you never win that race, sweetie. You can never outrun your old dreams about yourself. You'll be good for her that way, I think, remind her why she got into music in the first place."

"Really?"

"You sure helped me."

Kit smiled and looked down at the table.

Then they talked about details. She asked if she could borrow his car to go home and pack. She'd bring it back in the morning and they'd taxi to the airport to meet Joyce.

Before she left, they held each other for a long time. She kept talking about how excited she was. What an adventure.

He held her close but looked beyond her, out the window. He could barely make out the shape of the big tree in the yard. Something wasn't right. What was it, what was it? What was wrong?

Nathan almost felt like he was being punished as he put on his old suede jacket to go into Harvard Square and brood. Wasn't he supposed to be past all this? But something was wrong, beneath his thoughts, and he needed to know what it was.

He left the house around three in the morning. Everything was asleep. He didn't think at first, just tried to find his feelings, head down, hands in pockets, walking slowly up Craigie Street. He forgot to take his shortcut but there was no noise on Mass. Ave. to remind him to turn away. He didn't realize he'd taken the long way until he found himself beside the ancient church cemetery at the edge of the square. He leaned against the wrought-iron fence and stared at the flat stone markers, jutting out at odd angles.

What was wrong? What could possibly be wrong? It was a damn fairytale come true. Was it Kit? Joyce? Him? His ghosts breathing in his ear? He didn't think so, but he decided to go through the list. Something wasn't right.

He turned right on Church Street and saw Palmer Street and the sign for Club Passim. To his right was the Mexican restaurant. It usually had a grill fire going, filling the air with the scent of wood smoke. Too late for that. He thought about the gatherings there after his classes and smiled.

He looked over at the basement stairs leading down to Passim and felt a rush of contentment; he no longer had to scold himself when he saw the place. It didn't remind him of his failures, and he knew now that it had never meant to. How could he have gotten it so wrong, believing that even this most welcoming of places was not welcome to him?

He walked down the soft brick of Palmer Street. It was just an alley, really, once a place for wagons and carriages to unload their wares. Now it was more of a patio than a street; cars weren't allowed on it anymore. Everything was quiet. He heard his boot heels click on the old stone. What was wrong?

He thought about Kit and dismissed any notion that his feelings for her had changed. He loved her, adored her. Could he be jealous? Nonsense. That had never been in the air between them. Worth asking but no, that's not it.

Joyce? Would it bother him to see her parade her stardom? On the contrary. He grinned, thinking about the guilty pleasure it would be to watch Joyce in the wings, night after night, as Kit's star began to outshine hers. And it would; he had little doubt of that. He would also enjoy the mature friendship growing between them. No, those ghosts were gone.

So what was it?

He came out onto Brattle Street and looked over at the old yellow Blacksmith House, which had inspired the Longfellow poem about the village smithy. Old. He remembered Kit's words outside the supermarket as her eyes filled with tears:

You sing love songs about dead people, traditions, but from long ago.

Like living is something for other people.

You have to love everything in your life; you don't get to choose.

You're the only one around you who doesn't love you.

He shook his head and turned left up Brattle. When it met Mass Ave. he went straight, onto meandering Mt. Auburn. He could see the shopping complex called the Garage on JFK Street, once a hotbed of live-music clubs. Gone to pizza joints and chain stores.

Was it touring again that bothered him? The road? He'd thought his traveling days were over, but a bit of his wanderlust had returned. He'd never traveled first class; it would be fun to see what he'd missed. Jets and downtown hotels instead of backroads and cheap motels. Room service.

And he would not be alone. Most of all, that. He would not be doing it for himself. He remembered what Kit had said as they walked back to the dressing room after her set:

I couldn't have done any of it without you.

Not true. She needs to believe in herself.

He crossed Dunster Street and looked down at the bumpy brick sidewalk, cresting and dipping like tiny hills. He looked at the rows of darkened shops and cafés. No people anywhere. The square was strange without people. Didn't there always used to be people?

He walked past the Hasty Pudding theater, still prim and Edwardian, a lonesome relic of the old square. He came out onto Mass. Ave. across the street from Harvard. He turned right, barely aware of where he was.

He wouldn't be the headliner this time; maybe that bothered him. He'd be Kit's sideman. Was that it? Sniffing the world at the end of somebody else's cork? He'd always been proud that he ran on his own fuel, even when he was running on empty.

But he wasn't starting a career as a sideman. This was for Kit. Accompanying her had always been a joy. And he loved the work; it was a new way to use his musical muscles. Even more than with his own songs, it required hard, passionate listening. The essence of music. There was something pure about not having to worry about the other things, the career things, the show-biz things.

He especially loved it when the audience wasn't hearing him, just feeling him. Sometimes he could see the moment when they felt his guitar lift the sound. But nobody looked at him, nobody knew where the lift came from. Their eyes never left Kit. He loved that. So what was it?

I felt so safe that I could fly anywhere.

Couldn't have done it without you.

Not true, not true. He remembered how troubled he'd been when she said that after her set. It was flattering, of course. But it felt like she might actually believe it, and it simply wasn't true. She was all she needed on that stage, and she needed to believe that.

He turned right on to Bow Street, which took him back to Mt. Auburn and into the square. He walked past the upscale bistro that had once been the home of the legendary Club 47, where Joan Baez and Tom Rush got their start. Before his time. There actually were things that were before his time. He looked in the windows and saw only white tablecloths and poshness. No ghosts.

He thought about how his life was when Kit entered his life and how differently he saw the world now. But did she change him? She didn't mean to; she said that again and again. Mostly, she showed him ways he had already changed.

First, there was the sheer challenge of her: this beautiful, brilliant woman falling in love with him. That wasn't possible if he was anything like the person he'd thought he was. A woman like Kit wouldn't have time for someone like that. She'd be kind, the way she was with everybody. But she wouldn't want him in her life, the man he thought he was when he met her. And yet she did.

He remembered how hard he tried to understand that, how much junk in his head had to be tossed out for him to see how that was possible. A woman like Kit.

And yet, what she loved about him had been there all along, down in the important places where he'd shuttered out the good light, waiting for someone clean and honest to burst in, like sudden sunlight, open the blinds and force him to see how many precious things remained. Forcing him to see himself as she saw him, as she saw the man she loved.

So, in the end, she showed him how much he had not changed, how many good things he'd clung to, at such a cost. When she stood up to Joyce, she displayed the best of what connected them to each other.

I want to live in a world where everybody is important.

That's Nathan's world.

He walked back into the Square and up to Mass. Ave., crossing the street to Harvard Yard, with its black wrought-iron fence and tall, forbidding gates.

I think what you do is important, Nathan.

The Church Street gate was locked for the night. God, it was late, wasn't it? He didn't think he'd ever seen that gate locked. Maybe the library gate was open, up by Plympton Street. He walked over to see, strolling alongside the fence and the soft redbrick of Harvard. He rolled a hand absently along the iron spikes.

He would miss his house, of course, and all his small, pleasing habits. Deciding what to have for dinner based on which shop owner he wanted to chat with. One would want to talk about sports, another about music, always trying to change the subject to Greek music. Another would talk excitedly about the book he was reading. Knowing your neighbors: there's another vanishing art.

But his landlords were going to look after the place. Maybe after some steady work on the high end of the music business, he'd finally be able to convince them to take some money for the home they'd given him. Probably not. In fact, he'd have to be careful about that. He'd hurt their feelings if they thought he saw them as people who wanted his money. You're like family to us, they told him.

You're the only one around you who doesn't love you.

The narrow Plympton Street gate was open, and he ducked into Harvard Yard. He walked past Widener Library, with its grand stairway, and into the main yard.

The crisscrossing sidewalks were empty, all that fine young energy asleep. The lights were out in the redbrick dormitories, with their neat white trim. The trees in the yard were almost close enough for their branches to form a ceiling over the walkways. But the branches were bare now, stretching like thin old bones in the purple night sky, almost incandescent above the soft glow of the sleeping city.

It felt strange to be here without people. Everything about Harvard Yard was designed for quickstepping feet, intent chatter, busy minds, and the hubbub of people with things to do, promises to keep, miles to go before they sleep. Empty now, a barren landscape.

I couldn't have done any of it without you.

Not true, not true.

He walked diagonally across the yard, looking up at the gray stone of University Hall. In front sat old John Harvard, the school's founder, in his stately bronze chair and proper colonial garb, leaning back, book in lap, a startled expression on his face, as if he'd been reading a story aloud and looked up to find his listeners gone.

Nathan thought of everything Kit tried to make him believe about himself and how she had slowly made him see that they were true. How could he look into her face, see how much she believed they were true, and not believe them himself? She made them true. No, that's not quite it. They were true. She made him believe that.

Full of love, everything you do, full of love
Every single thing.
I think what you do is important, Nathan.

He stood up and walked across the yard, to the inside of the locked Church Street gate. He could barely make out the sign for Palmer Street.

His eyes lost focus and his new song came into his head. He hummed it to himself.

All that is true
And the only way through,
Is to find my way back home to you.

Home. Home.
Everything you do, every single thing.

He turned and leaned his back against the gate, stuffing his hands into his coat pockets. He looked searchingly at the night sky, and the air felt like winter coming.

Every single thing you do.

"Of course," he said, and a single tear ran down his cheek. "Of course."

Kit walked into the kitchen a little after ten. Nathan was at the table, drinking coffee. He didn't smile when she came in. Maybe that's the first thing she noticed, the first thing that seemed wrong. She looked at him and her smile froze. Somehow, without knowing, she knew.

She said nothing and walked quickly into the living room, through the whole house, and back into the kitchen. Without knowing, she knew.

"You're not packed," she said. Her voice was frail, frightened.

"I'm not going."

She leaned heavily against the refrigerator. "What?"

"I'm not going, Kit."

"What do you mean you're not going? What do you *mean*?" She pushed herself off the refrigerator, walked into the living room, and back into the kitchen.

She stood there, staring at the floor. "No, no, no," she said under her breath, pounding her heel in time to the words. "No, no, no." Her voice rose. She looked around the walls, then at him.

"This can't be happening," she said. "Everything was perfect. Everything is all right now."

"Everything is all right."

She took in a sharp breath. "How can you say that?" she said, almost whimpering. "How can you *say* that? Nothing is all right. Not now. *Nothing* is all right."

He looked at his coffee cup and back up at her. How to start? He turned from her and looked out the window. She waited. A single bird flew wide across the morning sky.

"No, it's not all right," he said, turning back and looking at her. "Of course it's not all right. But it's right. It's what it's supposed to be."

"How can you *say* that? What do you *mean*? Nothing is right. Not if you're not going. *Nothing* is right." Her voice was fragile. Everything that happened last night and it all came out so perfectly, all so perfect. Until now.

"You don't need me," he said, his voice sad but steady. "Not where you're going now. And I—"

"How can you say that, Nathan? Of course I need you. I—"

"You want me. I know that. And you want to need me. But you don't, not really. Not where you're going."

"That's not true. You heard us last night; how can you…your guitar was so close to mine. It made me feel safe, helped me play and sing…I felt so—"

"I know, sweetie, and I love doing it for you. But you don't need me for that; you don't. Everybody's eyes were on you up there, just you. You're all they're going to want. They barely noticed me."

"They felt you. I felt you."

"It's nothing Joyce's guitarist can't do for you. You know that; you know that."

He leaned forward in his chair. "Don't you? Because you need to know that. It's *important* that you know that. You are all you need up there."

She shook her head and looked at the floor. She had to know that was true.

"But on the road, my first time on the road," she said, trying another tack. "Making the new record." Her eyebrows jumped. Aha. "There's the new record, Nathan. I'll need you for that. You know how nervous I—"

"You've made a record. You know what you want; you know how it works. And you know where to find me if you need to. But this is Joyce's label, Joyce's show. She'll be there for you, and you couldn't be in better hands. After last night, I'm more sure of that than ever. I've never been where you're going now. And she has."

"Yeah, but Joyce, well, you saw her last night."

"I thought about that. And I feel even better about you two working together. I'm so glad you said all the things you did. All the things you needed to say."

He stood up and leaned against the counter by the window. He looked at her and smiled softly. His face showed how he felt about her and he wanted her to see that. To know that.

"You declared yourself last night," he said. "Who you are, what kind of career you want. Where you stand. Joyce heard it and accepted you, on those terms. Your terms. More than accepted you; she's even more sure you're the one she's looking for. That's exciting, Kit."

He leaned his hands back against the counter. "And it means it's going to be fine. You two are going to do good work together. I know that now, more than ever. Important work."

Kit leaned against the refrigerator and stared into his sad but steady eyes. She started to say something, stopped, and her shoulders slumped. Stumped again. She narrowed her eyes. There must be something.

"But this could be a big break for you, too," she said. Her voice rose and she pushed herself off the refrigerator. "I always wanted that. Don't you want that? Joyce says she still likes your music. I've been thinking about this. A lot. You could make a record, too; you could—"

"My work is here, Kit. You showed me that and you made me believe that it's worth doing. That it's important. Remember? I have my own work to do. And it's here."

She looked around the kitchen, eyes darting, searching for something, anything. This can't be happening. Everything was perfect.

"It's only one tour," she said. "It's not like we're moving to L.A."

"Isn't it?"

She stared at him. The tour, then recording in L.A. Then Europe with Joyce while the album was being pressed. Then the album release. The video. Media junkets. Album tour. Then touring again with Joyce. All mapped out. She was going away for…no, she was just going away.

"It's not, like, forever or anything," she muttered under her breath, as if she was arguing with herself now.

"No, it's not forever," Nathan said, lifting himself off the counter. For a moment, his face brightened. Then he leaned back, shook his head, and sighed. "But it's now. Your now. My now."

Her eyes flinched and flinched again. Going. Away. And then, gradually, he saw her eyes shift, soften, and settle. She was quiet for a long time.

He knew it was hitting her now, the same thought that came to him by the iron gate at Harvard. She was beginning to see how everything each had done in loving the other had led to this moment. Had made it inevitable.

Everything he had done to help her believe in herself, to believe that this music was her home, and to understand how much that meant. To prepare her for the road she was taking now, and to show her that she was strong enough to take it.

Everything she had done to make him believe in himself, to see that his work had value, that it was important, and that he still had much to offer the world.

They looked at each other for a long time, saying nothing. How could they have not known it? How could they have not seen it as clearly as they did now? Because they were in love, simple as that; because they were so much in love.

"So the home in your song," she said quietly, "it really isn't me, is it?"

"I never could have found it without you."

"Oh, I don't know. I think you were always there. You just didn't know it for a while."

"Hardest kind to find. Where do you look?"

She smiled, finally, a small smile. Then her eyes turned frightened again, but only for a moment. "I don't want…I never wanted…"

"I know, Kit. I know. Neither did I. Neither of us saw this coming. How could we?"

"You'll be okay then? Here, by yourself?"

Nathan looked around him, and his face filled with fear. Alone. Again. Then, as her eyes had done before, his eyes shifted, softened, and settled.

"No, I'll be fine," he said, unable to look at her. "In a while. After a while."

When he could look at her again, he said, "I'm not afraid of my memories anymore, Kit. Because of you, because of what you brought into my life. What you made me see. I can't tell you how much that means. There aren't words…no words…" His voice trailed off. He was crying.

They said nothing, looking at the floor, and then at each other.

"So you're home now," Kit said finally.

"Yes."

She looked into the living room, and her eyes fell on Nathan's stereo. She looked at it, shaking her head sadly. That old stereo.

She turned back to him and said, "It's good to be home."

"Yes, it is."

They were quiet for a long time. Then they walked to each other, held each other. And said goodbye the only way they could.

The Songs in Revival

Footloose, words and music by Chris Smither, Homunculus Music. Smither's version is available on the CD titled It Ain't Easy. www.smither.com

Remember the Alamo, words and music by Jane Bower, Vidor Publications, Inc.

So Long It's Been Good to Know Yuh, words and music by Woody Guthrie, TRO-Folkways Music, Inc. Guthrie's version available on Dust Bowl Ballads, Buddha Records. woodyguthrie.org.

Cluck Old Hen, traditional.

Colorado Trail, traditional. Author's version available on All That Is True, scottalarik. com.

Pretty Saro, traditional. Author's version available on All That Is True, scottalarik. com.

Wild Mountain Thyme, traditional.

Do You Really Want to Hurt Me?, words and music by Michael Craig, Roy Hay, Jon Moss, George O'Dowd (Culture Club), EMI Virgin Songs, Inc.

Pastures of Plenty, words and music by Woody Guthrie, TRO-Folkways Music, Inc. Guthrie's version available on This Land Is Your Land: Asch Recordings Volume 1, Smithsonian-Folkways Recordings. woodyguthrie.org.

Plane Wreck at Los Gatos (Deportee), words and music by Woody Guthrie, TRO-Folkways Music, inc. Judy Collins' version available on Judy Collins 3 & 4, Wildflower Records, judycollins.com.

This Land Is Your Land, words and music by Woody Guthrie, Ludlow Music, Inc. Guthrie's version available on This Land Is Your Land: Asch Recordings Volume 1, Smithsonian-Folkways Recordings. woodyguthrie.org.

Kit Palmer's song *Winter* inspired by *February,* words and music by Dar Williams. Adapted with permission of writer. Williams' version available on Mortal City, Razor & Tie. darwilliams.com.

Aginst Th' Law, words by Woody Guthrie, Woody Guthrie Publications, Inc. Billy Bragg's version available on Mermaid Avenue, Volume II, Elektra. woodyguthrie.org.

Blow, Boys, Blow, traditional.

Frankie On the Sheepscot, words and music by Gordon Bok. Bok's version available on Peter Kagan and the Wind and North Wind's Clearing, Folk-Legacy Records. gordonbok.com.

Unquiet Grave, traditional.

One for Winter, words and music by Cindy Kallet and Gordon Bok, Timberhead Music BMI. Their version available on Neighbors, Timberhead Music. gordonbok.com.

Arlington (the song Kit writes during the nor'easters: "*Where do you go, little bird*"), words and music by Nicky Mehta. Fictional use by permission of writer. Available on 40 Days, by the Wailin' Jennys, Red House Records. thewailinjennys.com

The Gower Wassail, traditional.

Country Life, traditional.

All That Is True, words and music by Scott Alarik. Author's version available on All That Is True, scottalarik.com.

Rudolph the Red Nosed Reindeer, words and music by Johnny Marks, St. Nicholas Music, Inc.

One of These Days, words and music by Earl Montgomery, Altam Music. Emmylou Harris' version available on The Very Best of Emmylou Harris, Rhino Warner. emmylouharris.com.

The Death of Queen Jane, traditional.

Judas (the new song Kit sings at the big concert), words and music by Antje Duvekot, Pantjebare Publishing. Fictional use by permission of writer. Duvekot's version available on Big Dream Boulevard, Black Wolf Records. antjeduvekot.com.